West of Here

West of Here

A NOVEL BY

Jonathan Evison

ALGONQUIN BOOKS OF CHAPEL HILL 2011

Published by

Algonquin Books of Chapel Hill

Post Office Box 2225

Chapel Hill, North Carolina 27515-2225

a division of

Workman Publishing

225 Varick Street

New York, New York 10014

FEB 2 3 2011

Printed in the United States of America.

Published simultaneously in Canada by

Thomas Allen & Son Limited.

Maps by Nick Belardes.

Library of Congress Cataloging-in-Publication Data
    Evison, Jonathan.
        West of here : a novel / by Jonathan Evison. — 1st ed.
            p. cm.
        ISBN 978-1-56512-952-8
        1. Washington (State) — Social life and customs —
        Fiction.   I. Title.
        PS3605.V57W47 2011
        813'.6 — dc22   2010020224

10 9 8 7 6 5 4 3 2

For Carl,

who I think would've liked this one.

I will sing the song of the sky.

This is the song of the tired —

the salmon panting as they fight the swift current.

I walk around where the water runs into whirlpools.

They talk quickly, as if they are in a hurry.

— Potlatch song

West of Here

terra incognita

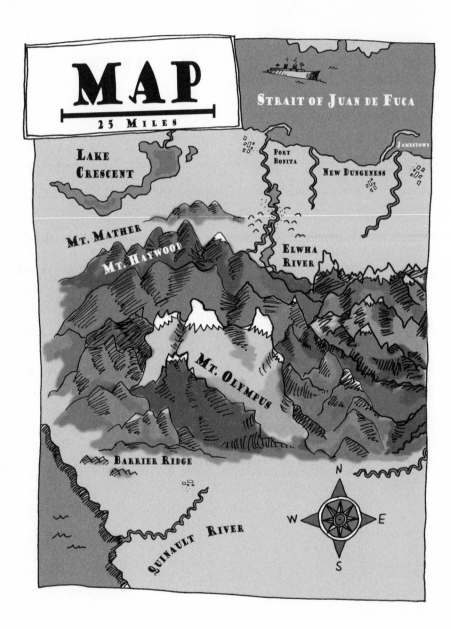

terra incognita

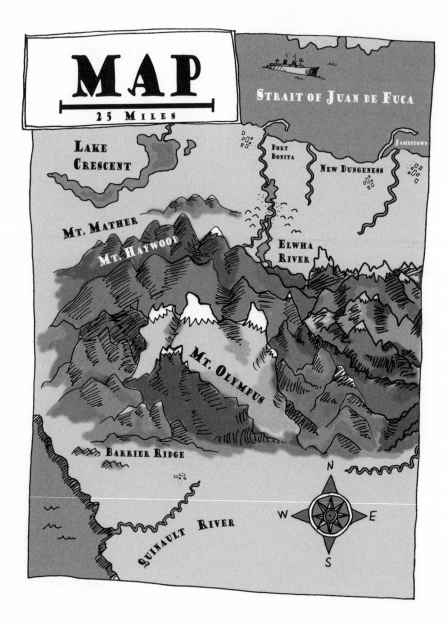

footprints

SEPTEMBER 2006

Just as the keynote address was winding down, the rain came hissing up the little valley in sheets. Crepe paper streamers began bleeding red and blue streaks down the front of the dirty white stage, and the canopy began to sag beneath the weight of standing water, draining a cold rivulet down the tuba player's back. When the rain started coming sideways in great gusts, the band furiously began packing their gear. In the audience, corn dogs turned to mush and cotton candy wilted. The crowd quickly scattered, and within minutes the exodus was all but complete. Hundreds of Port Bonitans funneled through the exits toward their cars, leaving behind a vast muddy clearing riddled with sullied napkins and paperboard boats.

Krig stood his ground near center stage, his mesh Raiders jersey plastered to his hairy stomach, as the valediction sounded its final stirring note.

"There *is* a future," Jared Thornburgh said from the podium. "And it begins right now."

"Hell yes!" Krig shouted, pumping a fist in the air. "Tell it like it is, J-man!" But when he looked around for a reaction, he discovered he was alone. J-man had already vacated the stage and was running for cover.

Knowing that the parking lot would be gridlock, Krig cut a squelchy path across the clearing toward the near edge of the chasm, where a rusting chain-link fence ran high above the sluice gate. Hooking his fingers through the fence, he watched the white water roar through the open jaws of the dam into the canyon a hundred feet below, where even now a beleaguered run of fall chinook sprung from the shallows only to beat their silver heads against the concrete time and again. As a kid he had thought it was funny.

The surface of Lake Thornburgh churned and tossed on the up-river side, slapping at the concrete breakwater. The face of the dam, hulking and gray, teeming with ancient moss below the spillway, was impervious to these conditions. Its monstrous twin turbines knew nothing of their fate as they hummed up through the earth, vibrating in Krig's bones.

Standing there at the edge of the canyon with the wet wind stinging his face, Krig felt the urge to leave part of himself behind, just like the speech said. Grimacing under the strain, he began working the ring back and forth over his fat knuckle for the first time in twenty-two years. It was just a ring. There were eleven more just like it. Hell, even Tobin had one, and he rode the pine most of that season. Krig knew J-man was talking about something bigger. J-man was talking about rewriting history. But you had to start somewhere. When at last Krig managed to work the ring over his knuckle, he held it in his palm and gave pause.

"Well," he said, addressing the ring. "Here goes nothin', I guess."

And rearing back, he let it fly into a stiff headwind, and watched it plummet into the abyss until he lost sight of it. He lingered at the edge of the gorge for a long moment and let the rain wash over him, until his clinging jersey grew heavy. Retracing his own steps across the muddy clearing toward the parking slab, Krig discovered that already the rain was washing away his footprints.

storm king

The storm of January 9, 1880, dove inland near the mouth of the Columbia River, roaring with gale-force winds. It was not a gusty blow, but a cold and unrelenting assault, a wall of hyperborean wind ravaging everything in its northeasterly path for nearly four hundred miles. As far south as Coos Bay, the *Emma Utter*, a three-masted schooner, dragged anchor and smashed against the rock-strewn coastline, as her bewildered crew watched from shore. The mighty Northern Pacific, that miracle of locomotion, was stopped dead in its tracks in Beaverton by upward of six hundred trees, all downed in substantially less than an hour's time. In Clarke County, windfall damage by midafternoon was estimated at one in three trees.

Throughout its northeasterly arc, the storm gathered momentum; snow fell slantwise in sheets, whistling as it came, stinging with its velocity, gathering rapidly in drifts against anything able to withstand its force. In Port Townsend, no less than eleven buildings collapsed under the rapid accumulation of snow, while some forty miles to the southwest, over four feet of snow fell near the mouth of the Elwha River, where, to the consternation of local and federal officials, two hundred scantily clad Klallam Indians continued to winter in their ancestral homes, in spite of all efforts to relocate them.

It is said among the Klallam that the world disappeared the night of the storm, and that the river turned to snow, and the forest and mountains and sky turned to snow. It is said that the wind itself turned to snow as it thundered up the valley and that the trees shivered and the valley moaned.

At dusk, in a cedar shack near the mouth of the river, a boy child was born who would come to know his father as a fiction, an apparition lost upriver in the storm. His young mother swaddled the child in wool blankets as she sat near a small fire, holding him fast, as the wind whistled through the planks, setting the flames to flickering and throwing shadows on the wall.

The child remained so still that Hoko could not feel his breathing. He uttered not a sound. A different young mother might have unwrapped the infant and set her cool anxious fingers on his tummy to feel its rise and fall. But Hoko did not bother to check the child's breathing. She merely held it until her thoughts slowed to a trickle and she could feel some part of herself take leave; and she slept without sleeping, emptied herself into the night until she was but a slow bleating inside of a dark warmth. And there she remained for several hours.

In the middle of the night, the child began to fidget, though still he did not utter so much as a whimper. Hoko gave him the breast, and he clutched her hair within tiny balled fists and took her nourishment. Outside, the snow continued in flurries, and the timber creaked and groaned, even as the wind abated near dawn.

Shortly after sunrise, the shack tottered once, issued a long plaintive moan, then collapsed in a heap. There followed a flash of fire and ice, and one dull moment of confusion, before Hoko extricated herself and the child from beneath the rubble and hurried the infant through the veil of snow toward the safety of the longhouse, oblivious of the burns up and down her arms.

Her father was already awake when Hoko burst into the longhouse clutching her newborn son. He did not look up from the fire.

"Shut the door," he said, and fell back into a dense silence.

FOR SIX MONTHS, the boy would have no name. For six months he would remain anonymous in the eyes of his mother, until finally Hoko gave him the name Thomas Jefferson King. But he was soon given another name. Upon meeting the mute blue-eyed child for the first time, George Sampson, a Klallam elder who lived in seclusion upriver, gave the boy a different name. Indian George called him Storm King.

succeed

In 1889, upon the behest of a public clamoring for adventure, and a press eager to package new discoveries, thirty-four-year-old Arctic explorer, Indian fighter, and rugged individual James Mather was consigned to conquer the last frontier of the Washington Territory, mere days in advance of its statehood. The sum of Mather's orders, as issued by Governor Elisha P. Ferry himself in a champagne toast and roundly endorsed by the expedition's underwriters, were as follows: "Succeed."

The vast uncharted interior of the Olympic Peninsula, between the Strait of Juan de Fuca and the rockbound coast of the Pacific, was ripe for discovery. For centuries the region had fueled speculation among seafarers, and for centuries the rugged obstacles it presented discouraged even the heartiest explorer. Viewed from the strait, as Juan de Fuca allegedly viewed it in 1579, the heart of the peninsula comprised a chaos of snow-clad ranges colliding at odd angles, a bulwark of spiny ridges defending a hulking central range like the jaws of a trap. The high country was marked by gaps so steep and dark that the eye could scarcely penetrate them, and all of this was wrapped tightly about the waist with an impenetrable green blanket of timber.

When viewed from Elliot Bay on a clear day, the leeward side of the Olympics presented another dramatic facade: a sheer wall of basalt inclining suddenly and precipitously from the banks of Hood Canal, stretching some hundred miles along the western horizon, so steep in places that snow would not stick to the face of them. Indeed, the Olympics presented to Seattle no less than a mile-high barrier to the unknown. And by 1889, the unknown was fast becoming a finite concept.

That Mather chose to launch his expedition in the dead of one of the worst winters on record is less a testament to his poor judgment than his determination to be the first in breaching the Olympic wilderness. He was harried from the outset by the fear that someone would beat a trail to his destiny before him, and this fear was not unfounded. Within a year, no fewer than a dozen expeditions would set out to penetrate the Olympic interior.

With little data to support him, Mather selected the narrow Elwha River valley as the point of entry for the party's crossing. The river ran flat and shoal at its mouth, and the wooded bottomlands seemed to offer an inviting path through the foothills and over the divide. Moreover, the proximity of Port Bonita, just east along the strait, would allow the party a base for their operations during the muddy weeks of trailblazing into the foothills.

Mather and his party of five set out from Seattle aboard the steamer *Evangel* on December 7, 1889, fully outfitted for a six-month expedition, though unprepared for the fanfare that greeted them upon their arrival in Port Bonita. Morse Dock was wrapped in silk bunting, with a dozen coronets sounding "The Spanish Cavalier." Men, women, and dirty-faced children formed parallel lines and watched the parade of trunks emerge from the hold and move serpentine through their midst. Mather himself, a bear of a man, crated a sizable trunk on his shoulder, unaided, gritting a bearded smile as he passed through the crowd. At his heels, untethered, came a pair of big fine bear dogs.

Near the end of the line, seeming to Mather out of place, a small native child seized his attention. Boy or girl, Mather was unable to ascertain, but the child, lithe and moonfaced, squinted fiercely with pointed blue eyes as he passed.

When he reached the staging area, Mather hefted his trunk onto the growing pile, and before he'd even ventured to get his bearings, was met by a very pregnant woman, with a very earnest handshake, and a frazzled knot of hair atop her head.

"Mr. Mather, is it?"

"It is. And you are?"

"Eva Lambert of the *Commonwealth Register.*"

Mather glanced past her at the muddy hillside and the ragtag assembly of wooden structures riddling the shoreline, then eyed doubtfully the colorful floppy bow dangling from beneath Eva's shirt collar. "A social register? Here?"

"A newspaper, Mr. Mather. The region's *only* newspaper. And not *here,* but *there,* over the hill at the commonwealth."

Mather smiled down at her through his formidable red beard. He snuck a glance at her belly pushed tight against her blouse, then another at her tiny left hand and saw no band adorning it.

Neither look escaped Eva's notice. "No woman, Mr. Mather, should have to wear seven pounds of underwear. Furthermore, marriage is not a career."

Mather beamed his amusement down upon her once more, scratching his big shaggy head. "So, then, no hearth and needles for you, is it?"

Eva smoothed the cotton blouse over her belly and looked right up into his smiling brown eyes. "It was not my intention to stir your playful side, Mr. Mather. I was hoping to ask you some questions."

Mather could not ignore the heaviness of her breasts but resisted the impulse to look at them. He looked instead at her jawline, sleek in spite of her condition, and the feline complexity of her carriage. "Ah," he said. "You want answers. Well, if that's what you're after, I'm afraid you're out of luck. I've made an exclusive with the *Seattle Press.* They ask the questions."

"And who else owns your expedition? Who else has designs on our resources?"

"I'm afraid those are questions, Miss Lambert." He shifted distractedly, removing his elbow from its perch, as another parcel was hefted onto the pile. "Sitka," he called out to one of the bear dogs sniffing among the crowd. The dog came zigzagging back and planted herself at his heels, whereupon Mather rested a huge hand on her head and left it there.

"Well, then," said Eva brightly. "Perhaps you have some questions for me. Perhaps you'd like to ask me about the commonwealth? Perhaps you'd like to know where our colonists stand on the subject of corporations? After all, the colony *is* a corporation, albeit not a greedy unsympathetic one, like some."

Mather looked about the dock restlessly. The native child, whom he now presumed to be a boy, was still standing nearby, staring at him.

"Do they serve whiskey at this colony of yours?"

"Buttermilk, perhaps. And eggnog is not out of the question. In any event, I assure you our hotel is superior to anything you'll find here in town."

"Ah, well, I'm afraid we've already made arrangements in town."

"Well, should you find them lacking anything in the way of refinement, please call on us, Mr. Mather — that is, call on me. The colony is scarcely a mile from town. We have a theater, you know? And razors."

"A theater. Is that so?"

"There's a vaudeville running this week that is positively scandalous from all reports."

"Scandalous, you say?" Rarely had Mather experienced a woman so forward and undaunted.

"Perhaps we'll see you there, Mr. Mather. Good day." Without further ceremony, Eva turned on her heels.

Mather watched her backside as she went. She walked with conviction but also with grace, soft steps and undulating hips. After a half-dozen steps, she turned.

"Mine is the door with the wreath," she called over her shoulder.

Soon she was swallowed up by the crowd. Turning to resume his duties, Mather's eyes landed once more on the native boy, who was presently tilting his head sideways as he continued to stare at Mather. Something was amiss with the child; his spastic movements, his broad forehead, his apparent lack of self-awareness. The boy was an imbecile. Smiling uneasily, Mather resumed his work.

WHAT THE OLYMPIC HOTEL, with its splintered beams and crooked eaves and buckled floors, lacked in refinement, it offered in proximity to the Belvedere just across the muddy way. The Belvedere, for its part, lacked all refinement but offered whiskey in excess, and a venue to conduct interviews. In spite of its high ceilings — the flimsy construction of which did not inspire confidence — the Belvedere was choked with tobacco smoke. The establishment was a hive of activity and chatter when the party arrived in late afternoon. Perhaps a hundred men, more than half of them standing, crowded the bar. An inventory of their hats alone spoke of the Belvedere's clientele; top hats and coke hats and westerns and cattlemans, homburgs and Dakotas and Sinaloas. Wide-brimmed and narrow-brimmed, tall and squat; of felt and leather and Italian straw. Mather even spotted a lone cavalry hat in their midst. The men beneath them were every bit as dynamic as their haberdashery; clean-faced and stubbled and mustachioed, lean and wide, tall and short, stooping and straight. But every one of them — big or small, wealthy or impoverished — shared an appetite for new possibilities. The same spirit that drew them each to Port Bonita in the first place accounted, too, for the palpable air of excitement in the Belvedere, as Mather and his men made their entrance.

In his station behind the bar, John Tobin, the Belvedere Man, smiled at his own good fortune. At the behest of said proprietor, a line of stools was vacated. All eyes were on Mather and his men as they approached the bar.

"We've been expecting you," said Tobin.

"I can only hope we don't disappoint," Mather said, claiming a stool.

"All around?" said Tobin.

"The house," said Mather gesturing grandly.

When Haywood cocked a dubious brow, Mather patted him firmly on the back. "Not to worry, Charlie. You can thank the *Press*."

Following a round of whiskeys that took nearly a quarter of an hour to procure, Mather and his men, aided by a handful of volunteers, shuffled several tables about, fashioning a makeshift interview station in the far corner of the bar, where a crush of men began to form. The din of the bar soon proved to be a distraction, so for a small price, Tobin was persuaded to grant Mather use of one of the upstairs rooms, normally reserved for the carnal pursuits of his patrons.

A tired mattress was condemned to a corner, and a desk was moved in from the office. A line of men soon formed up the stairs. For the remainder of the afternoon and deep into the evening, Mather and Haywood conducted interviews.

Tobin himself was among the first to volunteer.

"Whatever you find beyond those mountains, I hope it ain't more Indians."

"Not likely," said Mather.

"Not likely at all," Haywood concurred.

As the evening progressed, no less than two dozen young men pleaded their cases to join the expedition. They hailed from Pennsylvania and Nebraska and Indiana and Ohio; tradesmen, cattlemen, and miners, and even an out-of-work dentist with three fingers on his right hand. Too, there were men who were born and raised in Port Bonita, and New Dungeness, men who'd spent their lives hunting and trapping and logging the hill country from the Elwha to the Hoh. Some of them purported to possess firsthand knowledge of the interior, though invariably upon further inquiry revealed themselves to be ignorant of the mountainous terrain that lay beyond the foothills.

And not all of the men were young. A trapper by the name of Lofall, a West Virginian by way of Missouri, the owner of a dilapidated set of teeth and a gray beard of remarkable proportions, bigger in fact than Mather's, claimed to have navigated the Elwha to its point of origin. When pressed for further information, however, Lofall professed to know the circuitous route to the origin of every river and the least resistant path over every range. It was Lofall who would eventually convince Mather that the Elwha was navigable by flatboat, a conviction that would greatly alter the course of the expedition. For all his enthusiasm, the trapper could not, however, allay Mather's incredulity upon hearing his tallest tale of all.

"When I come out onto the bank — like I say, the river is running low and she ain't too wide, it being late summer — I see it there on the other side, howling like the devil himself. Holding two big river rocks and crashing them together like cymbals. At first I figure it for a bear, standing on its hind legs. But I'm telling you, this was no bear. Didn't howl like any bear, that's a fact. And it didn't have a face like no bear. This was half a bear and half a man, God as my witness."

"Were you armed?" inquired Haywood.

"Yes, I was. And, to be truthful, I can't say why I didn't go for my rifle. I suppose because . . . well, to be perfectly honest, I was scared stiff. Didn't know what exactly I'd be shootin' at."

Later, Mather and Haywood would question the Indians about Lofall's alleged bear-man, and the Indians invariably smiled knowingly but claimed to know nothing. The Klallam, he learned, were a tribe at odds, having splintered in two tribes, neither of which were to be trusted. The Siwash Klallam, wintering at Hollywood Beach, were said to be drunk and unreliable for the most part, while the Klallam at Jamestown, some twenty miles east along the strait, were said to be religious zealots, blinded by temperance and a hatred for whites. Mather opted to question the Siwash Klallam because of their proximity. Their camp was strung out for a half mile or more along the strait east of the harbor, comprising a loosely knit webwork of sagging tents, lean-tos, and odd ménages of shake and tin and canvas that defied classification. Among these habitations, a number of wooden frames had been constructed, festooned with laundry and cured fish carcasses. The gravel shoreline was littered with canoes, heaping from bow to stern with all manner of worldly possessions, from nets to baskets to iron skillets. Fires burned, or rather smoked, in uneven intervals up and down the beach, around which old Klallam women hunched to no purpose, and an occasional drunk was sprawled out.

Mather found the Indians to be every bit as forthcoming, if no more helpful, than the whites. An old woman wrapped in at least four shawls told Mather of a central basin awaiting them beyond the divide, surrounding a vast alpine lake, into whose chill waters all rivers flowed, an idyllic portrait soon corroborated by a half-dozen Klallam. They told of a wide fertile valley brimming yellow with mountain lilies. A land teeming year-round with elk, deer, and all manner of game. However, it was also noted upon nearly every occasion that the natives dared not venture into this paradise. Most were wary to even speak of the reason why. A Klallam elder calling himself Indian

George was finally persuaded to explain the matter of a certain fire-spewing bird god who nested there.

"Many years ago, too many to count, the hungry Siwash sent a hunting party deep into the mountains in search of ranging elk," the old man explained. "The hunting was good there. The elk were plenty and offered themselves to the hunters, who were very grateful. But when Thunderbird discovered that the Siwash had entered his home, he grew angry, and he descended screeching from his snowy perch, and swooped down on them, and the beating of his wings uprooted whole forests in front of him. And when he arrived with his deafening caw, the earth heaved. He opened great chasms in the earth, which swallowed the hunters. And Thunderbird dumped mountains and rivers upon the Siwash. And they did not die courageously, our hunters, but begging for their lives. Only a few managed to survive the wrath of Thunderbird, and this they did not manage on their own — they were spared by Thunderbird as messengers to warn the Siwash."

Apparently, the message was still alive and well in 1889, though Mather paid no heed to this warning, nor the bulk of the information he collected at Hollywood Beach, reasoning that the natives were dangerously susceptible to parable and could not be trusted to provide any credible information about the lay of the interior. Mather did, however, find their stories entertaining and judged the Klallam at Hollywood Beach to be in every way superior to the Crees and half-breeds he fought in Manitoba.

AFTER TWO DAYS of inquiries, the party found their guide in the person of a twenty-eight-year-old Klallam named Abraham Lincoln Charles. Charles was said by a number of his people to be an excellent hunter, fisherman, and tracker, with an impressive knowledge of the Elwha and the surrounding valleys.

It was observed by one elderly Klallam that Abe Charles was "the best hunter of all the Siwash" and that he never got lost, not even in the driving snow.

"Even if he doesn't know where he is, he knows where to go. The Little Earths live inside his head."

The young Klallam struck an impressive figure. At six foot three, he was nearly Mather's height but leaner and harder. He wore a Mackinaw jacket of Yukon wool and cut his hair short like a white man. Abe Charles was soft-spoken and measured in his delivery, two qualities that never failed to engender confidence in Mather, probably, he was willing to admit, owing to his own vociferous and impulsive manner. Moreover, Abe Charles did not drink. The young Klallam promised to be a welcome addition to the expedition.

Upon the eve of the party's initial push into the interior, however, Abraham Lincoln Charles would stealthily pack his bag by the light of the dying fire and steal quietly downriver into the night.

port bonita

On the afternoon of December 14, in the year of our Lord 1889, the good steamer *George E. Starr* chugged around Ediz Hook in a driving squall, her bowels belching hemlock and cedar, as she pulled into ragged Port Bonita. When she landed at Morse Dock, nobody clamored to greet her. Only a few tatters of wet silk bunting were left to mark the occasion when young Ethan Thornburgh strode off the *George E. Starr* onto an empty dock, clutching a lone leather suitcase, with the wind at his back and his silver-eyed gaze leveled straight at the future. He might have looked like a dandy to the casual observer, a young man of some distinction, all buttoned up in a brown suit with tails, freshly coifed, smelling of camphor and spices, his cleft chin clean-shaven, a waxed mustache mantling his lip like two sea horses kissing. But upon closer inspection, visible through the shifting mothholes in his wool trousers, a trained eye might have observed the shoe polish daubed on his underwear or the fear in his silver-eyed gaze. One might even have glimpsed the yellow blue remnants of a shiner beneath his right eye.

Ethan stood tall and lean on the dock, flattening his lapel, as he gathered his bearings. This did not take long. The town ran only one direction. Indeed, it had nowhere else to go, hemmed in as it was by heavy timber and steep inclines. There was only Front Street, a ragtag row of structures running east to west in an arrangement that suggested jetsam spewed on the shoreline.

Skirting the muddy creek that ran down the middle of Front Street, Ethan passed a feed store and a darkened real estate office before he came upon the Northern Pacific office. Smiling inwardly at the town's prospects as he peered through the mud-spattered glass, he found the premises empty. Along the fringes of the creek, the street was heavily rutted and thick with the churned-up mud of wagon teams, though presently Ethan saw none about.

At the Olympic Hotel, he came upon a rather rough looking gent with wild hair and a permanent scowl, who was leading two mules. When Ethan inquired as to the direction of the commonwealth colony, the stranger looked him up and down at length, squinting like a marksman.

"What is it you want with the colony?" he said.

"I want to locate it," said Ethan.

"Hmph," said the stranger. He spit on the ground and jerked his thumb once toward the east. Ethan tipped his hat as he mounted the sodden boardwalk.

Clomping clear-headed past the smoke and laughter of the Belvedere, Ethan was determined to pass without incident. He'd sworn off those immoderate houses of woe. What need of whiskey, he thought, drawing a deep breath, when the rare air of Port Bonita was free for the taking? With purpose and resolve, he proceeded for eight or ten strides before surrendering finally to temptation. Just a nip for courage, he assured himself. A little cheer to color the cheeks. A toast, as it were, to the adventure that lay ahead. Just enough so Eva wouldn't notice.

Ethan took a stool and, in spite of local custom, removed his hat and set it on the bar before him, revealing a head of straight dark hair parted cleanly down the center. Casting a look around the establishment, it occurred to him that the Belvedere did not live up to its name. In fact, not only did the saloon fail to offer the grand view its namesake promised, it conferred no view whatsoever, save for a partial vantage of the flooded street, obscured further by the mud-caked windows.

The Frontier Room, thought Ethan. Now *that's* the name for this saloon. Promptly he produced a small pad and the dull nub of a pencil from his coat pocket, whereupon he jotted his newest idea alongside two hundred other flashes of inspiration, including the Walla Walla chip (a variation on the Saratoga chip — made with sweet onion), the electric stairs, the electric pencil sharpener, the magnetic coat hanger, and a flatulent comic revue titled *Will-o'-the-Wisp*.

Replacing pencil and pad in pocket, Ethan turned to the gentleman next to him — a dough-faced fellow of forty or so, with a steam-shovel jaw — and extended a hand.

"Thornburgh, Ethan. Pleased to make your acquaintance, Mr. . . . ?"

Dough Face eyed Ethan doubtfully. "Whatever you're selling, mister, I'm not buying."

Undaunted, Ethan forged ahead. "You're certainly not, my friend, because *I'm* buying. Barkeep! Two whiskeys," he called out to Tobin.

The pale man still did not offer a hand. "Dalton Krigstadt," he said, as Tobin poured out the whiskeys.

Lowering his hand casually, Ethan looked his new friend up and down: denim trousers, leather boots, coarse hands. "Let me venture a guess," he said. "Woodsman?"

"Nope," said Krigstadt, staring straight ahead.

"Mason?"

"Nope."

"Railroad man."

"Nope."

"Hmm. Well, then, I'm beat. What's your line of work?"

Krigstadt suppressed a sigh. "Mostly, I haul things," he said.

"Ah, transportation! Where would we be without it? Especially here, where things are always moving. To transportation," said Ethan, raising his glass.

Krigstadt offered a less than enthusiastic nod and promptly shot his whiskey in a single throw. "What about you?" he said, wiping his mouth.

"I, Mr. Krigstadt, am a businessman."

Krigstadt eyed him doubtfully, once more; the flashy mustache, the ill-fitting jacket, the moth-eaten trousers. "What sort of business would that be?"

Ethan smiled and slid his empty glass forward for a refill. "Presently, sir, that remains to be seen. My background is in accounting. But I've come here to make a new start, Dalton. May I call you Dalton?"

"That's my name, ain't it?"

"Yes, of course. You see, Dalton. I've come west because I'm tired of toiling for others. I want to work for myself."

Krigstadt spun his empty glass. "Don't anybody work for themselves when you get down to it. Less he can make money out of thin air."

"Exactly my point," said Ethan. "You're a wise man, Dalton Krigstadt. A wise man, indeed."

Krigstadt slid his empty glass forward on the bar just as Tobin replenished Ethan's.

Two more rounds ensued, during which Ethan elucidated at some length upon his status as *an idea man.* Krigstadt offered little encouragement beyond the act of sliding his glass forward each time the barman approached.

After roughly an hour, Ethan, whose neatly parted hair was now mussed, referred to his pocket watch, plucked his hat off the bar, and stood to leave.

"Well, then, Dalton Krigstadt. It's been a pleasure. I trust in a town this size we shall soon meet again."

"Probably," said Krigstadt.

On his way out of the Belvedere, pleasantly flush from the whiskey, though not so flush, he imagined, that Eva would notice, Ethan stopped to inquire more specifically as to the colony's location. On this occasion, he solicited a one-eyed gentleman with what appeared to be gristle in his beard, whom he found leaning against the splintered rail of the boardwalk, carving a naked female form out of a potato. The result was a decidedly stubby female form. The artisan paused long enough to subject Ethan to a thorough visual inspection, whereupon he gruffly issued the coordinates "over the hump."

Ethan trod onward in the pitchforking rain. His mustache took on water and began to wilt. His heel was squeaking and his suit was heavy with rainwater by the time he arrived at the foot of a stumped and muddy hogback on the east end of town. Twice he lost his footing clambering up the muddy path and on one occasion very nearly lost his suitcase down the stubbled hillside.

As he crested the hump, he got his first look at the colony below. He took out his pipe, packed it, and attempted to smoke in the rain, as he looked down upon the Utopia for which Eva had abandoned him. The model commonwealth, free of working-class turmoil, free of labor strife, free of corporate tyranny, in short, the solution to the Chinese problem. A mill, a boat shed, a theater, a hotel, a schoolhouse. A cluster of little white houses huddled together like Indians on the shoreline. Doomed to failure, thought Ethan, all of it. Human nature would never allow for cooperation on such a scale. But it was nice to think so. How orderly the colony appeared clustered on one side of the hill, with the ragged outpost of Port Bonita on the other, how refined in comparison was its very conception. Yet, it was Port Bonita that called to Ethan, not the colony. Port Bonita, with its crude and youthful vigor, its laughing, belching, bawdy can-do spirit. A pugnacious town, Port Bonita, a fighter, and a damn good bet. It was Port Bonita into which Ethan would invest all his of faith and energy. And one day, God willing, he would invest his fortune there, too.

A full two minutes passed in contemplation before Ethan took notice of the spindly native child standing downhill of him at a distance of some twenty feet, arms akimbo, impervious to the rain. Clearly, there was something odd about this round-faced boy, if indeed, it was a boy. His lips were moving silently. Odder still were the child's glacial blue eyes, almost as pale as his own, which seemed to be focusing on some distant point beyond Ethan. Glancing back over his shoulder, Ethan found himself hemmed in by a muddy hillside.

"Boo!" said Ethan, swinging around.

But the child did not budge.

"Don't frighten easily, eh? That's good. That'll get you far, son. What's your name?"

The boy remained silently fixated on his distant point.

"I see. Silent, too. That'll get you even further. My name is Ethan. Ethan Thornburgh. Remember that name, son. One day it will mean something."

The boy tilted his head slightly to one side and squinted.

"Not convinced, are you? Well, that's okay. I should think you're not alone there. No, I'm rather used to that by now. But let me tell you a little secret, boy. A man's destiny is not in the eyes of others. It's in his own. And that, my young friend, is as good as any bank note."

Covering one eye with his hand, the boy tilted his head to the other side.

Ethan did the same.

The boy took a step forward, and Ethan, too, stepped forward. When the boy stepped back again, Ethan followed suit. This dance continued for several minutes. When it became clear to Ethan that the boy would win any war of repetition, he emptied his pipe with a tap and replaced it in his hip pocket. Thumbing the thin roll of bills in his pocket, he surveyed the mud-spattered condition of his trouser legs and laughed.

"Good day," Ethan said, doffing his soggy hat to the boy. He then turned and began trudging east down the squishy path toward the colony.

THOMAS FOUND HIS MOTHER seated alone by the fire at the mouth of the creek. The rain had let up, but the fire still hissed, unfurling a ribbon of black smoke toward the shoreline. Thomas sat beside her. His lips stopped moving. His mother did not look up but out across the strait. Thomas scooted closer, but still she did not acknowledge the boy. Upbeach to the east, a chain of six fires at roughly even distances unfurled their own black ribbons into the wind. Thomas could hear, just above the lapping shoreline, the low chatter of his people and occasionally the shrill voice of a white man in their midst.

an honest woman

But for the cedar placard reading LAMBERT, and the lone decorative flourish of a holly wreath fastened to the door, Eva's plain white house, quaint and ugly, was all but indistinguishable from the thirty small houses huddled around it. Nothing Utopian about it, to Ethan's way of thinking. The thought of the place made him restless.

The Eva who greeted Ethan at the door, just as he was straightening his waterlogged salmon pink tie, was clearly not the bustle-and-petticoat Eva who had abandoned him in Seattle, but rather a new incarnation, replete with divided skirts and a hard little bun atop her head, and a floppy hand-painted tie. However, it was apparent at once, as she stood fiercely in the doorway, jaw set, with one hand on her hip and the other on the bulge beneath her white blouse, that she was the same hardheaded Eva Lambert who had twice refused his hand.

"Oh, Ethan, no," she said, blocking his way. "Do you never learn? Have I not been brutally honest with you?"

"Brutal, yes," said Ethan. "Are you going to let me in?"

"What happened to your eye? You look awful. You've been drinking."

"I had a skirmish in Seattle. Now, may I come in?"

"You've always been less of a physical coward than a moral one."

"I've changed," he said.

"I've not," she said. "But come in if you must."

Eva led him to a cluttered sitting room, where Ethan sat himself down. He commenced rolling up his muddy trousers, removing his squeaky shoes and wet stockings, and setting his feet on the quilted pad of a sizable divan, where his toes set to wiggling, as he finessed his wilted mustache back into shape.

The room was populated by an upright piano, a pair of balloon-backed chairs upholstered in red velvet, and no less than three curios, riddled with bric-a-brac ranging from exotic butterflies and souvenir spoons to gleaming silver urns and porcelain gravy boats. It occurred to Ethan that the room's tumultuous decor was probably not so different from the furniture of Eva's mind. There was nothing plain about Eva. No tight hair bun could belie the frazzles; no high-necked blouse could button up her spirit.

"All right, Ethan, what are you doing here? The condensed version."

Ethan could not look at her. His eyes sought the clutter all about him and lit upon a little cluster of porcelain figurines arranged in a half circle atop a tasseled runner: a man, a woman, a boy, a dog, and two penguins. "There's an honest woman in you somewhere, Eva, I just know it."

"Ha! An honest woman! Really, Ethan, what have you been reading? And just what is an honest woman? One unburdened by initiative? One without opinions, one without — "

"Damn it, I mean it! It's time to put aside all the rest of it and get serious."

"The rest of what? The rest of me? The rest of my life? Why is it every time a woman gets serious, she has to set something aside?"

"It's not like that! I'm not asking you to give anything up. I'm not asking you to come back to Seattle. I want you exactly as you are, not one bit different. I just want to join you, to make a life with you. The life we set out to make when we left Chicago. Be sensible, Eva. You could use a man around here."

Eva turned toward the window. The rain was coming harder. "Even if that were true, you're too late. We've sold the cows. The brickyard has closed. The opera house sits half finished like a monument to our failure."

"I don't mean here. And I don't mean in town, either. I mean out there." He gestured vaguely toward the window. "Gads, look at it out there! It's glorious, it's endless. It's up for grabs." He reached up and grabbed two possibilities out of the air, and closed his fists around them. "Why not us, Eva? You're a new woman, why not a new life?"

"What do you think *this* is?" she said, clutching her swollen belly with both hands. "How many people do I have to surrender my will to?"

"I'm not asking you to surrender anything, I'm asking you to be a part of something bigger."

"I'm leaving in two weeks," she said. "I'll not burden my child with any of this."

"For where? Seattle's all but burned to the ground."

"Back to Chicago."

"You mean, back to Daddy."

"However you prefer to look at it, Ethan. It's not my concern. Good luck with your new life."

"It's not right, Eva! A boy needs a father."

"Who says it's a boy?"

"Whatever it is!"

"And just what qualifies you to be a father?"

"I've already qualified," he observed, indicating her stomach. "Wouldn't you say?"

"Roses and moonlight are not qualifications, Ethan."

"And what is that supposed to mean? Just what do you think I'm doing here? Remember, Eva, it was you who walked away and turned everything upside down, you and all your new ideas. We were happy in Chicago."

"You were happy."

"We were happy in Seattle."

"You were, Ethan, not I."

Ethan jumped up from his place on the divan and did his best to pace about the little parlor. So crowded was the room that Eva was forced to press her belly against the window sill each time Ethan passed. She never got used to this thing out in front of her, this cumbersome otherness, impeding her movement, weighing her down. Darkness was beginning to set in over the colony. Eva watched as one by one the windows of the hotel began to glow with lamplight.

"Look," resumed Ethan. "You may think I haven't any prospects. I know what your father thinks of me, and your brother, too. And I know what my own father thought of me, and I can still hear him laughing. Yes, I've made some rash decisions, some imprudent ones. Yes, I don't always look before I leap. Yes, I nearly got jugged on account of some miscalculations, but that's all they were, miscalculations, simple arithmetic. I was never cut out for the work in the first place." Ethan abandoned his pacing and plopped back down on the divan with a sigh. His hands set restlessly to work in his lap. "But, Eva, you're wrong about me, you're all wrong. Just who do you think is going to civilize this place? Who do you think is going to roll up their sleeves and put this place on the map? Men like your father? Stodgy old capitalists with no vision, the bed partners of senators and congressmen? You think the man that's had every break in the world, the man that's been handed a life, you think he's got the gumption to carve out a life here? You think *he's* going to transform this place with the sweat of his brow? Isn't that why you came here? A new start? A different kind of life? One that was equitable, one that offered a man the same opportunities no matter who he —"

"Ech!" cried Eva, turning from the window. "Men, men, men, men, men! Did it ever occur to you for one moment that a woman could be more than a helpmate, more than some chicken-tending, child-rearing Madonna of the frontier, that a woman could roll up her sleeves? Who do you think built that schoolhouse? Furthermore, who do you think conceived of it?"

"I didn't mean —"

"You don't have to mean anything. It doesn't matter what your intentions are. This is about convention, Ethan. This is about turning a blind eye to the obvious, something all men seem to share an astounding capacity for. Especially here. If you think I'm going to settle for less than a new man, if you think I'm going to settle for a man who talks endlessly of prospects but can't even see the potential of the woman he professes to love, a man who talks about changing the world but can't even change his perspective, well, then, you're sadly mistaken. I'll no sooner put my faith in that man than in the bed partners of senators. This is not about what my father or anyone else thinks. This is about what *I* think. And do you know what I think? I think that you don't inspire confidence. I think that you cast ideas out in front you like an angler, then fall asleep with your hat pulled over your eyes before you ever get a bite. I think you have the common sense of a puppy. I think you have the — " Eva stopped herself short when she saw Ethan slumping miserably on the divan. She turned toward the hearth and the light of the fire. "That was unkind," she said. "Forgive me."

Ethan saw her softening before his eyes; he could feel her caving. She took the two short steps to the divan and ran her fingers through his hair. "It was unfair of me to say those things. I could just as easily say that you're as guileless as a puppy. Or as affectionate. And, oh, Ethan, I know you want to be an extraordinary man, and that's admirable. I know you feel you have something to prove, but I'm not asking you to prove anything, not to me, or my father, or anyone else. I'm only asking you to understand. I just . . . oh, I don't know . . . I want to make my way in this life on my own power — not my father's and not my husband's. The very idea of marriage seems so . . . I'm a *journalist*, Ethan. That's what I do. A *real* journalist. I'm wedded to my work."

"But I've seen the clippings, Eva. 'Cow Gives Birth at Megg's Farm,' 'New Bridle Path Proposed for Ennis Creek.' This is hardly the stuff of Helen Hunt Jackson!"

"It's a start, Ethan. An opportunity."

"You're going to be a mother, Eva. I'm going to be a father. Does this not change things?"

She heaved a sigh, and left off stroking his hair, and moved to the corner of the room and lit a lamp, whereupon she returned to the divan and sat down beside him. "Oh, let's not talk about it. I'm famished," she said. "Have you eaten?"

crooked thumb

From the mouth of the Elwha to the base of the foothills, the settlers trail cut a muddy, circuitous path through a dark tangle of vine maple and alder. The path was rutty and obscure in places but relatively free of downed timber, and Ethan soon shook the chill of dawn as he scooted on his way toward the unknown. Occasionally he'd pass a claim, marked by a small clearing and a crude cabin, but never any sign of life. The land grab had begun. Men were claiming land but not making the requisite improvements, and Ethan knew well that he would have been within his rights to squat on these claims and call them his own. But he saw nothing in the periphery of these wooded bottomlands to inspire a claim. The timber was inexhaustible, and the river was close at hand to move it, but Ethan longed for something grander than timber.

In spite of a rather limp mustache and a watch-sized blister on the ball of his right foot, Ethan met the first leg of his journey with the ease of a purposeful stride. Neither the dank light of the understory, sodden and brittle with winter, nor the squelchy ground beneath his feet could temper Ethan's optimism. Twice the trail met with the confluence of a small stream, and on both occasions a tree had been felled for the purpose of crossing.

At mile four, Indian George Sampson had a claim in a small meadow along the near bank where the river ran wide. Unable to ford the high water, Ethan drank coffee with the old Indian in the murky light of the cabin, where he soon deduced that Indian George did not share his love of easy conversation. But at the very least the old fellow seemed to endure it with a certain enthusiasm, frequently nodding and raising an eyebrow on occasion. When Sampson did speak, the Salish was to Ethan an indecipherable cascade of sharp syllables, mostly with *q*s and *k*s, and Ethan found himself nodding his own head and raising his eyebrows. In the end, resorting to crude pantomime, Ethan was able to elicit George's aid in crossing the river by canoe, only to discover during their crossing that the old man was not only in possession of a considerable store of the Queen's English but was in fact a formidable conversationalist, inquiring as to the progress of the opera house being erected next to the colony hotel, the railroad said to be soon arriving from the east (in spite of their vacant offices), and the great fire that was said to have consumed the white man's settlement in Seattle.

"Why didn't you say anything before?"

George shrugged. The slightest of smiles played at the corners of his mouth. "You didn't ask."

On the far bank, Ethan left George with a handshake and some soggy biscuits. The old Indian gratefully accepted this bounty, which he would soon pass on to the boy, who would refuse the boat and swim across the river clutching the biscuits above the water.

With a final wave to George, Ethan reshifted his load, hefted his new rifle, and proceeded upriver along the left bank until he picked up the trail. As he began to gain elevation, the path diverged from the river and the ground was mottled with snow. The understory thinned out considerably, allowing the eye to penetrate further into the wooded interior up the hill. The sound of the river grew fainter as Ethan plodded on, preceded by the fog of his own breath.

On the far side of the first rise, Ethan met with a swamp, where, from the higher vantage of a rotting cedar, he paused to smoke his pipe and chart the least treacherous crossing. Three days later, Mather's mules, Dolly and Daisy, each cinched up to the tune of two hundred pounds, would bay miserably at the prospect of this crossing and would eventually become hopelessly mired, unburdened of their loads, and finally extracted, forcing the party to circumnavigate the swamp by a steep overland route, adding a half day to their journey. Ethan considered such an option but decided to meet the challenge head-on in spite of the chill.

He removed his socks and trousers, replacing his boots on his bare feet. Shivering, he refastened his bundle, and set off in his underwear to conquer the soggy terrain. He soon found himself mired in bog water well past the knee, his boot heels heavy with the suck of mud, pulling himself along by the limbs of bare alders.

As he mucked his way through the swamp, his body grew warm from the effort. He found his thoughts ungovernable. Flashes of Eva and the baby (a son, God willing, to whom he would assign the name Ethan Eben or perhaps Ethan Allen), flashes of a life yet to be lived, a bounty to be plucked out of the wilderness for the taking. And no rustic life, either — no buckskin jackets and boiled hams, but a life with electricity and running water and chamber music by firelight, a life of consequence, of virtue and good fishing, a life of ever-perpetuating golden opportunities. And maybe a saloon. Why not? Tasteful, of course, nothing Eva would object to. Just a piano player and a civil game of poker. And maybe the occasional pleasure of a whiskey or a half bucket of beer. Everything in moderation, of course.

Ah, but who was he kidding? What did he know of moderation? When had he ever capitalized on opportunities? An inventory of his life would show that he'd squandered opportunities at every pass — his education, his trade, every chance he ever had of winning the heart of the woman he loved. Eva was right. He did not inspire confidence.

This self-doubt was short-lived, as Ethan emerged from these ruminations at the head of a canyon in a small, clear meadow, just as the sun darted out from between clouds. From this vista he could see straight up the gut of the valley and over the foothills to the rugged snow clad peaks of the divide, where a marooned cloud bank unfurled its wispy arm into the valley. A hundred feet below him, the Elwha thundered through a narrow channel of mossy rock.

Ethan stood in his boots and his jacket and his muddy underwear on a rock spur jutting out over edge of the narrow abyss, and the hairs of his legs stood on end as though electrified. Here was something grand beyond all expectation. Transfixed by the raging flash of the river, he felt the thunder of it in his chest as it vibrated up through the rock. He felt the wild brute force of it in his spirit.

ALL AFTERNOON THE BOY could hear the determined thud of Ethan's ax reports echoing through the little valley, along with the crackle and peel of felled timber and the snow-muffled blow as it settled to earth. He watched from the wood line as Ethan dragged each length across the meadow through the snow to the bluff, where he cleared a level spot of snow and began notching saddles in the wood. He worked like a white man. He threw himself headlong at a job as if were he to stop the job would throw itself headlong back at him.

And it did. For Thomas heard the plaintive cries of agony and the tide of invectives aimed at heaven when Ethan crushed his thumb wrestling a log into place. The thumb began to swell immediately. Ethan packed it in snow as best he could and cursed himself at length as he leaned against his new home: half a cabin, twenty feet square, three logs high. The thunder of the Elwha was just loud enough to drown out the dull throbbing of his thumb, just hypnotic enough to set his mind wandering again into the future.

Ethan Eben. Ethan Allen. A fine boy, either way. From good hardy stock. Thornburgh and Lambert. A boy to make his father proud, a boy to set upon his shoulder, a boy to watch him shave, to walk at his side, a boy with whom to fish the chill paradise of these mountain waters. A boy he could guide with the steady hand of experience, through the labyrinthine complexities of life, so that he could avoid his father's folly, absolve his father's failures, and rise to the top of the heap. And he would build that boy into a man, and nobody would ever call that man small or petty or mean.

Compared to a son, a broken thumb was nothing.

THOMAS SQUATTED IN the hollow of a buttressed cedar. Sixteen was the number of trees that were not cedars. One was pointing its finger. Thomas tried not to stare at this one. The sound of the river began with a roar and ended with a hiss, and the sounds were perfectly balanced to Thomas's ears, but he wished he could hear more hiss. He wanted to be *in* the hiss, so he made his way down the hill to the mouth of the canyon, where he met the shallow bank and followed the river around the rugged tangle of a bend that was not yet called Crooked Thumb. Here the river eddied and swirled and hissed, and the roar was further off up the canyon where it belonged.

Thomas squatted on a smooth wet rock until dusk, fingering water-filled dimples in the surface of the stone, tickling the moss with his toes, and listening for voices in the hiss as his lips moved silently over words that came out of nowhere. His grandfather swore that the silent words were stories trying to get out. Indian George Sampson said they were spirit voices whispering inside of him. Thomas did not question the meaning of the words. The words were to the boy like a clock ticking inside of him, marking the days of his life, so that looking back, these days were not invisible, they were a record, a history, a proof. The Potato Counter had his books full of numbers and schedules. Thomas had his silent words.

LEANING AGAINST THE half cabin, Ethan's body grew cold with inactivity, and his teeth began to clatter as dusk settled in. He set to work making camp with his good hand. Finding no shortage of deadfall along the wooded fringes, mostly alder and spruce, he soon dried his boots and warmed his aching thumb by a raging fire. He used his last biscuit to make a poultice with snow water; he battered his hand with it and wrapped it in a sock so he wouldn't have to look at it. And again it was not long before he forgot the injury altogether beneath the roar of the Elwha. When he was no longer certain whether he was asleep or awake, he made a bed of spruce boughs inside his roofless cabin and lay on his back exhausted but not beleaguered. Aching but not miserable. Half asleep but fully awake to all of life's possibilities.

ETHAN STIFFENED UPON hearing the first holler, for that's what it sounded like, a deep holler, or a howl, clearly audible over the rushing Elwha. Then a series of whoops not unlike an owl's. They seemed to originate from the far side of the chasm, somewhere up the hillside. After the second holler, he bolted upright beneath his wool blanket. But it was not until the third call garnered a surly response from the near side of the chasm that Ethan found himself clutching the Winchester in his good hand.

He sat rigid and silent for the better part of a half hour, as the two calls volleyed back and forth over the chasm, drawing closer to one another as they moved downriver, until it seemed the near call came from no more than fifty feet directly behind Ethan on the bluff, and its counterpart answered from just over the gap. Ethan took the sock off his hand and eased his head up over the log wall like a prairie dog, leveling his rifle at the night. He heard what sounded like guttural voices whispering in tongues all about him in the canyon, a confusion of voices that seemed at once to circle the canyon and the inside of his head, and he wondered again whether he was asleep or awake, until he heard something large clatter through the nearby brush on a downriver course. And in that moment, Ethan felt the pale flame in his stomach flicker.

He had a good mind to squeeze off a blind round into the night, to dispatch a thunderclap of human braggadocio and send it echoing through the valley like a challenge, but somehow he could not summon the nerve. Instead, he coaxed the glowing coals and fed them until they raged, then squatted by the glow of the fire, holding his rifle. Never had Ethan felt quite so alive.

becoming

On the eve of the party's final ascent to base camp, where they would cache the last of their supplies before taking aim at the rugged interior, Mather and his men enjoyed venison steaks at the Olympic before crossing the muddy hogback to the colony for a night of theater at the Pioneer, where a certain burlesque musical extravaganza — having enjoyed its inauspicious debut at Wallack's Lyceum Theatre some four decades prior — enjoyed a warm reception from colonists and a few Port Bonitans alike.

At intermission, Eva and Mather retired to the drafty foyer, where a twelve-piece cornet band honked its way through the "Washington Post March," moving Mather to comment that the band sounded *a bit gassy tonight.*

"You seem amused by our efforts, Mr. Mather," said Eva.

"I confess, I am slightly. While I admire the spirit of it, I really do, I just think that . . ."

"And what spirit is that?"

Mather took a quick inventory of his general surroundings. The plank floor protested beneath his shifting weight. "Optimism, I suppose."

Eva found herself appraising Mather's beard, and the dirt caked beneath his fingernails, and for no reason at all she thought of Ethan. "The opera house will be on a much grander scale," she assured him.

"That's not what I mean," said Mather.

"What do you mean, then?"

"I see a general lack of organization at work here. I see women, children, and tradesmen, but I don't see anyone swinging an ax. I see them painting landscapes. I should think that before I put up an opera house, I'd put that mill to better purpose and get some industry in place. And I'd do something about those natives. They may look it, but they're not beaten yet."

"We're not trying to beat them, Mr. Mather."

"What, then? Join them?"

"They may join us, if they wish. Or we can simply coexist."

Mather smiled. "Nice of you to think so." Against his will, his gaze wandered again to Eva's swollen belly, which never failed to stir and confuse him.

Equally stirred and confused, Eva pulled her shawl about her.

Mather scanned the foyer for occupation. "I was given to understand that you were leaving for . . . Chicago, was it?"

"No," she said. "I believe I'm digging in, for better or worse."

"Mm."

"I have more faith in *women,* children, and tradesmen than you do," she said, turning from him slightly. "Not all of us were built to wander."

"Ah," said Mather doubtfully.

Eva could feel his eyes upon her, as she presumed to search the lobby for someone or something. And indeed, Mather's eyes were upon her, and his imagination compelled him further still. Where exactly was the grace in this defiant little woman, with her sleek jaw and thin neck and distended belly, if not in her defiance itself, in the challenge it presented him with.

"And the railroad?" he inquired.

"It will come," she said. "Sooner than later. They're setting up new offices in town."

"Yes, I've heard. But I've heard the same in Port Townsend and New Dungeness."

"You doubt it?"

Mather cursed himself for not leaving the subject alone, for never resisting the urge to conquer expectation. "I've been wrong before, and it's cost me a good deal of trouble and embarrassment. And I'll probably be wrong again someday. Still, I see no logical reason why Seattle shouldn't be the hub."

"And build this hub out of rubble?"

"Still, Seattle is a *town*, with all due respect. Don't think a fire is going to hold a town like Seattle down. They have electricity. They have banks. They're not printing their own money."

"Perhaps not. But then Seattle hasn't our wealth in unknown quantities, either. You yourself called this place a gateway not two days ago."

"Yes, but gateway to what, to where? There's rugged country out there. I'm guessing as rough as anything I ever encountered on the Mackenzie or anywhere else. That's no barrier range, Miss Lambert, whatever it is. And should this wilderness not surrender its bounty, what then? What becomes of this place?"

"Then, I suppose, we have no choice but to be a gateway to ourselves."

Throughout the second half of the show Mather snuck sidelong glances at Eva in the half-light, watching the quick, sharp proceedings of her mind in each frown and smile. His favorite expression was anticipation, for in those moments when her mind was suspended and awaiting, her little mouth stuck open in the act of flowering, and her eyes wide with innocence, the overall effect was childlike and charming. And when, during a moment of anticipation, he ventured to set his hand on hers in the warmth of her lap, she did not object.

After the show, Mather insisted on seeing Eva home by the light of his lantern. As they wended their way down the path, both were in high spirits.

"You're not afraid of the Thunderbird, Mr. Mather?"

"I should like to see his nest. And I fully intend to by spring."

Occasionally, their shoulders grazed one another as they walked.

"What spirit drives you to these enterprises, if I may ask?"

"You might be surprised," he said.

"Very well, surprise me, then."

"What if I told you humility."

"Ha!" said Eva. "I would have hardly guessed. I might have guessed vanity."

"There is that also, I won't deny it. And adventure and the promise of wealth. But more than anything, there is humility. Nature is not easy to conquer. She has a competitive spirit. She *will* humble you, Miss Lambert, and I've found that when she does, a man can be quiet in his heart. Besides, I like a challenge. And what's become of the father of your child?"

Eva felt her face go hot. "Pardon me, but I don't see where that's your concern."

"Perhaps not. Except that not ten minutes ago you were holding my hand."

For a silent moment they walked down the path in a puddle of light. Eva could feel her will weakening toward Mather, just as sure as she could feel the broadness and warmth of his big body beside her.

"Nothing has become of him, if you must know. He purports to be in the process of becoming as we speak."

"Becoming what?"

"That I cannot answer. But I trust he has the will to become something."

"Never underestimate the will," said Mather.

Just before the fork in the path, a young Indian woman overtook them and proceeded down the path toward the beach.

"Thomas!" she shouted. *"Can qeyen ceq!"*

Eva and Mather cut off to the right, soon arriving at Eva's doorstep, where Mather offered her an elbow up the steps.

AFTER MATHER LEFT Eva at her doorstep on the eve of his departure, he found himself adrift in the night, in no hurry to return to the Olympic, where he knew sleep would not have him. Instead, he wandered down the path, his thoughts focused inward toward some uncharted awareness.

How do we measure our lives, Mr. Mather?

That depends upon who we are, Miss Lambert.

And who are you, Mr. Mather?

It struck Mather, as he drifted further down the path, that despite all of his discoveries, despite his ceaseless charge at the unknown, all of his endless plotting and mapping and naming, he was willfully lost in himself. What was all of this exploration, this restless trek onward, if not cowardice dressed up in snow shoes? Fear with a hundred-pound bundle on its back. What was the purpose of his exploration, if not escape?

FROM HER PLACE at the window, Eva watched Mather's retreat, wondering what it was that so compelled her about this man. God forbid, it was those same qualities that repulsed her: his hulking sturdiness, his feral beard, his appetites. Was it that he charged at the unknown like a billy goat? That he was so unconcerned with the delicacies of convention, that he spoke frankly at all times? Or was it as rudimentary as the confidence in his stride and the bedrock of his convictions?

Eva scolded herself for this line of thinking and turned her thoughts obediently toward Ethan, who already might well have frozen to death or drowned for all she knew. Yet she could not bring herself to worry about him, for Ethan Thornburgh was nothing if not resilient. Landslides may rumble in his wake, rivers may flood behind him, but Ethan would emerge unscathed. The thought of him brought a smile to her face. Was Ethan not blessed with his own rugged brand of optimism? Was it not his good intentions more than any weakness of character that accounted for his follies? Was there not a great deal of sincerity beneath his toe-wiggling, mustachioed charm? And was he not eager to forge a path for his son, to build himself into an example? Wasn't he throwing himself fearlessly into the unknown, just as sure as James Mather?

Turning from the darkened window, Eva lit a candle and replaced it on the mantel, then perched on the edge of the divan and draped her shawl about her shoulders, resting her hands on the warmth of her belly.

BENEATH THE BOAT SHED, Mather leaned on a scaffold and loaded his pipe. A hundred yards in front of him, the bonfire still cast a dancing yellow glow on the Pioneer. The night rang with laughter, and sing song, and the conspiratorial tones of a community with big plans. But Mather did not wonder at their conversation, nor long for the fellowship of any man. Had he been standing on the wayward side of the Olympics, he could not have felt more remote. Nor could he have felt less compelled toward his own future.

And who are you, Mr. Mather? What spirit drives you?

FOR ALMOST TWO DAYS, Hoko did not see Thomas, but this was not unheard of, even in winter. She could not prevent his wanderings. Once, when Thomas was barely six, Hoko had followed the boy up-creek for the better part of two miles. He moved like a nimble shadow through the forest. She often lost sight of him. She thought she had lost him for good where the creek met the river in a bubbly confluence, only to discover him standing twenty feet behind her. The journey home had been a dance, with Hoko leading, only to find that she was following, stopping, only to find that he had already stopped, and when she arrived back at the fire, she found him there, squatting on his haunches, his lips silently at work.

Other times, his wanderings did not take him so far. Hoko would find him in the yard behind the Olympic Hotel, standing on a log, with his head tilted sideways and one eye covered, or pacing the dock with uneven strides, counting the planks and stepping over cracks. Sometimes she found him tracing circles in shallow water with a stick, or picking up stones along the strait, only to reorient them on the shoreline. But more often than not as of late, she found him shadowing one white man or another through town.

On the third day of Thomas's absence, Hoko lost her appetite. Late that evening, when the snow began to fall in earnest, gathering in drifts along the low bank of Hollywood Beach, she cursed herself, and cursed Thomas, and left the fire in search of him.

Front Street was only shadows and a pale orange flicker burning behind curtained windows as Hoko skirted the creek and ducked beneath the boardwalk calling for Thomas among the jumble of pilings. She could feel the thrum of life up the street in the darkness from the Belvedere, where white men gathered at all hours without occasion. As the buzz of activity grew nearer, her thoughts grew fainter. She passed two white men leaning in the doorway, speaking gruffly in low tones. When she felt their gaze upon her, she was a stranger to herself.

She crossed the stumped and rutty hogback in the snow. Beyond the hulking boat shed, the Pioneer Theater was bathed in the glow of a large bonfire, ringed with the sawtooth shadows of a dozen people hunkered around it. From down the path, Hoko could discern the uneven cascade of their voices woven with laughter, and the popping of the fire. The little theater was still emptying its restless cargo into the street as Hoko approached. Women were fastening their bonnets, and men were unpocketing their pipes, and children were catching snowflakes on their tongues in a swathe of yellow light.

When Hoko passed through their midst, all but the children paused in their tracks and stopped laughing, and no man tipped his hat. Cutting back along the Hollywood shore, she found the canoes pulled further upbeach than usual. The snow was not sticking on the shoreline, though it was accumulating in the wooden boats. An icy wind was knifing off the strait, and the fires burned slantwise with the force of each gust. Hoko could feel the rumble of the tide beneath her step, as she scanned the perimeter of each fire for Thomas, with no success.

She came upon Abe Charles squatting alone by his fire. As always, he was dressed like a white: laced leather boots and a wide-brimmed hat, a shirt of Scotch wool, and a buckskin jacket. He had a pipe in his pocket, and a rifle at his side.

"I'm looking for my boy," said Hoko.

Abe spit into the fire and it hissed. He looked up at the swirling snow. "The spirits are running about," he observed.

No matter how Abe cultivated his whiteness outwardly, he was still hopelessly Indian in his superstitions, a fact Hoko registered with impatience. "Have you seen him?"

"Maybe he's chasing them."

"Have you *seen* him?"

"No. But I saw your father, and I thought I saw a ghost."

Without comment, Hoko left Abe squatting by the fire and continued west. She could feel his sad eyes on her back as she trudged along the strait crunching clam shells. When she reached the mouth of the Elwha, she hiked upriver along the rocky bank the short distance to her father's home, a weather-beaten structure, part cabin, part shack, sagging beneath the weight of its roof. There was a time when the boy's wanderings brought him regularly to his grandfather's, where the boy would keep silent company with the old man, seated on the porch for hours, watching the tree line undulate, and listening to the crows gathered in the maples. It was her father who taught the boy to build fish traps in Ennis Creek, and string nets, her father who told him the stories of Kwatee and the Great Spirit, and Thunderbird, her father who filled the boy's head with words. But that was before her father began looking for answers in bottles. When the boy returned one afternoon with bruises and scrapes, Hoko forbid him to visit his grandfather. Yet the boy continued his visits, almost daily, in spite of her will, until the day he returned with a fat lip and a knot on his forehead. After that, the boy stopped his visits completely.

Already, by the time Hoko arrived at her father's house, several inches of fresh snow had gathered on the roof of the crude little structure, which listed slightly to one side beneath a great bare maple, several hundred feet off the left bank. The door rattled on its hinges when Hoko knocked. When her knocking failed to elicit a response, she pushed the door open, and it issued a squeaky protest.

The fire burned low, and a feral stink pervaded the little shack. Her father was asleep in a chair in the far corner of the single room, in the glow of the dying fire. His blanket had slipped off his lap, but still clung to his ankles. Hoko knew it was whiskey sleep, because it was always whiskey sleep now. As she drew nearer, she could smell the stink of him, like rotting plums, and she guessed that he had fouled his pants, as had become his custom. How long before drinking made him so small that he became invisible to himself?

"Father." She could hear the rasp of his breathing. She gave him a shake. "Father."

Slowly his eyes opened, and he looked up at her.

"Father. It's Thomas. I think he's lost."

His expression was fixed, as though the words meant nothing to him.

"Listen to what I'm saying. He's been gone two days. Nobody has seen him." She shook him again, which caused him to smile stupidly. "Have you seen him? Has he been here?"

The old man's smile withered. He narrowed his eyes suspiciously. Without warning, he all but leapt out of his wooden chair, as though startled from it. The chair reared backward and rattled to the floor, and the old man's feet became entangled in the blanket, and he fell forward to the floor with a crash.

Hoko rushed to his aid. Kneeling beside him, she began to roll him over on his back, but he swung around on his own strength and began to thrash about, swinging his arms, and kicking his legs, and letting loose a terrible shout. With an errant fist, he caught Hoko under the jaw, and she reeled backward before scrambling to her feet.

He struggled hopelessly to regain his own footing as Hoko fled the cabin into the night.

the invisible storm

Ethan huddled beneath his wool blankets, hopelessly alert, still clutching his rifle with his good hand. What howling beast of the night was this that spoke in guttural tongues and circled the inside of his head? What frame of mind was this that he could not distinguish the real from the imagined? And what exhilarating new fear was this that defied expression?

The snow finally let up altogether shortly before dawn. Ethan emerged shivering from beneath his blankets. His thumb was crooked and swollen but mercifully numb. He did not dwell on this state of affairs but immediately applied himself to reviving the coals.

Thawing his bones over the fire, Ethan scanned the little valley laid out before him in a veil of white, no mark of man upon her. The country seemed less rugged beneath the snow, and the valley seemed wider. By the light of day, the wilderness appeared to harbor no mystery from him, nor present any threat to him. In fact, it seemed to beckon him. Ethan turned from the fire to reach for his bundle and spotted at fifty yards a doe grazing on the fringe of the woodline. Ethan could scarcely believe his good fortune. Breathlessly, he went for his rifle. The doe paid him no mind and continued to graze as Ethan took aim, steadying the rifle with some difficulty in the bridge of his numb hand. As he locked in on her, she looked up and froze momentarily. That's when she gave herself to him. He saw himself hitting her before he ever fired.

When the shot rang out with an echo, the rifle jerked back, and the doe gave a lurch, but did not fall. She righted herself, then careened forward and to the side as if to go down, but caught herself once more, and staggered a few steps before darting into the woods without her former grace. Ethan gave chase. He lost sight of her almost immediately. He came upon the spattering of blood in the snow but hardly paused to look at it. He scrambled up the hillside, and after twenty hard-earned yards he stopped, out of wind. He quieted his breathing and raised his rifle and scanned the cluttered understory for any sign of movement. But there was only stillness.

After a fruitless hour of reconnaissance, which failed to yield so much as a stray track or broken limb, Ethan settled for a breakfast of dried prunes, a spot of bacon grease, and a handful of flour. The flour, however, did very little to slow the progress of the prunes and the grease, and Ethan was forced to pause frequently in his labors as the day progressed.

His thumb rendered him all but useless with an ax, so he began the business of running his lines with a length of alder he reckoned to be a hundred links, planting stakes along his way. It took him the better part of the day to reckon 160 acres, which extended south into the valley and east across the narrow canyon, a crossing that warranted considerable effort. He descended the bank near the mouth of the canyon, following the river around a sharp bend where a chaos of logs glutted the stream, causing it to alter its course into two sluices running swiftly around the edges. Ethan crossed the logjam and ascended the canyon on the far side to the bluff until he was opposite his cabin. With one arm, he felled and limbed another thin alder and began running a line up valley. And even as he executed this job, his mind set to work on the future.

How long before a road replaced the settlers trail? How long before the clatter and clang of industry ringed the harbor from Ediz Hook to Hollywood Beach? How long before other men of vision, men with furry gray eyebrows, clutching leather attaché cases, looked upon this place and saw the profound and inexhaustible possibilities? How long before money came pouring in from the east upon the hot rails of the Northern Pacific? How long before Port Bonita replaced Seattle as the jewel of the Washington Territory, Washington *State*, before it became a western terminus rivaling San Francisco? And who would join him in hitching their fates to this town, these hills, who would work beside him in harvesting the bounty of this wilderness, paving this road, ringing this harbor with industry? The fine ladies and gentlemen of the commonwealth colony? The rugged denizens of the west end? Certainly not the Indians. And wasn't it fitting that in a place comprised purely of potential, a failed accountant with no reputation, five hundred dollars, and a moth-eaten suit should help lead this charge toward civilization? For wasn't this man, in essence, all future?

UPON HIS RETURN JOURNEY, Thomas crossed the river again at Indian George's, where he found the old man tanning a hide by the blue smoke of a fire. George left off working and watched Thomas shake the water from himself on the bank of the river like a wet dog. He directed a craggy smile at the approaching boy. Thomas tried not to look at the old man's teeth, which were pointy in three places and too far apart.

In a dream, as a child, George received a song, and the song was in Twana, and spoke of an invisible storm. Until George met the boy, he didn't know the meaning of the song. Now, he thought he knew. The invisible storm lived inside the boy.

"Your mother will be worried."

Thomas tilted his head and covered his eyes. When he uncovered them, George was still there.

"Have you eaten?"

Thomas cast his eyes down at his feet, and his lips began silently working on his words.

"Come. I've got something for you."

Thomas followed him to the cabin door, but would go no further. On one occasion Thomas had entered the cabin, when he'd followed a pair of enormous curly-haired white men upriver. Thomas had not liked the smell of George's place, or the fleas. Everything was too close together. It was dark, not night dark, but day dark.

"Yes. Okay. I'll bring it out. Go. Sit in the canoe."

But when George reemerged with the sourdough and jam, he found the boy exactly where he left him, except part of the boy was no longer there. His eyes were far away. He began to quake as though a cold hand were squeezing his insides, and his teeth began to knock, and his eyes looked ready to burst from their sockets. Suddenly, he jerked once, as though struck by a bolt of lightning, and went perfectly still.

George was not alarmed. In fact, he took the shaking as a good sign. "I brought bread. Jam," he said. "Come to the canoe."

Thomas did not budge.

"Okay, here. We'll eat here." George brushed snow from the stump of a maple and sat down with the bread and the jam. Thomas stood in place, accepting a hunk of bread when George extended it but refusing the jam.

Thomas ate in silence and avoided looking at George's teeth. But he listened to the old man intently throughout the meal, and he enjoyed how, after a while, George made it a conversation all by himself. Sometimes there were words Thomas had not heard before. He put his lips silently to work on these words.

George talked like a white man. That is, he talked a lot. More than his grandfather, even. Thomas believed that this was because George was lonely, not because he did not like silence. It was said that George had once had a wife, a young Squaxin woman, and that he'd lost her to smallpox. It was also said that he'd lost her to the bottle. It seemed she was the only thing about which George did not speak.

Not only did George talk a lot, but Thomas also found George unique among Indians in that he'd lost his taste for salmon. He refused, in fact, to eat it. Not chinook, not coho, not silver, not even blueback from the Quinault. Niether smoked, filleted, nor slathered in whiskey.

"The river is choked with salmon of every variety," George complained. "I can hardly pole my canoe through them. I've been here many winters, and what do you think I ate all those winters? Yes, that's right. I ate salmon. And more salmon. I have prepared this fish in a thousand ways, and it always tastes the same. I am done eating salmon. Trout, I will eat, fried in a pan. But not salmon. I will not even grease my saw with salmon oil. I'm finding that I like sourdough bread, though. The bread sticks to the inside of my stomach and I like that. It smells funny, but that's okay."

Thomas smelled the bread and found that he rather liked the smell, sharp but smoky, not smoky like the Belvedere, but outdoor smoky. He liked that it tasted almost like it smelled, but not exactly. And indeed, the bread really did stick to the inside of your belly, and Thomas liked that, too. He wondered why anyone would put jam on it.

"Your time is drawing closer," said the old man. "You must know that. You must keep clean for your tamanamis, so you have no smell. You will get sick when he comes for you."

The boy was poking holes in the melting snow with his toe. His lips were not moving. His eyes were no longer far away. George could feel the invisible storm gathering inside the boy. Someday it would gather enough strength to unleash itself. And George believed it would come out like a dream-song for all the Siwash to hear.

"More sourdough?"

Thomas nodded without looking up from his feet. George tore off a hunk of bread and presented it to the boy, who immediately brought it to his nose upon receiving it.

"Have the Shakers come for you yet?" George wanted to know. "If not, they will come soon. From Jamestown. They'll want to put you to work, and that may be a good thing; you could do worse. They think the spirits are evil, but they have only given them new names. Don't go with them. Wait until your time has come. Wait until the day you become a man. Only then can you decide what to do."

George disappeared into the cabin again and shortly reemerged clutching a length of leather dangling what looked like a bone filed to a point. Presenting it to the boy, who was intently smelling his sourdough as he turned it round and round in his hands, it occurred to Indian George that sometimes the spirits worked in mysterious ways.

"Maybe one day you'll meet the shark that's missing this tooth. Or maybe it'll be another. The shark is the truth."

The boy hardly seemed to notice when George strung the necklace on him.

NEAR DUSK, ETHAN set out from the little bluff to scavenge windfall from along the edge of the wood line. It was cooling down again, and the trees no longer dropped snow pats in the meadow. Ethan passed once more the spatter of blood left by the doe that morning, and he felt a pang of hunger. The heat of the blood had left small craters in the snow.

It took Ethan less than fifty yards of scavenging along the wooded fringes to fill his arms. Just as he was about to circle back to the bluff, something caught his eye in the meadow to the south, a dark figure sprawled in the snow, about halfway to the head of the canyon. He set his load down where he stood, and set off to examine the figure.

The doe was still breathing after all those hours. The breath bubbling from her nostril had tunneled a hole in the snow. Dark blood had coagulated around the ragged edges of the entry wound, where the shot had shattered her shoulder, exposing the bone.

She'd lost a lot of blood. It spread out around her in the snow in the shape of a bell. Ethan could not gauge the extent of her suffering, nor did he wish to. The look in her eye was weak and placid.

He went for his rifle.

When he returned, he put the barrel to her temple and could not help but look into her eye once more, and when he did the trigger seemed to resist his pull.

He dragged the carcass all the way back to the cabin, leaving a bloody swathe in the snow as he progressed. He returned for his wood, tended the fire, and dressed the doe according to some vague notions. He found the hide to be tougher than he anticipated. The work was messy, and Ethan discovered that the job did not entice his appetite, and he wondered at his own vitality. But later, forcing himself to eat, he found that the fresh meat put his stomach at ease, and not long after dark he was heavy with sleep.

potato counter

DECEMBER 1889

Hoko knew that Adam would have questions because he always had questions; it was not only his job to ask questions but his line of defense, too. In his days with the census, his inquisitive nature had earned him the name Potato Counter among the Klallam, for he had counted everything under the sun, every chicken, horse, and potato, it seemed.

Hoko watched him, his wide-brimmed hat pulled low over his forehead as he strode down the beach toward her with the heavy determined steps of a white man, as though the ground were not there to accommodate his steps but only to slow his progress. When he drew near, she could see the cruelty in his blue eyes without looking up, she could see his set jaw, and his straight upper lip, and feel the rock hard stubbornness of his will and know that it was etched in the lines of his stubbled face. Hoko also knew, however, that something soft in him still remained, where she herself had hardened. She knew that Adam would not sit by the fire, he would stand, because he always stood.

"Where is the boy?" he said.

"Around," she said.

"Around the school?"

"Yes," she lied.

Adam peered east down the shoreline past the long line of canoes and fires. Maybe a hundred Indians were scattered up and down the beach in groups. There were a few civilized faces among them.

"You haven't been about the Belvedere with a bucket of clams, have you? Because I've heard talk. And I need no more proof than the drunkenness up and down this beach to know that whiskey is in good supply."

"I have no thirst for it," she said.

"Has the reverend been about?"

"I don't know. I have no thirst for that, either."

"Hmph," said Adam, looking back down the beach. "Well, this is no good. This is no damn good. Look at you people."

Hoko said nothing. Out beyond Ediz Hook, she saw the gray black plume of an approaching steamer, even as the wake of the last passing steamer was still lapping at the shoreline.

Without the census on which to hang the information he collected, Adam discovered the realm of general inquiry was an uncomfortable one for him, especially with Hoko.

"Yes. Well. How are you, then?" he said, finally.

"I am the same."

"And the boy?"

"He is the same." Hoko did not look into his eyes but kept her gaze locked on the blurry outline of Vancouver Island. The place had once seemed so close.

"What do you do for money?"

"Things for white women."

"What things?"

"Tend to their children and laundry."

"Well, try tending to your own."

The words hardened in Hoko's ears like wax.

"I have something for the boy," Adam pursued. "Back at the hotel."

"He needs nothing."

"It's a book of lists, he likes lists. It's bound in leather."

"I know the book," she intoned.

Adam glared down at her, and something in him tightened. "Don't act superior, woman. Because we both know the truth."

Hoko gazed impassively out across the strait. "Yes," she said. "The truth."

Adam's hand shot up in a flash, but he caught it there before it could act further, and he lowered it slowly. As he strode past her, he gave her a push on the back of her head. "Just send the boy to me. I'm at the Olympic."

At the third fire Adam came upon, two Klallam men were scuffling on the ground, and a third was reeling drunkenly around the periphery of the action, shouting lewd encouragement at the combatants. All three wore flannel shirts. The face of the circling man was very dark and badly pitted, and seemed to be made out of stone. He reminded Adam of the Klallam chief Chet-Ze-Moka, whose funeral he had attended, a decent white man's burial. Chet-Ze-Moka, who had seen the coming of the first white settlers and lived in spite of himself to see the death of the founders. Chet-Ze-Moka, whom civilization had baptized in rum, whom the white man called friend, then dubbed clownishly the Duke of York, whose proud chieftaincy was reduced by Adam's father shortly before he died, some say stinking of liquor.

"Who sold you the liquor?" Adam asked Stone Face.

The Indian stopped circling, but his eyes did not stop circling in his head. "If I told you," he said, with a smile, "I couldn't get more."

The two on the ground stopped scuffling, and looked up, beaming stupidly. One of them spit out a tooth and laughed.

Stone Face put his hands in the air, affecting his surrender. The two on the ground rolled over each other, laughing, whereupon Stone Face kneeled and pretended to pray. This brought more laughter.

In Salish, Adam said to the men, "You shame your fathers," and continued on his way. He heard the Indians laughing as he went.

So thick was the Belvedere with tobacco smoke that Adam's eyes began watering almost instantaneously. Even the Indians, he observed, in their crude structures, had enough sense to leave a hole in the ceiling. There were twenty or more men about the barroom and Adam estimated a dozen more on the mezzanine. He didn't venture a guess at how many more might be debasing themselves in the flea-infested rooms up the stairs.

Nobody stopped talking upon Adam's entrance, or paid him any mind at all, except for Tobin himself, who was behind the bar with his arms crossed. He sported a rather showy mustache, which struck Adam as too youthful for him.

"Well, well," said Tobin. "Skokomish not keeping you busy, eh?"

Adam did not take a seat at the bar. He stood at arm's length, frisking Tobin with his steady gaze. "I'm here to file a report."

"Drink?"

"I'm working."

"Didn't stop your father, you know? And he did a hell of a lot of good work up and down this peninsula. Your father was a — "

"I'm not him," said Adam.

Tobin uncrossed his arms and reached for a bottle. "That's for certain," he said. He poured out two glasses and pushed one toward the edge of the bar in front of Adam.

"John, I need to ask you some questions."

Tobin emptied his glass in one pull, and wiped his mustache. "You just missed the good reverend. I believe he went straight to the top with his report."

"Don't try my patience, John. This is very serious. I want to know who's selling these natives liquor. And I want straight answers."

"Certainly not me. I don't want their business. And I don't want their filth around here."

"There's no room for more filth around here," observed Adam, surveying the interior. For all its rough-hewn qualities, its rugged beams, its softwood floor, scuffed and splintered and buckling toward the center of the room, its burled walls and crude framing and dirty windows, it was always the frivolous touches around the edges of the Belvedere that struck Adam, the gilded mirror behind the bar, the velvet coat-of-arms tacked on the wall, and oddest of all, the yellow and green floral painted glass goblet atop the piano. The overall effect was that of a bear in lipstick.

"Fair enough," said Tobin. "You and the reverend are welcome to agree on that count. But then, not all men are made of the same stuff."

"You've got no holes in the floor I should know about back there, have you, John? No special buckets of clams?"

"Have a look," said Tobin, reaching for the second glass of whiskey.

"I'll take your word for it," said Adam. "But remember, you're not above the law, and they're not below it. I intend to find out who's selling them the liquor."

Tobin set the empty glass down in front of Adam. "And how would I know that?"

"Because if it's not you, it's your competition, and I know how you feel about competition."

"You know damn well it could be any Chink from here to Port Townsend. It could be a transient. It could just as easily be any one of these cranks from the colony. I don't know, and I don't care. I've had it up to here with Indians. They're a blight to themselves and everything around them. They should have left with the others."

"You're right about that, John. But they didn't. They're still here, and they're bent on staying, and until the law says otherwise, I'm here to protect them. Whether or not that makes me popular." Adam turned to leave. "If you think of something," he said, over his shoulder, "I'm at the Olympic."

"Sorry about your father," Tobin said.

Adam turned back around and shrugged. "Had him for forty years. Some people get considerably less fathering than that." Adam doffed his hat, and strode out the door. "Good day to you, John."

galloping gertie

DECEMBER 1889

Gertie McGrew gathered the folds of her generous skirt as she glanced down on the hazy barroom from the balcony. Governing her red tresses, she watched Adam take leave of Tobin, walking a little too tall under the weight of his burden. Among men, none were more complex than the ones she'd never slept with, and Adam was still among that dwindling number. Gertie could not be sure why she trusted Adam, but it had something to do with forsaking his father, who had exhibited an appetite for brutality that only the quiet ones seemed to possess. Tobin was also a quiet one. Descending the staircase, Gertie could feel his critical eyes on her and avoided his gaze.

"What are you looking at?" Tobin said.

"My feet."

"The hell. I see how you've been lookin' at me for weeks. The next time I catch you, I'll skin you. Now, mind your business. That little waif from Dakota wouldn't be on the nod, would she? Fell asleep under a stable hand yesterday afternoon."

"Maybe the lumber camps have worn her out. She's popular, if you haven't noticed."

Tobin spit on the floor and frisked Gertie with his eyes, head to toe. "If I find out you're lying, I'll have my pound of flesh."

"You'll have that anyway," she said, the hem of her skirt dragging across the dirty floor.

Gertie crossed the threshold into the afternoon air and turned her coat collar up against the chill. Though it was reckless to test Tobin's limits, and she knew it, somehow Gertie had convinced herself that she was at an advantage. It was true she ran a brisk trade, that she kept her girls clean, attentive, and clear of the opium. It was true that her sarcasm and her ability to absorb a punch inspired a sort of frightened respect in Tobin, and even truer that Tobin had a weakness for her carnal expertise, whereas he never partook of the other girls. Lately, she was beginning to fear him, though. Lately, she was beginning to think about making a run for it. Not that she had a plan, like most whores who ever managed to get themselves free had, not that she'd set by a little money every week like a sensible whore would have. No, mostly she indulged San Francisco like a daydream in her idle moments. She liked to picture herself as a lady instead of a whore, walking cobbled streets instead of muddy sloughs. She knew it was silly, and she kept it to herself. Sometimes she liked to picture herself filling her days with whatever it was ladies filled their days with — she imagined museums, coronations, high tea. But her imagination could never go too far with this picture before she ran out of the ever important details to populate it. Usually, she fell back on images smaller and grayer: herself working in a laundry on Polk Street, living alone with a Siamese cat and a parakeet who knew her name. Gertie imagined herself cooking, growing herbs on her window sill, buying shoes with her paycheck, and eating in restaurants with checkered tablecloths. Maybe she'd allow some dark Italian to take her to shows on Friday night and steal a few kisses on her doorstep.

Raising her wide freckled face along with her tattered skirt hem, Gertie traipsed south down the boardwalk with her chin held high, past the realty office and the livery to the dry goods store, where dusting off a crude bench, she seated herself, crossed her legs a little less than demurely, and looked out over Front Street, wishing she had a bottle of whiskey. Across the street at the Olympic, a filthy old Indian was reeling in the mouth of the alleyway as though he'd been struck by lightning. His head lolled about dazedly as he took one step forward, then one back, then one to the side, and repeated the sequence again and again without making any progress. Within moments, a trio of loggers spilled out of the Olympic and clomped north down the boardwalk, pausing at the mouth of the alley to watch the old man flounder. They made crude sport of the Indian for a minute or so, mocking and taunting him, calling him Chief Firewater and the like, until finally the stooping man with the burned face gave the old fool a push, forcing him backward into the mud, where he struggled miserably to regain his feet. The trio erupted in laughter. Gertie was glad Tobin wasn't there to see it. Surely, he would've been amused.

A team of six horses strained north down Front Street, heads down, shoulders slick with sweat, their nostrils huffing white plumes of protest against the cold air as they inched their way forward past the druggist's. A huge length of fresh timber carved a furrow of mud and manure in their wake. Two doors down, the postmaster flipped his shingle and locked his door for the lunch hour. Gertie knew his lunch would include a visit to the Belvedere, specifically a visit to Peaches, the new girl who had taken to whoring like she was born to it.

Out of the dry goods doorway strode a strange haughty creature, a practically dressed women, very pregnant, who seemed to be in a hurry, trailing cornmeal from a ruptured sack.

"Looks as though you're leakin', ma'am," said Gertie.

"Pardon me?"

"Looks like your sack went and sprung a leak. There, near the bottom."

When the woman still failed to react to this information, Gertie wrested the bag from a startled Eva, turning it over on end, and handed it back with the breach on top, at which point Eva finally grasped the situation.

"Thank you," she said.

"Which way you headed?" said Gertie.

"I'm quite all right," insisted Eva.

"I can see that. I only asked which way you're headed."

"Toward the commonwealth."

"Mind if I join you halfway?"

"I suppose not," said Eva. In fact, Eva was pleased to be distracted from the knowledge that she'd secretly come to town not for cornmeal but with hopes of seeing James Mather before the expedition set out.

"So," said Gertie. "You folks really a bunch of crackpots over there?"

"Is that what you think?"

"I don't think either way. But that's what I hear. Whole town says as much."

"Tell me, Miss . . . ?"

"Gertie McGrew."

"Tell me then, Miss McGrew. Am I a crackpot to believe in my own dignity?"

"Some might say. In my trade, anyway."

"Am I mad to believe that every American ought to have the opportunity of liberty and the pursuit of happiness? That the wealth of this young country should be dispersed somewhat evenly without regard to birth or entitlement or sex? Am I mad to believe that a woman can do anything a man can do?"

"I'd say you're mad on that count, most definitely."

"Hmph," said Eva. "Spoken like a woman who makes a living debasing herself."

"Well now, I may be debased, but don't get the idea for one minute that I'm doing it to myself, your highness. And as for a woman being able to do anything a man can do, I'll just say I haven't met a woman yet who could live three weeks without bathin' herself. And I haven't found one yet that delights in killin' small things like a man does."

"I suppose there's some truth to that." Eva stopped and offered a handshake. "I'm Eva Lambert. Pleased to meet you, Gertie."

"Likewise, Miss Lambert."

"Do call me Eva. Won't you join me for a tour of the colony?"

"I'm afraid Hogback is as far as I go, Miss Lambert. I'm due to be debased again any minute now."

"You treat it as though it were your calling."

"Maybe that's why I'm good at it." It occurred to Gertie that Eva would probably make a hell of a whore, too, if she'd ever let her hair down and put all that willfulness to some use. "Well, then, I best be getting along."

"If you should ever change your mind and find yourself in the commonwealth," said Eva. "Mine is the door with the wreath."

"I'll certainly keep it in mind, Miss Lambert."

"Eva."

Gertie turned, lifted the hem of her dress, and took three steps toward the Belvedere before Eva beckoned her once more.

"There's always room at the commonwealth, Gertie."

Gertie thought about telling her that there was always room at the whorehouse but checked herself. "I'll keep that in mind, Miss Lambert."

labor

Long before *Old Anderson* came huffing and puffing around the spit into Port Bonita, Jacob Lambert had surrendered his steak and egg breakfast to the straits. His stomach was still mutinous, along with his general outlook, as he set foot on Morse Dock, and gazed upon the ragged settlement laid out in front of him. Unlike so many hopeful young men preceding him, Lambert saw no potential in any of it. A beach littered with savages huddling around fires. A muddy hill bristling with stumps. A cluster of oversized tool sheds, some of them on stilts, emblazoned with crude signs, masquerading as commerce. Not a brick building or a gas lamp among them. And all of it hemmed in by an impenetrable wilderness. He could scarcely wait to leave.

Front Street did little to elevate his opinion of Port Bonita. He did not venture to lay a gloved hand on the rail, as he crossed the boardwalk. He raised his pressed pant legs and walked gingerly over the muddy hogback, not once losing his footing. But for a little mud on the toes of his shoes, he arrived on the far side none the worse for wear. He knew exactly where to go. Everything was oriented precisely as Eva had described it in her letters. And yet all of it was so much less than she described. Nobody was more susceptible to delusion than the ideologue. Who, but a Utopian, could turn mud into mana?

For the second time in a week, Eva found herself unpleasantly surprised by a caller as she opened the door to reveal her older brother, Jacob, brow deeply furrowed beneath the brim of his bowler. He stepped past her into the cramped foyer before she could say a word, and took a cursory look around. "Pack your trunks," he said. "I'm taking you home."

"You're doing no such thing."

He grabbed her about the soft part of her arm.

She gave a cry and yanked her arm free and began immediately to rub the smarting area.

"Pack your trunks," he said. "I won't argue, and neither will you. I'll warn you not to defy me, Eva. I'm in a foul mood. I fully intend to be home within the month, so you haven't time to mount a resistance. Father has gone to great expense to —"

"And what are you? Father's new man?"

"I'm your brother. Now, get a move on. There's nothing to discuss, here, Eva. You've had your little Utopian vacation, and I'm taking you home. Don't be a fool." When he noticed that Eva was on the verge of tears, his manner softened. "Oh, Eva, be reasonable. This is no place for a child, and you know it. Let go of all this Haymarket Square nonsense, and come back to Chicago. You can't very well spend your life painting seascapes and wallowing in the mud. Look around you. You need proper medical facilities. Now, I've been three weeks coming to get you; I've had much unpleasantness along my way, including fisticuffs with your young suitor Thornburgh in Seattle, and frankly, I'm just about out of —"

"I won't go, Jacob," she proclaimed, wiping her eyes. "I don't care what anybody else wants. This is what I want."

"And what exactly *is* this, Eva? No proper road, no electricity, no bank, no school, no —"

"There's a school," she said. "And there's a *newspaper*, Jacob! How can you fail to see the significance in that?"

"A month ago you said your commonworth was a failure."

"Common*wealth*."

"You said they'd oversold the idea, that the people in town were unfriendly, that they deplored the colonists, that the weather was insufferable, and suddenly —"

"Well, I changed my mind, Jacob! I'm entitled to that!"

"You're entitled to a lot *more* than that! And damn it, it's time you start taking advantage of it instead of squandering every opportunity presented to you."

"I'll make my own opportunities, thank you very much. I'm perfectly capable of —"

"Of what? Look at the fine mess you've made of things! Pregnant, no husband, no father, living in a — "

"There *is* a father."

"Oh, dear God, Eva, stop this nonsense, right now. That scoundrel is no more worthy of you than this place is wor — "

Suddenly, Eva cried out, her eyes as big as saucers.

"What is it?"

Eva clutched her belly and cried out again.

"Good Lord," said Jacob, searching madly about the foyer for he knew not what.

WEARY OF VENISON, Ethan was squatting by the fire at dusk in the shadow of his roofless cabin, frying a sockeye in a skillet, when he was startled by a voice.

"Hello again."

Ethan spun around to discover Indian George standing three feet behind him on the bluff. The old Indian looked clownish in his ill-fitting white man clothes. He wore a high-buttoned waist coat, ten years out of fashion, and a shapeless felt hat atop his head. There was a dirty yellow bandanna tied loosely about his neck.

"Sorry," said George.

"Lordy," sighed Ethan. "You startled me. I didn't hear you coming."

"I tried to whistle," said George, who attempted once more without success. "The air won't sing for me."

"How did you find me?"

"A white man is not so hard to track."

Ethan finessed the skillet with his good hand. "Well, you're just in time for dinner."

George could not bring himself to look at the salmon; the thought of it made him queasy. "I ate already, thank you." He squatted by the fire, but when he was confronted by the pungent odor of the fish rising from the skillet, he sidled back a few feet. "Your thumb is no good," he observed.

"Crushed it," said Ethan.

"Ah." The old Indian surveyed the little valley in the waning light. Beyond the foothills, the peaks of the divide were socked in by dark cloud cover. More heavy snow was imminent. George had visited this very spot as recently as high summer, when the evening hours were filled with the ghostly trilling of marmots and the tin whistle of thrushes from across the canyon.

"What brings you up here, George?"

"Postmaster sent word. It's your woman. Her time has come."

Ethan dropped the skillet and practically leapt to his feet.

"Sit," said George. "We're out of day. We'll have to wait for morning."

"But we can't wait! I have to be there!"

George broke into a craggy smile. "Not really, you don't."

Thus began the longest night of Ethan Thornburgh's life. Oblivious of Ethan's hand-wringing preoccupation, or perhaps because of it, George talked incessantly throughout the ordeal. Ethan had never heard an Indian talk at such length. His voice flowed as constant and steady as the Elwha. He sung the praises of sourdough bread endlessly, complained about the preponderance of salmon glutting the Elwha, wondered aloud as to the origins of the *first* sourdough bread, inquired as to whether Ethan happened to know where he might acquire some different *varieties* of sourdough bread, and just when it seemed he'd exhausted the subject altogether, Indian George pulled a half loaf of sourdough from his coat pocket and commenced eating it pinch by pinch. But even the tough, impossibly dry bread could not slow the river of his voice.

And all the while, as George's voice sounded in the night, punctuated intermittently by the popping of the fire, Ethan's thoughts raced and bounded in his head. He shifted restlessly on his haunches. Morning seemed so remote that it would never arrive. He ached to be in town with Eva. His only comfort was the knowledge that all the parts of his new life were fitting perfectly into place, engaging harmoniously as though by some process of mechanization: Eva, Ethan Jr., all the blessings that were due to him as a man. In those moments when his mind took firm hold of this idea, he sunk into a sort of reverie. And it was during one of these reveries that Ethan was struck as though by lightning with the single greatest idea of his life, the one idea among all those scribbled notes and tossed off scratchings that would prove the key to unlocking his future. What serendipity, what power of fate was this at work, that he had only to stumble upon his destiny, had only to wade through a swamp in his undershorts, to claim this canyon without even knowing why, to squat on it and daydream until the moment arrived when its purpose was delivered to him? The heat of inspiration suffused his whole body.

Indian George stopped talking when he saw Ethan climb mechanically to his feet and proceed, as though in a trance, to the edge of the chasm, where he stood looking down at the dark restless form of the river rushing through the canyon. And after a moment, Ethan began to laugh, a big hearty gregarious laughter that wracked his body and filled the night. The laughter of a god smitten with his creation. And Indian George began to laugh, too, not even knowing the source of his own mirth.

THOMAS STOOD JUST inside the door of Adam's sparse little room at the Olympic. His cheek had only recently stopped stinging from the slap his mother had issued him upon his return from the hills.

"Go to the Potato Counter," she'd told him. "He's at the Olympic."

With a bittersweet hard candy lodged between his cheek and gum, Thomas's lips set silently to work over the handwritten columns inside the leather bound book. Adam went about the business of packing his open bag on the bed, now and again sneaking a sidelong glance at the boy. The twitches were getting worse. They were coming in fits. Adam observed a new strangeness in the boy. He seemed at once closer and further away. His expressions were less benign, sharper. He was lean and spindly and round-faced as ever, but there was something in his bearing that suggested manhood.

Some of the handwriting was slanty, and some of it was in a loopy hand, and the columns were uneven, which Thomas liked, but not too uneven, and the feel of the leather spine was smooth and cool in his hands. He did not like the columns with the numbers, the way the fours were too different to have the same meaning, and how all of the numbers kept changing their meaning, how they didn't really mean anything until they were attached to something else. And he didn't like the way that some of the zeros didn't connect. He liked the ink blots, but not the ones touching the letters or numbers that didn't come first, and not the ones at the top of zeros. Thomas liked the words better than the numbers. They were even less exact than the numbers, but they told better stories than the numbers, which could only go up or down.

"What do you make of all that, boy?" said Adam, fastening the leather straps of his bag. "Hmph. Can't say as I understand what the devil you find so interesting in any of it, considering it can't possibly make any sense to you, but I'm glad of it."

Adam found himself wondering with a pang what would become of the boy. He was liable to start getting bigger and stronger. What if the fits got worse? Who could control him? What if he hurt somebody? Adam's worst fear was that he would be forced to take action himself. There was nobody here to shepherd the boy, nobody to keep him under control, not even a watchful eye to monitor his condition. Hoko seemed to exercise little influence over his wandering ways. Many of the natives stubbornly clung to the belief that the boy was gifted and could not see the curse for what it was. And just what was it, anyway? Adam could not say, but it was not a gift. At best, the white world would treat the boy with stepmother kindness, Adam reckoned, but then, they'd treat him that way anyway. God forbid he should ever take to the bottle and become unmanageable. There was no getting around Jamestown, no getting around the Shakers. He must put the boy among them if he was to have a chance. Even if it meant separating him from his mother. It was the only way.

"Look at me, boy."

Thomas did not look up, but continued appraising the columns of words and numbers.

"Thomas, look at me."

Thomas looked up from the book. His lips stopped moving.

While some of the Klallam believed the boy could see many worlds,

Adam was not convinced he could even see one. Sometimes he felt sure that the boy's blue eyes were sightless, which accounted for their strange distant appearance. And yet the boy moved gracefully through the world, so how could this be?

"You quit running off now, you understand? You stick by your mother. Watch her. Do what she does. And quit following white men around, unless you've got something useful to offer them. Do you understand? Because I suspect you understand a lot more than you're letting on, boy. I suspect you know the difference between right and wrong. And that's something. It may not seem like much, but it's a lot. Just keep knowing right from wrong, you hear me?"

Thomas heard him, but he was not really listening. He was looking across the room at the shaving mirror on the foot of the bed. More precisely, he was looking at the reflection of almost but not exactly half of the window and was straining to see what was in the reflection of the world outside the window. But he could not quite apprehend the reflection. So he looked out the real window and could see a light snow beginning to fall, and then he looked back out the reflected window, but it wasn't snowing there.

Watching the unwitting boy, Adam resolved himself once more on the matter of Jamestown. "I'll be back through town in a week or two."

Thomas moved to the foot of the bed and picked up the mirror. He did not look at his own reflection, but turned his back to Adam and looked at Adam's reflection over his shoulder.

"Stick by your mother," said Adam's reflection.

onward

When confronted with the resignation of Abraham Lincoln Charles, the party's Klallam guide—who had taken leave stealthily from base camp the previous night, leaving only his rations—Mather was nonchalant. "Fairy tales," he mused, slapping Dolly kindly on the hindquarters. "They take to them like children. Boogeymen and Thunderbirds. Sometimes I think they make them up so that they don't have to confront their real fears."

The rest of the party went silently about their tasks. Haywood was fidgeting impatiently with the altimeter, an open notebook in his lap. Runnells was squatting by the fire, renesting the skillets and packing the coffee away. Reese was cleaning his rifle beneath the cover of a fir, with Moose, one of the bear dogs, at his feet. And Cunningham was somewhere out in the brush with a case of the trots. The snow had turned to slush during the night, and now the rain came straight down in big heavy droplets. The tents were heavy with it. And the slate gray sky promised more to come.

"Better that he spooked now than later, I suppose," pursued Mather. "Let's cinch up these mules and beat a path to the promised land, shall we? We've lost a guide, but we've gained some flour. And we've still got Dolly and Daisy on our side."

"A couple of plugs," observed Reese, from behind a walrus mustache. "I practically had to beat the fat one with an ax handle to get her stirring this morning."

"A mule, despite its reputation, can be finessed, Reese. Unlike that stubborn pair of cayuses you attempted to secure from the natives."

"Finessed? A mule? You're out of your mind, Jim."

Mather rather liked the stubbornness of mules, enough to afford them a good deal of patience. The trick, to Mather's way of thinking, was to harness their will. This was done gently, not overtly. The world was no more a black-and-white proposition to a mule, he reasoned, than it was to a man. Beat them, and you only exhausted their will. Charm them, and they would give you their life force. Mules had served him well all the way up the Mackenzie River. And despite what Reese had to say, Mather had a good feeling about Dolly and Daisy. They had sturdy legs on them, and broad backs.

"You'll see," said Mather. "These two will serve us well."

Four hours later, Dolly and Daisy were put to the test. When faced with the very swamp Ethan had crossed in his underwear, the mules refused to proceed farther than ankle deep in the muck, braying in protest at the prospect of crossing. Mather offered them gentle encouragement, patting their heads, scratching their backsides, nudging them along with a hip. After several minutes, these methods still failed to inspire movement in the beasts, and Reese began flaying them with the butt of his rifle, in spite of Mather's entreaties. Dolly and Daisy began plodding forward incrementally. Within a half-dozen steps, however, they were mired to the belly and could proceed no farther, could not even rear up in spite of their efforts. Runnells and Haywood were forced to unload the cargo and haul it out of the swamp, as Mather and the others backed the braying mules out with considerable effort.

They were a half day making three trips along switchbacks down the thickly wooded gulley to the river, where they staged their supplies at the foot of a narrow canyon. In addition to the large stores of flour, sugar, coffee, and pemmican, their cargo included tobacco and whiskey and fishing tackle and bacon grease, oilskin and canvas and blankets and axes and whipsaws and rifles. Also among the supplies were Reese's tools for mineral prospecting, Cunningham's medical supplies, and Haywood's survey equipment.

The oilskin was no match for the relentless rain, nor did the canopy of timber offer much protection from the downpour, as they plodded down the gulley with the last load of supplies. Dolly and Daisy were cooperative beneath their slackened loads. They handled the mud-slicked terrain with relative ease. The dogs bounded ahead at all times, now and again sniffing. The morale of the party remained upbeat through the dreary weather. Haywood moved with a spring in his step. Cunningham, the untested professional man, kept a vigorous pace, to everyone's relief. Reese and Runnells bantered about everything from bear hunting to suet pudding.

Mather was at the head of the group, preoccupied by the spirit of adventure. The complexities of living had been pared down to the minimum, reduced to the business of steady progress. The lay of the land was no more rugged than a few small canyons broken with gulleys and streams.

The canopy was high, the understory dense, but not so thick as to tangle up the mules. The downhill route was sodden in the bare spots, but the thick groundcover of fern and salal allowed for passable footholds. All things considered, the terrain was quite easily navigated, but then, they were still miles from the high country.

In the late afternoon, the party set up camp on a high bank overlooking a logjam, just around a bend from the mouth of a narrow canyon, where the river could be heard roaring through the chute. Runnells gathered deadfall and started a cooking fire while Cunningham and Haywood pitched the tents and unburdened the mules. Reese gathered his tackle and headed for a deep hole just above the logjam where, to the disbelief of the whole party, he caught no fewer than fourteen fish of five varieties in a twenty-minute period.

"They're catching themselves," he exclaimed. "The river is practically bubbling with them."

Restless to move forward, Mather set out up canyon with his rifle for the purpose of collateral exploration. After a quarter mile up the wooded incline, he emerged in a small clear meadow, where the valley opened up in the shape of a teardrop. From this vantage he caught his first glimpse of the divide, its steep snow-clad ridges festooned with clouds. On a bluff overlooking the canyon, Mather spotted, to his surprise, a cabin, and made his way toward it through the snow. An Indian with a yellow bandanna fastened about his neck in the manner of a cravat was at work on the roof. The Indian nodded to Mather, took note of the rifle, but kept to his work, notching a crossbeam with a hatchet.

Mather set his rifle aside and sat on a stump, whereupon he packed a pipeload. He watched the Indian work for several minutes without comment. It was almost as though Mather was not there.

"A fine spot you've picked here," said Mather, at last.

"Fine spot," concurred George, dismounting the roof beam. "But I didn't pick it. It belongs to somebody else. You may have passed him."

"I can't say that I did. We left the trail a few miles back. We've been back and forth through the gorge with our supplies. We're headed for the divide. For the Quinault, actually."

"Mm," said George.

Mather was amused by the Indian's attire. While most of the natives were content with cotton twill and flannel work clothes, this one seemed to fancy himself something of a clotheshorse. Not only did he wear his bandanna in a ridiculous manner, he wore a waistcoat and wool trousers, and a small-brimmed hat.

Mather extended a hand. "The name's Mather. My party's just downriver."

George shook his hand. "I'm George."

Mather offered George his grip of tobacco, which George declined.

"When do you expect this somebody back?" Mather inquired.

"I don't know him well enough to say. It was his woman's time."

That the woman was Eva did not occur to Mather. Had this occurred to him, he might have inquired about the matter in greater detail. "You work for this man, I take it?"

"No."

"He's an Indian?"

"No."

"Do you suppose he'd mind if my men and I staged our supplies here for a day or two? We've got a boat to build."

"And you're going to Quinault?"

"That we are."

"In a boat?"

"As far as it's practicable, we are. We've got well over a thousand pounds of fortifications."

"Mm. Yes," said George, gravely.

"What is it?" said Mather.

George proceeded to explain that several miles upriver, through the next gap, lay a second, larger canyon, and that if they were determined to build a boat, they'd be better served to build it there, beyond the head of the canyon. They'd never navigate a boat through the canyon, not even a canoe. When Mather asked him what lay beyond the second canyon, George could not say.

"Ever know anyone who's been beyond that?"

"When I was a boy, there was a Quinault woman who used to bring her children over the mountains every summer to the Elwha to see her people."

Mather grunted a laugh. "A woman with children, you say?"

George laughed, too, not really knowing why. "Yes."

"How did she get by the Thunderbird?" mused Mather.

George scratched his neck, and looked toward the divide, as if the answer might be found somewhere amid the lofty ridges. "That's a good question."

Mather smiled. "What would you say if I crossed those mountains, and when I returned, I told you I encountered no Thunderbird?"

"I'd say you were lucky."

"Indeed, I'm lucky. And I've little doubt that my luck will hold out where this Thunderbird is concerned."

George was still looking for answers in the high country. "But then I'd say you were unlucky."

"Unlucky?"

"Yes. Because you couldn't see the world underneath the world."

"Ahh."

So amused by all of this was Mather that he invited George to join the expedition for dinner. George accepted but upon arriving at the camp downriver was disappointed to discover Runnells filleting salmon with a buck knife. His spirits improved drastically, however, when he spotted a frothing crock of what he presumed to be sourdough starter near Runnells's feet.

Mather was gregarious throughout dinner, a veritable master of ceremonies, eliciting conversation from George for the entertainment of his men. George obliged, and dined happily on sourdough, while the others inhaled the fourteen salmon among them, leaving only the discarded skins ringing the edge of the fire, where smoke curled off of them in tiny plumes. Afterward, they smoked by the fire, and Mather uncorked the whiskey and passed it around. George did not partake of the whiskey but continued eating sourdough in little balls. Mather persisted in coaxing stories out of the old Indian. George did not disappoint. Gazing intently across the dancing yellow flames at Mather and Haywood, George told the men of the Great Spirit who had looked over his people for thousands of years. He used his hands to conjure the Great Spirit out of the air and show it to them. And when the white men could not see the Great Spirit, George released it just above the lapping tongue of the flames, and it rose like smoke, and even Mather felt something in his spirit rise, even as something else pinned him to his seat. Outwardly, however, he expressed only amusement.

George told the party also of Kwatee, and how Kwatee changed the world, how Kwatee had murdered Chief Wolf and wrote a song about it, and fled, and made the rivers and the rocks, and how he made deer and elk and beaver out of the early people, and how he had once killed a shark from the inside of its stomach. And when George spoke of Kwatee, his eyes were smiling in the firelight, and his hands painted pictures in the air, and the eyes of the white men were dim with confusion, though the smiles were still pinned to their faces.

George told them of Wren, and how Wren shot a ladder to the sky to try to get the sun back from the man who took it away; so too did George shoot a ladder into the sky, and the white men couldn't see it, though they all looked up anyway. But it was their nemesis Thunderbird above all else that the white men wanted to hear about, Thunderbird, with his great curving beak and his eyes glowing like fire, and his breath that uprooted forests. Thunderbird, fire and rolling ice, clutching Killer Whale in his great horny talons, as he rocked the valley with his deafening war cry. And when George spoke of Thunderbird, he still painted pictures in the air, but his eyes no longer smiled.

When George finally took leave, long after dark, without the aid of a lantern, he clutched in his palm a lump of Runnells's sourdough starter. When asked by Cunningham how he would see his way back in the dark, George explained, to the mild amusement of the party, that he'd already seen his way.

That night in the tent Mather dreamed he heard strange voices circling his head, but he could not put faces to the voices, and he could not apprehend the words they spoke. He was awakened in the night by a powerful howling from the riverbank, which was unlike the howling of any wolf, or the lowing of any bull elk, or the drunken clowning of any man he had ever heard. And beside him on his back, beneath the patter of rain on the canvas tent, Haywood heard the wailing, too, rising like the lament of some grizzled bagpipe, punctuated by an owllike whooping. But neither man would ever speak of it to the other.

In the morning, amid a light drizzle, they ate a breakfast of gilletes and salmon skins, and there was little conversation around the fire. They broke camp and hauled three loads to the head of the canyon, where they cached the supplies in Ethan's cabin. Even as they jockeyed the parcels around, consolidating their loads, George was at work on the roof. Shortly before the party departed, the Indian enlisted their help in hoisting a crossbeam, which the men were happy to do.

"This friend of yours is indeed a fortunate man," said Mather to George, as he straightened the load on his back. "He's made a fine companion in you. Give him our thanks. Perhaps we'll meet again."

But that was the last George ever saw of Mather. As the party set off, George watched their single-file retreat from his place on the roof. And the farther their figures receded into the little valley, the bigger the valley appeared, until the bigness of the valley swallowed them altogether.

minerva's feet

Such was the brevity of Eva's labor, so determined was she to deliver the child and be done with it, that by the time Jacob returned with the midwife, both parties panting heavily from having traversed the hogback and crossed the colony at a frantic pace, Eva had already birthed the baby and severed the cord. She propped herself against the larder, in the darkest, coolest corner of the kitchen, clutching the wailing infant lightly to her chest.

The infant girl was ostensibly healthy and in good color, and she possessed a formidable set of lungs. Peering down at the crinkled face, Eva rested two fingers on the distended belly of the thing, which was warm to the touch. She was humbled and repulsed by the weakness of it. Its groping, helpless little hands, bunching themselves into fists, moved her to wish it was back inside of her, where it was merely an obstacle. Now, the complexities were manifold; now, the thing was no more a part of her.

The appearance of the child inspired a striking turnabout in Jacob's behavior. He relinquished all proprietary airs toward his sister. With motherhood, she had earned his respect at last.

"You've done good, Eva. My God, she's exquisite. What will you call her?"

"Certainly not Ethan," she said.

By the end of the second feeding, it was apparent that something was wrong with Eva. She was on fire. She'd grown faint and blotchy. Her pelvis was in a vice. Once again, Jacob was pressed frantically into action.

When Haw was summoned by the postmaster's son from his tiny root cellar in New Dungeness, he was at work by candlelight, grinding tortoiseshell into a fine powder with a pestle. The young man told the

Chinaman, whom he insisted on calling Huey, that a girl child had been born at the colony that morning and that complications had set in with the mother. Doc Newnham was unavailable. Haw collected a dozen herbs and several jars in his leather bag, tucked his braided queue beneath a wide-brimmed hat, wrapped his coat about his lean frame, and mounted the waiting carriage.

The trek west up the peninsula was a plodding and muddy affair. On two occasions the wheels became mired, and Haw was forced to dismount the carriage and leverage the rear wheels out of their ruts as the young man drove the horses forward. In both instances, Haw emerged mud-spattered, much to the young man's amusement. But for occasional speculation concerning the state of the road before them, both men were mostly silent throughout the journey.

They arrived at the foot of the hogback shortly before dusk. A smattering of loosely knit colonists met Haw's arrival in town. As the carriage rattled through their midst, Haw could hear the whispers of pig-tailed devil and Chink upon their lips, could feel their eyes burning holes in him, and tried his best to appear solemn throughout the procession, though a familiar panic was at work in him.

Jacob greeted Haw at the stoop. "You'd think they'd never seen a Chinaman," he observed.

Haw liberated his queue from beneath his hat and stepped into the little house. "Or maybe too many," he said.

The midwife was cradling the infant before the hearth. The child fidgeted in her arms, whining and chortling at every turn. Eva lay propped up in bed, weak-eyed and feverish in the lamplight. In spite of her condition, she greeted Haw coolly, and would not look him in the eyes. Jacob had been nearly an hour in persuading her to see the Chinaman, whose filthy, ragged appearance did little to inspire confidence in either of them. His very presence seemed to alert Eva's suspicions. As he readied himself, spreading a cloth upon the chest of drawers and scrupulously laying out his herbs on it, she scrutinized his every move for peculiarities.

"Pot," he said, at length. "Fresh water. Also, glass. Teacup."

Jacob set out for the pot and water.

Eva noted that the Chinaman touched nothing nor performed any action with his right hand. Every task was executed with the left hand. He would sooner employ the use of his chin than the use of his right hand. His every move was deliberate, decisive, careful, and yet she distrusted him. The moment he drew close enough that she could smell him, she was surprised to discover that his smell was quite like that of a forest. She was further surprised by the lightness of his touch when, finally, he employed the use of his right hand, which he'd reserved for the express purpose of checking her pulse. First, he checked it at the wrist, then at the neck, keeping count silently with his lips. Eva shuddered inwardly as he set his right hand flat on the bare skin of her abdomen.

Jacob returned from his charge. Haw took the pot of hot water and the glass from him and set them both upon the chest of drawers. He poured out a small glass of liquid and brought it to Eva's bedside and instructed her to drink it, which she did hesitantly. He took the empty glass from her and set it back on the chest, then began sprinkling herbs into the pot of water: leaves and stems and roots, *dong guai* and *shu-di-huang* and dried rhubarb. He instructed Jacob to boil it on the stove and inquired about the whereabouts of the doctor. Jacob told him that Newnham had been summoned west of Joyce, where a logging mishap had occurred along the Hoko River.

As Eva sipped the hot elixir, her eyelids grew heavy. She was glassy-eyed and perspiring profusely. Finally, she slipped off into semi-consciousness. For the next two hours, she faded in and out of this state, plagued by feverish visions, ink blots and ghostly tracers in the lamplight. At one point it was snowing in the room, but the snow was black and sizzling hot on her skin, and the voice of her brother seemed to be coming from the mouth of the Chinaman. And the Chinaman looked in turns like the devil and the face of the moon. Mercurial thoughts flitted in and out of her head, impressions she could no more apprehend than she could stand upon her own strength and walk out the door. She sensed dimly that the world had lost all order, that she had no dominion over the events shaping her consciousness.

ETHAN LEFT THE head of the canyon shortly after dawn, his spirit electric. He could not move nor even think fast enough to keep pace with the future as he strode down the mountain. He took no change of clothes on his journey, only his pipe, a bit of fish, and a crust of bread. The trail was fraught with calamity from the outset: washed out and riddled with downed timber. A quarter mile downriver from the head of the canyon, he turned his ankle on the rutty path, forcing him to slow his pace.

By the time he rejoined the trail on the far side of the swamp, he had walked off the pain of his ankle, but he rolled it once more, not half an hour later, while fording the river. His feet were pulled from beneath him, and he reared backward in the current, jamming his crooked thumb upon the rocks. He watched helplessly as the river took his bread and fish. When he reached the far bank, he was forced to build a fire and dry his clothing by the heat of it. A light rain needled his naked back as he huddled against the chill for several hours.

When at last Ethan stormed into the little white house an hour before dusk, he did so with a considerable hitch in his gait and his right arm pressed firmly against his stomach, as though held in place by an invisible sling. Upon confronting Jacob in the foyer, it was apparent at once to Ethan that something was wrong. Wrong enough to negate any unfinished business between the two men.

Ethan bore little resemblance to the man Jacob had confronted in Seattle. The elements had beaten all airs of the dandy out of him. His face had not seen a razor in weeks. His cheeks were sallow, and filth gathered in the creases of his forehead. His hair was wild, his clothing was rough, soiled in patches, and the air all about him stunk like a dead campfire. But Jacob recognized for the first time some singularity of intent in that silver-eyed gaze.

"Where is she?" said Ethan. "Am I too late?"

Jacob rested a hand upon Ethan's shoulder, and Ethan did not shrink from it. "She's not well. We're hoping her fever will break. But . . ."

"What about the baby? Is the baby okay?"

"The baby is fine. She's sleeping in the parlor."

"She?"

"Yes. Your daughter. She has no name of yet."

Ethan squeezed past Jacob to the sitting room, now further crowded by a white bassinet. He peered down into the blanketed nest, not quite knowing all that he was looking at, nor what course of action to follow. When Jacob entered the room, Ethan looked to him for instruction.

"Should I let her sleep?"

"She's your daughter. Perhaps an introduction is in order."

Ethan lifted the baby from the bassinet with his good arm, cradling her head in the crook of his injured hand; the child did not awaken. Instantly, Ethan's disappointment fled. He was overcome by her delicacy and diminutive grace; her tiny fingers clutching at his shirtfront, her dark downy hair and its smell of newness, the impossibly delicate veins ribbing her pink eyelids. He could not resist running his crooked thumb over her wrinkled forehead. She was everything the wilderness was not: delicate, vulnerable, small. And she was everything worth taming it for. It was no longer enough to prove something to the world, to distinguish himself for the sake of distinction, to conquer in the name of Ethan Thornburgh. Taming the Elwha was no longer a dream in itself but a means to an end, and that end was to bring civilization to the feet of his daughter, to ensure that she grew up in a world with electricity and a thousand other modern conveniences, so that she should never be forced to sweat and toil in the mud, never have to expose herself to the crushing forces of the wilderness, even to profit by it.

"Minerva," said Ethan. The word had just come to his lips. "Her name is Minerva, by God."

ETHAN AND JACOB sat vigil with Haw throughout the night, as the lamp burned low. Eva's condition did not improve. All the color drained out of her. Her bouts with consciousness were infrequent. Her speech was a riddle. Haw alone held out hope. He checked her pulse obsessively, daubed the sweat from her forehead, and at one point administered a poultice of crushed herbs and tea on her fore-head, neck, and wrists.

When hunger awoke Minerva during the night, Ethan went to her, and gripped her softly with calloused hands and hoisted her from out of the crib, breathing deeply of her hair. He held her close and rocked her gently; he reassured her in low tones, all to no avail. He was powerless to soothe the child. Her cries were horrific, pinched and phlegmy, earnest beyond all proportion. It was agony to hear them. Finally, he put the child to her mother's breast, and held her there, where she fed, unbeknownst to Eva.

What if this child should have no mother? The thought was black and inescapable. That Ethan's lover lay dying on the bed was of sub-ordinate concern. Surely, no God would take this child's mother. But as the night wore on, he began to reason that God had forsaken him and, worse, had forsaken his child. And so Ethan invested his faith by degrees in the one agency that might possibly exercise any influence over Eva's fate. He watched intently each methodical step of the way, as the Chinaman attended her. He looked for signals in Haw's con-centrated manner, but he did not ask questions or try to impose rea-son upon the Chinaman's methods. Whether it was rational science or devil's magic, it was Eva's only hope. And so he watched sleepily as Haw's movements played shadows on the wall, listened to the soft patter of Haw's feet across the wooden floor, breathed the fragrance of a dozen herbs, until at last, Ethan fell asleep in his straight-backed chair.

Eva's condition worsened as the night unfolded. Her pulse was wild with feverish rhythms, she twitched on occasion and issued plaintive moans, until suddenly, shortly after dawn, her fever broke in an in-stant. Only Haw was awake when she regained her senses, and only Haw watched a healthy color suffuse her face as outside the day broke cold and clear.

the river

The general consensus among the Mather expedition held that with each homestead the men passed on their way through the teardrop-shaped valley and into the next gap, they had for certain passed the outermost settlement. Time and again they were disappointed by a small clearing or a crude snow-covered structure. Not until they reached the foot of the second, larger gorge did they truly leave the last vestiges of white settlement behind.

The snow kept on through the day and into the next, and the sound of their own plodding snowshoes was muffled, as were the echoes of their voices. There was five feet of accumulation in places, and for this reason Mather cut his blazes low on the trunks of trees, so that come spring the blazes would be at eye level.

The party dug in a half mile beyond the head of the big canyon and chose a low sandy bench just below camp as the site for boat construction. From the felling of the timber to the caulking of her hull, the boat took them the better part of four days. The dogs got into the bacon the first night, making off with all but precious little of it, so that breakfast each morning thereafter consisted of gilletes and coffee. The weather was not cooperative. Each morning the timbers were heavy with ice, and it was necessary to thaw them for several hours over the fire. They smoked the green wood until it was light as cork. They curved the timbers at stem and stern by heaving them with a lever arrangement. They caulked the hull with oakum and pitch until she was watertight and dubbed her *Lucy*. She was thirty-by-five at the beam, two feet deep, and decked forward and aft for bowman and steerman.

After the finishing touches were applied to *Lucy*, the men lowered the stores down the rutty bluff and packed them tight into the hold.

Reese then persuaded Daisy and Dolly aboard with the butt end of his rifle before passing the reins to a waiting Cunningham. They dragged the boat into the riffle and held her fast by the towlines. They stood upon the bank amid a light snow, where Cunningham halfheartedly attempted to solicit heavenly intervention on behalf of the expedition, leaving Reese to roll his eyes. Finally, with considerable effort, they pushed off into the current.

The boat took fairly well to the water, though she rode low beneath the weight of the stores, her nose cutting into the water beneath the rapids. Mather manned the bow pole, with Haywood at the steering oar, while Reese and Runnells struggled for footing along opposing banks with the tow line, accompanied by the dogs, who alternately bounded ahead and sniffed along the bank. The boat dragged against the swift current. Progress was extremely hard won, as the river proved itself to be a more formidable challenge than anyone expected. Surely, this was not the same river that ran flat and shoal at its mouth, the same river that promised smooth passage to the divide. This was a rock-strewn beast boiling with rapids, a heaving, roiling, serpentine devil. Where the river did not run wide, it ran braided in chutes and timber-choked shallows. Footholds were hard to come by on either bank. Reese and Runnells spent the better part of their time waist deep in the numbing current, the wind and snow in their face.

Time and again, the boat hung up on rocks and snags, and several times the force of the current overwhelmed them, and they were pushed back into the rocks they had worked so hard to clear, colliding with such violence on one occasion that Daisy reared up in the boat, and Runnells lost the towline momentarily. Mather was nearly thrown from the deck into the rapids. And Mather's heart thrilled on that occasion, for he found no triumph in surrender, nor even in the spoils of victory, but only in the perilous clutches of the battle itself. That's the answer he should have given Eva, that's the spirit that drove him. Only in adventure were the senses fully engaged, the life force fully harnessed, the intellect fully immersed. Only then could one feel the magnetic forces of chaos pulling them toward the true nature of all things. And only when these forces dragged you by the collar to the very precipice of terrible understanding, and forced you to look down into the abyss, only then did the fighting begin in earnest, only then were you truly alive.

When they crashed against the rocks, Mather laughed like a madman, even as he regained his balance, and when a quick glimpse at Cunningham revealed that the latter had lost all color, a warmth suffused the lap of Mather's pants, and he did not fight it, but joyfully let it spread down his legs.

"Ha! What were you expecting, Cunningham, Lovers Lane?"

A quarter mile upstream from the collision, two giant firs, six and seven feet in diameter, lay fully across the river. The men were forced to drag the boat to a rocky bar and tether the mules. They regrouped over a loaf of wet sourdough, a small fire, and a pan of warm water. It took the remainder of the day to cut through the downed trees with hatchets and whipsaws. And though the chore greatly depleted their store of dogfish oil and elbow grease, it did not deplete their optimism.

Spirits were high around the campfire. Prune pie and whiskey fueled their celebration. Cunningham alone seemed rattled by the day's events. He chewed at the stem of his pipe and stirred the fire restlessly. Reese was uncharacteristically giddy, at one point patting Dolly upon the muzzle with something resembling affection. Despite having spent the first half of the day chest deep in the chill rapids, clutching a frozen towline that tore his hands to tender shreds, Runnells felt a warmth in his bones. Even the mild Haywood, who preferred polite deference from the forces of nature to the grueling business of conquest, could not help but revisit the day's adventures with relish.

At the end of the night, as Mather lay in the tent, wrapped in his shell of woolen blankets, staring into a blackness that may well have been the back of his eyelids, he afforded himself an image of Eva, and what it might have been like to feel her body pressed against his own in the darkness. He soon fell asleep.

DAWN SNUCK INTO the tent, as though with the slightest stirring, she might withdraw back into the night. The morning was cruel — dark, blustery, but not quite ominous. Yesterday's triumph still cast the palest of light on the new day. The tents were sagging with ice when the men awoke, and Mather discovered crystals in his thick beard; leaning up on his elbows, he shook them off like a bear might have, with three big sweeps of the head and a pawing motion. Outside the tents, the snow came down the valley in windblown sheets, stinging his face and hands. The coals were completely dead. The pemmican was tough. But the coffee sharpened his senses and awoke his spirit.

They found the boat's hull mired in ice, and even before they could begin the day's journey, they were forced to hoist her up on blocks and put the fire to her. When she was dry, they recaulked her hull for good measure. It was early afternoon before they packed the boat back up, dragged her to the edge of the bank, and guided her into the water. Beyond the two firs, the river ran deep and narrow for a stretch, and the boat dragged against the current like never before. Footing was impossible along the steep banks, and Cunningham was useless with the towline. Reese battled hard, knee deep in water, scrambling for footholds between the slick rocks. His grasp was all but frozen to the towline.

Emerging from a high-banked gulch they hit a tough stretch of flat white rapids which offered no possibility of circumnavigation. Mather rode them straight up the gut for a hundred glorious feet, grunting, and roaring, and laughing and cursing, before it became impossible to gain headway, and Mather and his men submitted to defeat. They eased her back down river to the nearest possible landing, a narrow stone promontory along the left bank.

Forced to portage the cargo, they guided the empty boat to the head of the rapids, and pulled her over a knee-high fall of jagged rocks, an effort requiring as much guile and tact as brute strength. The chore left every man exhausted. They ate gillettes and did not linger by the fire.

That night, the snow relented, along with the biting wind, and even the current was in good humor throughout the next morning, during which they covered the better part of a quarter mile. Mather felt confident that the worst was over, that the river would lead them through the remainder of the foothills to the divide, where they would face a bold new set of challenges in the high country.

The river ran flat for a quarter-mile stretch, offering relatively little resistance. By midday, they'd wended their way through the next gap to the base of yet another dark fold of steep wooded hills, the tops of which were shrouded in mist. The closer they drew to the interior, the more rugged and dramatic the lay of the land revealed itself to be. The hills grew more imposing with each successive layer, from the rolling foothills below the first canyon, to the hulking ogres that followed. The hills they now confronted were heavily buttressed, great shouldered beasts that sprouted out of the earth as though they were still growing, still pushing their way up, opening chasms and shaking off boulders, shedding their igneous skin as they reared upward toward heaven. And still the party was nowhere near the outer perimeter of the larger ranges, still they had hardly ventured twelve miles from the mouth of the Elwha. How far was paradise? Where amid this chaos of mountain terrain was the golden valley?

A short ways into the dark cleft, they hit a foul stretch of rapids, where the river emerged from a chute of basalt and promptly met with the confluence of another churning stream. The Elwha was a frothing cauldron, the roar of it deafening. Cunningham lost the rope repeatedly, but Reese was able to hold her each time, until sweeping around the port side, Reese lost his footing and was caught in the current, relinquishing the line as he was pulled under by the rapids. The world flashed on and off as the river took possession of him.

The instant Reese lost the line, the mules reared, and the boat was forced back by the current with such sudden violence that she spun forty-five degrees, and Haywood lost the steering oar, and the boat crashed upon the rocks. Haywood and Cunningham and Dolly were all thrown free of the boat and swallowed up by the river in a terrible instant. But Mather hung on, even as the boat broke free of the rocks with a groan, even as it spun out of control. She was taking on water through the hull, over the sides, everywhere he turned. The remaining mule was now on her feet and pitching violently backward. The world had come undone. Mather's head was spinning with a delectable violence. He was one with the chaos, immersed in the savage truth of all things, when the stern was wrenched out from under his feet, and he was struck as though by a bolt of lightning, and time, as he knew it, ceased to exist.

rebuked

Something was strangling the life out of Mather, some cold hand had gripped his torso like a vice, and pulled him beneath the rapids again and again, swept him along against his will, and Mather would have surrendered gladly to its pull, if only he could have drawn a single breath. Instead, he fought desperately for air, blacking out in spotty flashes. Above the dull roar of rapids he heard the dogs barking on the bank and heard the panicked baying of Daisy, still captive on the unmanned boat as it careened out of control. A blurry figure lighted upon the far bank, splashing into the shallows, shouting between cupped hands. Suddenly, something grabbed hold of Mather by the waist and dragged him under the riffle, grappled desperately with him, entangling him in its clutches. When he fought his way to the surface and managed at last to fill his lungs with one desperate gasp, he found himself face to face with a deathly pale Cunningham, who was still clinging for dear life to Mather. A wide gash had opened across Cunningham's forehead. Not until Mather glimpsed the naked fear in Cunningham's eyes did he feel the tingle of his own sharpened senses, the electric chill of fear down his spine. And it was fear that gave Mather the strength to shoulder Cunningham, fear that drove him in hard-fought increments toward the bank, even as the rapids shot them farther downstream, until Mather at last managed to get his feet underneath him and stop their terrible progress, wading to shore with the dead weight of Cunningham still clinging to him. Upon terra firma, Cunningham stood and walked upon his own strength.

The dogs came first. Sitka lit out from the underbrush and nearly bowled Mather over when she reached him, licking his face and pawing at his shoulders as she balanced on two legs. The other dog came down the bank, wet and panting, but nonetheless enthusiastic. Runnells appeared a few moments later, alone, limping along the far bank. He was hatless and his pants were split down one leg. He threw his arms up and shrugged, then nodded and lowered his head and kept walking until he was directly across from Mather and Cunningham, where he crouched on the bank and put his head in his hands.

For a half hour they walked the banks calling for Reese and Haywood until little hope remained in the frayed edges of their voices. They sat and waited, Runnells on the far bank, and the other two men opposite, until Cunningham swore he heard the braying of a mule from up the hill. Mather listened intently. Soon there was a great ruckus in the understory behind him, the clatter of snapping limbs and a sharp exclamation laced with superlatives. Haywood emerged from the brush leading Dolly. And behind the mule came a disconsolate Reese dragging his heels.

They found Daisy a quarter mile downstream pinned between two rocks, grinning hideously with her shattered jaw rent in opposite directions. Her legs were twisted into impossible configurations. But in her final miraculous act of stubbornness, she was still breathing weakly. Mather could not bear to look at her. The brutality of her disfigurement, that a life could be ripped apart so violently and thrown aside like a thing, seemed a violation of all that was natural. That the thing should continue to breathe and suffer in such a maligned condition was sickening. The dogs would not let Daisy lie, and Mather shooed them away angrily. Without a rifle to end the mule's misery, he was forced to stave her head in with a hefty stone. Her skull caved like a melon, and Mather would not soon forget the sensation of it.

The boat somehow defied the rapids long enough to clear the narrow passage the men had cut through the firs. She crashed on the rocks not five hundred feet upriver from the sandy bench of her conception. Her hull was battered well beyond repair and the hold was ruptured. The stores had been scattered. The collective force of the expedition had been scattered, as though the wilderness had swallowed them up and spit them back out in pieces.

The men regrouped above the sandy plateau, where they'd established a camp a week earlier. In the clearing, they spread out all that remained of the stores. The losses were heavy but sustainable; most of the flour was lost, and nearly all of the meat, though it had been little to begin with. The sugar and coffee were total losses. The camera was lost, along with some of the survey gear. However, three of the five rifles had survived with no apparent damage. A single grip of tobacco had survived, albeit waterlogged, along with a precious little whiskey.

Reese built an enormous fire fed by the brittle skeletons of alders. The fire roared like a furnace, burned hot and smokeless, and the points of its flames lapped at overhanging limbs twelve feet off the ground. The entire camp bathed in its glow. The men gathered around the fire, as close as they could bear to stand, and felt the hot wind of it on their faces. Nothing was said. The whiskey was uncorked and imbibed sparingly twice around the circle. Now and again, someone tossed a dry fir bough into the inferno, and the tiny needles sparked and flitted like gunpowder as the fire consumed them in bursts of white light. And when the flames died down, the men sat on rocks and licked their wounds and contemplated the rumbling in their bellies. Haywood scribbled madly in his journal, which had survived miraculously unscathed, wrapped in oilcloth in what remained of the hold. Runnells mended his pants with a needle and thread, his swollen ankle propped upon a round of cedar. Reese cleaned the rifles, one by one. Cunningham, the gash on his forehead dressed with the aid of Haywood, huddled nearest the flames. He could not seem to get warm, his teeth clattered frightfully.

Mather leaned back against his rock, hypnotized by the fire. He felt at once dull and lucid as he watched the ring of orange coals pulse around the perimeter of the flames. All the adventure had been drained out of him, his manic appetite for the wild and undiscovered had waned, at least temporarily, and his mind set to other more familiar wanderings. His preoccupation with Eva Lambert had become, weeks into their journey, a source of profound irritation to Mather. He was shamed by it, yet in his quiet moments he gravitated toward the thought of Eva like a moth to flame. The only act that might have relieved the shame and discomfort of Mather's yearnings was unthinkable, that is, to have confessed to Haywood or, worse, to Reese, that the mere thought of a women's swollen belly should cause his heat to rise.

mummery

JANUARY 1890

When Adam sent the boy away from his room, Thomas walked out backward, still clutching the shaving mirror in front of him at arm's length, navigating his way through the threshold and down the stairs by way of its reflection. After a moment, Adam could see the boy through the dirty window, walking backward down the middle of Front Street, entranced by the reflected world as it came to him over his shoulder.

Adam clasped his leather case and snatched it off the foot of the bed, then made his way down the groaning stairs. In the lobby, he came upon Reverend Sheldon, who was talking emphatically in hoarse tones at the desk clerk on the subject of the latter's moral fiber. The clerk listened impatiently, as one who knows a punch line, now and again scanning the lobby as though looking for an escape. Adam tried to soft-shoe past, but the reverend caught his eye and, without pausing in his harangue, signaled Adam to stay put by suspending a chubby index finger in the air.

"Fortitude," Reverend Sheldon declared. "I'm talking about real guts, real moxie. That's what you lack, son, moral fortitude, what the whole of this frontier lacks — and make no mistake, it *is* a frontier, gentleman, statehood or no statehood. And the evil oppressor that clouds these brackish backwaters, gentleman, is the devil himself, and the moral turpitude he inspires from all quarters. Look around you. Why he's got you virtually surrounded, from that godless colony there, to those savages on the beach, to that abomination directly across the way. Remember, it's the weak that run for the hills. The strong stand their ground and fight in the name of Alm —" Here, the reverend gave way to a fit of violent coughing, during which he employed the suspension of his other index finger to indicate that his thought was not yet complete. The cough rattled in his barrel chest, doubled him over with its force, and his balding head turned bright red. He recovered at last, short of breath, sniffling, his eyes awater. "In the name of Almighty God," he rejoined with considerable effort. Even as the clerk was grumbling a defiant *Amen* beneath his breath, the reverend turned his attention to Adam.

"I'm told you're off to pay the natives in Jamestown a visit, Adam. It shall be my pleasure to join you as far as New Dungeness."

Lacking both the patience and temperament required to find the reverend amusing, or in any way refreshing, the journey by carriage was interminable for Adam. Not only was the going slow over the muddy, rutted road, but the reverend, needing no encouragement from Adam whatsoever, spoke to no end on all matters right and moral, returning more often than not to the subject of the natives, a sore subject indeed, as he'd enjoyed so little success converting them.

"Powder and lead, that's how they Christianized them in Vancouver's day. And why not? What has all this *Great Father* nonsense profited us? I once met your beloved Chęt-Ze-Moka. He was drunk in a wigwam with his genitals hanging out. One of his wives had a black eye. These are not wayward lambs, Adam. They're savages down to their very souls. Born in sin. Salvation is beyond them. They're every bit as bad as the Chinese. I've witnessed their ceremonies, their potlatches, and what have you, and they're evil incarnate. Slaughtered dogs and idolatry. Face paint. Mummery." This the reverend punctuated with a rasping cough, which gained momentum and soon racked his entire person. His eyes began to bulge and take on the desperate aspect of a drowning man, and his cheeks soon glistened with tears. Still, the moment he could apprehend his first breath, he persisted in his sermon. "They ate the dog, Adam, ate it raw. They blackened their faces. They crawled around wearing lizard heads, like men possessed."

Nearly half of the road was washed out by a slide two miles east of town, and the carriage could scarcely pass without succumbing to the steep hillside. The snowfall was steady and wet, slush by the time it hit the ground. The wheels churned up brown muck and threw a fine spray of grit in their wake. However, the traveling beyond the washout was relatively smooth. Adam might have let the road lull him to sleep, were it not for the reverend.

"Shakerism is not the answer. Shaking bells instead of rattles, defiling the name of Jesus Christ. Quivering like jellyfish. That's no route to salvation. They're still the warring, slave trading, superstitious heathens they were a hundred years ago. Three hundred years ago!"

Here, in the ruddy-faced reverend, with his high-minded moral vision and irrational fear of the natives, was Adam's father revisited. And hadn't Adam himself held these tenets of superiority to be true until he met Hoko? As a young man, hadn't he felt that his father had been justified in reducing the chieftancy of Chet-Ze-Moka? Hadn't Chet-Ze-Moka exhibited a dearth in the qualities of leadership? And didn't this lack of leadership, along with the chief's penchant for drunkenness, point to some weakness of character?

Adam remembered the funeral, remembered his father slandering the chief under his breath, even as the eulogy was being delivered. And young Adam's only objection to these slanders was that his father's voice might draw attention. It wasn't until later, until Hoko, that Adam understood the qualities of leadership, understood that these qualities were not universal, that chieftancy to the Klallam, from its very conception, did not adhere to the same perimeters as the Great White Father, did not impose its will with a heavy hand where matters of free will were concerned, did not always issue edicts or make decisions or speak on behalf of the speechless.

The reverend was still talking when they came upon a lone figure walking east along the road.

Adam called for the driver to stop, but the reverend, upon inspecting the traveler, instructed the driver to proceed.

HAVING SUCCESSFULLY COMPLETED his herbal ministrations upon Eva, Haw was not afforded the benefit of a carriage ride back to his root cellar in New Dungeness. Instead, he set out on foot through the soggy snow, his herb bag slung crosswise across his shoulder, his queue tucked beneath his wide-brimmed hat, as he slogged through the muck. He had trekked roughly four miles east when he heard the rattling approach of the carriage at his back. The carriage slowed nearly to a stop, then started again with a lurch. Then stopped once more.

Haw sat with his hands piled in his lap across from the two whites and did not venture to speak. The lean and rugged man wore a stubbled growth of beard and had an irritable gaze that forever sought freedom from the cramped quarters of the carriage. He wore his hat low on his forehead. He seemed to be holding in a sigh, as he peered out between the half-drawn curtains at the passing landscape. The portly one with the sweaty forehead was talkative to the point of distraction. This, Haw soon gathered, must be the source of the other man's irritability. The fat one had a deep, productive cough, which frequently doubled him over and seemed the only thing capable of slowing down his opinions. In those rare moments of silence afforded by the fat man, Haw listened to the squishing progress of the horses.

Throughout his ramblings, not once did the fat man condescend to address or even look at Haw.

". . . all this talk about nation building and industry, and they've left God right out of the equation. Now, that's what I call arrogance."

Adam reckoned the miles to Jamestown to be about six by the time they passed the elk herd moving through Messing's homestead.

". . . how does one build a nation under God, when all the work is being perpetrated by the mongrel races? . . . how can one possibly expect to fly the flag of heaven over this godforsaken outpost, when there's a coolie under every rock . . ."

The Chinaman looked impassive. Adam wondered at his English. He wondered also at the contents of Haw's bag.

". . . the missionary approach is obsolete. At some point it becomes necessary to divide and conquer the spiritually bereft. At some point you can't indulge them, at some point you've got to rain fire and brimstone down on the Sodomites of this world, Adam."

When the reverend surrendered to his most violent fit of coughing yet, when his face turned red as the rising sun, and his eyes looked fit to burst out of his head, Haw was moved to action. He pushed the doubled fat man upright and placed the palm of his right hand lightly upon the reverend's windpipe, and the coughing decelerated almost immediately. With his free hand, Haw rummaged in the leather bag around his neck, producing a small brown bottle, which he opened dexterously with one hand and placed beneath the reverend's nose, instructing him to breathe. A pleasant odor pervaded the carriage. The reverend soon gathered his breath, but before he could resume talking, Haw presented him with another bottle, this one a little larger, and instructed the reverend to partake of it. When the reverend declined, Haw encouraged him further.

"Sip sip. No whiskey, no whiskey. Medicine."

The reverend conformed to Haw's wishes, in spite of his own, and sipped from the bottle. Haw resumed his own seat, leaving the bottle to the reverend, who grimaced as he wiped his mouth and tried to pass the bottle back to the Chinaman.

"Sip sip," said Haw.

The fat man complied, a little less than tentatively on this occasion, and soon resumed his monologue. "To begin with, we've got to level the Indian classes, roll up our sleeves and stamp out this potlatch business once and for all . . . burn this Babylon to the ground . . . obliterate this cesspool of iniquity . . ."

But as the Reverend progressed his tongue grew heavier, and his opinions lost their razor sharpness, and Haw smiled inwardly. The difference in the reverend was not lost on Adam, who seemed finally to have released the sigh he'd been holding in for so long.

Within a half mile, the reverend was awash in a dull silence, and his eyes were glassy, and he slumped so that his head and shoulder were pressed against the vibrating side of the carriage, and the smallest of smiles took shape upon his lips. And neither Adam or Haw could belie their own smiling eyes when their gazes crossed.

jamestown

JANUARY 1890

The reverend, having slept through his stop at New Dungeness, was still out cold late in the afternoon, even as the carriage lurched to a stop in Jamestown. Adam tilted his hat to Haw, ducked out of the carriage, and hopped off the runner into the slushy road. He dug in his pocket, settled with the driver, doffed his hat once more, and began trudging down the squelchy lane toward Lord Jim's house.

Fifteen years prior, Lord Jim, refusing to accept the conditions of relocation, rallied a handful of Klallam to pool five hundred dollars for the purchase of some two hundred acres of cleared meadow and sandy beach along the strait east of New Dungeness. They left the lower Elwha and the Siwash behind and moved some twenty miles east. They burned the cedar stumps out of the ground; planted wheat, potatoes, turnips; began raising chickens and swine. They built a village facing the water of thirteen houses and a little white church, and they named it Jamestown in recognition of Lord Jim. They started a temperance society and collected signatures from every last denizen of the village. But in seizing their destiny, they had unknowingly surrendered federal recognition. It would take 107 years to win it back.

Soon after the inception of Jamestown, Lord Jim brought the Shaker religion to his people, and they took to it, whole congregations of them signing the cross over and over, stomping loudly counterclockwise in a circle, shaking their rattles and ringing their bells, and trembling like oil on a hot skillet as they received their songs. Almost universally, the whites condemned them for these blasphemies, though Adam, having no misgivings with the Shaker church, was unique among his fellow agents. To Adam's way of thinking, anything that inspired temperance in the natives was not to be discouraged.

Perhaps of all the Indians Adam had encountered in his ten years of service, from Neah Bay to Puyallup, Lord Jim possessed the finest command of English and also the healthiest sense of irony. It was Lord Jim who, in the year of the census, dubbed young Adam "Potato Counter," though in recent years, the old man had taken to calling him *cayci*, meaning "busy one." It was also Adam's impression that Lord Jim was, at times, in love with the sound of his own voice. And though the old man was still weak with fever as he sat across from Adam in his straight-backed chair amid the waning light of early evening, his voice was still strong.

"My heart cries for the Siwash," he said. "They know just like we know, *cayci*, about the futility of resistance. The Great Father has taken our shamans, taken our right to fish."

Out the window, a wall of fog was creeping in steadily along the shoreline. The old man gazed at it as if he could see right through it. "The old ways are gone," he observed. "And for this reason, we embrace change. Because we want a future, *cayci*, and we want to build this future ourselves. That is why we purchased this land on our own, so it could not be taken from us. That is why we plant potatoes and wheat. That is why you will find not one drop of whiskey in our midst, even as our brothers the Siwash are drowning in it. And *that* is why I brought the Shaker religion to Jamestown, *cayci*. Because my people need something to believe in besides the Great White Father. Because the Great White Father will not cure what ails my people, he *cannot* cure what ails us. He speaks volumes but doesn't keep his word. He still does not honor the treaty that bears my father's signature, the treaty to which your own father was a witness. And I realize this is no fault of yours, *cayci*. You've been a friend to the Klallam, even in the long shadow of your father. And whatever I thought of your father, still, I am sorry for your loss. And I wish his shadow had died with him. And like you defy your father, even in death, we defy the Great White Father. But we do not defy him with violence; we defy him with acceptance. We are impoverished, *cayci*, but we are sovereign. Maybe not as Indians, but as a people."

"That's why I'm here, Jim."

"Because the whites have heard our grievances at last?"

"Because of a boy."

"And what boy is this?"

"He lives among the Siwash at Hollywood Beach."

"Yes. I know of the boy. The spirit chaser, the Storm King. I've heard it said that he can produce thunder and lightning out of the air."

"You heard wrong. He's just a boy."

"I've heard differently. I've heard he walks in two worlds."

"He walks alone in the world of his own head," said Adam. "That's all. But he's a fine boy. Smart. Strong. I want him to come live here. In Jamestown, with you, or whoever you see fit."

"On whose authority does he come to live here?"

"His mother's."

"And where is she? What ails the mother that she can't care for the boy?"

"The boy is wild. He needs structure, or trouble will find him."

THERE CAME A persistent rumble from above, but inside the big rumble were many little rumbles made of many different voices. There were thirty-one cracks of light, and one knot-shaped hole that danced with candle flame near the center. In the front, there was a great yawning mouth of light that opened with a groan and closed with a crash, swallowing the shadows within. The shadows had voices but no reflections, had footfalls but no faces. Sometimes when the shadows passed through the cracks of light, and the footfalls were heavy, a squiggle of light wavered in the mud puddle near the boy's feet. The ground was squishy beneath his heels, and the wooden piles were blistered and sticky to the touch. The air was heavy with the smell of creosote. When the piano started playing, the rumbling only increased in intensity, and the wood planks issued sighs and creaking complaints from all about the flickering knothole. The reflections were invisible, as if they did not exist, but Thomas knew they were there, somewhere behind the implacable surface.

Suddenly the piano rode out on a gaping beam of light, only to be muffled an instant later with a crash. There came three heavy footfalls down the back steps, and a dark form descended. At the bottom of the steps, the dark form crouched and concealed a wooden box beneath the foot of the steps. There followed a whistle, a cough, the acrid stink of tobacco.

A moment passed in silence. The dark form broke wind, cleared its throat, and issued another whistle. Finally, it ascended the steps and was swallowed once more by the musical light.

Soon there came footsteps in the slushy snow, and the light of a lantern approaching, and voices talking low, drawing closer. Indian voices.

Suddenly there were upside-down faces, two of them floating hollow-eyed and ghoulish, melting like candlewax in the pale quivering lamplight.

"I see only six."

The one holding the lantern bent nearer to the box, and the ghostly light caught Thomas crouching between the piles.

"Hey!"

Thomas made a break for the alley side, but one of the men caught firm hold of his ankle, and the boy slipped and fell, and he felt the cool sting of the mirror as it sliced open his palm. The light whirled around as though the world were turned on end and shaken, and an avalanche of shadows descended on Thomas as he scrambled madly to break free of the hand. The back door crashed again and harried boot clomps skipped the second step and rounded the corner at a trot, accompanied by a confusion of voices.

"There!" said one voice.

A rough hand wrested Thomas about the collar.

"Got him!"

Thomas bit into a line of fat knuckles. There came a terrible scream, and the grip relented, and the boy kicked his leg free and scurried out from beneath the Belvedere. Clutching his broken mirror in his bloody grip, he began to run.

He fled the alley as fast as his feet would take him and rounded the corner. He slipped on the slushy path as he leapt for the boardwalk, and his chin struck the wooden edge with such force that his vision went inky and his ears set to ringing. A rough hand grabbed him by the collar and swung him around. The mirror slipped from Thomas's grasp, careened off the boardwalk, and landed in the mud near his feet.

Thomas recognized the Indian by his dark, pitted face. He'd seen his grandfather keeping company with the dark man in recent months. He was Makah, not Klallam. His breath was rank with fruit. He was called Stone Face.

"Gotcha!" he said.

A white man soon appeared over the Indian's shoulder. He was the Belvedere Man, the one with the mustache. "What have you got here?"

Stone Face laughed. But in a chilling flash he turned serious and shook Thomas violently by the collar. The white reached in and tried to wrest control of Thomas's collar. "Gimme that," he said.

But Stone Face swung around and leered at the white. "Stay back!" he shouted, trailing a long strand of saliva. "I'll take care of it."

"You damn well better," said the white.

"Go!" said Stone Face. And he wheeled around and slapped Thomas across the face with the back of his hand, and only then did the white turn away and walk back down the alley.

Stone Face forced Thomas into the alleyway. He slammed the boy up against a wall and shook him fiercely. Thomas did not cry out.

"What do you think you're doing under there, huh? Who said you could be there?"

When Thomas did not answer, Stone Face doubled him over with a punch to the stomach. He straightened the boy up and leaned in so close that Thomas could not bear to open his eyes.

"I asked you a question, boy!"

But Thomas issued no reply. There were tears streaking down his face. His nose was running. His mouth was trembling as he struggled to gather his breath.

This time Stone Face spoke in Salish. "What business have you got under there?" And when the boy failed to respond yet again, Stone Face slapped him. "Talk, boy!" He grabbed a fistful of the boy's hair and shook his head violently. *"Nex' t'cuct!"* He glowered at the boy, waiting for some reaction. But the boy only winced. Finally, the situation became clear, and Stone Face relinquished his grip. He smiled and pinched the fat of Thomas's cheek. "Ha! *Nac!*" He pushed Thomas to the ground. "Couldn't talk if you wanted to," said Stone Face.

littlenecks

The clams were thin and watery this season, and Hoko knew the boy would not eat them, but she dug them out anyway. Ediz Hook was pitted with them at low tide; littlenecks squirted all about her. She worked with her sleeves rolled up past her scars, nearly to the elbow, and it was comforting to sink her wrists into the coarse sand and feel the suck of the water as it rushed in to fill the breach. After two-dozen littlenecks and a handful of butter clams, Hoko paused where she squatted, and looked over the bay at the little town, smoking and churning, expanding before her very eyes. For weeks they'd been felling trees on the bluff above the town, and little cabins were popping up among the smoldering slash piles; it was as though the town were lowering its shoulder and pushing its way into the wilderness. And yet the bigger the town grew, the less room it afforded her people. As she walked down the spit toward Hollywood Beach, it looked to Hoko as though the town were trying to crowd the Klallam out altogether, push them right off the edge of the land into the strait. Their ragged little camp was besieged by progress, hemmed in, just as the town had once been hemmed in by the wilderness. But the Klallam were no longer lowering their shoulders and pushing back at their opposition.

At Hollywood Beach, Hoko came upon Abe Charles sitting in his canoe, mending a net with the expert precision of a woman. He was still dressed like a white but not as much as usual. He was hatless. His rifle was nowhere to be seen.

"I thought you took the whites into the mountains," said Hoko.

Abe did not look up from his work. "Something visited me up there. The spirits turned me back."

"Spirits," she said flatly. "And where are these spirits now?"

Abe shrugged.

"How is it that these spirits will guide one man down a mountain but lead a whole people to ruin?"

Abe remained intent on his labors, feeding out net with his right hand. "That sounds like the white God you're talking about."

"What good are the spirits to us? The only spirit I see is whiskey."

Abe glanced up at her, his fingers continuing their work.

Hoko pulled her sleeves down over her scars.

"The spirits may speak," he said. "But they don't always listen."

Gazing out over the strait, a scowl took shape on her face. "Indian talk," she said.

Abe focused once more on the net. "You've grown hard."

Hoko did not deny it.

"Hard, like your father."

"My father is not hard. My father is weak. You don't know my father."

"Maybe not," he said. "But I did once. Just as I knew you once." He draped a length of net over the side and untangled a corner. "Did you find the Storm King?"

"I found my son. There is no Storm King. His name is a lie. The spirits are a lie. My boy is called Thomas, and he is just a boy." Hoko hefted her bucket.

"That could be," observed Abe, finessing a hard little knot with busy fingers. Then, as though the two subjects were synonymous, he hastened to add, "Those clams will be watery. I've got venison."

But Hoko was not interested in venison. She walked off down the beach toward her weak fire and her quiet sullen ways. As Abe watched her go, an old hunger stirred in his belly, and he felt the familiar ache of wanting in his jaw. If only life were so easy to untangle as a net.

the afterglow

Eva's little house had become so stuffy and constricting in the days
following Minerva's arrival that it may have been a tomb. Confined
to her bed upon strict orders from the Chinaman, she found herself
restless and ill at ease, and she actually rather missed the feverish
state of semiconsciousness that had previously gripped her. Ethan
and Jacob were no longer content to stick to neutral corners, nor willing to harbor the slightest misgiving toward one another, but hovered
forever about Eva in tandem, beaming like a pair of vaudevillians, as
they tirelessly delivered chicken broth and biscuits to her bedside,
hectoring her to consume them *if not for herself, then for the baby.*
Still worse, her neighbors landed upon her tiny cottage with an endless procession of bread loaves and pewter-molded desserts, stamping
their feet on the porch upon entering, disrobing in the foyer, and proceeding directly to Eva's bedside, whereupon they began poking and
prodding at Minerva, stroking the downy soft spot atop her crown
and cooing nonsense in her ear, commenting time and again on her
father's likeness, until the weight of the child began to feel like a stone
altar on Eva's chest. But what troubled her most was the suffocating
effect of her own smallness. In the face of such blessings, she loathed
herself for her ingratitude, loathed herself for loathing the baby, for
refusing to call it by name, for wanting to rebuke its whimpering so-
licitations, for wanting to pinch its fat, tender arms when it nibbled
too hard on her nipples, for wanting to cast her neighbors back into
the cold with their tidings, and for wanting her brother and her lover
to resume their hostilities. This last wish was futile, for in the dreadful interminable hours of suspense that marked Eva's infirmity, the
two men had forged an alliance that grew stronger with each soiled

diaper. Minerva, by her very appearance, had sealed the two men's fortunes together.

To see Jacob nodding his approval gravely at the pitch of Ethan's excitement, to see him furrowing his brow in consideration of Ethan's outlandish scheme, was bad enough. But to be imprisoned by motherhood, bound to a featherbed and shackled to the insatiable demands of another, while the word *destiny* crackled in the air like electricity between the two men, was more than Eva could endure. How was it that destiny forever attached itself to men? How was it that men presumed destiny to choose them? And what was the act of this presumption but to relinquish responsibility for their actions? And who was left to shoulder the burden, to suffer the consequences of these actions? While the men carried on about *putting the river to work* and *illuminating the darkness,* what great destiny had attached itself to Eva, if not domesticity?

It was agreed upon by the two men that as soon as Eva regained her strength, Jacob would accompany Ethan back to the homestead and see firsthand what grand possibilities the canyon presented. Until then, Jacob said he would make no promises, but Eva could see that her brother had already made up his mind. The fever was alight in his eyes, the spirit of adventure had seized him; the boy in him had awakened and the man was not far behind.

For six days, long after she had regained her strength, Eva remained in bed, saddled by Minerva and plagued by a simmering rage in her chest. Ethan returned by degrees to his dandified ways, his kissing seahorses and moth-eaten trousers, while Jacob grew rough around the edges, splitting alder with a day's growth of beard, talking about *town* as though it were really a place, about the homestead as though he had carved it out of the wilderness himself. The words *progress* and *labor* were upon his lips, even as the words *financing* and *easement* took shape on Ethan's.

When Ethan and Jacob finally took leave one gloomy morning in January, Eva met their departure with dread and relief. From the window, with Minerva fidgeting in her arms, Eva watched them go — Ethan lighting the way with his silver-eyed gaze, walking tall beneath the weight of his bundle, Jacob a half-dozen paces behind, newly outfitted from top to bottom for the backwoods, from rifle to whipsaw, tottering slightly beneath his load.

While neither city life nor the silver spoon had prepared Jacob for the rigors of backcountry travel, he proceeded at a steady pace in Ethan's wake as they trudged along the rutted settlers trail. He could scarcely keep his eyes on the sodden path. The scale of this wooded cathedral was out of proportion with anything Jacob had ever known or expected; colossal timber, wide as a steam engine at the base, tall and straight as the steel-framed towers springing up in Chicago, spread out in endless stands, with bark so deeply furrowed that a man could hide his whole fist in the coarse folds of it. Now and again, as they skirted the river, Jacob caught a glimpse of the Elwha through the trees, a flashing silver serpent as it roared down the mountain. The valley narrowed as they left the bottomlands behind, and the hills closed in on them from either side, until Jacob could see their snow-capped tops looming through the canopy. That he should be instrumental in taming this wilderness seemed impossible. That God had intended it to be tamed was a wonder in itself.

There was no fire burning at Indian George's, and his canoe could be seen tethered to the far bank. Ethan gathered with no small relief that his Indian friend was still upriver at the homestead. Popping his head into the dank cabin, Ethan could see at once that something was amiss. The cabin had been turned upside down and inside out. The larder was upended in the corner of the room, where a ruptured sack of flour had erupted beside it, spewing a crescent of fine white dust upon the uneven floor. The lantern lay shattered in a puddle of kerosene, with the Holy Bible facedown beside it. Ethan suffered a pang of guilt as he surveyed the damage. He comforted himself with the knowledge that he would reward George for his loyalty and could not help but wonder how he'd earned such devotion in the first place.

The river was too fast and high to ford. Ethan and Jacob were forced to grope through thick brush along the bank for several hundred feet, until they reached a rocky bar, a short distance beyond which Mather and his men a week prior had felled a hemlock four feet in diameter for the purpose of their crossing. Backtracking along the far bank, Ethan and Jacob picked up the trail near George's canoe and proceeded up the incline.

The trail leveled out in a small meadow bordered by a stream on the far side, running perpendicular to their path. Ethan spotted a buck at the stream's edge and froze in his tracks. The beast did not startle easily; it stood still as a statue but for the plume of its breath in the cold air. He had no fewer than twelve points and was as big as a horse. Jacob had seen such antlered heads adorning walls in Chicago and Peoria and Detroit like trophies, but nothing in the glass-eyed gaze of these enormous heads had prepared him for such majesty. It did not occur to him, as he locked eyes with the beast, to level his rifle. It was as though the buck's gaze held him captive. By the time Ethan whispered the directive, it was too late; the instant Jacob raised the rifle, the buck lit off into the brush.

A little ways north of the swamp, they scrambled up a rock spur that jutted out of the steep hill flanking them to the west. Dangling their legs over the side, they lunched on a half loaf of tough bread and a handful of smoked oysters. Even through the thick expanse of forest, they could hear the river in the distance, and when Jacob was moved to comment on the power of it, Ethan thrilled with propriety.

Soon after lunch they reached the bog, which was covered in patches by a thin crust of ice. The two men cut through the gulley, plowing their way down through four feet of snow. They were fighting their way back up the incline when the crack of distant gunfire froze them in their tracks.

THEY CAME FROM the north, traveling up canyon along the wooded edge of the far bank, two of them, both heavily bearded, outfitted with packs and rifles. From his place on the knotted stoop, a post that had grown all too familiar in Ethan's absence, Indian George recognized neither man. Though he could hear the brash tenor of their voices from across the chasm as they shouted back and forth, he could not discern their words. There was something crude in their manner, but George could not say what exactly, whether it was their ragged clothing or the way they slung their rifles so casually at the hip, as though they belonged there. The presence of the strangers did not alarm George, however, until they began pulling up Ethan's stakes along the eastern line and lobbing them into the canyon.

When George emerged from the darkness of the cabin clutching Ethan's Winchester and a pocketful of shells, the strangers had vanished. He swung around the east side of the cabin, peering south along the rocky cleft, but he saw no sign of the two men. He scanned the wood line up and down the chasm, but they were nowhere in sight. Tentatively, he resumed his seat on the stoop, set the rifle aside, and listened.

Within a half hour, George heard voices from downstream. This time they were along the near bank, just below the head of the trail. He took up the rifle once more and slunk downhill toward the tree line. When he was parallel with the voices, he stopped. He could hear footfalls over the packed snow, and soon he glimpsed the two figures through the trees and squatted low as they passed. He picked up their trail and followed them stealthily a short distance, until he reached the wood line, where he watched the men cross the clearing toward the cabin. The taller man unburdened himself of his pack and ducked his head as he entered. The other man circled the perimeter like a sentry, arriving back at the stoop just before the tall one emerged with a kettle and a cast-iron skillet. He laid his rifle down on the stoop, along with the pilfered cookware. The short one then crossed the threshold into the cabin, emerging moments later with a pair of boots. He sat down on the stoop and wrestled his own shoes from his feet and aired them out. The tall man wasted little time in picking them up and slinging them into the abyss.

For ten minutes, George watched the men from his place along the edge of the clearing, clutching the rifle and wondering at his loyalty to a white man he hardly knew. It was soon apparent that the intruders had no intention of leaving. The two strangers surveyed the canyon in every direction, scratching their beards, shaking their heads, carving out invisible lines in the air. They stopped to smoke, and the lanky one produced a flask from his hip pocket. He took two sips and was about to take a third before the stubby one wrested it from him.

Kneeling in the brush, George's foot began falling asleep, and he grew impatient with watching. The flask of whiskey became a source of contention between the two men, who wrangled for control of it. The tall one managed to maintain possession of the flask and held it above his head, well out of reach of the little man, who jumped up and down like a terrier trying to reach it.

George leveled his rifle, took aim above their heads, and squeezed off a round. The shell struck the cabin a foot above the tall man's head and rained splinters down on him. Before either of the thieves could snatch up their rifles, George squeezed off another round, which sent the men scrambling for cover.

He had them pinned in the cabin and made a deliberate approach, fishing for shells in his pants pocket as he came. When he reached the stoop, he tossed their rifles aside and ordered them out of the cabin. They complied with their hands out in front of them. The short one came first with snot in his beard. The tall one was still clutching the flask.

"We wasn't plannin' on nothing," the short one said.

"Shut up," the tall one said.

George shepherded them down the stoop and half way across the clearing before the tall one made a break for the woods. George leveled his rifle and took aim between the shoulder blades of the running man, who kept his arms in the air even as he fled. George fingered the trigger but did not fire. The barefoot man soon broke after his companion, and George lowered his rifle.

A few minutes later, Ethan and Jacob, still huffing from their clambering ascent of the gorge, came upon two bearded strangers a half mile from the homestead. They were seated shoulder to shoulder on a downed portion of cedar at the foot of a snag. They had no packs or rifles. The short one was barefoot.

house calls

Had Doc Newnham not commented on the foolhardiness of the Mather expedition during his house call that morning, as he prodded Minerva with all manner of shiny instruments, James Mather might have been the furthest thing from Eva's mind.

"Shouldn't be surprised if they're all dead of pneumonia by now. That is, if they haven't starved to death," said Newnham, donning his stethoscope. "I spoke with the man myself — this Mather, I mean — not three days after his arrival. He had me remove some sutures from his thumb. Said he stitched them himself. Hmph. Well, it was my opinion that the man was arrogant. At the very least naive."

The thought of Mather out there fighting for his life in the belly of the wilderness caused nothing to thrill in Eva. Her face, which had grown pale and thin, did not color at the mention of his name, her eyes, rimmed with dark crescents, did not light up. Hardly was her curiosity aroused. Whatever crude thing she may have felt for James Mather had long since been swallowed by the darkness. Neither did the thought of Ethan or her brother offer Eva any light. Nothing had moved her in two weeks. Winter seemed to get gloomier by the day. Eva found herself fighting a heaviness of heart and limb unlike anything she'd ever known. Sometimes the child would wail for half an hour before Eva could summon the will to climb out of bed in the morning. She'd been to town only once in two weeks' time. Hoko came for the laundry and to tend to the baby twice a week. What little time Eva could steal from the child, she spent not writing or reading or painting, but sitting in a dull stupor.

"Arrogance seems to be epidemic in these parts," pursued Newnham. "What do you suppose Washington, D.C., is going to say when they find out these squatters have broken the reserve? Do you suppose

Little Ben is just going to stand by and watch as a bunch of rubes and rustics carve up his billion-dollar country? Do you think his benefactors will allow such a thing to happen? I hardly think so. And what about the arrogance right here in this colony? Printing your own money! Ha! Turning your back on the great republic. This place is no longer some distant frontier, it's to be a state, and it shall have order, you'll see."

Minerva, with her intermittent cough, raspy breathing, and snot-encrusted nose, suffered, according to Newnham, from a common cold.

"Steam inhalation daily," prescribed Newnham, clasping his bag shut. "A few drops of camphor in a warm bottle nightly. And keep her away from that Chinese devil."

Newnham secretly believed that the child's coldlike symptoms were not due to wet feet or a winter chill but were extensions of a maternal neurosis. He had noted in a previous visit that the young mother neither wore a wedding band nor doted on the girl physically. It was true. Eva was no doting mother. Though she exercised the utmost patience in serving the child's needs, her approach was in no way effusive. She did not tickle Minerva's belly, nor marvel at her soft skin and tiny fingers or the cherubic roundness of her face. Eva told herself that she no longer resented the child, in spite of all she'd been forced to abandon in the name of Minerva: her independence, her professional life, her vitality. Likewise, she told herself that she didn't begrudge the child for everything she'd been forced to endure: scabbed nipples and swollen feet and the constant state of servitude. But worse still were the hours without Minerva, when she had no purpose at all to move her, those horrible interminable hours spent by the window, gazing out at the snow, aching dully from the inside out, until Eva felt herself sinking into a dark morass of loneliness and apathy out of which she was powerless to see.

Thus, in spite of Eva's rather low opinion of Newnham, the thought of his departure inspired a certain desperation.

"Will you stay for a cup of tea, Doctor?"

"I'm afraid I've got other matters to attend to," Newnham lied.

"Surely they can wait a few minutes?"

"I'm afraid they cannot, Miss Lambert. I must be on my way."

Newnham made as if to stand, lifting himself a few inches off the ottoman, before Eva set her hand on his knee. "Just a cup of tea. Something to warm you up before —"

"I really must go," he said, rising.

From her station at the window, Eva watched the doctor go; clomping through the knee-deep snow, past the sagging boatshed toward the hogback, and she felt herself sinking once more into the depths of despair.

When Minerva began to whimper from her crib, and then to cry, so too did Eva begin to cry.

***

HAVING LOST ANOTHER trick to Peaches, a turn of events that mercifully escaped Tobin's notice (along with just about everything else since Adam began poking around his whiskey trade), Gertie leaned suggestively against the end of the bar, displaying her ampleness to a slow house of the usual suspects: trappers and loggers and steaders, dirt-caked and full of whiskey, entrepreneurs from points east, cleaner behind the ears, but even filthier between the sheets, and of course the postmaster's son, by whom Gertie could set her watch. Business had dropped off along with the general excitement in the days since the expedition departed, although Peaches seemed to stay busy enough, a fact Gertie bore with a burgeoning resentment.

Three stools down, Gertie overheard Doc Newnham gossiping out the side of his thin mouth as Tobin busied himself with a rag.

"Turned her back on a fortune back east — seems she got it in her head to save the world by writing newspaper articles."

"I wonder if she could do a man a decent favor?" Tobin said.

"I daresay that favor might have teeth," commented Doc.

"Spirited, eh?"

Doc tossed his whiskey off and grimaced at the heat of it. "Not like she used to be. Used to put a bug in my ear about every social cause you can think of — used to carry on about corporate tyranny and feminine self-sufficiency every time she opened her trap. Seems her opinions have all dried up along with any mothering instincts she may have had. What's more, she's driven her man to the hills — and I can't say that I blame him."

"Sounds like she might make a good whore."

"Little proud for that. But if you say so, John." Doc pushed his empty glass in Tobin's direction.

The sky was low and the cold air smelled of smoke when Gertie stole out of the Belvedere later that afternoon. Choppy at the shoreline, the strait was slate gray and flat beyond the breakwater, where a pair of steamers crossed paths, one bound for Seattle and the other huffing west against the receding tide toward ports unknown. Yesterday's snow had been ground to muddy slush by the time Gertie hoisted her skirt and coattails up past her knees and crossed the hogback to the commonwealth. The colony seemed all but deserted in the late afternoon. The largest building in the settlement, nearly twice the size of the boat shed, was still a work in progress, though it looked to Gertie as though the elements were already taking a toll on the exposed structure. For all its fastidious charms, the village as a whole was not weathering the winter well. Paint was chipping all about, roofs were sagging. The little houses, nearly identical in shape and dimension, sat beside one another in three neat rows, a proximity and arrangement that Gertie found oppressive. In spite of her frequent disparagement of Port Bonita, the careless disorder of its design — if one could call it that — the town appealed to her reckless impulses. In spite of its inevitable growth, Port Bonita expanded in ragged disarray as though it were surprised by its own growth. While the colony spoke strongly of containment, Port Bonita pushed restlessly at its borders wherever it could find room.

Gertie located the house with the wreath near the end of the line, its chimney puffing blue smoke, its windows glowing with pale lamplight in the dark afternoon. After the third knock, Eva came to the door in a plain gray dress with a squarish neckline, her hair piled carelessly atop her head in a lopsided bun. She smiled at Gertie as a weary soldier might smile at the arrival of fortifications.

"Miss McGrew, what a pleasant surprise."

Gertie could hear the wailing of an infant from another room. "Miss Lambert."

While Gertie removed her coat and stamped her feet free of slush in the foyer, Eva put the kettle to boil, straightened her dress, and finessed her bun into shape. Gertie noted the dark crescents beneath Eva's eyes. The child's protestations continued from the backroom, unheeded. Finally, Gertie crossed through the den to the nursery, where she hoisted the baby girl from the crib and cradled her in one arm. The child's whimpering began to subside immediately. She was a delicate child. Hardly a bit of adipose in the arms or belly. Her breathing was raspy and a little shallow, but Gertie found the girl exquisite nonetheless. What impressed her the most was the alertness in the child's blue-gray eyes. Unlike most infants, this one seemed to have a keen awareness of her surroundings.

"I wouldn't have taken you for the mothering type," said Eva, from the doorway.

Gertie reached with her free hand into the crib for the child's quilt, wrapping it about the infant, who began immediately to root. "Actually, I'm just the sistering type," Gertie said. "Five little sisters and a baby brother, in another life."

Eva watched as the infant began to tug at the bosom of Gertie's dress, and Gertie ran a delicate finger over the child's face from cheek to cheek as though she were drawing a smiley face there. That Gertie could soothe the child so easily left Eva feeling both grateful and bitter.

"What became of them?" Eva said.

"The boy died of the fever before his teeth ever broke. Made my father, who always wanted sons, none the more pleasant, though it was one less mouth to feed. Not that there was enough to go around after the fact. Two of my sisters took to whoring in St. Louis, and two of them joined the convent. Jury's still out on the youngest."

"Why did you come west?"

"The wind blew me as far as Idaho, where I met Mr. John C. Tobin, a man with big plans and the money to back them. And the rest is history, as they say. It's been written before, so I won't bore you with it. And what brought you out here, if I might ask, Miss Lambert?"

The kettle began to moan softly from the kitchen. "All the while I thought it was my Utopian ideals, but now I'm beginning to wonder if I wasn't chasing a man, or at least the ideal of a man."

"You?"

"The irony is not lost on me, Miss McGrew. It's just beginning to sink in."

"And when it sinks in?"

"I shan't allow it to," said Eva, turning to tend the kettle.

It occurred to Gertie that Eva might be the most complicated woman she'd ever met, and that was saying something. Whatever was bending Eva on the inside, it was not of the garden variety. It seemed as if her will were bending her one way and stubbornness were bending her another. But whatever tempered such a stubbornness, and where it resided, was beyond Gertie's comprehension. The child had fallen asleep in Gertie's arms. Looking down at the girl, her little fists balled in front of her, Gertie felt a rush of warmth. Only then did she begin to feel the weight of dead possibilities. How many possibilities, such as the one sleeping in her arms, had she rid herself of — how many at the hands of Doc Newnham alone? An entire population. No precautionary measure seemed to suffice. That she was still not barren after all these years made matters all the more troubling. The moment Eva returned and set the tea down atop the dresser, Gertie handed the child to her.

"What if I told you I liked it, Miss Lambert?"

"Mothering?"

"Whoring."

"I'd say you were lying."

"What's that word you modern women are always moaning about? Objectification? What if I told you I liked the objectification of it? Not the relations part, not the black eyes and the chafed thighs and the rank taste of a man's payload, but the getting outside of myself part. What if I told you I took comfort in being an object?"

"I'd say that was sad."

"What if I told you," Gertie said, "that I thought you could use a good debasing yourself?"

Blanching, Eva turned toward the fire. "Then I'd say you were vulgar."

"And you wouldn't be the first."

Composing herself, Eva turned back to Gertie with her chin held high. "And what if *I* told *you* that you might put those convictions of yours — which you obviously have no reservations about voicing — toward some better use than whoring yourself?"

"Many find me useful, Miss Lambert. I'm practically all used up, according to some. But what did you have in mind?"

"You say you like to be outside of yourself — you like to be an object. Then why not be an instrument to some higher purpose than demeaning the tenets of womanhood for the rest of us?"

"Listen, dearie, I've had Jesus, God, and the Ghost fed to me more ways than you can count, from Bibles to sticks, and it hasn't stuck yet. And I promise you this much: your Virgin Mary has done more damage than all the whores from Babylon to Port Bonita."

"I'm not talking about God. I'm talking about society."

"Society?" said Gertie. "I see how it is: I try to make a whore out of you, and you try to make a social crusader out of me. It's like a vaudeville comedy. Very clever. Hard to imagine making any kind of a difference, Miss Lambert. But why don't I send a telegraph to Little Ben, care of the capital, and see where we go from there?"

"Anybody can make a difference, Gertie."

"That could be, Miss Lambert. But it takes a certain type to be a whore."

paradise awaits

The snow started up again shortly after the party bedded down the previous night, and by morning it had turned to steady rain. Down the hill it came, running in muddy rivulets through the camp. The snowpack grew dense and heavy with moisture, and much of what was stuck to the canopy plopped to the forest floor all about them in lumps. The weak winter light of midmorning filtering through the trees might have been dusk. They were down to one mule. The dogs were beginning to whimper with hunger. Overland travel conditions could hardly have been worse than the heavy waist-deep slush. But Mather held out hope that a good frost that night would make for hard snow and good traveling in the days to come.

With nothing to eat but prunes, which they exhausted long before they could fill their stomachs at breakfast, the men enjoyed little opportunity for leisure that day. Haywood, Reese, and Runnells, the latter upon a swollen ankle, hunted throughout the day without success, managing only a single shot between them. Though still well within the winter range of elk and deer, having not penetrated beyond the last of the green foothills, the fauna was scarce, in part, Haywood reasoned, owing to the incomprehensibly vast size and ruggedness of the country. A half-dozen elk herds might be rendered invisible by the dense wooded hollows stretching out in every direction, so that only dumb luck might betray their presence.

Cunningham remained in the tent most of the day gathering warmth. Now and again he emerged to relieve himself and huddle by the flames from which he still could draw no heat. Inwardly, he cursed himself for undertaking the expedition. He had been of little use as a doctor; indeed, he was powerless to soothe his own aches, and as an explorer he had proved to be a liability more often than not — a light load bearer with a big appetite, a boob with a rifle, incompetent with a towline. Of all the men, Cunningham pined most acutely for the family hearth. As with the others, he had neither sent nor received any word from his family in over a month. He missed the comfort and routine of civilized life, the poached eggs and newspapers and umbrellas of it. He yearned for the hours and minutes of civilized life, a tempo that could be controlled and manipulated, doled out, sectioned up, and spent, unlike the shapeless drudgery of day, night, day, night.

The spark of adventure still had not touched the torch of Mather's fervor since he dragged Cunningham bleeding from the Elwha, a fact that Haywood was keen to observe.

18 January 1890
Though I am loath to express my uneasiness with our intrepid leader in recent days, I can't help but think that the others don't feel some similar discomfort with his behavior. Yesterday, when the snow was still falling heavily, and the rest of us organized gear beneath cover, Jim sat perfectly still in the clearing on a low stump in his shirtsleeves for the better part of an hour, until the snow drifted halfway to his ankles. He does not inspire confidence. When he left for the river today, he forgot his tackle and lost nearly an hour of daylight trekking back downriver to retrieve it.

Upon his return from the river, the hunting party hopefully awaited Mather's arrival at camp. When at last he crested the high bank, clutching only a steelhead and a trout, neither an ounce over three pounds, the dejection of the party was palpable, though nobody dared give it voice. Dinner weighed in well short of a feast.

The temperature did not drop, and the hard frost Mather had hoped for did not follow. However, good fortune did visit the expedition the following morning. Haywood, in fact, was quick to credit providence for this good fortune, when in the crepuscular light of dawn he was awakened by the stirring of canvas. Rolling over with the expectation of finding Cunningham answering the call of his tiny bladder, Haywood was dumbstruck to discover that a doe had poked her head into the tent and proceeded inward well past the shoulder. More improbably still, she did not startle as he went for his rifle, or flinch as he leveled it, or blink when he pulled the trigger and the shot rang out with the sting of powder.

Cunningham awoke screaming as the doe toppled upon him, pinning his lower half. The sudden appearance of blood and cranial tissue spattered in a wide arc upon his bedding did little to calm him. Unpinning himself in a desperate flash, Cunningham all but leapt from his bedroll and scurried out of the tent in his stockings, much to the amusement of Haywood. Much ado followed as the beast was dragged from the tent and promptly dressed.

For the next three days the weather did not break, and the hard frost did not come, but the curative powers of fresh meat upon the party's morale were considerable. By the time Cunningham devoured his second venison steak, his fever had disappeared and his teeth had ceased clattering altogether. His strength and humor returned with each mouthful.

The second afternoon Reese bagged a small black bear whose misfortune it was to amble into camp and set the tethered dogs to barking. Haywood was moved to comment in his journal upon the docility of the beast, who did not so much as raise her hackles as the dogs snarled and yipped and Reese scrambled for his rifle.

19 January 1890
Indeed, the beasts are veritably giving themselves up to meet our appetites. That this bountiful place should provide such sustenance at this elevation (the altimeter reads 1,450 feet, though surely we must be higher), and at this late season (even the bears needn't slumber their winters away for lack of food), may be further testimony that paradise awaits us over the divide.

There was laughter all evening as the fatty bear meat popped and crackled in the skillet, and the remains of the whiskey was passed around the circle. They savored the very last of the spirit in ceremonious conjunction with the liver, which melted on their tongues. It was decided in the spirit of competition that each man should design and construct for his load his own means of overland portage.

Masticating slowly, his shaggy brow furrowed, Mather conceived of a travois made of alder, which amounted to a wheelbarrow on runners. Cunningham, meanwhile, striking various thoughtful comportments of his own, conceived of a sledge with bowed vine maple runners. Reese and Haywood settled on towropes, reasoning identically that anything more elaborate would simply prove cumbersome and unwieldy over the rough terrain. Not content to wait for morning in executing his design, Runnells, basking in the glow of the fire and the whiskey, began constructing a nondescript contrivance somewhere between a toboggan and a sled that he named the *Buggy*, upon which it was generally agreed all classification was lost.

The weather finally broke, and morning brought the hard frost they'd been awaiting. The party was collectively healthy, rested, and optimistic, even Mather. But nowhere was this upswing more evident than in Cunningham, five pounds heavier and immeasurably stronger, who had shaken his misgivings about the expedition and constructed his maple sledge with a certain whistling relish.

Mather constructed his travois with the slight alteration that he was forced to build the stanchions and deck of fir, having burned most of the cedar readily available to them. Though Runnells effected a few painstaking refinements in the frame of the *Buggy*, these alterations were invisible to the others, and he spent a good deal more time admiring his ugly duckling, convinced that he alone would subdue the elements with the marvel of his conception. Haywood watched the others work with the keen interest of a knowing father.

Before they even set out, the clouds returned in earnest dragging sheets of wet snow. Within an hour of breaking camp, the snow defeated all but the mule. The *Buggy* was a shambles. Mather's travois wilted. Even the towropes proved ineffective against the drag of slushy snow. Cunningham's sledge had weathered the trail best, though its maple runners had straightened out somewhat and were forever mired beneath the crust. Finally, all vehicles were abandoned in favor of the time-honored mode of backpacking.

The river had lightened their loads considerably, but they steadily gained elevation as the day unfolded, carving switchbacks through the timber for hours upon end. The oil clothing was useless against the wet snow, prompting Mather to abandon his altogether rather than endure the weight of it. The going was brutal, though Dolly suffered the worst of it, wincing frequently beneath her load as the skin of her ankles was rubbed raw by the snow.

Even well rested and nourished, the men were out of steam long before the daylight ran out. They ate the last of the doe and a good deal of the bear and slept hard that night. Mather dreamed, not a dream, but a slow heavy pulse, like a heartbeat from the center of the earth.

and beyond

When Ethan and Jacob reached the head of the canyon and emerged in the snow-blanketed meadow below the bluff, the grandeur of the scene was lost on neither man. The valley was a bowl of glorious white, and beyond the foothills the rugged snowcapped peaks of the divide loomed in dramatic relief, crisp against a backdrop of deep blue sky. And right in the middle of it all, Ethan was overjoyed to see his little cabin transformed. Not only did it boast a cedar shake roof but sturdy steps and a porch and, wonder of wonders, a river rock chimney belching black smoke into the whitewashed valley. Ethan could not have been prouder of these improvements had he made them himself.

When the men were halfway across the snowy meadow, Indian George emerged on the stoop waving. And waving back, Ethan grinned ear to ear, but even as he grinned, the thought of George's pillaged cabin was heavy upon his mind.

George was eager to relay his recent adventures, but before he could even begin, Ethan informed him of the chaos that vandals had visited upon his cabin, and George nodded gravely, the lines of his forehead gathering. He took flight without a word, a rifle that Ethan didn't recognize slung at his hip.

Ethan turned and walked right past the warm glow of the cabin to the edge of the bluff with Jacob in tow. The two men peered down into the narrow chasm. A silent moment passed as they watched the river roar through the chute.

"We'll transform this place, Jake, for a hundred miles in every direction. Our dam will be a force of nature." Ethan unpocketed his pipe and tobacco and packed a bowl and puffed, relishing the endless possibilities of progress. "A glittering city will take shape along that strait, Jake, you wait and see."

And standing there on the lip of the gorge with a stiff wind rocketing past his ears, his arm draped over the shoulder of the man whom he hoped would soon be his brother-in-law, Ethan envisioned a glorious future for Port Bonita, twenty, thirty, a hundred years and beyond.

onward

kid stuff

JUNE 2006

Though the strait was still a vaporous wall of white beyond Ediz Hook, the fog had broken inland but for few wisps and tatters, and the sun angled in weakly from the southeast, illuminating the Red Lion Inn, where a UPS truck was idling out front and an old fellow with a walker and a blue windbreaker was inching his way across the parking lot toward the stairs to Hollywood Beach. At Front Street, Curtis felt a little pang as he passed Anime House. He didn't bother checking the alley to see if the box was still there, where he'd abandoned it three days prior. Curtis had attempted to sell his comics to Anime House in an effort to finance an eighth of weed. The whole thing turned out to be a colossal hassle. He'd hauled the cumbersome white box all the way to school on the bus. It wouldn't fit in his locker, so he had to empty the box of its contents, stacking the entire Marvel Universe individually, vertically, and in reverse alphabetical order, from *X-Men* to *Avengers,* in his locker, amid a corridor bustling with morning traffic — the squeaky shoes, the jostling, the stray knee in the back. Now and again, he paused in his duties long enough to consider an issue.

Here was John Proudstar as Thunderbird — he of the long black tresses and blood red headband, pictured boldly on the cover of *X-Men* #95, the very issue in which Thunderbird dies in the exploding plane of Count Nefaria. Here was Chris Bachalo's *X-Men* #193 cover, awash in golden hues. The issue in which another Indian hero, the Apache Warpath — looking suspiciously like Thunderbird sans headband — comes to avenge his brother's death. Only now could Curtis see they were just making fun of Indians. The ubiquitous feathers and tomahawks, the bright red skin, all that spiritual garbage. As much as Curtis despised them all, the truth was that up until a few short years ago, he had loved them, too: *Exiles, Alpha Flight, X-Men.* Curtis had liked the idea of outcasts banding together. He had liked the idea of turning misfortune into strength. He had liked the idea that the imperfections of history could be repaired. He loved the heroes for being bigger than life, loved them for saying the things people never said, taking the actions people never took, but ultimately, he identified with them for their superhuman weakness more than their strength. For in their weakness, he recognized himself.

Curtis couldn't throw the stupid box away after he'd unpacked the comics, because he still needed it to haul them downtown, so he'd been forced to drag the empty thing with him to lit and consumer studies (both of which he was nearly failing), where, try as he might to keep the box tucked under his desk, it invariably stuck out into the aisle, arousing curiosity from every angle. He bailed on driver's ed third period. He'd never have a car anyway, so what was the point? He stole away down the empty hallway to his locker, reorganized the Marvel Universe, shouldered the box, and walked it in the spitting rain all the way to Lincoln and Front.

He could not deny a certain nostalgia upon entering the shop, with its glass cases smelling of Windex, its store-length rows of countless titles scrupulously organized in their wooden bins. He could do without the Warcraft posters and the game rentals, but otherwise it was the same: everywhere color and the competing odors of dust and newness.

Flipping through Curtis's collection, the counter guy, a dude about forty, could not disguise a certain nostalgia of his own. "Ha! *Rom Spaceknight* — a comic based on an action figure nobody bought. No way, you gotta be kidding me, *Luke Cage, Hero for Hire*? Hmph. Look at that afro. Micronauts — *another* comic based on an action figure nobody bought. Boy, kid, you've got some real turkeys in here."

Curtis could have done without all the commentary. He just wanted forty bucks. Maybe fifty, so he could buy a pack of smokes, some Doritos, and an Excalibur down at Circle K.

"Twenty bucks for these," the counter dude said, peering over the rim of his reading glasses, clutching a stack that included most of the *Fantastic Fours*, *X-Men*, some *Daredevils*, and the crown jewel of his collection, Marvel Two-in-One annual #1 (featuring the Ever-Lovin' Blue-Eyed Thing and the hopelessly gay and outdated Liberty Legion).

"That's it?"

"Look, I just don't move a lot of this seventies stuff, kid. *Luke Cage, Hero for Hire*? *Rom Spaceknight*? Sorry, but I couldn't give that stuff away."

As it turned out, neither could Curtis. He tried to give the rest of the box to the guy for free, so he wouldn't have to lug the thing back to school. No dice. Begrudgingly, he salvaged all the Native American crap and left the rest in the alley by the Dumpster.

The day had only gotten worse for Curtis after abandoning the comics. Still twenty bucks shy of that elusive eighth, he'd returned to school, stashed what was left of the Marvel universe in his locker, and proceeded to Coleman's office to deal with the stupid job shadow bullshit he was getting roped into in order to pass Gerke's class.

"What about shadowing one of the elders?" Coleman had said. "Or somebody from the Tribal Council? Or the Jamestown Heritage Museum? They might even have an internship for you down there."

Coleman wasn't even Indian. He'd just married an Indian so long ago that he'd managed to convince himself he was Indian by association. The ponytail, the politics, the ugly sweaters. On his desk, a leather stitched pencil cup with beads and tassels.

"Why not keep it local?" Coleman persisted.

"It is local," Curtis observed impassively from behind a curtain of black bangs.

Coleman frowned his guidance counselor frown.

They'd never let him forget it — Coleman, the elders, the guy from the fry bread stand at Sunday market. They were always ennobling the tribe, clinging to the past with a grip so tenuous it was almost silly — potlatches, totems, canoes. Please. Like he was going to carve a totem or ferry people around in a canoe? Why couldn't his people just adapt? And what were they trying to sell him, anyway? Curtis was no dummy. He'd done his research. He'd read the history books. He knew that being a Klallam back in the day wasn't all communing with nature and dancing with spirits. He knew about the slave trade. He knew about the Hudson's Bay Company, and the Dungeness Massacre. He knew about the violence and hatred the Klallam had visited on the Tsimshians as well as the whites, how they'd burned them and decapitated them. Funny, but you never heard the elders singing that tune. They were always trying to get you to succeed, to do the tribe proud, *give back* to the community. Give what? For what? The stupid casino?

Coleman was pensive. He picked a ball of lint off his ugly sweater, considered it, lobbed it over his shoulder, and scratched his ear with a sigh. "All this acting out — the bad grades, the skipping, the attitude — is this about your dad?"

Curtis heaved his own sigh and looked out the window. "Why does everything have to be about my stupid dad? Ancient history — there's a class I could pass."

"I was just wondering whether — "

"No, okay? No."

"But maybe if you just — "

"I'm fine. Seriously . . . can we stop?"

Why was it that somebody was always there to offer unsolicited advice? And they always wanted to talk. *Let's talk,* they'd say, *tell me about it, you'll feel better,* but mostly they'd ask, *Why are you angry?*

"What are you angry about?" Coleman wanted to know.

"I'm not angry. I'm annoyed."

"Do you want to talk about it?"

"Of course I don't want to talk about it. I don't want to talk at all. I just want to *not talk,* okay? Do we *have* to talk? Couldn't I just listen? Couldn't you just tell me a bunch of stuff about how it's going to be for me if I don't *get my grades up,* and how I ought to *embrace my heritage* and *take responsibility for myself,* and I'll just sit here and listen? Or maybe you could just *not say* all those things this time and just give me all the papers and stuff I'll need to fill out for the job thing."

For once, Coleman didn't say anything.

AMBLING DOWN THE sunny side of Front Street toward the center of town, in no hurry whatsoever, Curtis took a small comfort in knowing that whatever bullshit awaited him at High Tide Seafood that afternoon, it couldn't be as bad as three days ago. He passed the boarded storefront that was once Pop's Restaurant and, before that, Charlie's. The only thing left now were the big brown letters RES-TAURANT, partially obscured by a FOR LEASE sign, and in the window, hanging crookedly, half of a waterlogged menu. Prime-rib dip $7.99. Surf-and-Turf $9.50. Curtis paused briefly at Coho Unlimited, Port Bonita's premiere tourist boutique, with its regionally famous window display: an explosion of stuffed giraffes and ceramic chickens, and faux-Indian art, phony muskets, and wooden seagulls, and mermaid-encrusted fondue bowls. There was a five-foot chainsaw-sculpted salty sea dog captain named Old Ned, smoking a pipe by the door. There were racks and racks of postcards near the front entrance. *Gateway to the Olympics. Hurricane Ridge. Thornburgh Dam.* And though there were no tourists about, a four-hundred-year-old poster in the window boasted 30 PERCENT OFF OF ALL STOCK! Next to this hung a yellow flyer:

Dam Days, September 2–3!
Come celebrate over 100 years of Port Bonita history!
Featuring Live Music, Logging Competition, Chainsaw Carving
   Contest, and World-Famous Salmon Bake
Proudly presented in part by your neighbors at Wal-Mart.

Fucking Wal-Mart. They killed everything. Curtis could hardly recognize this place anymore. He was almost embarrassed to admit that as a child, Port Bonita had seemed like a glorious place, the center of the universe, and Dam Days had seemed a grand occasion marked by fry bread tacos and brass bands. Now it seemed stupid: a bunch of fat whites and sad-looking Indians mulling around Lake Thornburgh as if there were anything to see, anything to celebrate but a hulking mass of useless concrete and a lot of chain-link fence. As if Port Bonita were anything else but one big fucking Wal-Mart.

A half block later Curtis passed Gertie's, where even at three in the afternoon, a handful of sketchy-looking dudes and one old lady with yellowing bleach blonde hair stood out front smoking cigarettes. She looked like Skeletor. They all looked like Skeletor.

Curtis fired up a Salem. Deadsville, that was this place.

Sasquatch Field Research Organization

Report 1017 (class B)
Year: 2006
Season: Spring
State: Washington
County: Clallam
Nearest town: Port Bonita
Nearest Road: Elwha River Road

OBSERVED: The following events happened roughly two miles above the Thornburgh Dam along the Crooked Thumb trail, the first week of April 2006. This area has had a lot of sightings (mostly class B) over the past several years, so I was not completely surprised by the events of that night. In fact, my purpose out there was to call-blast after dark (using uncompressed digital recordings of the Snohomish Whoop-Howl and Del Norte calls), employing a Peavey JSX 212 cabinet and a 120-watt Joe Satriani Signature Head. Loud as hell. I used a 12-volt marine battery with 300-watt square-wave inverter for juice. I had to make three wheel-barrow trips in with all my gear, which I could hardly fit into the Goat (my '73 GTO 400ci sport coupe).

My plan was to get in early and stay put, hunker down, and drink a few brews in the dark (but I wasn't drunk during any of what transpired; with the amp and everything else, I could only carry four beers on the last trip — I can't even feel four beers). I'm an experienced hiker with a lot of cryptoid-tracking experience (I had a class C encounter off of Highway 112 near Joyce 7/6/99, as well as a possible class B near Hoko River 9/11/2003. Both sightings, nos. 0645 and 0914, are in the SFRO sightings database). I am also very familiar with the area, having lived my entire life here (Bucket Brigade class of 84!). Lastly, I know what a bear sounds like. I've hiked Crooked Thumb many times. Above the dam along the western shore of Lake Thornburgh is a lot of second-growth fir and hemlock, which has seen a little harvesting in recent years, but most of it is protected, or supposed to be. I parked at the slab and hiked to just shy of mile marker 2. I employed the use of a scent mask (Dave's Pop-Up Scent Canisters combo kit with detachable wick — got it at Big Five). I also hung pheromone chips around my encampment. These I acquired via a guy on the Internet and are supposedly the same chips utilized in the Quachita Project in 2001, made of part-human and part–great ape pheromones. They don't really smell like anything, but I'm not a Bigfoot (although I wear a size 13).

The Elwha might be dead below the dam, but above the dam it is still wild. I've been told by hikers it is some of the wildest and most rugged country anywhere. My theory as to why the Crooked Thumb trail is proven to be a hotbed for sightings in the past, and why I've chosen this area as the focus of my field research, is because it is heavily tracked by deer in all seasons. This allows the Sasquatch an abundant food source in the winter months. Also berries are prevalent (huckleberry, thimbleberry, salmon berry) and there is an accessible freshwater source via both Lake Thornburgh and the upper Elwha. The trail is broad and flat for the first few miles allowing for easy migration, but the lake is otherwise hemmed in by mountains.

After my camp was set up, I hunkered down until dark. The anticipation gets creepier the darker it gets and the less you can see. About an hour after dark I blasted my first call (a ten-second Del Norte). As anyone who has ever call-blasted knows, to hear these sounds amplified is incredibly eerie. It was extremely dark, and the moon was hidden deep behind cloud cover. I'm not afraid of the dark, but I'd be lying if I said I wasn't afraid of this dark. This is a big kind of dark. I never get used to it. A third-generation NVD is at the top of my wish list right now. (I saw the Night Optics D-300G-3A goggles at Big Five for a little over 3K — I should've bought them!)

I waited nine minutes before my second blast (another Del Norte). I got no response to the vocalization, but I did hear something move in the brush uphill from me (probably a deer). I decided to try a few tree knocks on a nearby fir. For this purpose, I brought a 33-inch, 31-ounce Louisville Slugger Triton Softball bat (also a Big Five purchase). I wrapped the barrel of the bat in a half inch of duct tape so it would lose the aluminum sound and make a good thud. After a series of four syncopated knocks, I listened for a few minutes and received no response.

I waited seven more minutes before blasting a Snohomish Whoop-Howl. My neck hair stood on end when four seconds later I got a faint response from (I'm guessing) a quarter mile to the west. The response did not sound so much like a Snohomish as it did a Skamania Howl. It was the most chilling thing I've heard in my life. I suddenly felt extremely cold and I actually got the shivers and my teeth were chattering together. The other thing is that I suddenly felt like I had to go to the bathroom.

I waited about sixty seconds with my teeth chattering, when I heard another vocalization from the west. This was particularly alarming because this thing was moving pretty fast. The second vocalization sounded considerably closer. I immediately blasted another call and got a response seconds later. The closest one yet. My hand was shaking badly. I could hardly press play. I'll be honest, I was about ready to get the heck out of there. I didn't like the way this thing was coming after me. Suddenly, from the east I heard the strangest vocalizations I've ever heard. It sounded like talking, like somebody speaking in tongues and it was very close, in fact it was all around me, as if I were being surrounded. I was so scared at this point that I almost blacked out. I huddled up in a ball, clutching the Louisville Slugger.

The vocalizations were really deep, deeper than anything human. They were fast. They kind of floated on the air. I can't quite explain it. The smell was pretty strong, like skunk cabbage or rotting garbage. I couldn't really tell how close they were because to tell you the truth even though my senses were sharp, I wasn't sure I could trust them. My heart was beating in my ears, and that may have affected my judgment. I really cannot say how much time passed. I kept expecting them to walk right into the camp. In which case I would've probably had a heart attack. But at the same time (and this may sound weird) I felt more alive than I've ever felt before. My whole body was like one big nerve ending.

Finally, I got up the balls to turn on my headlamp and jump up and swing the beam of the light in a circle at the woods all around me. I can't say for sure what I saw. All the shadows were disorienting. But there was definitely movement in the woods. I saw something big move behind a tree, and I heard brush snapping behind me. As I swung my head to the north, I thought I saw another big shadowy figure move through the beam of my flashlight, too quickly to identify but big enough that it could only be one thing. It was moving away from me, scrambling up a steep embankment. From west of me came another chilling vocalization that almost gave me a heart attack. It was more of a screech than anything else, similar to the Gifford Pinchot recordings from fall of '96. After a minute, I began to realize that they had all moved off, and a few minutes later I heard another vocalization from the west, pretty far off. These things were fast. It's hard to imagine anything moving quite that fast in the dark.

I'm still not sure how many there were, but if I had to guess I'd say there had to be at least three because of the directions of the vocalizations and the forest noise. I know what I heard, and I don't care who thinks I'm crazy.

I did not sleep one wink. I kept making noise throughout the night. It was by far the longest and most terrifying night of my life, and for sure the most memorable (even more memorable than the night I scored 39 points against North Mason in the '84 regionals). As soon as it was light enough to see out, I started loading my stuff out. On the way back to the Goat on the second trip, I noticed something that looked like animal scat (see Also Noticed).

ALSO NOTICED: On my second load back to the car in the morning, about two-tenths of a mile east of my camp, I noticed what I believe to be fresh Bigfoot scat. It was really big. It looked like a big melted caramel or something. I sent samples to SFRO for analysis, but they were returned with a nasty letter from the postal service. I later gave the samples to SFRO investigator Greg Beamer who sent them to Central Washington University for analysis.

OTHER WITNESSES: None. I do all my cryptoid-tracking solo to avoid forest noise. In this case I wish I would have brought somebody. It would have been a lot less scary, and I might have collected better data instead of curling up in a ball clutching a baseball bat.

ENVIRONMENT: This is a thickly wooded area running along the lake shore on a high bluff. As I said earlier, there is abundant game along this trail. My camp was approximately two miles above the trailhead, which obviously isn't that far, but as experienced cryptoid-trackers know, most sightings happen in the ecotone.

Report submitted by: Dave Krigstadt
Follow-up investigation pending.

the shadow

"Krigstadt! Your shadow's here," said Jared. "And I need an invoice for those clams FedExed off to Fletchers ASAP. As in, before lunch. And don't forget to order wet-locks. I'm not eating another two hundred pounds of coho because you for — "

"Yeah, I got it. I got it." Krig made a show of rifling through some papers on his desk. When he was sure Jared had turned, he grabbed his nuts. "I got it right here."

Jared disappeared into his wainscoted office.

"Little prick," Krig mumbled. It was one thing to take orders, but to take them from a little ass-munch like Thornburgh, who'd only been there five months, was almost too much to endure. Goddamn little senator's son — just like the CCR song. Where the hell was Thornburgh when Krig led the Bucket Brigade to the regional championship on the glory of his sweet stroke and sure-handed crossover, huh? Where was he when Krig dumped in thirty-four against Forks? In eighth grade, that's where. On top of all that, who was pulling honor roll two years in a row? That's right, Krig. Not as dumb as he looked. He was even in philosophy club for a while, with people like Edward C. Posniak and Katherine Lewis, but the geniuses were even smugger than the jocks. And their humor was insufferable. C'mon, seriously, Spinoza jokes? The point is, it wasn't about brains, getting ahead; it wasn't even about who you know, because, well, Krig knew everybody in this town. It was about, it was about . . .

Swiveling around in his squeaky office chair, Krig discovered an Indian kid standing in the doorway of his cubicle. The boy, at least he thought it was a boy, looked about thirteen, but he had to be older. The counselor lady said she was sending a junior. His baggy gray T-shirt read: WHAT THE HELL ARE YOU LOOKING AT? His jeans looked like a wolverine had gotten to them. He wore his greasy black hair to the shoulders, framing a perfectly round face. He was squinty-eyed and impassive. Krig thought he looked baked.

"So," said Krig. "You must be my shadow, right? Curtis? Chris?"

Curtis or Chris didn't say anything. He just stood there.

"Okay, then. Let's do this thing. You got a notepad or anything? Aren't you supposed to take notes or something?"

The kid shifted his weight, just barely, from one foot to another.

"All right, then, fuck it," said Krig. "Let's get started. First things first: I'm Dave, the production manager around here. You can call me Krig. That little prick in the brown office is Jared. He's the GM. That stands for Gay Man."

The kid didn't even blink. Tough nut to crack, thought Krig. Figures he'd get a weirdo. I mean, really, what kind of kid wants to work *here* when he grows up? Why did he ever agree to this job-shadow bullshit in the first place?

"So what do you know about this place? You know what we do here?"

The kid gave no indication one way or another.

"Right. Well. We process seafood, since you asked. About four million pounds a year. Most of it salmon. Sounds like a lot, right? . . . Right. But before you get the idea you're gonna just waltz into a job here after graduation, you oughta know that we're the last commercial fish processor in Port Bonita. This whole industry went tits up around here long before your old man ever squirted you out, even before logging hit the skids. There used to be like twenty of these places working around the clock. The whole harbor was lined with them. My old man and my uncles and their old men all used to do this shit. Back in the day, my great-grandfather used to pull hundred-pound chinooks out of the Elwha — June Hogs, they called them. That was then. Most of the fish are in Alaska now. There ain't beans for fish around here. So you see, kid, it's all about sustainability — but I'm not here to give you any history lessons or environmental crap. All you need to know is this: you wanna process fish in P.B., you're working for me. And this here," Krig said, indicating his murky cubicle with a panoramic sweep of his hand, "is the nerve center of High Tide."

The kid was apparently unimpressed. Sullen little fucker, eh? Wait'll he's spooning fish guts for a living. Wait'll he's squaring his tab at the Bushwhacker five nights a week at closing, pining for some waitress who looks like a mud shark.

"Any questions before we get started? . . . Okay then, good. Let's walk you through this. Out there is the processing center."

They stepped out of Krig's cubicle and walked a short ways down the corridor, past a big blurry window, through a heavy door and down some metal stairs. The processing center was a cement gray cavern reeking of fish, a hissing, rumbling dungeon in the bowels of the plant. Curtis saw his mother slitting bellies near the front of the line. She looked stupid in her rubber apron and her paper hat. She waved. Curtis ignored her.

"You know Rita, huh?" said Krig. "Rita's cool. So, how do you know her?"

Curtis didn't answer.

The closer they got to the line, the more deafening became the hissing and rumbling, so that Krig was forced to project his voice over the racket.

"That big fucker right there is a hydraulic tote dumper. Fish comes in, that fucker picks it up, slaps it onto this fucker here — this is the conveyor — and *boom*, we're locked and loaded. First the cutters — *thwack* — there go your heads. Next, we slit the belly, slice the neck, and scoop out the guts. Then we slit the bloodline and bleed the fucker. We spoon the bloodline, rinse the bitch, and — *boom* — this fucker's ready for market. Any questions? Good, I need a smoke."

Curtis followed Krig out back to the parking lot, where Krig offered him a smoke. Curtis accepted with the slightest of nods.

"So, what, you don't talk?"

Curtis lit his cigarette and let the question pass.

"Suit yourself," said Krig, pocketing his lighter. "You smoke weed?"

The kid arched an eyebrow.

"Yay or nay?"

Curtis tendered another slight nod.

"Well, then, I'd say it's about four twenty, how about you? C'mon, time for a safety meeting."

Curtis followed Krig around the back of the warehouse, past the loading dock, and across another dirt parking lot to a lobster red GTO.

"This is the Goat," said Krig. "Pretty sweet, huh? 'Seventy-three. Got it off of some schlub who lost his nut down at Seven Cedars."

"Cool," lied Curtis.

In the car, Krig procured a slim joint from an Altoids container in the glove box. "Kind of a pinner," he said, by way of an apology. "But I gotta maintain at work."

Krig sparked it and took greens. "This shit's the chronic," he said, holding his breath. "No sticks, no stems, no seeds. *Whoo-ee gimme some-a-that-sticky-icky-icky.*" He passed the joint to Curtis and exhaled a cloud of blue smoke, which hung in the air.

Curtis thought the guy was an idiot. How old was this guy, anyway? He had to be older than his mom. He took a long pull and passed the joint back to Krig.

"So, what," said Krig. "You're an Indian, right?"

Curtis didn't say anything.

"That's what I thought. I got a buddy who's an Indian. Doesn't pay shit for taxes. So, you believe in Bigfoot, or what?"

"Nah," said Curtis.

"I thought all Indians believed in Sasquatch."

"That shit's made up."

Krig took another pull from the joint, which was down to a nub already. "Yeah, well, you never know," said Krig, exhaling. "I've seen some shit."

"You were high."

"Heard, anyway. Couple of them. And I've seen a pile of dookie about this big on the Crooked Thumb trail."

"Yeah, and I'm a medicine man."

Krig let the subject pass. Nobody wanted to believe him. "So, how do you know Rita?"

"I live with her."

"She's your sister?"

"Yeah, right."

"Your mom?"

"So what?"

"So nothin', just asking. What about your old man?"

"Nothin' about my old man."

"That's cool. I gotcha." Krig handed him the joint. Curtis hit it and looked out the window. "So, your mom's like single or whatever?"

"She's whatever."

Krig let this subject pass, too. Better not to push it. "So, this is seriously what you wanna do when you get out of school?"

Curtis shrugged it off, still gazing sullenly out the window.

"It's not exactly glamorous, as you can see," pursued Krig. "It may seem like good money, but —"

"But you're doing it."

"Well, yeah, that's true," said Krig, reaching for the joint. "As long as I can remember. It was different back when I started, though. It's different now. If I was you, I'd blow this town."

"Well, you're still here."

"That's what I'm saying. I just mean if I were *you*, I'd go to college and party my ass off and get a degree or whatever so I'd have some options, you know?"

"I gotta go," said Curtis, opening the door.

"Later," said Krig.

Stubbing the roach out in the ashtray, Krig watched Curtis go. The kid ambled across the lot and crossed Marine without looking. He headed south toward Front Street. Weird little dude. But Krig was willing to give the kid a break. He was a little antisocial, but whatever. Who could blame the kid?

Krig checked his eyes in the rearview mirror, fished an Altoid out of the glove box, and reminded himself to order wet-locks.

SOMETIMES IT WASN'T enough for Jared to hide in his office, where Dee Dee was likely to molest his solitude with inventory discrepancies, or Don Buford from Prime Seafoods might call to badger him about the ALS charity golf tournament in Sequim next weekend, or worst of all, Janis might call to dispatch him on some errand — color swatches from Sherwin-Williams, Bubble Wrap from Office Depot — thus negating his lunch hour, which Jared preferred to spend sleeping in the SUV (and why not, it was costing him six and change per month?). But sleep wouldn't have Jared this afternoon, as he reclined in the driver's seat of his GL-450. After five months, the job was getting to him. It wasn't the stress; the workload was manageable enough. It was the nature of the details now populating his life, the things he was forced to think about, all the shit that rolled uphill instead of down. For instance, the wet-locks that Krigstadt would no doubt forget to order (again), and the two hundred pounds of coho that would subsequently thaw (again), resulting in a phone call Thursday morning (again) from an irate retailer in Spokane.

How had his life been reduced to such trivialities? What happened to expectations — his and everyone else's? He was a Thornburgh. Thornburghs didn't ponder the shipping cost of canned clams, didn't fret about the flagging market for pickled herring in the southwest; Thornburghs authored public policy, they legislated, they built dams out of mountains and put towns on maps!

But wasn't he being a little hard on himself? Was it really owing to some flaw in his own character that he had wound up here, in what ought to be the prime of his life, with nothing more to show than a dwindling trust fund and a head full of canned crab? Where were the opportunities? He had his ducks in line; he was networked, educated, sufficiently energetic. And contrary to the perception around High Tide, Jared had put in his time — maybe not in the trenches but at least in the classroom. So where were the rivers to be dammed, the policies to be forged? How did one fashion a future from smoked oysters?

A tap on the window startled Jared from these meditations — it was Dee Dee, clutching a fax. Jared lowered the window with an electric whir.

"This rush just came in from Longview," she said. "Oh, and Don Buford called about your tee time on Saturday."

the bushwhacker

When Timmon Tillman stepped off the 136 bus in Port Bonita into a mud puddle, with $843 in his wallet and a letter from the parole board testifying to his status as a reformed ward of the State Corrections Center in Clallam Bay, nobody was there to greet him, which is exactly how Timmon Tillman preferred it. When the board asked him what future he envisioned for himself, Timmon told them simply, "A place of my own." When they asked him what kind of work he'd like to do, he told them, "Something with my hands." And when, in conclusion, they asked him if he had a goal in life, Timmon said, "To live my life one day at a time."

But what Timmon had wanted to say was, "To be left alone."

In the Circle K, he bought two pepperoni sticks and a Snapple. The clerk snuck furtive glances at his tattooed hand: the washed-out gunmetal blue Egyptian ankh (which looked more like an upside-down gingerbread man), the would-be bar code, which having presented his cell mate Gooch with far too great a challenge from a design standpoint resulted in an amorphous blotch on Timmon's wrist, and above the knuckles, a single word scripted in a scrolling cursive hand: *onward!*

Timmon left his four cents change in the Kool Menthol penny tray and started drifting toward the center of town under a steady drizzle. The mountains were socked in from the foothills to the ridge, and the strait was hardly visible through the haze. The speeding cars on U.S. Route 101 threw a gritty spray in their wake, and when he closed his eyes, the sound of the swishing tires sounded almost natural to Timmon, like the surf. But the moment he opened them again he longed to be outside the prison of himself. He could almost feel the fizz of tonic on his tongue, the warm suffusion of vodka in his belly. The world was teeming with possibilities, and the overwhelming majority of them were too excruciating to ponder: a nowhere job, a crummy motel room, an issue of *Juggs* — then what? The endless reiteration of hot plate dinners and naked lightbulbs? The perpetual sound of his own spinning wheels? How was marking time any different on the outside?

Only the thought of a steak dinner brightened Timmon's outlook as he booked a room at the Wharf Side, where there was nothing even remotely surreptitious in the appraisal of the carbuncled old desk woman when she looked Timmon up and down with particular attention to his tattoos.

"The coat hangers stay," she wheezed. "And we like to keep things quiet around here."

"Yes, ma'am," said Timmon.

The room afforded Timmon a dramatic view of an auto body shop, a Chevron, a Jack in the Box, and a Taco Bell. The walls were orange, the pea green carpet was piebald, and the residue of twenty-year-old smoke clung to the yellow drapes. The bathroom was so small that in order to stand in it, the door had to be shut. There was a rusty ring around the shower drain. Something smelled like mop water.

Timmon unpacked his duffel bag: some jeans, a windbreaker, some socks, a pair of prison-issue black rubber flip-flops, and a copy of Whitman's *Leaves of Grass*, which might have been kicked there from Peoria. *O me! O life!* He arranged these things sparsely about the room in an attempt at hominess. And looking upon his work with a hollow ache, he fled the room immediately in favor of the open air.

It was still dumping rain at dusk. The sky was low. The mountains remained invisible. The unmistakable odor of deep-fried fat hung in the air. Timmon trudged north past Taco Bell, brimming eerily with light in the gathering darkness. Jack in the Crack, Chevron, the Dollar Store. He could have been anywhere. He proceeded over the hump and onward.

In the murky confines of the Bushwhacker, Timmon ordered a vodka tonic and leveled his gaze on the bartop in front of him, avoiding even the most casual eye contact with the bartender or anyone else. Despite lethal doses of Whitman's tireless curiosity and optimism, which he spoon-fed himself daily in the dank perimeters of his cell, Timmon's most recent stint in prison had done little to awaken his curiosity in people.

When his drink arrived, he left it in front of him on the bar like a challenge, where it stayed until the ice melted and the fizz went out of it and dew drops formed on the outside of the glass. Knowing all the while that if he drank it, the fierce determination to win would come surging back immediately, but knowing also the boomerang effect morning would bring, all the terror and madness and self-loathing. What was this compulsion to escape, to be beholden to no man? And why was it he could only seem to achieve freedom in the reeling, slobbering stages of drunkenness, those very stages he could never remember in the morning when he awoke in holding cells with his zipper unfastened and lumps on his skull? Why, like old Walt, could he not be afoot and light-hearted upon the open road, healthy and free with his path before him? Where were his hearty appetites, his slumbering passions? Where betwixt these green islands were his subtle refrains?

When his steak arrived, Timmon had no appetite for it. He could do nothing but ponder the dim prospect of his future. Eight hundred and forty bucks. Eight twenty-five after the steak and the vodka, both of which would remain untouched. Beyond this paltry sum separating him from total destitution — amassed under the state's supervision at the wage of $1.15 per hour, collating Wal-Mart circulars as a means of personal empowerment and social elevation — the future was even bleaker food for contemplation. The infernal struggle. The paperwork. The standing in lines. The people with their suspicions, and worse, their charity. The smell of those curtains.

At least Don Gasper gave him a couple of leads. Gasper said he was coming back to P.B. himself when he was sprung. Said he knew everybody. Said it was a kick-ass town. But then, look at Gasper. Guy couldn't even burgle his own grandmother.

AN OFFICE, THE first of many, thought Timmon. Well, sort of an office. More of a cubicle with mottled brown carpet and a fishy smell. A guy in a rubber apron and boots was leaning back in his chair, looking at Timmon's letter of recommendation without really looking at it. He kept looking instead at the gingerbread man.

"So, wait a minute," the guy said. "Didn't I see you at the Bush-whacker last night? Shit yeah, I thought you looked familiar. I was eyeing your steak." Krig handed the letter back to Timmon. "I don't need this shit. What are you gonna steal? Goddamn halibut?"

"Don Gasper mentioned that —"

"Don Gasper's a tool. I played JV with the guy. He's what we call a go-left. No fucking right hand. Just box the fucker in at the top of the key and force him right. He'll settle for some weak-ass jumper every time. Gasper. Pfff. What a prick. I haven't seen that guy since our ten-year."

Thornburgh came striding down the corridor toward Krig's cu-bicle. Krig promptly swung his feet off the desk.

"Where's my wet-locks, Krigstadt? I've got two hundred pounds of coho sitting down there and no wet-locks."

"I'm on it, I'm on it," said Krig, with a salute. "Done and doner, sir."

Jared heaved a heavy sigh. He thought about saying something but decided, exhaustively and at length with a rather drawn expression on his face as he appraised Krig, that it just wasn't worth it. Turning on his heels, he marched across the hall to his office.

"Prick," mumbled Krig, who replaced his feet on the desk. "You're one lucky sonofabitch, Tisdale, you know that? And I'll tell you why. We got a hundred and twenty thousand pounds of salmon coming through here next week, and I'm short-handed on second crew. You think you can hose down fish? Spoon out guts? Maybe drive a forklift if you're a good boy? It ain't brain surgery, but you'd be surprised at how some of these dumbfucks could screw something up. Do these sound like skill sets you possess, Tisdale? Because if you can do that, I don't care if you tattoo a pentagram on your forehead. I need fast, reliable processors. In fact, I might even be able to shuffle some things around. Better hours. How does first crew sound?"

It was apparent even before Timmon donned his apron the following morning in the locker room that Krig had decided to take him under his wing, a fate Timmon would have cheerfully traded for eight hours of solitary confinement. Krig was intent on grooming him. Krig believed in second chances.

"I figure you give a guy a break, right? Even the playing field. P.B.'s all about fresh starts. Used to be, anyway. Hell, look at Thornburgh's great-great-whatever. Guy got here with a plug nickel after they ran him out of Seattle, and now half of P.B.'s named after him."

Krig was inexhaustible. He kept talking about his Goat. Three times he commented on Timmon's stature. "You *sure* you didn't play any roundball?"

At six foot six, Timmon was weary of this assumption. The answer was no. No, no, no. He never played basketball. He was gangly, having grown all at once one excruciating sophomore year that saw his pants cuffs ascend halfway to his knees and his Adam's apple push against the inside of his neck as though it were trying to break through. Everything grew but his dingus. He'd gone out for JV and was the first man cut. He ran the court like a wounded marionette. He launched hopeless bricks at the rim. He couldn't even set a decent pick he was so skinny. He hated basketball. And still, the whole world insisted on foisting basketball upon him, as though it were beyond the realm of possibility that a tall guy related to the world as anything but one big fucking basketball game.

Krig walked Timmon through every phase of processing: demonstrating with knives and spigoted spoons various feats of prestidigitation upon fish carcasses as they made their way up the line, station to station. At lunch, Krig insisted on sitting with Timmon on the loading dock. He insisted on showing him the Goat, stipulating that Timmon sit in the driver seat. For one merciful hour, Krig left Timmon slitting necks on the line unattended, but even then he was a lingering presence, frequently prairie-dogging over his cubicle and peering through the smudged Plexiglas window to check on Timmon's progress. Worse, he insisted on driving Timmon to the Wharf Side in the Goat, spiriting him away instead to the Bushwhacker for happy hour, where Krig proceeded to describe in stultifying detail the texture, scent, and miraculous size of what he determined to be Sasquatch dung at a nearby lake.

The second day was hardly better. Krig's presence was suffocating. He persisted with the basketball. His growing familiarity toward Timmon was harder to endure than anything Gooch had ever visited upon him in the darkness of their cell. At least Gooch didn't like basketball. It hardly mattered to Timmon what Krig's intentions might be or what doors Krig might open for him. Timmon didn't want a break. He just wanted to be left alone.

At lunch, he narrowly escaped Krig under the pretense of meeting his parole officer.

"No prob," said Krig. "You can take an extra hour if you need it. You need a ride?"

FRANKLIN BELL WAS the first black person Timmon had seen since he left Clallam Bay. He was a little guy with salt and pepper hair, whose stature was diminished still further by a giant avocado-colored desk, in whose squeaking bowels he presently scanned for Timmon's file. It was soon apparent that Bell compensated for his size with a hard-nosed exuberance.

"Taylor, Temple, Thatcher, Tillman, *bam! Thankyouverymuch.*" He pulled the file out, kicked his feet up on the desk and perused the contents of the manila folder, humming all the while a tune vaguely familiar to Timmon. Was that Don Henley? Was the black dude humming Don Henley? Bell tapped his foot in time, bobbed his eyebrows up and down, and kept on humming as he scanned the file. It *was* Don Henley! "Boys of Summer."

Thirty-six, thought Franklin, doesn't look it. Same age as the boy would be right now. Had it really been that long? Chasing the thought from his head, Franklin continued his humming survey. String of priors and two strikes. Nothing violent. Kid doesn't look so tough when you get past the ink. Mother deceased, father deceased. Couple of community college classes. No driver's license.

Finally, right about the time Henley saw a Deadhead sticker on a

Cadillac, Bell slammed the folder shut on the desktop. "Free at last! So whaddaya gonna do with that, Tillman? You gonna squander that opportunity?" But before Timmon could answer, Bell answered for him. "Hell no, you're not. I'm here to make sure you don't." Bell spun around in his chair and opened a brown mini-fridge from which he produced a green and red carton. Kicking his legs up once more, he took a long pull from the carton, which left a thick white mustache upon his upper lip. Bell was apparently oblivious of the mustache.

"Mm-mm. I like me some eggnog, Tillman. *That's* goodness. Like mothers milk. I know what you're thinkin', too, you're thinkin', 'Now, what kinda dude drinks eggnog in June?' Well, now, you take one look out that window and you tell me it looks like June, Tillman. Looks like goddamn Christmas to me." Bell offered the carton to Timmon, and when Timmon declined, he took another pull himself. "*Damn,* that's good. I gotta special order this shit. Damn near four bucks a carton this time of year." Bell set the carton down and picked up the file again. "Native son," he observed. "South-side boy myself, Tillman. South Halsted, one-bedroom apartment with four brothers and a sister. They tore that pesthole down, good riddance, paved it over with an interstate. Where you from?"

"Lincoln Park," lied Timmon.

"Mmm," commented Bell, doubtfully, glancing down at the gingerbread man and the blotch on Timmon's wrist. But it didn't bother him that Timmon was lying. He could empathize with the guy. Franklin knew what it was like to want to shed one's beginnings. He'd been running out from under shadows as long as he could remember. "Been a long way down, eh, son?"

"Didn't take long," said Timmon.

"Fast worker. That's good, Tillman. At least you're decisive. We can work with that." Bell drained the carton, spun around in his chair and let a jump-shot fly. It clunked off the rim of the green garbage can. He shrugged it off, and smiled. He still had an eggnog mustache. "Well," he said. "Least I'm still in the game. Let's talk turkey." Bell folded his arms and leaned back even farther in his chair, which issued some plaintive squeaking. "Just what do you plan on doing with your life, son?"

"Gettin' by."

"That it?"

"That's plenty."

"That what they taught you in corrections?"

"Somethin' like that."

"Why Port Bonita? Says here you were in Aberdeen before your last stint."

Timmon glanced out the window at the rain and shrugged. "Why not?"

"Plan on settlin' down, do you?"

"Suppose so. Can't go too far now, can I?"

"This ain't no land of milk and honey, Tillman. I'm just warning you. A man needs to create his own breaks around here, a man needs to show a little hustle if he plans on gettin' anywhere, you follow? Ain't squat for work, and plenty of competition. Consider yourself lucky to have a job."

Timmon nodded.

"Plenty of riffraff in these parts, too. How are you at resisting temptation, Tillman?"

Timmon cast a vague glance out at the rain once more. "Why comes temptation, but for man to meet and master and crouch beneath his foot."

"Say what?"

"Browning."

"The pitcher?"

"The dreamer."

Franklin looked impressed, nodding his head slowly and hoisting an eyebrow. "Reader, huh?"

"Not by choice."

"Says in the file you're not a big talker."

Timmon gave a nod.

"Well?"

"What's to say."

"Fair enough, I suppose. How about listenin'? Do much of that?"

"I hear a lot."

"Good start, Tillman, I like your style. You're a man who bides his words. A listener. Good set of ears can get a man a long way. Don't stop listenin' to them dreamers in your head, boy. They know somethin'. And I know a thing or two, myself. And I want you to listen up, and listen good, because sooner you realize what I got to tell you, sooner you can make your life a masterpiece."

It did not occur to Timmon to envision what sort of masterpiece Bell had created out of his own life, that is, a sixty-hour workweek, peptic ulcer, studio apartment behind a bowling alley, twenty-three consecutive months of excruciating celibacy. Instead, Timmon found himself clinging to Bell's exuberance. And why not? Maybe there was a fresh start awaiting him at the end of Bell's soliloquy. Maybe Port Bonita would prove to be a departure from Aberdeen. Or Lawrence, Kansas. Or Chicago. Gaspar said it was a kick-ass town. Krigstadt had made the place out to be some kind of Shangri-la for self-starters and misfits. So why not lean into Bell's enthusiasm, why not listen to his promise of fresh starts, even if it meant setting certain realities aside?

Franklin could feel it, too — the kid was listening. These were the moments when he scored his victories. These were the moments that sustained the sterling record. This is where you broke a guy's patterns, convinced him to try new approaches to the same old shit. This is where you convinced him to run a different team out there for the second half, convinced him to believe. These were the moments when the momentum swung. And if Franklin could push hard enough, he could turn a guy around, undo the first half as though it never existed.

"You're the master of your own destiny, Tillman, and that's a fact. Wrap it in all the poetry you see fit. Because that's the truth. A man can pick his destiny. I've seen it. And he can do it right here in Port Bonita, too — with or without the shit economy and neverending rain. This is ground zero for your life, Tillman. So whaddaya gonna do with it? You gonna foul the nest, again? You gonna ignore your past mistakes? Surrender to your own apathy? Or"— here, Bell swung his legs down off the desk and practically had to stand on his chair in order to reach across the desk and seize Timmon by the collar — "are you gonna reach into the future and grab life by the *nutsack*?"

Bell made it seem tactile. Almost like an act of aggression. Timmon could do aggression.

"You gotta dare to dream, Tillman. I got dudes like you comin' in and out of my office all week long, smellin' like fish — down in the face, angry folks. And you know why? 'Cause they're chickenshit mother-fuckers! I say, shit or get off the pot, Tillman! Quit wastin' this bureau-crat's time and go waste some more of his tax money sittin' your white ass in a jail cell." Releasing his grip, Bell lowered himself back into his squeaky chair then stood, walked to the corner, picked up the eggnog carton, and dunked it. He sat back down in his squeaky chair. "That there's a high percentage shot. And that's how you do it, Tillman. You gotta slam dunk your life. Think about the future you want for yourself. When you figure that out, the rest is easy. Find a hole, get yourself a head full of steam, grip that rock, and drive to the hoop. And like the man says, 'Don't look back, you can never look back!'"

LATE IN THE evening, having left his sweet-and-sour chicken half eaten in front of the television, where the M's were about to drop their third straight to Anaheim, Franklin found himself — contrary to the wisdom of Don Henley — looking back. A light mist shone in the purple streetlamps, as he walked his bull mastiff around the parking lot behind Port Bonita Lanes. He could hear the faint crack of pins, and the general hum of activity from within the sagging gray edifice. Farther off, he could hear the swishing of light traffic on Route 101.

He'd lied to that kid today. No getting around it. *Dare to* dream — as if anything were that easy. *Ground zero for your life* — as if anything were that definite. He should've tempered his optimism. He'd made all of Port Bonita seem like it actually gave a shit. He'd made it sound like he himself gave a shit. He should've given it to Tillman straight. He should've said, "Son, I ain't gonna lie to you — it's sink or swim. And keepin' your head above water ain't exactly the stuff of fairy tales. But it beats the joint."

He should've done the practical thing—told the kid to keep his nose clean, told him to keep collecting a paycheck and stay out of bars. Told him this town was no different than any other town with a Wal-Mart and two Mexican restaurants. Instead, Franklin had inspired him, stirred up those dreamers and poets. He could see that green light in Tillman's eyes, even as he left the office. But how soon would that fade? How soon before a shit job in a shit town seemed like a dead end street? Next time, Franklin decided, he'd tone things down a bit, prepare Tillman to lower his expectations slightly. Tell him his life may not look like Hugh Hefner's right away—at least not for the foreseeable future—but it could look a sight better than three-square and a Ping-Pong table. A guy could buy his own groceries, watch TV on his own time, get an apartment behind Bonita Lanes. Boy like Tillman needed practical advice, not poetry.

FRANKLIN BELL'S PEP talks actually worked for a while. Two sessions, anyway. On both occasions, Timmon had exhibited a slight spring in his step when he returned to High Tide from his two-hour lunch, donned his rubber apron, and took his place on the line. But after the third meeting, there was no spring in his step. Gutting fish, he tried to see the hole, tried to grip the rock. But the only hole he could see was so deep that he couldn't see out of it, and the only thing he was gripping was a headless fish. And when Krig came up behind him and set a familiar hand on Timmon's shoulder, inquiring whether he planned on joining him for happy hour, the die was cast. Timmon swept the hand off like a tarantula, shed his apron matter-of-factly, hung it on a peg, and walked calmly across the processing room toward the back entrance.

The instant Timmon strode out of High Tide and let the door close behind him with a metallic clatter, his future was delivered to him in a flash of weak sunlight. Surrendering to the one decision that could conceivably make his dream a foreseeable reality, a bitter little pellet dissolved in his stomach. Suddenly, he burned to throw himself head-long at the future. The solution to his life was right in front of him.

He had only to beat a trail to it. It was all so tangible. Risky, perhaps, dangerous — by no means a cakewalk — really, a cold hard business when you got down to it but thrilling and boundless. And it was his for the taking.

Timmon patted his wallet in his front pocket, still $618 thick. Plenty for where he was going. He smiled at the thought of it, marched with purpose and determination across the dirt parking lot, past the Goat, and across Marine without looking.

THE NEXT WEEK, when Timmon failed to appear for his fourth parole meeting, Franklin left his office depressed and went home to his studio apartment. Arriving home, he plopped down on his bile colored sofa and patted Rupert's big square head.

"Well, Rupe. We finally lost one."

setting free the wild

JUNE 2006

Bringing her mother had been a mistake. So had wearing khakis and a sweatshirt. Of course Beverly would disparage the place. Of course she'd focus on the negatives, batting her heavy eyelashes like Gloria Swanson as she commented innocuously on the overabundance of shade, puckering her bee-stung lips as she benignly observed the northern exposure or the proximity of a precarious alder to the carport. No matter, the roar of the river and the rugged mountain seclusion. Never mind that the place was a steal at $78,500, with owner financing.

"But Hill, honey, it's not even a cabin," observed Bev, standing beneath the shade of the badly weathered gazebo. "It's a trailer."

"But, Mom, the river. Just look at it."

"Isn't the river dead? Isn't that what you're always telling me?"

"All that's gonna change, Mom. That's what I've been telling you. Once the rehab starts, things will be — "

"*If* the dam comes down."

"The dam's coming down, Mom."

"That's not what the *Register* thinks."

"The *Register* is owned by a bunch of cronies trying to sway public opinion, Mom. As soon as the feds buy the dam, they'll decommission the whole . . ." Hillary trailed off when she noticed her mother wasn't really listening but looking in her compact.

"Honestly, Hill. You and your causes."

Bev puckered her lips, and stepped cautiously down from the gazebo into the long grass. "It's still a trailer, Hill. What's wrong with your apartment?"

"It's an apartment, Mom. For starters, I don't own it, and on top of that, people walk on my ceiling. It's claustrophobic."

"Well now, Hill, this little . . . *place* can't be over four hundred square feet."

"Yeah, but look around you."

Beverly cast a vague look around. "Is there electricity?"

"Of course, there's electricity."

"What about after the dam?"

"The dam isn't a public utility, Mom. It has nothing to do with my electricity, or anyone else's. And the truth is, I don't even care if it has electricity. I *want* to diminish my carbon footprint. I *want* sustainability. I *like* that it's rustic."

"Your great-grandfather's homestead was rustic. This is a trailer, Hill. It's got no resale value. And just for the record, I know all about green living, dear. I don't buy anything at Wal-Mart except for plants — Rory's is just too damn expensive, and I don't want to haul pampas grass all the away across town in the Suburban. So don't think that I don't know a thing or two about the environment. Listen, Hill, I'm not here to talk you out of this, but the trailer's a teardown, and there's a good reason why the lot is so cheap — it's ten miles from town."

"That's what I want."

"Oh, Hill, all this stubborn independence, all this feminine self-sufficiency. Have you really thought this out? How are you supposed to meet people? How are you supposed to entertain? Tell me you haven't given up on men completely. Trust me, honey, you can learn to love them."

"I'm not gay, Mom."

"It's okay if you are, Hill. The point is, you can learn to love them. The benefits of a — "

"I'm *not* gay."

Doubtfully, Bev looked at Hillary in her square-cut khakis and sweatshirt, then over her shoulder at the muddy Silverado parked in the driveway, a mountain of filthy five-gallon buckets and a two-cycle gas genie heaped in the bed.

How was it possible that her own mother still wouldn't believe her? No, Hillary hadn't had a steady boyfriend in eight years or paid sixty dollars for a haircut. No, she didn't wear makeup. Yes, she was self-sufficient. Yes, she drove a pickup. Yes, her work clothes de-emphasized her figure. But you try scrambling up riverbanks in a skirt and heels, you try navigating Forest Service Route 2880 in a Miata. Sometimes Hillary thought her mother was merely symptomatic of a bigger problem: Port Bonita, with its willful ignorance, and lack of imagination, its stubborn backwoods resistance to progress of any kind. Even the fashions arrived ten years late. Port Bonita, where orange juice was still just for breakfast, where mixed marriage was still divisive and gay marriage was a scourge, where any guy with an earring was a fag, where any woman who drove a pickup or cropped her hair short or embraced utility over design was a lesbo.

In a way, Hillary felt sorry for her mother. There was something admirable and sad in the way her mother strove so hard to resist the inevitable. Hillary could scarcely imagine the sheer force of will or the leap of imagination required to outrun a truth as pervasive as middle age, to convince oneself that dating a twenty-eight-year-old Motocross enthusiast, wearing seamless panties, or pumping your chest full of saline, made any sense at all, when you were three years shy of Social Security, and osteoporosis was just around the corner.

"Look, Mom, if it will make you feel better, I've got a date Saturday."

Beverly perked up. "With a guy?"

"Yes, Mom. With a guy."

"Who is he? Where did you meet him?"

"I haven't. Genie set it up."

"DeMarini?"

"Of course."

Bev fought off her disappointment at this news and kept the smile tacked to her face. She'd always suspected Genie DeMarini of being a lesbian. "Well, that sounds hopeful."

"Trust me, it's not."

"Oh, Hill."

"Mom, there's more to life than men," said Hillary, immediately realizing she was not helping her cause. "What I mean is, just because I'm not with somebody doesn't mean I wouldn't like to be with the right person. I've just chosen not to make it my life's work."

"Well, you could at least try *attracting* someone, Hill."

Hillary knew that the comment was not intended to be cruel — there was the note of well-intentioned suggestion to it, which made it all the sadder to her ears.

"You hate it, don't you?" Hillary said. "This place."

Bev waved at a mosquito and looked around vaguely, her eyes landing on the Silverado in the driveway. "Oh, I don't hate it, Hill. I'm just not sure it's a good investment, dear. I just think you should look into something closer to town."

incomplete

Thomas remained on the ground for a moment and listened to the footsteps of the dark Makah receding. Groping in the mud all about him, Thomas dredged the broken mirror out from beneath the boardwalk. He tried to wipe the reflection clear with the palm of his bleeding hand but succeeded only in smudging the glass still further. The tool had been rendered useless; the world it revealed was cracked and muddy and bleeding. But the boy continued to clutch it anyway as he clambered to his feet. In spite of an instinct to flee, Thomas felt the stronger pull of his hatred. The boy's heart was still racing as he followed the Makah's path to the far edge of the Belvedere and down the alley. His breathing had quieted by the time he reached the head of the alley, at which point he could hear Stone Face talking to his companion, the little one, whom Thomas recognized as the one called Small Fry. A third man's voice silenced them both. Thomas could not decipher his words. Ducking under the building once more, down among the pilings, he drew closer. He could see two sets of legs at the base of the steps. The third voice came from above, from the top of the steps. He could hear it now. And he recognized it as the Belvedere Man.

"You best have the same idea of taking care of something that I do. If this comes back to me, you're finished. Do you hear?"

Stone Face consented with a grunt. The two sets of legs walked away. Bottles rattled and clinked in the wooden box. Thomas crawled out from beneath the building and hurried after the two Indians. They trudged the length of town along the base of the muddy hillside, with Thomas trailing them at a safe distance. The wind kicked up, and it began spitting rain. The tar paper roof of the Olympic Hotel set to flapping here and there.

When the boy drew too close, his footsteps — ginger though they were — finally betrayed his presence. Stone Face stopped in his tracks and swung around.

"What's that?" he said, to Small Fry.

"What's what?"

"Didn't you hear?"

"Hear what?"

"Shhhh."

Thomas was flat on his belly in the mud. The grit of soil was on his tongue, and the lingering taste of blood. He was still clutching the tool, reflective side down, in his outstretched hand.

Stone Face started creeping back in Thomas's direction.

"It was nothing," said Small Fry, holding the box of bottles.

"Shhhh."

Stone Face crept closer still.

"This is getting heavy," said Small Fry.

"Shhhh."

"It was only the wind."

Stone Face stopped abruptly and stood perfectly still not twenty feet from where Thomas lay. The wind was blowing fiercely in the treetops up the hill. Limbs clattered in the understory. The roof of the Olympic Hotel flapped its intermittent signal.

"Told you it was the wind," said the little man. "C'mon. You carry this."

Satisfied, Stone Face turned around and rejoined his companion. When they reached the base of the hogback, the two men hunkered down in the mud, leaned against the hillside, and uncapped one of the bottles. Stone Face drank greedily. After a few passes with the whiskey, the two Indians rose to their feet, and Stone Face hefted the box of bottles. Thomas could see the difference in their comportment almost immediately as they proceeded up the hogback. They bumped each other occasionally as they shuffled along, and the bottles jumped around in the box. They said nothing, as they trudged up the hill. Thomas did not venture after them until the two men had crested the rise on the colony side, at which point he made a mad dash up the

hogback. By the time he crested the hill, he could see the shadowy figures of the two men cutting behind the boat shed toward the strait.

Thomas caught up to the men just as they began hiking through a
field of long grass. He squatted low, listening to their whisking progress. Now and again, he sprang to his feet and shot forward through
the grass in bursts like a jackrabbit.

The two Indians arrived at the shoreline a half mile east of Hollywood Beach, at which point they turned back toward the distant fires,
ambling along the water's edge in a stiff wind, passing the bottle back
and forth.

"Why did we take this way?" Small Fry wanted to know. "This is
a circle."

"Because, stupid. This way we came from somewhere else."

Thomas found little need for stealth, as he followed the two men
with the bottles at a distance of a hundred feet. They were blinded
by whiskey. Small Fry was laughing a lot and began to spin in circles
as he walked.

"Shut up," said Stone Face. "Quit playing."

A quarter mile from the nearest fire, the two men followed a narrow trailhead up the slope. Thomas followed them at a short distance.
Small Fry started humming a white man's song.

"Quit singing stupid songs."

"You quit."

"I'm not singing, stupid."

They paused yet again along the trail to set the box down and un-
cap the whiskey. As he brought the bottle unsteadily to his lips, Small
Fry began to retch, and Stone Face seized the bottle from him, just
before the small man dropped to his knees and retched again. Stone
Face wiped the rim of the bottle with the sleeve of his shirt. He looked
at the rim disgustedly before sipping from it. After he put the cap
back on, he kicked his slumping companion.

"C'mon," he said, and picked up the box.

But Small Fry didn't get up. Instead, he lay down on his back in the
wet grass.

"Get up."

Small Fry only moaned.

Stone Face jostled him with a foot. "Stupid pig. Get up."

When Small Fry failed to comply again, Stone Face simply left him there on the ground. "Stupid Indian," he said, proceeding up the trail.

Thomas stepped right over Small Fry, who rolled over with a groan and looked up at him with lolling yellow eyes. And reaching up as if to touch Thomas, he moaned.

A quarter mile further on, the Makah left the box of remaining bottles in a small clearing by the side of the trail. Grasping his own half-empty bottle, he approached within mere feet of Thomas squatting in the brush and began to urinate, swaying considerably as he emptied himself near the boy's feet. He laughed at the unwieldiness of his own body. Thomas clutched the mirror in his sweaty palm, as Stone Face gathered himself and fastened his pants and squatted down on his haunches about ten feet in front of the boy. He began to hum the same white man's song that Small Fry had been humming.

Thomas crouched in the brush in perfect silence. If he was still enough, he could forget where he was, and if he could forget where he was, he could turn invisible. That's how invisibility worked. Soon a chaos of hushed voices converged on the trail in front of him, both male and female. Thomas soon recognized them as Klallam voices, and among them he thought he could discern the dry, aching voice of his grandfather.

"Shush. Over here," said Stone Face.

They congregated around the box. Six in all, two women among them. The Indian from Port Gamble was there, the one who sometimes passed out beneath the boardwalk.

"Be careful," his grandfather said.

"Give me that," said Stone Face.

A bottle dropped to the ground and shattered in the grass more like an egg than a bottle.

For an instant, everybody froze. Then, like a bolt of lightning in the darkness, an arm shot out, striking his grandfather square in the face. He cried out and fell to his knees.

"Look what you did, old man," said Stone Face. "Now you've got none."

The Indian from Port Gamble laughed, and one of the women laughed. Clutching his nose in his hand, the old man reached for the box, but the Indian from Port Gamble kicked his arm away and laughed once more. This time everybody laughed. They uncapped their bottles and gravitated to neutral corners and squatted. There were only four bottles. One of the women shared with her man. The old man scrambled on all fours over to the other woman, who pushed him away.

"Get out."

"Please," he said.

"Get."

The old man slunk over to Stone Face and reached out to him hopefully. "Just one."

"None for you, old man. You've had enough."

"Just one. Please, just one."

"Okay, just one." Stone Face held out the bottle. But when the old man reached for the bottle, he slapped his hand away. "Go."

He began to writhe in agony. "Please," he kept saying.

Finally, Stone Face gave him the bottle, and so greedily did the old man partake of it that the liquid overflowed from his mouth and ran down his face, and Stone Face wrestled the bottle back from him and slapped him across the face.

Hunkered beneath a dripping maple, Thomas felt the icy tingle of a rivulet running down his spine. His jaw tightened. Rising to his feet with a rustling of vines, he stepped out into the clearing and walked ten steps until he stood right in their midst, unafraid.

But nobody seemed to see him there. The boy hoisted the mirror aloft, so that its muddy face was pointing out at them, and gritting his teeth, he spun a slow, furious circle, pointing the instrument at each of them in turn.

But it was no use. He was invisible.

Gripping the mirror fiercely, he marched out of the clearing and rejoined the trail, where he again came upon Small Fry, sprawled flat on his back in the middle of the path, chortling like a pig in his sleep. Thomas had a mind to defile Small Fry, to step on his face, to spit on him, but he could not bring himself to do it. Emerging once more at the trailhead, Thomas walked to the water's edge, where he tossed the mirror aside, disgustedly. The first wave washed over the mirror and receded, leaving a smattering of tiny shells upon its surface. The second wave took hold of the mirror and dragged it out into the surf.

Thomas marched west toward Hollywood Beach.

dangerous ground

Hardly had Tobin emptied himself in Gertie's mouth than he pushed her head away and hitched his pants, checking his pocket watch as though he had a stage to catch.

"I want you back on the floor in ten minutes," he said.

"But this afternoon you said —"

"Never mind what I said. Turn twenty dollars between now and eight o'clock, and you're free to watch the end of the show with the rest of the crackpots. But I'm warning you, don't make it a habit. I'll be damned if I'll have that colony whore putting ideas in your head, you hear? You're not some lesbian preservationist. Your daddy's not a wealthy industrialist. Your daddy was a rapist, and you're a whore."

There were days, not so far removed, when Gertie would've talked back to Tobin. Back then, she had ground to stand. Back then, it was worth taking it on the chin. This was her house, she was the draw: Gallopin' Gertie McGrew, the most generous working girl west of the Missouri. Could suck a billiard ball through a drainpipe. Once rode a man so ragged he couldn't get back in the saddle for three days. The fact that Gertie continued to manage the house, that she still governed the girls and ran the trade, was little more than a technicality anymore. How long before Peaches or some other young girl elbowed her out?

Tobin turned back to Gertie on his way out the door. "And nobody's paying you to spit."

Shortly after the dinner hour, Gertie took it in both barrels from a Wichita rug merchant, accounting for half of the twenty dollars she presented Tobin shortly before eight o'clock. The other half she paid herself. The ground was muddy beneath her feet, as she navigated the back alley toward Hogback, hoping to make the colony by intermission. Her thoughts were already stuck derisively upon Tobin when her approach startled his two Indian stooges upon their nightly charge. The dark one straightened up alertly while the small one shrunk in his shadow with the box of bottles.

"Oh," said the dark-faced one. "Just you."

Probably, she would be stepping over them on her way back. Probably, they would both foul themselves before morning. Strange that she pitied them when she had no sympathy for drunks. Strange that she should view them as innocents when she knew that they were not to be trusted. But left to their own devices, they did less damage than most. They only wished to recover that which had been lost. But clearly, theirs was a hopeless cause.

Once, in a courageous moment, she'd said to Tobin, "You're killing them. Why do you do it?"

He just looked at her with those laughing eyes and that cruel smirk. "Quit answering your own questions, whore. And quit asking them, while you're at it."

Gertie arrived midway through intermission, where she found Eva awaiting her beneath the wooden marquee, dressed unseasonably light, her pale cheeks flushed, her breath visible in the night air. Gertie apologized for her late arrival.

"I'm pleased you could come at all," said Eva.

Though Eva assured Gertie that the Opera House was to be on a grander scale than the theater, Gertie was not altogether unimpressed by the plank floors and high-vaulted ceiling of the theater. The lack of decorative flourishes lent the place an austerity that Gertie had never liked in churches but liked everywhere else.

Collectively, the colonists cut a strange figure. There was something somber in their utilitarian dress, in the way they carried themselves a little more upright than most. The men were all clean-shaven and clean beneath the fingernails. The women seemed plain at first glance, but some — and none more than Eva — were quite striking upon closer inspection.

The revue itself was a comedy of errors, and not a particularly good one. The leading man, a reedy fellow with pattern baldness, had a stutter that worked to tragic rather than comic effect. The buck-toothed ingénue, who looked like a whore Gertie once worked with in Colorado Springs, bungled her lines repeatedly. Still, Gertie enjoyed herself in spite of the scandalous whispers elicited by her presence, though she was relieved to take the open air when it was over.

Walking side by side with Gertie, Eva could not help but think of her not-so-distant stroll down this very path with James Mather, then, as now, flush with a certain posttheatrical buzz, aglow with some ineffable human electricity that she found both thrilling and terrifying. For those few thrilling moments with Gertie, without Minerva, Eva's bones did not feel heavy.

"I've been thinking about what you said," Gertie observed. "About making a difference."

"And?"

"And you're right. Even a whore can be of some service to society if she puts her mind to it."

"It was unfair of me to judge you. I'm a hypocrite. What utility have I served the greater good?"

"You've inspired me," said Gertie. "That's a start."

Eva felt a warm rush of blood in her face. "Forgive me if I'm dubious. But I'm afraid my facility to inspire anything is highly suspect."

Seizing Eva's hand, Gertie pressed it firmly against her own. "It's not true," she said. "Long before I ever took to whoring, I knew I was no damn good. The fact is, whoring was about the first thing that made me feel like anything at all. Like I had some kind of influence. I was good at it. And I know how funny that must sound, but nobody ever told me differently. Not even Jesus Christ himself ever made me feel like I could be anything but a whore. And maybe I can't. But Miss Lambert — Eva — you're the first person to convince me that a body's more than just the station assigned them, that a person is made up of choices."

only temporary

When Curtis got home, the Monte Carlo wasn't in the driveway. The front door was locked, and the key wasn't under the mat. Circling around the side to the kitchen window, Curtis wondered why his mom bothered. She trusted a criminal with her heart, but she was afraid of being robbed by strangers? What was there to take, anyway? The TV? You'd need a furniture dolly to haul it. Wriggling through the kitchen window onto the countertop, Curtis knocked a coffee cup out of the dish rack as he pulled his legs through. The mug bounced a few times on the warped linoleum but didn't shatter.

A quick check of the fridge confirmed what Curtis already suspected, that there wasn't much to eat. He snatched a Silver Bullet from the top rack, a box of Rice Chex off of the counter, and retired to his room. He locked the door and plopped down on his springless mattress. It was a dank little retreat, especially in winter, when the sun cut its arc in the southern sky, reaching the high window for but a few precious minutes per day in late afternoon, whereupon it was forced to contend with a dirty and mottled screen. But even in the half-light, the creeping gray blotches were visible in the corners where moisture had leached in through the outside wall. The chaos of the room was decidedly oriented toward the floor, around the mattress, where clothing was strewn about and heaped in piles and the lamp listed to one side near the head of the mattress. Next to the lamp lay a can of black Krylon, a paper clip corroded with pot resin, along with the shredded remains of the pencil-and-ink work he'd torn from the walls a week earlier in a fit of disgust.

The stack of salvaged comics lay fanned out under partial cover of mateless socks and black T-shirts. The room may not have been glamorous, but it was his. If Randy came to live with them, he'd lose it, for sure. If Randy came to live with them, things would be fucked. Worst-case scenario, they'd relocate again, probably even farther from school, deeper onto the rez. His mom would go back to tiptoeing around, focusing all her energy on Randy, who'd reject her at every turn. Best-case scenario was more of the same.

Snapping on the lamp, which immediately toppled sideways onto its shade and was left uncorrected, Curtis popped his Silver Bullet and reached for the stack of comics. Between handfuls of Chex, he started flipping through issues, no longer ordered, not even by series. He paused briefly on *Alpha Flight* #2. Olivetti's pencil work kind of sucked when you really looked at it. His character didn't bend — even Mister Fantastic looked stiff.

Curtis liberated an issue of *Exiles* from its plastic jacket and perused it. Calafiore had a surer hand than Olivetti with the pencil — maybe too sure; his musculature was overwrought. Even Mister Fantastic looked beefy in Calafiore's treatments. Calafiore's figures smiled when they should be grunting, grunted when they ought to be smiling. But the real problem was the stories. The whole premise of the Exiles was preposterous: holes in the fabric of the time-space continuum had created alternate realities. The Exiles traversed these alternate realities, trying to undo the damage and set the omniverse in order.

Curtis tossed the issue aside without returning it to its protective sleeve. He drained his Silver Bullet in one long gulp and squashed the aluminum can like the Hulk, tossing it in the general direction of the wastebasket. He thought about reaching for the pencil and pad but reached for the Krylon instead.

WITH THE STOP-AND-GO traffic on Front Street, it was nearly six thirty by the time Rita got home from work. Finding the door locked, she fished in her purse for the key. The tendinitis in her wrist was throbbing. Forty tons of Alaskan chum in three days and still two days left in the week. Then what? A double at Gertie's on Saturday and maybe a hot bath and a frozen pizza on Sunday. But what was she complaining about? Money was money. With enough overtime,

she could buy Curtis a car by the end of summer, so he could drive
to school senior year, even get a job, if he wanted one. Maybe then,
he wouldn't be so isolated, maybe then he'd make some friends. Bar-
ring unforeseen expenses (the Monte Carlo), Rita could clear an extra
four hundred bucks this month and the same next month, hopefully.
She saw a red '92 Accord for fifteen hundred out in front of Murray
Motors.

Setting her handbag down on the kitchen table, Rita liberated her
hair from a ponytail and shook it out in long black waves. There was
a day when she might have combed it out. Instead, she opened the
refrigerator and snatched a Coors Light, lingering in the sickly light
to contemplate the rest of the fridge's contents. She should've stopped
at Albertson's. Popping her Silver Bullet, she sat at the kitchen table,
fished her Merit Ultra Lights out of her bag, and sparked one up, exhaling a thin blue cloud into the kitchen.

She didn't see Curtis's book bag lying around anywhere. The bedroom was conspicuously quiet. The front door had been locked. Most
likely, he was out wandering again. Yesterday, on her way home between shifts, Rita had passed him walking along the ditch on South
Ennis with his head down. When she slowed down to offer him a ride
home, he'd refused. When she offered to turn the car around, and
drive to KFC for takeout, he'd even refused that. And in an act that
struck Rita as aloof rather than defiant, he hadn't even tried to hide
his cigarette. After three and a half years, he still hadn't forgiven her
for Dan. How differently things might have turned out if she hadn't
chased Dan off that night. She would've never got the phone call.
They'd probably live in a house, a real house, like the old one on South
Tenth, something that didn't creak and groan under the weight of
each step, something without monstrous green carpet, something
with two bedrooms and decent water pressure. But most important,
she'd still have Curtis. She lost both of them the night Dan screeched
out of the driveway for the last time. Randy could never replace him,
and she knew it. But at least Randy had helped them keep the house,
if nothing else. For a while. When he got busted, they had little choice
but to relocate without his income. Rita had been telling herself for

thirteen months that the move was only temporary, maybe as short as three months, depending on parole. Then they'd get a place, maybe not the old place on South Tenth, but a bigger place, somewhere closer to the river, off the rez.

IT BEGAN ON the mattress with a slow shudder; once, twice, as the icy fumes ran up Curtis's nostrils, past his eye sockets, to his brain stem. Inky black ghosts converged from all corners, swimming figure eights in his peripheral vision, and the only sound was a slow bleating from the center of the earth. Behind the veil, an orange glow pulsed like the heart of a dying sun, beckoning him, as the ghosts swam playful circles around its glow. And soon Curtis forgot he was in his room, on a mattress, trapped in an imperfect time line. Soon he forgot that he was anyone at all, but only some*thing*, something slipping, slipping, falling, forgetting.

The forgetting ended when the canister slipped from his grasp and thumped on the carpet. Soon came successive raps on the locked door. A voice, his mother's voice, reached him through the fog.

"Curtis? Are you in there? "

The world was still a thousand pinpricks under Curtis's scalp, as he wiped away the moist halo around his mouth and rolled over on his shoulder, facing the wall.

"Go away," he heard himself saying.

kilt lifter

JUNE 2006

Having been forced to work the line in place of Timmon for the remainder of the first shift, Krig smelled even more like fish than usual
when he took his customary stool at the Bushwhacker for happy hour.
By his third Kilt Lifter, the general irritability that had marked the
end of his workday had been replaced by a very specific and very acute
self-contempt. How had he managed to offend Tillman? How did he
always manage to offend, alienate, repulse, or suffocate? Even as a
starter on varsity, Krig had found himself an outsider, and never for
lack of effort. Familiar to all, loved by nobody. It didn't seem to matter
how much towel slapping and dick waving he engaged in during the
week any more than it seemed to matter that he shot a league-leading
68 percent from the field. Come Friday night, Krig often found himself alone in the parking lot of Payless or the ferry terminal, nursing
a Mickey's Big Mouth in the front seat of his primer-riddled Camaro,
listening to Jethro Tull. And not because he had tragic acne, or he
was insecure, or he lacked social currency, but because he was bad
with what his guidance counselor called boundaries. And wasn't he
still making the same mistakes? Still jumping the gun? Still trying
too hard?

The fact that such a concept as trying too hard even existed was
troubling to Krig. Did he shoot 88 percent from the stripe senior year
because he tried too hard all those nights in the driveway shooting
free throws blindfolded? Did he find that little extra spring in his
hops come the fourth quarter because he tried too hard to condition
himself? Why should a guy like Jared Thornburgh, who didn't try at
all, walk into a job as general manager? Why did the Thornburghs of
the world succeed as if it were their birthright while the Krigs should

be forced to endure years of loyal service, pulling guts and slitting necks? Talk about boundaries. Jealous? Just pissed off. Okay, jealous. Of course he was jealous! Why should Thornburgh have a smokin' wife like Janis while Krig dabbled in online dating? And even in that arena he proved to be an abject failure. Boundaries. On paper he looked great: production manager of the largest (okay, *only*) commercial seafood processor on the peninsula, respected member of the amateur cryptozoological community, athletic build (aside from a little paunch), nice car, good conversationalist, fun (loves happy hour, classic rock, car camping), seeks SWF who enjoys same . . . seeks SWF with varied interests . . . seeks SWF . . . seeks anyone, really.

"You ready for another, Dave?" It was Molly. The mud shark. The only person in Port Bonita to address him as anything but Krigstadt or Krig, because she was an outsider, a transplant from Aberdeen, and Krig liked that. Molly, meanwhile, had given Krig little indication that she liked anything about him, not even his 40 percent tips. Ever since he started talking his Bigfoot bullshit the second night she worked there. Beyond a nod of recognition each night as he took his stool at the bar, Molly exuded an air of indifference, tinged with the slightest scent of annoyance.

"Is that a yes or a no?"

"Does the pope shit in the woods?" said Krig.

"Uh. No, Dave. Last I checked he didn't. Kilt Lifter?"

"Yeah."

Fucking boundaries. But, really, what did he expect? As far as Krig knew, no woman in the history of the world had ever looked into a guy's eyes and said, "You had me at Bigfoot." But wasn't that the foot he always got off on? As soon as he was nervous in a social situation, didn't he start yapping about Bigfoot and other cryptozoological anomalies? Chupacabra. The Minnesota Iceman. Why couldn't he just shut up about it? Why was he so convinced Bigfoot existed in the first place? Really, what had he heard that night? Could he really say? Could all the follow-up investigations in the world really change that? When had he taken that leap of faith? Long before the events of May 6 on the upper Elwha, that's for sure, long before even the class C sighting out in Joyce back in '99. He'd gone looking for that one, too. Just like Roger Patterson. Who's to say he didn't see and hear exactly what he wanted to?

Sasquatch Field Research Organization

Report 1017 (class B)
Follow-up Investigation by SFRO investigator Greg Beamer

I met the witness six days after he filed the original sighting report. Initially, Mr. Krigstadt was too frightened to return to the scene of his encounter above the Thornburgh Dam. After some persuasion, Mr. Krigstadt finally consented to accompany me to the spot, where we scanned the area for tracks. We found nothing conclusive. However, it is worth noting that our search was conducted following two days of heavy rainfall. There were a number of broken tree limbs in the surrounding area at heights of six to ten feet, and one possible hair sample, which has been sent along with the scat sample to Dr. Kurtz for analysis. Mr. Krigstadt is, in my estimation, a credible witness. He has a good knowledge of Sasquatch behavioral patterns and utilizes a scientific epistemology. But what I found most convincing was Mr. Krigstadt's very palpable uneasiness about returning to the scene of the sighting. I've seen this fear and felt it myself. Mr. Krigstadt was more than willing to cooperate with the follow-up investigation and even volunteered to transport the samples to Dr. Kurtz in person. Both samples came back inconclusive.

Verdict: Inconclusive

kilt lifter redux

What Krig had not told Greg Beamer as they walked the upper Elwha above the dam that dewy morning in May was that he had endured night terrors for the past five days: feverish, twitching, adrenaline-addled ordeals, the likes of which he'd never known. In an effort to ward off the visitations, Krig began sleeping on the sofa, fully clothed with the lights on, medicating with even larger than normal quantities of beer and weed and falling asleep in the glow of the television to the innocuous fare of Nickelodeon. But it was no use; even *SpongeBob* was no match. So vivid and terrifying were these dreams that Krig had actually begun to question whether his experiences on the upper Elwha might have been a dream. Further investigation had yielded nothing. Even the poop was inconclusive. Perhaps Krig had dozed off that night on the trail. The possibility even occurred to Krig that he had not gone upriver that night, at all. But then clearly he had awakened on the Crooked Thumb trail clutching a Louisville Slugger, clearly he had humped all that gear back to the dam in three trips, clearly he had received a parking infraction.

There was, of course, another possibility. Once, several years prior, following a fruitless Singles Night at the Seven Cedars Casino, during the course of which Krig had nearly fractured a woman's fifth metatarsal on the dance floor, doing the Sprinkler to Gloria Gaynor's "I Will Survive," Krig had met an old Indian at the bar afterward. The guy must have been two hundred years old. He couldn't have been an inch over five three. His face looked like melting wax. He had little skin tags all around his eyes.

"Meriwether Lewis Charles," he said, pushing his empty coffee cup aside. "Around here, they call me Running Elk. Or Lew. Don't order the decaf. It sucks."

He had the voice of a much younger man; secure, unwavering. Even his carriage was that of a younger man. He sat straight in his stool. He was a sharp dressed little guy, too; white suit, white shirt, white tie. His gray ponytail was secured with a decorative leather band.

"I saw you dancing," he said, staring impassively straight ahead. "You move like an elk."

"Yeah, I'm kind of a klutz," said Krig. "I tend to get into other people's space. You know, boundaries."

"An elk is graceful," Meriwether observed. "Your step is springy. The fat woman was in your way. Bah! Women are always in the way. What do you call that dance?"

"The Sprinkler."

"Mm."

The old fellow went back to staring impassively straight ahead, fingering the rim of his coffee cup.

"Buy you a drink?" Krig asked.

"I'll have a Pepsi-Cola. Not the diet kind. The diet kind sucks. I find that it leaves an astringent taste in my mouth."

At some point during their conversation, Krig finally got around to asking Meriwether Charles the Bigfoot question. Meriwether smiled knowingly. "I know of the Sasquatch."

"And?"

Meriwether sipped his Pepsi, and stared straight ahead. "He comes in times of crisis."

"You mean because he's scared, or threatened, or . . . ?"

"No. To his host. When his host is in crisis."

"His host?"

"Whoever he visits. That is his host. And the only one who can see him. But many have seen him. My grandfather Abraham Lincoln Charles was visited by Sasquatch when he led Mather up the Elwha in 1889. That's when my grandfather gave up the white man's ways, by degrees, anyway."

"Nobody else saw him?"

"How could they?"

Though Krig didn't buy the spirit-form hypothesis, he did buy the old Indian some fried calamari right before the kitchen closed. To accept Meriwether Charles's conception of Bigfoot as a spirit form, Krig decided, was to ignore the large body of evidence: the Patterson footage, the Memorial Day footage, the Skookum Cast. One could neither photograph a spirit nor cast its image in plaster. In the end, it was the concrete evidence that had persuaded Krig that Bigfoot existed. And yet still he was persuading himself regularly as to the veracity of his own claims. Did he really know what a bear sounded like? Wasn't it possible that a cat could have made those sounds? An elk herd? Would Krig really know what an elk herd sounded like moving through the forest in the dead of night? Maybe not. But Krig still wasn't willing to buy the spirit-form hypothesis. Besides, who was in crisis? Not Krig. Sure, he was a little, what? — stuck, maybe? Okay, maybe a little stuck. Same town, same job, same barstool. But so what? He loved Port Bonita. What was out there that was any better than this? You had the mountains, the river, the strait, the fresh air. You had history.

Now and again, when Krig got restless, he bought a six-pack and drove the Goat the seventeen miles down to the Dungeness spit at night, where he stood high on the bluff, with a stiff wind rocketing past his ears, and looked west, back toward the lights of Port Bonita. Across the strait, over the moonlit whitecaps, the more impressive glow of Victoria, British Columbia, was visible, foreign and resplendent on the horizon, but Krig hardly looked in that direction at all. He always looked west toward Port Bonita. He could see Ediz Hook speckled with light, he could see the hulking shadow of the Olympics, awash in darkness. He could see KFC on the east end of town. He could almost see High Tide from his place on the bluff. And whenever he looked at P.B. like that, from the outside, all lit up and full of promise, it always called him back.

"Hey, Krig." It was Molly. "You want another, or what?"

the view from here

The elk and fried potatoes on which the Potato Counter had dined late that evening with Lord Jim did not sit well in the hours approaching midnight. The prospect of confronting Hoko about the boy's future in Jamestown weighed heavily on Adam's mind as he roosted on the edge of the bed in Lord Jim's guest room, wrapped head to toe in coarse wool blankets. Outside the wind was blowing fiercely off of the bay, rattling the thin glass window panes with each gust and setting the flame of the kerosene lamp to dancing.

Lord Jim had hardly eaten a thing at dinner. The old man had grown increasingly distracted as the evening wore on; it was clear to Adam that the chief was conflicted about the boy.

"And what if the mother should not wish to leave her livelihood with the Siwash, *cayci*? What then?"

"Then the boy must come alone."

"What does the boy want?"

"He doesn't know what he wants. He's a strange boy. He wanders. It's a wonder he ever comes back."

"And you are asking me to stop this wandering?"

"Yes."

"Mm." Lord Jim lapsed into silence. He speared a square of potato but did not bring it to his mouth; rather, he spun it on his fork and set it back down on his plate next to the others. "What is it, do you suppose, *cayci*, that sets the boy to wandering?"

"He doesn't know any better."

"I see," said Lord Jim, though he knew this was not true. A thing acts according to its nature; that is the way it has always been. Everything knows better. "And who is the boy's father?"

Adam shot a quick glance out the window. "He doesn't have one."

"Everybody has one, *cayci*."

"His father was lost upriver in a storm."

"This is true?"

"It's not important."

"And what is important, *cayci*?"

"That the boy be looked after."

Lord Jim retreated once more into silence.

"I will pay for his keep," pursued Adam. "And for the mother's, should she consent to come."

But lying on his back in bed, Adam knew Hoko would never consent to come; he knew she would fight him bitterly, and the knowledge made him restless. He stood and gathered his clothing off the straight-back chair. He dressed deliberately, as though the act of dressing might make his clothing warmer, fastening each button with care, tucking wherever possible. Bundled up, Adam stole quietly down the hallway to the back door, which creaked on its hinges as he opened it against the wind. Squeezing through a narrow opening, Adam passed through and padded down the wooden steps into the night.

The wind was whistling between the row of darkened houses. The scene was perfectly desolate, more desolate somehow than if the little houses had not been there at all. Adam turned his fur collar up against the biting wind and trudged in darkness toward the shoreline. The snow had not stuck to the shoreline, and Adam felt himself drawn to the water's edge, where he stood, face to the wind. Looking out over the choppy water, he could see the light of a distant steamer bobbing on its westward journey.

What if his life had taken a different path? What if he'd made different decisions, the ones he now knew to be the right decisions? Perhaps he would not be standing alone on the edge of the world at this moment but snug in bed with Hoko's warmth pressed up against him, perhaps he would know then the fullness of belonging: a hearth, a vegetable garden, and a boy he could call a son. Why had he allowed his father to influence these decisions? What was it that he so feared about his father? He held in contempt so much of what he stood for, and fought for, and yet Adam forever decided in life as though he had meant to please his father. And for this reason, though perhaps not this reason alone, Adam did not feel the fullness of belonging but the sting of an icy wind cutting his face like daggers.

The first time Adam laid eyes on Hoko, she was hardly more than a child, with a broad smooth face and downcast eyes. She moved with the thoughtless grace of a child, murmured softly to her cohorts, grinning like a child, as by dim light her slim fingers worked strings of coarse cedar bark into something resembling cloth. And yet she was a woman, lithe and sure like a woman, smiling knowingly like a woman.

Adam was little more than a young man himself, collecting data for the Census Bureau, a job his father had finagled him in spite of Adam's short list of qualifications. He wore the beard of a man, spoke in the low authoritative tones of a man, clutching his leather case like a man. But inside he was waiting to be found out like a boy. The man-boy spent the better part of a week sitting in the acrid blue haze of the longhouse on the bank of the Elwha, questioning the Siwash as to their numbers, quantifying everything under the sun — pigs and acres and salmon and death — an act that the Siwash could not be made to comprehend.

"What good is all your counting for my people?" Hoko's father had demanded. "By counting you only make the world smaller."

Adam felt the young girl's eyes on him throughout his stay, and on those occasions when he looked back at her, she invariably bowed her head, not in shyness, it occurred to him, but in deference. The more Adam felt Hoko's eyes upon him, the more he yearned to look back, an impulse that was not lost on her father, who was anything but pleased — indeed, no more pleased than Adam's father might have been.

"I have only one daughter," he said. "Mark that in your books."

ON THE FOURTH day, the Potato Counter left one of his slim leather books on the dirt floor beneath a bench in the longhouse. Nobody noticed when Hoko secreted the book away beneath her blanket. And nobody noticed when she took leave of the longhouse early in the chill evening, clutching the book flat against her stomach. Though she had little interest in the book itself — did not in fact so much as open it while it was in her possession — she had seized it reflexively, without a thought. She knew already what populated its pages, for she'd watched for several days as the Potato Counter made his notations — numbers, the language of the white man's stories. He asked questions and turned answers into numbers. Because numbers, he believed, were incapable of deception.

Hoko did not understand her intense curiosity regarding the Potato Counter, because it was new and came to her not through her mind but up through her body like a fountain.

Why had she taken pains by the river to rinse her face and tie her hair back and don the silver bracelet that had once belonged to her mother? What was it about the Potato Counter that stirred her so? Was it something he was — clear-eyed, sober, ruggedly handsome, perhaps? Aloof, unfeeling, distant. All she knew for certain was that she felt herself pulled toward him, as sure as if she'd been caught in a current.

At the Olympic Hotel, the desk man could not persuade Hoko to leave Adam's leather book in the clerk's charge. She was thus directed up the stairs to the second floor, where, at the end of the hall, she knocked on the door. Clearly, the Potato Counter had not been expecting anyone, particularly not a female caller, for he was shirtless and clutching a washcloth when he opened the door. He hastily retreated from the open door, where, out of sight, he wrestled a shirt on, and then beckoned the girl to step inside. When she entered the room, Adam was buttoning his shirt, with his face to the window. The room was empty but for the bed and a small end table, on which a tiny puddle was forming from the washcloth that dangled over the lip of a ceramic basin.

Buttoned up, Adam turned to face the girl, who looked more like a woman in the early evening light of the window than she had in the dull confines of the longhouse.

"I'm Hoko," she said. "Like the river."

"You've brought my book, I see. I hadn't even missed it. And here I'm supposed to be collecting information, not losing it."

She was gazing steadily at him now, and Adam could not withstand the power of her gaze. His eyes sought refuge in various corners of the room, as though he were looking for something, and indeed he wished he'd had something to offer her — a sweet, a biscuit, a cup of tea.

"Would you like to sit down?" Then, realizing that there wasn't a chair, he smiled sheepishly. "Hm. Well. Homey, isn't it? You could . . ."

Hoko perched on the foot of the bed with her hands in her lap, watching him silently, as Adam began to move without purpose about the room. Finally, he decided he was looking for somewhere to set the book and dropped it on the bed. He could feel her eyes upon him all the while.

"Sit," she said.

He sat beside her on the bed.

"Look here," she said.

When he leveled his unsteady gaze at her, she set her hand against his unshaven face.

"You should go," he said, regaining his feet.

She stood without taking her eyes off of him.

"Go on," he said.

But the moment she was gone he ached for her in spite of himself, so much so that he felt himself growing beneath his denim trousers, and he admonished himself for this.

Now, standing on the shoreline at Jamestown, sleepless and all but shivering as the cold wind cut him to ribbons, it occurred to Adam in retrospect that he had always held Hoko accountable for everything that had later transpired between them; had Hoko not forced him time and again to reject her advances, he would not have grown progressively frustrated by these temptations, would not have let his frustration harden into something akin to hatred.

When Adam turned toward the little village of Jamestown, he could see the lamplight still burning in the window of Lord Jim's house.

onward and upward

For nearly two weeks after their raft excursion had met its abrupt and disastrous end, the beleaguered Mather party contended with wet, heavy snow along their overland route. The elements proved to be a much bigger obstacle than the terrain itself. Though the hills were heavily buttressed and growing steeper along their upriver course, the Elwha valley continued to offer relatively wide passage. The country was still thickly wooded, but the understory had grown somewhat sparse, and the brittle vegetation offered little resistance against machete, ax, and boot. The slushy snow played havoc with their snowshoes. Further complicating their travels was the loss of Daisy. Down to one mule, the men traveled heavy in the shadow of their packs, forced to drag with ropes what Dolly couldn't bear.

But all was not somber at the end of each day. Supper, no matter how paltry, along with the comfort of a crackling fire, never failed to lift the party's spirits, if only a little. Layers of leather and wool were shed, clothing was strung on lines to dry, aching backs were stretched and rested, bare toes wiggled in the firelight as the men dined on bacon grease and flour and a precious bit of meat. And they talked as men will talk, of exploits and dreams and even small defeats. However, it was generally but never verbally agreed upon that conversation should not veer toward the home fires, and so each man's domestic longings remained in isolation but were expressed without words — by silence, distraction, long looks into the fire.

In the art of conversation, Cunningham leaned heavily on his medical exploits in Tacoma: bullet wounds and shattered legs, two cases of typhoid, one emergency appendectomy performed on a bandstand amid an electrical storm, goiters the size of cantaloupes. Mather, for his part, told frequently of his formidable Canadian adventures, including the Riel Rebellion, in which Mather had narrowly escaped the Frog Lake Massacre.

Runnells continued to confirm his status as a man of few words, content to whittle sticks and organize stores, now and then assenting or dissenting with a grunt or a guffaw. Reese, meanwhile, proved increasingly preoccupied with the mule, by whom he began to station himself at mealtime, and whom was frequently in recent days — to the silent disapproval of the other men — the recipient of his supper scraps.

Haywood's silence was generally understood. While Mather might have led them, Haywood in large part directed them. More than anyone, Haywood observed, not only in the geological details that were his charge but also in the subtle underpinnings of the party's morale, the direction of the wind, the state of supplies, along with any and all signs of the promised land. Though he was usually scribbling in his journal — mapping, logging, musing — Haywood remained at attention around the fire, at times offering perfunctory commentary, even as he mapped and logged, but rarely initiating conversation.

"Now *those* were mountains, gentleman," Mather said one evening. "*These* are merely hills, bumps, trifles. Ask Haywood about the Rockies. Charlie, how big were the Rockies?"

All eyes turned to Haywood.

"They get bigger every year," Haywood observed wryly, without looking up from his pad.

"There, you see. And so will these mountains," said Mather. "That's a promise. All of this will get bigger. Whatever we put behind us in this wilderness, gentleman, will get bigger and tougher with each passing year. That's how it works. Take it from me."

Mather wanted to believe this — indeed, he used to believe it — but the truth was, he no longer held it to be true. On the contrary, the further he put things behind him, the smaller they seemed; his boyhood, the mighty Mackenzie, Eva. His most bitter grudges of the past were all but forgotten, his greatest sorrows and triumphs stirred but the weakest of flames. Only *now*, Mather knew, in the immediate, did the mountains *truly* look big, and the river run wide, only now could one feel their bigness and wideness, now, while your heart beat in your chest, and the hairs of your arms stood at attention, and death was the enemy.

That night, for the first time in twenty years, James Mather prayed — something neither the Indian Wars nor the perils of the tundra had ever inspired him to do. He prayed for clear skies and discovery, for danger and heartache and laughter, for a life beyond fear, a life that got bigger, really got bigger, as it receded. And after he prayed, he slept.

The temperature dropped overnight. The haze lifted. The skies cleared. Haywood was first to emerge from the tent shortly after dawn and taste the cold brittle air. Before he could enjoy three breaths of it, however, he spotted something on a high ridge several miles in advance of the expedition that nearly took his breath away.

22 February 1890

The silver light of morning revealed a most extraordinary and completely unanticipated spectacle on the ridge some two or three miles in advance of the party to the southwest: a thin blue ribbon of smoke curling its way toward heaven, from what appeared to be a rather sizable cooking fire. Needless to say, the party was at a collective loss as to the identity of who might be cooking over such a fire, having left all vestiges of human settlement behind weeks ago. Each speculation proved more unsettling than the last, from hostile natives (indeed, more than one Port Bonita Indian made mention of a tribe of "giant" Indians of a volatile disposition dwelling in these higher elevations) to the far more troubling possibility of a competing expedition. It was this latter possibility that saw us break camp with great haste and proceed directly to the source of the smoke.

What we found were natives, a hunting party of perhaps two dozen. There was a large store of elk meat being made ready for curing and a half-dozen hides in various states of preparation. The natives were clothed in hide outfits consisting of a pointed hood, shirt, leggings, mittens, and moccasins, and they were all in possession of snowshoes. We soon ascertained they were friendly and versed in the pijin Chinook, the implications of which were most humbling indeed, as we believed we had ventured where no man had ventured before, only to find a tribe of traders and hunters thriving amid this rugged terrain. They soon brought to our attention an ancient trail at the foot of the next ridge that led over the Devil's Backbone to — and I must pause here to confess that my translation may be imprecise — the place of no more. In any event, they made it sufficiently clear that they did not venture beyond that point.

We were treated to a feast by the natives, who exhibited a predilection for raw elk meat, a delicacy that we were all strongly encouraged to partake of but gracefully declined with the exception of our fearless leader, who ate ravenously, with no regard for the blood streaming down his face. He continues to exhibit curious and troubling behavior. On any given day of late, he oscillates between despondency and the sort of carefree eastern bravado that fails to convince. Moreover, he is reckless in a way I've never known him to be, both on the trail and with his words. Throughout the feast, he made merry, but his eyes darted about the proceedings like a man with designs. I find it increasingly difficult to trust his judgment. I'm not at all certain that the natives trusted it. These natives of the upper Elwha were altogether more primitive than their Port Bonita counterparts. They were in possession of a number of trivial artifacts from the civilized world, which were treated as objects of some reverence, including a brass key, and an L-shaped metal instrument with a wooden handle, which Cunningham soon identified as a cauterizer.

Well nourished, though admittedly a little discouraged by our encounter, and in Jim's case suffering from a mild gastric disturbance no doubt caused by the copious consumption of raw elk, we set off in the early afternoon in search of the ancient trail to the Devil's Backbone.

all the noise

JULY 2006

When Timmon Tillman set off from the Crooked Thumb trailhead, fully outfitted for the backwoods to the tune of $614, not to mention an additional $800 in stolen merchandise, five stolen library books (including the Olympic journals of Charles Haywood), an aluminum skillet, along with modest stores of jerky, rice, and Snickers bars, he had no intention of ever returning to civilization. His GoLite frameless backpack was anything but light. He had never fired a crossbow. He was on his second Snickers by the time he reached the dam. Never in his thirty-one years had he ever felt so free. At last, he was afoot and light-hearted with his path before him, his slumbering passions awakened, creamy nougat betwixt his teeth.

Having skipped his parole meeting, Timmon knew that Frank Bell was shitting bricks, just as sure as the district court had already issued a bench warrant with the name Tillman on it. If they ever caught up with him, he was fucked. But nothing, it seemed, could temper his optimism as he paused to marvel at the last vestige of civilization he would ever lay eyes upon, or so he hoped. Hooking his fingers through the chain-link fence above the spillway, he watched the frothing white water pound the river a hundred feet below. He found the low rumbling of the turbines unsettling.

Suddenly, there came the shrill laughter and frantic mirth of children from the parking slab behind him. Twenty of them, at least, which he figured for third-graders with a few adults in their midst, flooding out of a dingy yellow school bus and gathering in a chaotic scrum in the parking lot; frenetic, full of life, bouncing off of each other like dirty-faced electrons, clutching brown bags, bonking each other on the head with them. How long before life put the fear in them, the real fear, not the dark-closet-boogeyman fear, but the rational kind, the everyday kind, the kind based on facts and observations and the cold hard mechanics of the world? How long until they clutched their brown bags tighter and stopped bouncing off of each other? Timmon wanted a cigarette but resisted the urge.

The big people herded the kids in a squiggly line toward the viewing area, where they jostled for places along the fence, clutching the hexagonal links in their grubby fingers, tugging at the mesh, kicking it until it rung like shattering icicles, clambering up it despite the protestations of their chaperones.

The calmest child of the bunch, a saucer-eyed girl in red rubber boots and an unseasonably warm jacket, gravitated toward Timmon immediately and took her place beside him along the fence, a few feet removed from the others, where she peered alternately at the spillway and the sluice gate, sneaking frequent glances at Timmon's tattooed hand. He did his best to ignore her. But something about the dirty fur lining of her coat, something about those three long feet separating her from the others, would not allow him to.

One of the adults began issuing various edicts and instructions as to the occupation of their hands and feet during the presentation before she began reading from her blue factoid sheet, projecting her voice over the roar of the spillway.

"The Thornburgh Dam, which is over one hundred and twenty feet tall and produced over six thousand kilowatts of hydraulic power in its heyday with its twin turbines. It is named after Ethan Thornburgh and was completed in 1896 — *Trevor, give Charlie his lunch back this instant!* — the same year that saw the opening of the Sons of Peoria sawmill at the base of Ediz Spit — *Trevor, I mean it* — which became the county's largest employer for the next four decades until its closure in . . ."

"Psst. What's that blob on your hand?" the little girl said.

"Nothing," he said, looking straight ahead.

"Mm." She bit her lower lip and tilted her head a bit to one side. "It looks like the Liberty Bell, sorta. With angel wings."

Timmon had to look at her. Something in her voice melted him, and hearing it, a little cloud of regret passed over him, but did not linger. "Yeah, well, it ain't."

"Oh," she said.

Timmon could feel the persistent eyes of the girl on him again and tried in vain to ignore her curiosity. Sneaking a sidelong glance at her, he could see the downy blonde hair of her face glistening in the sunlight. It was a good face, honest. Not cute, just unsullied by disappointment. And that alone was enough to make her beautiful. But her beauty was fading. Give her a year. Wait till next summer when she was still wearing that jacket, and began to see herself from outside of herself, and three feet was no longer a big enough buffer against the rest of the world.

"What about that one?" she whispered. "What does *omward* mean?"

Timmon gave a little sigh. Loosening his grip on the fence, his manner softened somewhat. "*On*ward, dummy. Not omward."

"Oh. Well, what does it mean?"

"It means just keep going."

"Hm," she said, biting her lower lip once more. "Going where?"

Timmon gripped the fence tighter. He thought he'd just let the question pass, thought he'd just ignore her altogether. But then she tugged at the dangling strap of his backpack.

"Well," she whispered. "If you're going to keep going you've got to be going somewhere, because going isn't a place."

"Wherever," he sighed.

The girl furrowed her brow and scrunched up her mouth and set to work on the information.

". . . in nineteen ninety-two the Elwha River Ecosystem and Fisheries Restoration Act was passed to fully restore the ecosystem and native fish habitats by allowing reservoir sediments to naturally erode downstream. The act called for the removal of the dam by the year two thousand seven. However, in recent years the act has . . ."

"Wherever isn't a place, either," the girl whispered, finally.

Timmon fished a Camel out his GoLite and sparked it up. "Wherever like wherever," he said. "Like out there, like everywhere, anywhere, wherever, just onward."

The girl knitted her brow.

Timmon's voice, or perhaps it was his cigarette, attracted the attention of one of the chaperones, a stern little woman, squat and gray as a government building, who shot Timmon an icy glare and a frown as she took the girl by the shoulders and shepherded her away.

The girl looked over her shoulder, her little forehead still wrinkled. Timmon released his grip on the fence, hefted his pack, and took leave of the dam with a sense of relief. For a hundred yards he could feel the girl's eyes stuck to him.

The trail ran along a low bluff on the west side of Lake Thornburgh for a half mile, until it diverged in a southwesterly direction and began to gain elevation, switchbacking up the western slope of the valley. Clear-cutting had mottled the low foothill country in a checkerboard pattern and cut huge swathes into the steep higher elevations. Timmon passed no one along his way. By the time he stopped for his third Snickers at the top of the ridge, he'd put all thoughts of the little girl and civilization behind him. He sat on a downed tree and loosened his right boot, which was chafing his heel, and smoked a cigarette and looked out over the lake and beyond the valley, where he could see a series of rugged spurs spread out in a wide arc from the north to the east, some of them scarred by landslides on their steep faces. Surely, somewhere out there, on the banks of some nameless stream, at the foot of some nameless mountain, was a home for Timmon Tillman, two-time loser; a sun-dappled place where he could pass his days unencumbered by the existential hell of other people, a place to be left alone, a place so remote that the smoke of a campfire would not betray his existence. No more offices, no more leering desk clerks, no more meaningless toiling in body shops or clam factories. No more Gooch, no more walls, no more cells. Just wide-open spaces and bountiful wilderness, a place where he could engage the circle of life, no matter how grueling the business of survival might prove to be.

Crumpling his Snickers wrapper, he threw it on the forest floor and got to his feet. Spurred by a burning impatience, he trudged onward, down the ridge and over the saddle and through the next gap, where the trail leveled out in a narrow thickly wooded valley and rejoined the river along a low bank. The water flashed silver and white in the sunlight, and the roar of it was even greater than the roar of the spillway had been. Now and again as he plodded along the rutty path, he came upon horizontal blazes hatched deeply into the bark of trees at eye level, to which he gave little thought, until later, when reading Haywood's journal, he would come to realize the significance of these blazes.

Where to stop? Where to begin his new life? Onward! Onward through the broad-shouldered foothills and into treeless high country and over the divide until Timmon Tillman ceased to exist, until the past and the future ceased to exist and all that remained was the difference between life and death. By late afternoon, he was exhausted. A blister had formed on his heel. He stopped where the river emerged boiling from the mouth of a gray canyon, and sat on a massive rock, and unburdened himself of his GoLite bag with the clink of carabiners and the thud of his empty thermos, and smoked the last cigarette of his life.

He chose a small sandy clearing along the bank in the shadow of the canyon to set up camp. He spent twenty minutes wrestling his camospotted bivouac tent into shape. He gathered firewood and started a smoky fire. He ate jerky and another Snickers bar and wished he had another cigarette. Taking up Haywood's journal, he read distractedly for a few minutes until the sun began to set, whereupon he decided it was time. He fished the pint of Smirnoff out of his GoLite and uncapped it, then held it out in front of him and took a long hard look at its contents before braving a tentative sip. The old familiar sensations visited him at once; the icy-hot sting on his tongue, the shiver, the welling of giddy anticipation in his chest, as though he were standing on the edge of a precipice and couldn't wait to jump. The second sip was less tentative. On the third sip, he took the leap.

Within forty minutes, the pint was half empty and Timmon was the master of his own universe. Being master only meant letting go, surrendering, letting his thoughts drift of their own accord, until he laughed without cause, until the downy hair of a child's sunkissed face was no different than the notion of his own mortality, until believing was no different from disbelieving, until his dick was in his hand and his seed was spilling out into the river, and spilling, and spilling until he was empty of everything, until the emptiness filled him up and the fire died and he fell asleep face down beside his tent with his dick hanging out of his trousers.

deal breaker

Hillary had planned on ordering a single glass of the house red and nursing it through the evening. But by the time she parked the Silverado, wobbled across the gravel lot in high heels, and stepped through the double doors of the Bushwhacker, her nerves were already getting the best of her. She knew immediately that all bets were off. She was wringing her hands under the table when Molly arrived for the orders.

"I'll have a gin and tonic," she said.

"Y'all got eggnog?" said Franklin.

Molly arched an incredulous brow. "Uh, in like, *four* months we *might.*"

"Just give me a glass of milk, then."

He was older than Hillary expected. She hadn't expected salt and pepper. And blacker, too. Not that there was anything wrong with that. Strange that Genie had failed to mention it, though, since there were only about three black people in Port Bonita.

"Nice place," she said.

Franklin surveyed the Bushwhacker. Something smelled like fish. "Yeah," he said. "Not bad."

She was younger than Franklin expected. A little chunkier, too — but in all the right places. Still, Franklin couldn't seem to muster his characteristic exuberance. The loss of Timmon Tillman was still nagging him. He'd forgotten how much he hated losing them. It wasn't even about facilitating anymore. The knowledge that some tattooed knucklehead was out fixing leaky radiators instead of marking time was not the payoff. The payoff was the knowledge that Franklin was good at what he did, that he packed his lunch and got the job done — 317 consecutive times he'd gotten it done before Tillman walked through his door. How had he miscalculated?

"You seem down," Hillary observed, hitching up her blouse. "It's me. You're disappointed."

"No, no, far from it," he said. "It's work."

"Genie said you're a parole officer?"

"That's right."

"That must be interesting."

"Yeah, well, don't know about that. S'pose someone's got to do it."

The drinks arrived. Franklin wasted little time in getting started on his milk.

"So then, you must believe in second chances?" said Hillary.

"S'pose I do. Now that you put it that way."

"What about third chances?"

"Depends." Franklin wrinkled his face and set his glass down. He had a milk mustache. "This taste sour to you?" He slid the milk across the table to Hillary, who eyed it suspiciously, took a tentative whiff, and slid it back.

"Smells okay."

"Hm," he said. "Damn if it don't taste sour to me. So, Genie says you're some kind of environmentalist."

"I work for Fish and Wildlife."

"Yeah? You like a ranger or somethin'?"

"I do environmental impact studies."

"That so? Interesting," lied Franklin. The very word *environmental* conjured mosquitoes in Franklin's imagination.

"I don't wear a uniform or anything like that," Hillary said. "Mostly, I just count fish and measure silt levels — we're trying to predict how the landscape will react once the dam is removed."

"Yeah, I heard somethin' about that. Dude on the TV said the other day how that dam's on roller skates, that a fact?"

Hillary smiled politely, uncertain whether Franklin was joking. He seemed earnest enough. "That's just an expression. It means there's nothing under the dam but alluvial."

"Alluvial, huh? You mean like dirt?"

"Something like that. More like sand. Some people are afraid the structure will blow out before the restoration even begins."

"Inconvenient truth," said Franklin.

He had great teeth. Must be the calcium. Kind of an airhead, though. That she was attracted to Franklin Bell on some level came as a relief to Hillary. Not that she had butterflies. Not that she felt the flush of sexual attraction. Still, there was something there, a sort of magnetism. But then, how could she be certain that she wasn't just talking herself into this attraction out of some perverse sense of defiance? Had being called lesbo all these years finally pushed to her to the fringes of rural social convention? She liked that Franklin was black — it had to be a character builder in Port Bonita. She smiled inwardly at the thought of Beverly's reaction.

"Isn't truth just generally inconvenient?" she said.

Franklin flashed his nice teeth. "S'pose so," he said, sipping his milk.

"Before the dam there were ten andromonous fish species in the Elwha," Hillary pursued. "All but one of them is extinct now. And all of it could've been avoided with fish ladders."

"Fish ladders, huh? You don't say."

Franklin supposed he was still just a city boy deep down, still a son of Windy City steel and concrete, crowded el trains and noisy storefronts, because already he had a few questions that he was afraid to ask. For instance, how the hell's a fish supposed to climb a ladder in the first place? Also, this was the first he'd heard about fish being transsexual. How was it that after eleven years in Port Bonita, gateway to the Olympic National Wilderness, the mysteries of nature were still foreign to Franklin? Fish run, tree harvest, snowpack; these were just phrases, things, to be quite honest, he didn't even care to understand. The fact is, he could hardly stand the wilderness, it struck him as lifeless and dull. All those trees just standing around to no purpose. The deafening silence. The mosquitoes. Franklin felt no more at home in the wilderness than a giraffe might feel on the Dan Ryan

Expressway. The fact was, he was a little terrified of the wilderness. Given the choice, he'd rather stroll through Cabrini Green waving a fistful of cash at one in the morning than walk through Lincoln Park at noon. And yet, not only had he applied for a position in this outpost a decade earlier, he'd even passed up positions in Muncie, Detroit, and Indianapolis — urban locales all, and all of them exponentially closer to Chicago. Only later did it occur to Franklin that he'd been trying to outrun anything.

"Any kids?" said Hillary, as though she were reading his mind.

"Naw, nothin' like that."

"Me neither," she said.

"Never got around to it, I guess," said Franklin. "Heck, I can hardly take care of myself."

"I know what you mean."

In the ensuing silence, Hillary downed her G and T in an effort to soothe her nerves. Franklin followed suit with his milk, grimacing slightly.

"Needs rum," he said.

After the second gin and tonic, Hillary's nerves settled into a pleasant state of arousal. It felt good being tipsy. Franklin got better by the sip. Maybe he was different than the others. At least, he didn't talk about himself the whole time. Hillary felt something bubbling up in her chest that wasn't tonic, as though the evening might be leading somewhere.

Franklin was also pleased by the evening's progress. He wasn't forcing anything, like he had with the Longaberger basket rep from Port Townsend or the administrative assistant from the women's correctional facility in Purdy. Franklin was laying back, and everything was smooth sailing until shortly after the third round arrived, when Hillary asked him if he did much hiking.

"Heck no," he said, waving it off, with a grin. "It'd be a cold day in you-know-where before you'd catch me walkin' around out there. My idea of the great outdoors is a potted plant."

Like an anchor chain, disappointment plummeted down the back

of Hillary's throat. Franklin could see it and was determined to recover from the misstep.

"'Course I can't say I really ever gave it much of a chance. Never
cared much for baseball until I saw Wrigley Field. So I guess I could
be persuaded to give it a try. Can't really judge a thing until you've
tried it."

It wasn't that Franklin redeemed himself — because, let's face it,
this was a deal breaker — it was more that he tried to redeem himself
that kept Hillary from slamming the door on the evening's possibilities. Still, her interest was waning the more he tried to save face, and
Franklin could feel it. It was time to push it, he decided.

He smiled over the rim of his rum and milk. "I gotta say, blind date
and all, I wasn't expecting anyone half as smokin' as you."

Hillary felt her face color, simultaneously thrilled and annoyed at
herself for taking the bait. She had to admit she liked his directness,
if nothing else.

"Really," pursued Franklin. "Usually, I wind up with, well, you know —
not that I'm Paul Newman or anything. But a fine-looking lady like
yourself? Girl, you must be beatin' 'em off with a stick." Damn it, why
did he always start talking like Bobby Brown? Bobby Brown never
worked. It was too forward, it always had lewd undertones. But to
Franklin's surprise, on this occasion Bobby Brown worked, if not by
way of its intended effect, then simply by its directness.

Downing her G and T, Hillary felt the stirrings of an old recklessness. "What now?" she said.

seasons

One morning in early March, the suffocating cloud cover that had characterized the long winter finally lifted, and the cool crisp light of day slanted through Eva's frosty window. Pulling herself upright beneath the covers, she discovered at once that the heaviness was gone from her limbs and that a certain clarity and sharpness had returned to her perceptions.

As she padded across the creaking floor to tend to the stove, she paused at the sight of Minerva sleeping soundly in her crib, her tiny pinched mouth pulsing, her little fists clenched and twitching ever so slightly. For week upon plodding week, in spite of her tired limbs and dull senses, Eva had attended to the infant's every physical need. She had fed and bathed and clothed and quieted the child, and yet it was clear to Eva that she had failed miserably in the most basic measure of motherhood. She had forsaken her child, as sure as if she'd abandoned her on a doorstep.

After stoking the fire, and setting the pot to boiling, Eva retired to her desk by the window and reread her letter to Ethan for the fourth time, wondering if today were the day she would send it. Before she got halfway through the letter, however, just after *I was unaware that the practice of husbandry now extended beyond the perimeters of matrimony* and right before *I have a moral responsibility to society at large,* Eva calmly folded the letter twice, walked it to the kitchen and, pulling back the iron hatch, dropped the letter into the coals, which she set about stoking.

She'd been tough on Ethan, and she'd known it all along, known that those who'd abandoned hope would discourage hope in others, those who'd given up the pursuit of a dream — often long before the mad scramble had ever begun — would make it their business to obstruct the dreaming of others. And so it had been with Ethan. Eva discouraged Ethan's dreaming without ever having put her own shoulder to the wheel. Yes, she'd relocated two thousand miles away; yes, she'd adopted a belief system, a philosophy; yes, she'd chopped a little wood, donned a floppy bow, made flapjacks, painted some sea-scapes, and written a few ephemeral pieces for the *Register*. But how had she really suffered by it all? By not being taken seriously? By not being heard? If so, it wasn't for lack of complaining; she'd objected, dissented, refuted, opposed, torn down, cast aside, or dismissed ev-erything the world presented her. If she had lacked a sympathetic audience, it was no small wonder. And hadn't this child been part of Ethan's dream? And hadn't she denied him that, too?

When she could no longer see her own breath, Eva woke Minerva and lifted her from her crib, bundled in her nest of blankets, the mark of sleep still spread across her wrinkled face.

"Good morning," Eva said, smoothing the downy hair atop the in-fant's crown. "Things are going to be different now."

Receiving this intelligence, Minerva cooed once and grasped at the air with tiny fingers.

"And what have we here?" Eva said. "Ha, why it looks like little mit-tens! And a little scarf."

The girl began to fidget immediately, but suddenly Eva had pa-tience to spare. Hoisting the bundled girl up in her arms, Eva walked her out into the crisp bright morning, where the child fell silent in the brilliant light. How clear and miraculous the world appeared in the light of a new day. How enlivening that first breath of cold air, how wondrous the crunch of fresh snow. To the south, Eva saw the mountains as though for the first time, every chasm, every cleft, every sawtoothed ridge against a crisp relief of deep blue sky. How tiny and restless the colony, with its little white houses and busy little chim-neys, seemed in the shadow of such grandeur.

Minerva began to squirm in her arms. Lacking any immediate pur-pose, Eva plodded toward the hotel for the sake of plodding toward somewhere, until at last Minerva settled once more. Crunching down the snowy path toward the colony, she shielded the child's eyes against the blinding sunlight. In the distance, the pounding of a hammer could be heard, soon joined by the reports of a second hammer, and the laughter of children from the schoolyard. A woman with a shovel was clearing the steps of the half-finished Opera House. A handful of men were at work beneath the boat shed, three on deck with ropes, and two on the scaffold alongside the hull, calling instruction out to one another as they guided a timber into place. A carriage man readied his team in front of the hotel. Even at a distance, Eva could see the fog of the horses' breath. All around her was industry and purpose.

What am I waiting for? thought Eva.

The headquarters of the *Commonwealth Register* comprised one high-ceilinged — though narrow and extraordinarily cluttered — warehouse smelling strongly of ink. The nature of the clutter, strewn defiantly about in bold strokes — an unapologetic clutter — spoke strongly of the paper's editor, publisher, and chief author, W. Lane Griffin, a hawkish, prematurely aging, and altogether serious man, whose thin lips seemed somehow uncharitable, as though he were hoarding them beneath his ample mustache.

Griffin did not look up from his work when Eva made her entrance. As if to foil her entrance, Minerva began to fuss immediately.

"I want to start writing again," Eva said, by way of announcing herself, over the child's protestations. "And I want to write real stories. Stories that will make a difference."

Griffin bestowed a quick disinterested glance up at Eva and her child before resuming his work. As if on cue, Minerva began to cry.

"It appears you've got your hands full," he observed, scrawling furious notes on the pad in front of him. "This is a newspaper, not a nursery."

It had often occurred to Eva that Griffin was not forward in his thinking, only extreme, and inflexible, and loud. Indeed, if Port Bonitans expressed an aversion to their colonist neighbors, or an outright contempt, if they were in any way threatened by, wary of, or otherwise disgusted with the colony, it was likely owing to the opinions of Mr. W. Lane Griffin, voice of the *Commonwealth Register,* that is to say, voice of dissent, dissatisfaction, and outrage. In spite of his extreme worldviews and his radical beliefs, Eva found Griffin's views to be quite pedestrian with regard to the specifics of gender. He was no more progressive than her brother, and if Jacob's respect was hard won, it would be twice as hard to win Griffin's. And Eva knew that Minerva's caterwaul, now reaching a shrill crescendo when Eva needed it least, was certainly not helping her cause.

"I should think all that mothering would be enough to keep you busy," he shouted over the infant.

"I've got two hands," Eva called back. "And a brain. I'll manage just fine."

Just when it seemed Minerva had ceased her crying, the girl struggled for a few desperate gasps of air and started wailing anew.

Griffin ripped a page from his pad and started rifling through his desk drawer in search of something. "How would you like to cover the Broderson wedding?"

"That's *not* what I had in mind," Eva said, rocking the baby urgently.

"What then?"

"I'll bring you a real story," Eva said.

"Like you brought me a Mather story?"

"That's not fair."

"No?" said Griffin, looking up. "Bring me a story, then. A story that's not about the railroad, not about the reserve, not about Harrison and his cronies. Bring me something local with national implications, something of import, something to rally these laggard souls, to mobilize their ideals, to grab them by the lapel and shake the apathy right out of them. Bring me a cause."

"Count on it," said Eva, turning on her heels and marching out of the office. She might have been flush with triumph had it not been for Minerva's conniptions, which drew the attention of passing colonists. Though to attribute such motives to an infant shamed her, Eva couldn't help but feel that the child had wished to deny her course all along. That Eva actually resented the girl for this perceived subterfuge shamed her still further, as she rocked the screaming infant briskly in her arms.

the right thing

Adam awakened shortly after dawn to the trumpeting of Lord Jim's rooster beneath the window. For nearly an hour, he lay in bed on his back, staring at the ceiling through the fog of his breath, listening to the rooster scratch at the frozen earth beneath his window. Adam tried for the tenth time to envision a future for Thomas but discovered instead that it was hard to see beyond Hoko. He would take the boy without her blessings if need be, but he could not take him without her knowledge. When he heard the soft patter of Lord Jim's wife moving down the hallway toward the kitchen, Adam excavated himself from beneath a mountain of wool blankets and began to dress for the second time in five hours.

Shaving without the benefit of his mirror, which now bobbed on a gentle swell far beyond the breakwater of Ediz Hook, Adam cut his chin twice and pressed his thumb and forefinger firmly against the nicks until the bleeding stopped. Half an hour later, the cool air stung his face as he awaited the carriage to Port Bonita. Once again, he found his thoughts reaching backward to the beginning, though on this occasion, it was Hoko to whom he assigned his sympathies.

FOR NEARLY FIVE months, through the bulk of a rainy spring and all of a short, mild summer in 1880, Hoko had managed to disguise her bulge beneath unseasonably heavy clothing. Her mother was not alive to notice the change, and her father, whose once frequent and adoring gaze had fallen off precipitously since the afternoon he saw Hoko with the Potato Counter near the mouth of Ennis Creek, was completely unsuspecting of any change. That is, until the chill morning in early fall, when Hoko, stretching hides for winter with her father, reached up to lace a corner to the frame, and in spite of her bundled layers, revealed the thing for the briefest of moments, during which her father happened to notice. Before Hoko could lower her arms, he reached out and set his calloused hand on the thing, and a stricken expression took shape on his face. Hoko lowered her arms and lowered her eyes.

"Look what you've done," is all he said. She felt the sting before he even slapped her. That was virtually the last thing he said to her until the night of the storm, when the boy made his entrance into the world.

Adam had been quick to notice the change, much quicker than Hoko's father. He did not discover it hidden beneath Hoko's bundles but in her eyes, often evasive since the night of their coupling. Near the end of spring, he detected fear in the girl's eyes for the first time. And he saw something else in her eyes for the first time: a certain glaze on the surface. Seemingly overnight, Hoko went from a doe-eyed innocent to an embittered woman.

"The bigger I get," she once said, when Thomas was just weeks from being born, "the smaller you seem to get."

IF ONLY, ADAM thought, ten years later as his carriage rumbled on its way west, I could do it all over again.

Not fifty steps off of the carriage in front of the Olympic, Adam chanced upon Hoko, perched on the steps of the hardware store, clutching a white infant wrapped in swaddling blankets.

"Whose?"

"A woman's."

"What woman is that?"

"Why do you always ask?" she said, pointedly.

It was a fair question, and Adam knew it. He could never resist the urge to ask. He was still counting potatoes after all these years, still demanding accountability from everyone whose path he crossed. And how did he account for the gruffness in his tone after all these years when he spoke to Hoko?

"I've come for the boy," he said. "I've made arrangements. In Jamestown."

Hoko looked at Adam impassively, then down at the baby, who was beginning to whimper. She rocked the child until it settled, and said nothing.

"He'll be taken care of there," Adam pursued. "And there's a place for you."

"I have a place."

"A better place."

"I don't want a better place," she said. "Not for myself."

A young woman, presumably the infant's mother, emerged from the hardware store with a small steel trowel and a rolled canvas.

"Ma'am," said Adam, doffing his hat.

"Good day," Eva said, and turned her attention to Hoko and the baby. "For heaven's sake, let's get out of this infernal cold."

As Hoko was whisked away by the young mother down the muddy boardwalk, she looked back over her shoulder, and Adam would not soon forget the look on Hoko's face, softer than he'd seen it in years, stripped of all anger, drained of all passivity, her dark eyes large and wounded, painfully alive.

Slowly, and to Adam inexplicably, Hoko nodded her assent.

ADAM FOUND THOMAS alone beneath Morse Dock, standing with his arms akimbo and one eye closed as he stared straight up at the planks. The boy paid no mind to Adam's approach, and kept staring up at the planks. After a moment, he covered the other eye, then both eyes, then uncovered them again and squinted fiercely. Drawing closer, Adam saw a nasty scrape on the boy's chin, and bruising about his neck, and understood suddenly the reason why Hoko had consented to let him take the boy.

"Who did this to you?"

Thomas said nothing.

Adam took the boy's chin in his hand and inspected his face in closer detail. He poked at the bruises, and the boy winced. He ran a thumb over the scrape and the boy grimaced. Somebody had gotten the boy around the neck—that much was clear. Not Hoko, Adam knew, but more likely her father, who only got meaner with the passage of time. This, too, was Adam's fault. Her father had no thirst for whiskey before Adam had come along and upset the balance of his life. Now he was all thirst. Adam recalled the first time he'd seen him drunk — in the middle of the day, on what might have been the very eve of his grandson's birth. He was in town, spinning circles in the muddy snow and cursing the spirits. He spit and slurred his words. A string of saliva dangled from his chin. When he saw Adam, he stopped spinning and leered at him.

"*Tay-equin,*" he said, his smile curling in on itself at the corners. He wiped the spittle from his chin and raised his right hand, leveling a finger right at Adam.

"*Kwetceq,*" replied Adam soberly, turning his back on Hoko's father. But as Adam continued on his way down the street — which was hardly more than a muddy slough in those days — he could feel the man's finger trained on his back. In this manner, Hoko's father followed Adam at a distance of a few paces, past the Belvedere and the Olympic, halfway to the hogback. Adam had wanted to stop, to spin around and confront the old man. But he didn't have the courage. Deep down he knew he didn't have a leg to stand on. So he kept on walking, and Hoko's father kept following, pointing, sneering — silently, intently, hatefully. To this very day, Adam could feel that finger trained between his shoulder blades.

Letting go of the boy's chin and tousling his hair, Adam reflected that the violence visited upon him was a blessing of sorts. Without the scrapes and bruises, Hoko surely would have resisted his will. But to her credit, the boy's welfare outweighed her own stubbornness.

The next morning, following a half-eaten oyster omelet at the Olympic, Adam set out to retrieve the boy at the Siwash camp, when, at some distance, he spotted Thomas kneeling restlessly across the fire from his mother.

HOKO HAD RESOLVED herself to be firm, to instruct the boy rather than release him.

"If your father were here, he would be proud of you," she said. "He would tell you this is the right thing. Jamestown is where the Klallam will rise again."

The boy was fidgeting, drawing his shapes in the sand.

"Look at me," she said.

Thomas looked up at his mother with his distant blue eyes.

"Your father was a strong man; he would tell you to be strong. He would tell you to make him proud."

Thomas knew that no such father ever existed, that his father had not been lost in a storm, only lost to Thomas. But sometimes he imagined this father, anyway, imagined him living upriver, moving stealthily among the shadows of the deep forest. He imagined his father coming downriver to claim him someday.

"You must do what your father would want you to do," Hoko told him. An old guilt constricted these words. What was the purpose of the lie?

She reached out to him, but he did not reach back. "Go," she said, her heart turning to liquid. "Make your father proud."

THE BOY WAS restless in the carriage, continually pressing his face to the rattling window, turning his head from side to side, bobbing it forward and back like a rooster. At one point he balled his fists up and hammered his lap with them.

"Easy," Adam told him. "You've got to learn some control, boy. You can't be acting up like that all the time."

It seemed to Adam as if the boy's body had a mind all its own. He noted with relief, however, that Thomas was no longer twitching as he had been in days prior.

"The Shakers would just as soon have you twitching, I suppose."

THOMAS STOOD IN the squelchy road as the Potato Counter settled with the carriage driver. The village sat facing the water on the edge of a large flat prairie strewn with old stumps. The two rows of houses formed an almost straight line. The houses numbered fourteen in all, seven on each side, and they were mostly brown and red, but one of them was green. Looking down the middle of the street with his head tilted sidewise, first to the right, and then to the left, Thomas oriented himself. At the end of the lane stood a little white, steepleless church, tall and straight and mud-spattered along the lower edge. There were chickens at large in the muddy street, bobbing about aimlessly, and from across the meadow came the distant bleating of sheep.

The Potato Counter led Thomas right down the middle of the row of houses, and Thomas saw Indian faces peeking out from behind curtained windows, old men and women, mostly. There were no signs of children about the place. In a potato field beyond the town, Thomas saw a figure leading a horse toward the road. As they drew nearer to the shoreline, he could hear the lapping of the surf, and from somewhere behind walls he heard the dull ringing of bells.

Adam talked to the child as they made their way toward Lord Jim's.

"You're going to like it here, boy."

Thomas knew that the Potato Counter was only reassuring himself.

"You stick to this place, or I'll be forced to come after you, hear?"

It felt to Thomas as though they were walking slowly, for which he was glad. The smell of the place was not unpleasant, of low tide and manure and the heady smell of grassland.

"Your mother will come here to live someday soon. You'll wait for her, you understand?"

Near the end of the row, they came upon a red house with a sloping roof, whose shingles were affixed willy-nilly. Mounting the uneven steps with Thomas in tow, the Potato Counter tapped on the door, and an old fat woman, whose teeth were too far apart, greeted them there. She led them inside and down a hallway that smelled like cooking, to a room with no door, where an old man sat waiting for them in a rocking chair of rough hewn cedar, with a heavy blanket folded over his lap.

The old man smiled at Thomas, but Thomas did not smile back, did not so much as tilt his head or move his lips. The room felt big and small at the same time. Twice, with the old man's gaze steadily upon him, Thomas glanced over his shoulder at the doorless doorway. Sensing his uneasiness, Adam took his hand, and to his surprise the boy held it.

Lord Jim scrutinized Thomas head to toe, glimpsing things in those strange blue eyes that he could not comprehend, a world he could not penetrate. The boy did not shrink from his gaze. He stood straight. His lips began to work silently, and he clutched Adam's hand still tighter.

"This one has a strong will," observed Lord Jim. "This one doesn't forget."

"That I wouldn't know," said Adam. "The boy's a mystery to me."

Lord Jim nodded his head slowly. "He will reveal himself, *cayci*. And he will cease to be a boy."

When it came time for Adam to leave, the boy would not let go of his hand. Extracting it at last from the boy's fierce grip, Adam patted Thomas once on the head and turned to leave, avoiding the boy's eyes, which he could feel desperately trying to engage him. As Adam passed through the doorless doorway, Thomas tried to follow him, but Adam turned and held him there until Lord Jim stood on venerable legs.

"Don't be frightened, child. I've been expecting you."

The old man persuaded the boy to come back through the doorway into the room, which felt only big now, and no longer small at the same time. The old man retrieved a high-backed chair from the corner of the room and positioned it directly in front of his rocker.

"Come. Sit."

But Thomas would not leave the window. With the curtain pulled back, he watched the Potato Counter retreat, and it was as if something were pulling him through the glass.

forgiveness

It was spitting rain on Hollywood Beach early in the spring of 1887, when Joseph King came to ask his daughter's forgiveness. A steady breeze was blowing off of the strait, and a cloud of frenzied seagulls hovered above the receding tide. Beneath her mat shelter, Hoko was sitting cross-legged by a low fire. Thomas squatted beside her at a distance of several feet. Neither of them seemed to notice Joseph standing nearby. Hoko was looking straight ahead, as though in a trance, and the boy was looking down at his feet, scrawling shapes in the sand.

After a moment, Joseph approached a step closer to the fire and announced himself.

"C'tan ek?"

Thomas looked up at his grandfather, but Hoko did not. Soon the boy went back to his scrawling. When the silence became too long to stand in, Joseph ducked in under the roof and lowered himself by the fire across from his daughter.

"The salmonberries are out early," he observed.

"Ha-tec," said Hoko dryly.

Joseph lapsed into silence. Restlessly, he began to stir the fire. He continued to shrink from shame, but also from fear. He'd better speak now while he still had a mouth.

"I have come to ask for your forgiveness," he said at last.

Hoko still did not look at him. She spoke to him from a great distance. "If that's what you've come for, then you shouldn't have come at all."

"I'm sorry, I'm so sorry." Joseph looked briefly into the fire and then sought the evasive eyes of his daughter. "But you must understand. I was angry. *K'wesen.*"

Hoko's face hardened. "And I was scared, and alone. You understand? Just a girl. *K'wesen.* You disowned me, you blamed me. You stopped speaking to me. You made me feel like nothing. What is sorry, after that?"

Joseph lowered his eyes, which immediately sought refuge in the fire. "You're right, sorry is nothing. I am nothing. And only you can make me something again. That is why I'm here."

"Here, ha! Here is nothing. *Hiya? Uxw'k! There* is where I needed you then. Here you're no good to anybody."

"But I've come to — "

"You've come to a different place," Hoko said, looking right at him for the first time. "You are a different man; I am a woman. You chose these paths for us."

It was Joseph who diverted his eyes now. "But you are my daughter, my flesh and blood."

"*Hiya.* You have no daughter."

Thomas looked up from the sand to watch his grandfather walk away that day. He walked like a dead man.

undoing

The morning Randy was sprung, Rita called in sick. She combed her hair out in waves beneath the blow-dryer and tucked it behind her ears, how Randy liked it. She painted her toenails ruby red. She donned a denim mini and some pointy black pumps and a fake leather halter. Finally, she applied a smoky blue eye shadow and ruby red lipstick to match her toenails.

The strait was shrouded in fog so thick that Ediz Hook was not visible, but by the time she reached Wagner's Corner it had lifted, and Rita began to catch sunbeams through the low clouds as she wended her way down a deserted Highway 112. She bit her cuticles and smoked cigarettes and fought off the silence with KBSG. She caught the tail end of "Baby Love," all of "Brandy," and the opening bars of the Zombies "Time of the Season" before the signal gave out around Joyce, and Rita was left only with the swishing progress of the Monte Carlo as it sped toward Randy. Gradually her thoughts began to seep in to the silence. One thought in particular assailed her — the thought of how Curtis would never forgive her for taking Randy back.

But how could you explain the complexities of real world love to a sixteen-year-old kid, a kid who hid in his room doing God knew what with empty paint cans? A kid who had trouble forgiving, a kid who held grudges. A kid who was angry at the world. Rita softened at the thought of Curtis in one of two dozen oversized T-shirts, peering out from behind thick bangs. He was a good kid, beneath it all. She didn't deserve him.

When it had been just Rita and the boy, after Dan, and before Randy, things had been different. Curtis had made an effort. He looked out for her. When Rita dragged in come evening after working a double shift, when her wrist ached as though someone had cut a tendon,

Curtis made macaroni, brought her a beer and three aspirin, watched the news with her, and shared her sullenness. He never asked her for money. He was always on the lookout for deals as they strolled the aisles of Albertson's or the Dollar Store or Safeway. The Club Card had been his idea. He'd taken the move to the trailer well, all things considered, although she knew he hated the place. It wasn't until the calls from Randy started arriving from corrections that Curtis took a turn for the worse. That's when they stopped shopping together. That's when the door locking began. It got to where she no longer knew whether Curtis was home. When they passed in the narrow hallway, he was sullen and silent.

Any anticipation Rita had felt for greeting Randy turned to dread by degrees with the realization that her future was bound to look a lot like her past. That Randy, for all his charms — his lean musculature, his arrogance, his soft spot for pitbull puppies — was not likely to have changed, to have been corrected, as it were, one iota. Randy simply could not be undone. They could break him down, humiliate him, force him to his knees in the name of correction, but he'd only get harder. Sometimes Rita felt that Randy was her punishment for Dan.

When Rita arrived, Randy was already slouching outside reception in the rain, looking shorter and meaner than she remembered. His nose seemed crookeder. He was wearing jeans and a green windbreaker and black rubber flip-flops. His hair was cropped to a blue shadow and she could see the little pink scars on his head even at a distance. Rita made a quick inspection of her lipstick and her eye shadow in the rearview mirror as she pulled to the curb, where the Monte Carlo stalled.

Randy dropped his cigarette butt, ground it out with the toe of his flip-flop, and climbed into the car as Rita restarted it. He pulled out another cigarette. "I'm hungry," he said. "Where you been?"

"Sorry I'm late."

"Yeah."

"You look healthy."

"Yeah, well, what can I say? Ain't nothin' better to do in there than stay healthy. Got a light?"

The car ride was mostly silent. Rita could feel Randy's eyes on her but not enough, never enough. Mostly, he just smoked cigarettes and looked vaguely out the window. It didn't seem to matter what Randy looked at, there was always a level of disinterest in his gaze.

They stopped at the Hungry Bear where they hardly talked while Randy made quick work of a three-egg omelet and two bowls of peach cobbler. Rita had a green salad with dill pickle wedges in it. Picking absently through the iceberg, she noticed a new tattoo on Randy's wrist, just visible beneath the cuff of his jacket. It looked like an ice-cream cone with feet. She would come to find that it was the handiwork of someone named Gooch in his cell block and that the subject was in fact none other than Atlas shouldering his burden. And later, when she looked up Atlas at the library, it would occur to Rita that Randy shared absolutely nothing in common with Atlas, who was punished for his strength and determination, while Randy was punished for stealing cars and assaulting cabdrivers. And while Atlas carried upon his shoulders the pillars of heaven and earth, Randy's only burden was his own baggage. But none of this occurred to Rita as they sat at the Hungry Bear, beneath the constant scrutiny of the proprietor's eight-year-old daughter, who sat in the adjacent booth picking her nose and wiping it on the underside of the table, while staring unabashedly at what were for the most part silent proceedings.

Randy was apparently unaware of the child's surveillance. He kept staring at Rita's tits throughout lunch, until he was finally moved to speech. "Why you gotta put it on parade like that? That's bullshit."

They stopped by Gertie's around noon, just as Mickey fired up the big screen and started restocking the coolers. They drank two pitchers of beer on Rita's employee discount. They watched *SportsCenter* twice. Three times they ducked out for cigarettes.

"Got a lead on a job," he said, midway through the second pitcher. "Muffler shop off Lincoln."

"Mm," she said.

"What's that supposed to mean?"

Rita watched NASCAR footage unfold without really paying attention. "It means, that's great. I hope it pans out."

"It fucking better."

"There's a two-bedroom on Lauridson for six fifty," she said hopefully. "It's got a pool. And a parking garage."

"Pff. Like we need a parking garage for that shitpile."

"We could get a better car. We could fix up the Monte Carlo and give it to Curtis. He's sixteen now."

"Don't get ahead of yourself," he said, fumbling in his jeans pocket. "Give me the lighter, will you?"

They left Gertie's about two that afternoon and stopped at Circle K for a sixer of Schmidt Ice. On the drive back to the trailer, the Monte Carlo stalled twice.

WHEN CURTIS ARRIVED home around two fifteen (having skipped Enslow's class), he found the trailer awash in a blue haze of cigarette smoke. Randy's green duffel bag sagged off one end on the coffee table, along with three empty Schmidt cans. Randy's clothing was strewn up and down the hallway. Curtis could hear them fucking in his bedroom, where they hadn't even bothered to shut the door, his mother grunting with each shunt, her head, or elbow, or some other body part bumping the flimsy wall, as Randy talked to her breathlessly.

Curtis registered it all with disgust. Same old shit. How long before Randy started in with his jealousy bullshit? Before he started watching Rita's every move like a hawk? When she'd first started working at Gertie's, Randy used to come in and sit in her section and drink coffee for most of her shift. He waited for her in the parking lot after the restaurant closed. Finally, Mickey had told Randy that he couldn't sit in there all night long. Curtis had heard them arguing that night.

"Paranoid, my ass! Not with the kind of scumbags that hang out at that place," Randy had said.

How long before Randy started bossing Curtis around again like he had a right? How long before he came unhinged and started taking shots at his mom? Fuck if he was going to watch that bullshit all over again. Fuck if he was going to so much as look at Randy sideways. Especially not on acid. Why spoil one of the few things worth looking forward to? Dosing was the greatest escape yet. Better than sleeping. Better than drawing. Better than huffing. To peak on acid was to forget yourself completely, to turn yourself inside out, to broadcast what little mystery was left inside of you and then walk, and grasp, and wander with childlike wonder through a world of your own creation. That was the main thing, to feel like a kid again. Curtis could remember sitting perfectly still as a child, unfocusing his eyes watching the outer world swirl together in a corkscrew of humming colors. He could remember leaving his body altogether. But that was childhood. Ancient history. Now, he was forever stuck *right-fucking-here,* wherever that was — a million light-years from the humming corkscrew. But for ten bucks he could get close.

Curtis began to effect a quick escape, though not before he fished around in Randy's jeans for his wallet. There must've been three hundred bucks inside. Filching a pair of twenties, Curtis replaced the wallet and smiled inwardly at the thought of KFC and a two-liter bottle of Pepsi. On his way out the door, he snatched a half pack of Salems off the coffee table, along with a waxy red apple and half a Diet Coke.

The rain had let up and the sun was darting in and out of clouds, shining silver on the wet pavement. The acid began running a cold electric finger up the boy's rib cage and into his throat. Drifting toward the center of town, Curtis felt his eyes begin to outgrow their sockets. His stomach made a fist. The veil of reality began to take on that threadbare look, and Curtis knew that soon he would be able to see right through the fabric. He gave a shiver and fired up a Salem.

There came an instant when Curtis was coming on, when he knew he was about to relinquish his tenuous grip on the ordinary; it arrived as a ticking behind his eyeballs and a fluttering in his chest and a heartbeat in his skull. The world began to pulse with color, and invisible things began leaving their signatures all around him. And he gave into this slackening perception of the ordinary, so that he might glimpse the world underneath.

Now and again Curtis awakened in flashes and found himself in unfamiliar places — kneeling on riverbanks, riding in canoes, swimming through darkness toward an orange glow. He walked outside of his body and saw things he could not comprehend yet somehow recognized — tiny laughing people made of forest and sunlight. He witnessed himself, shivering on the bank of a river in an animal skin rug, his skin rubbed raw, waiting for he knew not what.

strange ways

Thomas slept on a straw mat at the foot of an empty bed formerly belonging to Lord Jim's daughter, Lila, who was in turn forced to share a room with her parents across the hallway. In spite of Lord Jim's entreaties, the boy would not sleep on the mattress and refused to sleep with anything but a goatskin rug, a state of affairs for which Lila chastised the boy endlessly. Some nights, early in spring, when the wind howling off the bay sliced through the thin walls and rattled the windowpanes, the boy awoke shivering and huddled about the flame of a candle for warmth. Other nights the boy was troubled by dreams. One dream in particular would not let him rest.

He dreamed of the Siwash standing in a field at the edge of a high bluff. It was the dead of night in the dream, and the moon cast a purple glow upon his people, who stood expressionless, as still as statues — 132 Indians in all, scattered along the edge of the bluff, with no one stationed closer to the edge than his mother, her braided hair pulled back tight, her arms at her sides, gazing hypnotically over the ledge, where a hundred feet below, a riotous sea pounded the shoreline. Behind the Siwash, the mountains reared up like shadows. Indian George stood near the boy's mother. He was wearing a scarf over his face, like he did when he cleaned fish for market. Flanking his mother on the opposite side, Abe Charles, dressed like a white, clutching his rifle, stood stupefied. Stone Face was not far behind Abe. The pits of his face were deeper in the moonlight. He was smiling, just barely. Next to Stone Face, Small Fry, peering out of yellow eyes, was smiling, too. Farthest from the bluff's edge, in the field of long grass, the boy's grandfather squatted on all fours, his toothless maw wide open as though he were screaming. But the old man made no sound. Nobody or nothing made a sound except for the waves assaulting the shoreline.

High on a hill, the Belvedere Man stood tall in the moonlight with folded arms. And looking down on the Siwash, he spat on the ground.

Four times the boy had the identical dream.

Thomas was instructed in many things at Jamestown. He was taught by Ida Hall how to milk a goat and to pin laundry on the line like a woman. By Cook Dan Solomon, he was taught how to mend a fence and shingle a roof. Begrudgingly, Lila taught the boy to lead a horse by bridle, taught him to round up chickens and pin them to a stump, and with an enthusiasm Thomas found unsettling, the girl demonstrated how to behead the hens with an ax, laughing as the headless things darted blindly and furiously about the yard.

The boy had a way with horses, a fact Lord Jim soon took note of.

"They trust you," he told him one day, as the boy ran a hand down the gray mare's neck and withers. "This horse is a good judge of character."

Much to Lila's dissatisfaction, the old man taught Thomas to ride on none other than the gray mare generally reserved for Lord Jim himself. The boy was a natural, though his style was unorthodox. He rode high in the saddle at a canter, like General Custer, with one hand clutching the saddlehorn. The mare was very responsive to the reins, although Thomas hardly made use of them. The beast anticipated the boy's every move. Every afternoon, regardless of the weather, the boy rode the mare — through the potato fields, across the creek, into the foothills to the banks of the Dungeness, until the two were as graceful as one.

At the end of each day, the boy was tired in a way he had never been tired. He sat every evening at the table with Lord Jim and his wife, and Lila, who pinched the boy under the table and ground her heel into his bare foot. Thomas did not care for Lila with her pointy gaze and cruel laughter. She often speared food off his plate when her parents were not watching, which Thomas did not mind so much at first, as he hadn't yet developed a taste for Jamestown food. They ate steamed turnips and potatoes and carrots. Lamb, and chicken, and more potatoes. Only infrequently did they eat fish, and hardly ever clams.

After a while, Thomas rarely thought of the Potato Counter, who had not shown his face in Jamestown since leaving him there, and gradually Thomas felt a sense of belonging in the little village. There were no bottles in Jamestown to darken the spirits of the people, no Stone Face or Belvedere Man to threaten them. Save for an occasional stopover by carriage, there were no whites at all in the settlement. The Jamestown Klallam were different from the Siwash Klallam. Lord Jim called them sovereign, which Thomas took to mean that they were like whites. They lived as whites with their eyes trained on the future. They dressed as whites and governed themselves as whites. And like whites they counted.

The Jamestown Klallam went to church daily, congregating in the mud-spattered building at the end of the row. In spite of his initial reluctance to enter its windowless confines, Thomas grew to be comfortable in the place, grew accustomed to the bells, which rang dully and tinnily like cowbells. He enjoyed arranging the candles on the prayer table. Each day he knelt upon a thule mat before the altar and configured the candles in a manner that was almost symmetrical. Always, he lined the crosses along the outside border, but not quite perfectly straight. And when the Shakers filed in clutching their bells, sober and calm, something happened to them in the holy light of the candles. They began to tremble like horsetails in the wind. They quivered and writhed, as the spirit coursed through them like an electric current, until the bells began to ring of their own accord. And Thomas found that he himself began to vibrate with the spirit.

Daily, Lord Jim sat Thomas down on the dusty floor at his feet and gave the boy puzzles and nettle tea to calm his perpetual fidgeting. The old man's face looked like a plum withering on the vine. His movements were slow and deliberate. His willowy voice burbled on like a stream.

"We do not need Bibles here. The gospel does not require a book," he told Thomas. "It is already written inside of us." Reaching down, he set his palm on the boy's chest and another upon his forehead. "The spirit sings inside of you. It sings in your bones. What does it say? Listen to what it says, Thomas."

Thomas listened for the spirit, which he soon identified as the simmering thing inside of him. Lord Jim urged Thomas to contain this thing, to let it work through him, rather than consume him. The spirit wrote words on the inside of the boy's head. Soon he began to string these words together, and the words set the boy in motion in a new way. He began thinking of things that were yet to happen, goats yet to be fed, fences yet to be mended. His wandering ways ceased. He moved about in his new world deliberately. His feet took him from one place to another, as though there existed nothing in between the two places. Even his mind, when it set to wandering, never wandered far before it arrived at some purpose. When he counted, the numbers became the things he was counting, and he no longer preferred odd numbers to even. A line was no longer a line, but a boundary, beyond which the boy was free to pass, if he pleased.

Thomas supposed that he, too, had become sovereign.

One morning, as Thomas was scattering feed for the hogs, he spotted Horatio Groves crossing a nearby potato field on foot. Thomas liked Horatio Groves more than all the Jamestown Klallam, save for his mentor, Lord Jim. Horatio often talked to Thomas as though the boy were not even there. Like Indian George.

Halfway across the field, Horatio dropped to his knees and began digging a hole in the ground with his bare hands. After several minutes, he pulled a small wooden box from the hole and dusted it off. Thomas was squatting behind the water trough now, watching intently as Horatio clutched the box close to his body and hurried on across the field, disappearing into the toolshed behind Cook Dan Solomon's house, where he closed the door behind him. Thomas watched the shed for a good while, but Horatio Groves never reemerged.

Later in the day, Thomas walked to Cook Dan's toolshed to satisfy his curiosity. When he pushed the slat door open on its rusty hinges, a blob of light flooded the little shed, illuminating Horatio Groves slumped in the far corner between a rusted plow and a tiny workbench, clutching a bottle to his chest.

"What are you looking at?" he said bitterly. "Shut the door."

Thomas shut the door but not before crossing the threshold, and now he stood in total darkness with Horatio Groves.

"Don't just stand there," said Horatio. "Speak."

When Thomas failed to speak after a moment, Horatio snorted. "You're not touched by spirits. You're just crazy."

Never had Horatio talked to him like this. Thomas heard a swish and the gurgling of liquid as it splashed against the bottle neck.

"You're nothing," observed Horatio. "Just like the rest of us."

The smell of the whiskey filled the dusty darkness.

"Get out of here," spat Horatio. "Before I wring your neck like an old hen."

Thomas backed up against the door, pushing it open, and this time Horatio Groves shielded his eyes from the light.

That night, the boy dreamed once again of the Siwash, but something was different. This time his people were not silent. This time Thomas heard the moans of his grandfather, lowing like a wounded bull. He heard Stone Face slurring his speech and Small Fry laughing. He heard the soft, frightened murmuring of Siwash elders gathering at the edge of the bluff.

In the night when the boy awoke shivering and huddled around the flame of his candle, one word was written larger than all the others inside his head as he stared into the flame, and that word was *ceqwewc*.

"To undo the damage," Lord Jim once instructed, "first, you must make them see."

greasing the wheels

Six dozen strong, eager men with big appetites, twenty and thirty and fifty years old, gnashing their teeth, shouting themselves hoarse, as they carved and hammered and blasted the canyon to dust for weeks on end. Twelve and fourteen hours a day, inch by inch, they did the impossible: they moved the river. From the vantage of the rip-rap bank, standing astride boulders, Ethan watched his destiny unfold, watched as load after load of gravel came down the mountain by flat-car to fill the breach, saw it dumped into the river by the ton, until at last, on a crisp clear afternoon in early spring, flanked by a foreman and engineers, Ethan watched the debris break the waterline, and he felt his heart thrill as the river began to back up into the diversion channels, creeping toward the flood plain. And still, Ethan was restless, still he yearned for the dam itself, yearned to see its concrete bulk rising from the canyon floor, yearned to feel the surge of the giant penstocks as they inhaled the river, its turbines churning water into luminous dreams. It wasn't enough to divert the river, or even stop it in its course; Ethan longed to see the power of the river transformed, longed to see its wild essence burning incandescent in sitting rooms and stations from Morse Dock to the east end.

And what to fuel these dreams of incandescence, if not the sweat of Port Bonitans? At what cost were dams and nations built? Money. Money for manpower and the infrastructure to support it, money for titles and acquisitions, and money to grease the wheels of fortune. Money for rails and rolling stock, money to grate inroads and clear timber, money to turn mountains into dust. Money for the great barge-mounted dredges soon to arrive from Seattle, money for concrete and the power to mix and move it. Every steel cable crisscrossing the canyon, every heavy-headed maul hammering the earth, cost hard currency. And the money flowed, arriving invisibly from Chicago to fuel the beast, but never without strings, always burdened by demands and unreasonable expectations. Still, the money came without fail, and Ethan put it to work.

And who to keep this revenue streaming but a man of Jacob's distinction, a Lambert and, by his very birthright, a captain of industry. Who better to see the big picture than a man from the east? Like brothers, they quarreled in the dusty light of the office, to the ceaseless accompaniment of blasting, like distant mortar fire.

"Don't be naive, Ethan. You can hardly expect them to provide the capital and not gain by it. They're not a bank, they're shareholders."

"They're investors, Jake."

"Precisely."

"*We* are the investment."

Jacob laughed. "I see. Is that how you see it? I rather think our shareholders are under the impression that a hydroelectric dam is the investment, Ethan. Or, to put it more precisely, the power that dam will one day generate."

"They'll get their share," grumbled Ethan. "That's what they paid for. But no more, I tell you. I don't intend to let them steamroll the interests of this town. Without this town, there would be nothing to invest *in.*"

"The town will benefit from the power, Ethan, that is the point, is it not?"

"And what of the profit, Jake? Who will benefit from that?"

"Gracious, you are naive, Ethan. You sound like my sister."

the taste

If success had a smell, failure had a taste. It tasted like gunmetal, and it was strong on Jared Thornburgh's tongue as he sat in his wainscoted office after hours staring at his half-eaten birthday cake. And what a paltry sight it was on its paper plate: a crumbling mound of angel's food with white frosting and an avalanche of jimmies accumulating at its base, baby blue and lemon yellow and fire engine red. How paltry *all* of it was — the wainscoting, the softball trophy, the gilded plastic nameplate, the Rolodex full of seafood retailers, the fucking golf poster: I'D RATHER BE GOLFING. The hell he would. He hated golf, hated everything about it, hated nothing more than the smug camaraderie of its proponents, the reverence they afforded the game, as though it were sacrosanct, some gentleman's rite of passage to walk around in the grass in a haze of martinis, swinging a club at a fucking ball for three hours. What the fuck did Don Buford from Prime Seafood know about sanctity? And the conversation. Ugh. One-upmanship. Big fish tales. And worst of all, business. Always beneath the gregarious laughter and the conspiratorial back-slapping and the air of nonchalance lingered the bottom line. That had a smell, too. It smelled like fish. His whole life smelled like fish. That was the real bottom line. It didn't matter what appearance he cultivated, what car he drove, what his handicap was, what his wife looked like — the inescapable truth was that it all smelled suspect. Oh, he was fooling people, no doubt. He saw them looking at his wife's ass (though he'd had little occasion to see it himself); he saw them admiring the GL-450 (with unit-body platform for maximum comfort and stability); he saw them looking up with contempt and admiration at his office from the processing line, as though he were the man behind the curtain, heir to the Thornburgh legacy, whose father had been a senator, whose father's father's father had tamed the wilderness, dammed the mighty Elwha, and put Port Bonita on the map. Sure, he was fooling them. But he wasn't fooling himself.

Just look at him now with a fucking stapler in his mouth (Ha! As if), and even that wasn't loaded. Look at him, alone on his thirty-second birthday, which Janis (being *tied up late* at work for the third night this week) completely forgot. And where was the rest of that family they planned? Where was the next generation of Thornburghs to comfort him, those sweet-smelling vessels of hope to ease the discomfort of living? Where were they to loll around at his feet in his hour of need? Janis had grown impatient after three months of trying, until finally she took to grasping his manhood with a sort of ferocity, as if she could scare an erection out of it. And when he finally managed to get over the hump, after eight therapy sessions and some little blue pills, Janis wouldn't have him. She just lay there beside him night after night like . . . well . . . like a dead fish.

And how sad had the birthday cake ceremony in the employee lounge been this afternoon, that grotesque cake glowing like something radioactive beneath the fluorescent lights. In cobalt blue frosting: HAPPY BIRTHDAY, BOSS! executed in a rather austere hand. And the card: no penguin in roller skates, no toad with a crown perched rakishly upon its head, not even a punch line, not even an exclamation point after Happy Birthday. Just Happy Birthday. There you have it. You were born on this day, and here you are thirty-two years later, still disappointing yourself, your wife, and the ghosts of your ancestors. And there it was, emblazoned with thirty signatures to which Jared could assign no faces, except for Dee Dee, who had warded off his only advance by wielding her pepper-mace key chain. Thank God they didn't have HR around here, thank God Dee Dee was the forgiving sort.

A few people took advantage of the work stoppage to smoke cigarettes out back. Krig was among them. The rest of them sang "Happy Birthday" with all the jauntiness of Gregorian monks. Nobody called for a speech. Jared cut the cake. People dispersed. And here he was three hours later in his office, the cake growing staler by the minute, the card propped open on his desk in some hopelessly lame stab at sentimentality. No plans. Big fucking success.

Jared knew the battle was over the moment it occurred to him that afternoon in front of the urinal—as he struggled desperately to pee while beside him Krigstadt thoughtlessly fired a wide stream at the porcelain—that in a certain way he envied a guy like Krigstadt, whom he envisioned, in spite of overwhelming evidence to the contrary, to be a happy guy, a hearty, prole-spirited average Joe, who drank canned beer with his buddies and had a thick-carpeted basement and watched football and hockey and wore T-shirts with winning teams emblazoned on them so that he could associate with a winner, and that was enough, the mere association. It was that easy. Raiders 32, Eagles 7. You didn't have to be the coach or the quarterback or the guy in the skybox—you just had to be the guy with the thick shaggy carpet and the Raiders shirt. No scrambling up any social ladder, no debilitating self-consciousness or acute status awareness, just a Raiders shirt that said to the world, "That's fucking right. What are you gonna do about it?"

Why tackle success when you could let the pros do it?

Jared finally mustered the energy to leave his office without knowing where the evening would take him. He figured he'd probably stop by the grocery store and buy a six-pack of Alaskan Amber and maybe some Thai from the deli, go home, watch *World News Tonight* on TiVo, or maybe, if Janis still wasn't home, *The Wizard of Ass.* Maybe he'd poke around online, look into that plat development deal Doug Westermeyer was talking about. Could be a good investment opportunity.

He waved to the Mexican cleaning girl on his way out, Maria, Estella, whatever. She waved back, but she wasn't smiling.

The Goat was still in the far corner of the front parking lot, and Krig's silhouette was visible in the driver's seat. His subwoofer was thumping. Jared checked his watch. Seven thirty. Krigstadt had been off for an hour and a half. What the hell was he doing out there? Maybe he needed a jump.

As Jared approached the Goat across the gravel lot, he saw the flash of an orange halo appear suddenly around Krig's head. And as he drew closer, he observed Krig chicken-necking in time to Aerosmith's "Dude Looks Like a Lady," his hand at his mouth as though he were kissing a butterfly, and a thin joint pinched firmly between his fingers, its little end glowing orange, unfurling a slinky plume of smoke toward the windshield.

Krig was apparently oblivious of Jared's approach, and the tap on the window caught him totally by surprise, yet he was not startled. He stopped chicken-necking and turned down the stereo, but he didn't hide the joint. He rolled down his window.

"What's up," Krig said.

Jared couldn't resist leaning slightly into the smoky interior of the car. The smell of the weed struck a sentimental chord with him. It reminded him, like only smells can, of freshman year at the U, his dumpy room at Delta Sigma Phi, the endless supply of cheap beer, the wonderful thoughtless immediacy of life.

"So what's up?" said Krig, a hint of impatience in his voice.

"You all right? I thought maybe your car wouldn't start."

Krig gave the fuzzy dash a firm pat. "Not the Goat," he said. "The Goat leaves no man high and dry."

Jared snuck a glance at the joint between Krig's fingers. The glance did not escape Krig's notice. "Get in," he said.

Krig was quick to forgive Thornburgh for being an ass-munch and was more than happy to extend the olive branch, but it was Jared who forged ahead once Krig announced that "the doobage was toast."

"You wanna grab a beer?" Jared said.

"Does the pope shit in the woods?" said Krig, who fished his Altoids out of the glove box and popped one in his mouth. He replaced the mints without offering one to Jared, checked his eyes in the rearview mirror, threw the Goat in reverse, and rained a rooster tail of gravel on the sidewalk as he tore onto Marine.

Krig slowed to a crawl once they hit Front. He settled low in the driver's seat resisting the urge to say every single thing that came to his mind, fighting off the instinct to engender familiarity too quickly. Boundaries. He had to remember.

If Krig was trying to erect boundaries, Jared was trying to tear them down. Why not? What was he protecting? What threat could the shag-carpeted domain of Krig's world possibly pose? Jared noticed Krig's ring as Krig gripped the wheel: a chunky gold band with a blue and gold pendant inlay — P.B. '84, it said. "I used to watch that varsity team," Jared offered. "The one with you and Lauridson and Richards. The Bucket Brigade."

They missed the light at Lincoln. Krig gazed out the side window across the Red Lion parking lot toward the strait. He couldn't remember what was there before that, but it was something else. The restaurant was called something else, too. And before that, it was just Hollywood Beach.

"Bucket Brigade, my ass. We blew it," said Krig. "We sure as heck didn't put out the fire against Aberdeen."

"That was just one game," Jared said. "You guys were unstoppable."

"Yeah, for three quarters. We folded, bro. I folded."

"You were a machine. Besides, Aberdeen had that Glovick kid."

"I was one for nine from the field in that semi game. I missed a free throw that could have put us up with a minute thirty-nine to go."

"Lot of time," observed Jared.

The light changed. The Goat crawled into the intersection. "We're talking about the lead though, bro. The *lead*. I was an eighty-eight percent free-throw shooter. They only had one time-out left. No way I miss that shot."

"I don't know, Krig. I don't remember any of that. I was in junior high. I just remember it was the best team we ever had."

Suddenly, no fewer than three fire trucks and a chorus of wailing sirens rounded the corner on Lambert headed in the direction of Wal-Mart. Krig promptly pulled to the shoulder and let them scream past.

"Wonder what that's all about?"

"Probably a fender bender," said Jared.

"Yeah, probably. So, you goin' to Dam Days this year?" Krig asked.

"Hell no."

"Why not?"

Jared waved it off. "What a bunch of self-aggrandizing bullshit."

Krig didn't know what to make of the statement. So he didn't say anything. What was wrong with Dam Days? Sure, the bands usually sucked, and the smoked salmon was overpriced, and the crowds were kind of a pain in the ass, but it was Dam Days, it was a tradition, one of the last decent things left in P.B.

"They want me to write some speech," Jared volunteered as they crested Hogback.

"About what?"

"About my stupid family and a bunch of ancient history I don't give two shits about. Screw that bullshit."

They drove in silence, past Payday Loans and the Wharf Side, past KFC and Taco Bell. They missed the light again at South Golf Course. Jared looked out his window across the deserted Rite Aid parking lot. The streetlights burned expectantly an hour before dusk. At night, this stretch of Route 101 glowed like the aisle of a convenience store. A guy could procure anything from 30-weight oil to Chicken McNuggets along this stretch 24/7/365, a guy could *Shop Rite*, could *Save On*, a guy could even *Think outside the bun* if he were so inclined. A guy could do virtually anything in Port Bonita he could do in New York, Philadelphia, or Chicago. But somehow it was all pretty sad.

"You know," said Jared, looking out across the expanse of empty parking lot. "It's funny how something can keep getting bigger even after it's dead."

Happy hour was over by the time Krig and Jared arrived at the Bushwhacker. Jerry Rhinehalter from Murray Motors was still at the bar, along with a couple of guys Krig didn't recognize. In the corner, a little black dude was having drinks with a familiar husky woman in heels. Was that Hillary Burch from high school — the one who almost bit Tobin's dick off? It *was* Hillary Burch. The little black dude she was with had a milk mustache. This town was getting weirder by the day.

Molly worked the bar solo. She was doing something new with her makeup, and her hair was pinned up over her ears. She looked like a mud shark in blue eye shadow and hairpins. One of her tits was hanging lower. But she made it work. Krig felt his heat rising when Molly came for their orders. Krig introduced his friend as "*Jared Thornburgh*," and though the name apparently didn't ring any bells for Molly, at least she saw that Krig wasn't drinking alone, at least the guy he was drinking with didn't smell like fish, at least the guy was wearing a dress shirt, a fact that might (Krig hoped) allude to his own upward mobility. And unless it was Krig's imagination, Molly was a little more attentive than usual that evening, a little quicker on the refills, now and again flashing a little shark smile when she came for their empties. To top it off, she actually made a stab at small talk, something she'd never done before.

"Hear all those sirens earlier? Crazy."

"Yeah," Krig said.

"Dumpster fire at Wal-Mart," she said, brushing some stray hair out of her eyes. "You guys ready for another round?"

Krig and Jared sat at the bar for two and a half hours, Kilt Lifter after Kilt Lifter, forging separate roads toward a collective past, summoning such points of reference as the Laurel Street stairs, the Lighthouse, and Swain's General Store, enlisting such local benchmarks as the crab festival, lavender days, and the Clallam County Fair. Gradually, their experiential roads began to merge, finally converging in 1986 at the grand opening of the Port Bonita Fine Arts Center, where Jared's dad delivered the keynote speech during the banquet. Krig worked as a busboy. The rest was history.

They ordered some hot artichoke dip. Jared caught Molly eyeing his wedding band as she delivered the dip but didn't say anything to Krig. In what proved to be the crowning moment of their burgeoning familiarity, Jared got Krig to admit that 1:39 was a lot of time, even with only one time-out left.

"The game doesn't end at one thirty-nine, Krig! A helluva lot can happen in one thirty-nine. Now, if you'd missed, say, *six* from the stripe, that's one thing, but *one* measly free throw with a minute thirty-nine left? C'mon, Krig. That's not a game breaker. Give yourself a break." Jared drained his Kilt Lifter. "And besides, nobody remembers the details."

If Jared was kind in his appraisal of Krig, he was merciless in his appraisal of himself. By his fourth Kilt Lifter, Jared could barely contain his self-contempt.

"But I *am* an ass-munch! You were right in the first place. I'm a class A prick. I fucking hate myself. My life is a fucking act, Krig. I've co-opted every bit of potential I may have ever had, and for what?"

After five Kilt Lifters, it was all over. Jared told Krig about the stapler. "I'm the biggest pussy you'll ever meet, Krig. You don't even know what a — *hic* — pussy I am." Jared pounded the bar with a fist, rattling the artichoke dip.

The little black dude shot them a look from across the room. Hillary Burch was fiddling with her blouse.

"C'mon," said Krig. "Let's get out of here."

Jared reached for his wallet.

"I got it," said Krig. Figuring the tab to be around forty, Krig dropped three twenties on the bar, but Molly didn't notice. He rearranged the bills and fidgeted with his wallet a little, and was slow pushing his stool in, but Molly still didn't notice. She was busy with Hillary Burch and the little black dude. But as Krig and Jared were on their way out the door, Molly called after them. "Nice meeting you, Jared."

Krig laid rubber pulling out of the Bushwhacker lot. Though he was smarting a little over the thing with Molly, he was determined not to blame Thornburgh. Thornburgh was okay. He liked Thornburgh. The guy needed Krig. The poor sonofabitch had damned near stapled himself. And on his birthday, no less. Look at him there slumping in the passenger seat. This guy needed to look his demons right in the eye or at least get so plastered that he didn't give a fuck. Krig swung into the Circle K parking lot and left the Goat idling.

"Back in a sec," he said.

Jared watched Krig lumber toward the front entrance. He could hear the muffled *doon-doon* of the bell as he entered the store. He fished his clamshell phone out of his pocket and snapped it open. No missed calls. Janis still hadn't remembered. He snapped the phone shut. Well, at least there was Krig. Jared was ready to submit his will to Krig altogether, go wherever Krig took him. Why not? Clearly, Krig knew something about having a good time. Tooling around drunk in the Goat was a lot better than playing golf with Don Buford. He snapped his phone open again and checked the time. Ten forty. Let Janis worry. Let her figure out that she'd missed his birthday and feel terrible. He turned the phone off, snapped it shut, and replaced it in his pocket.

Jared could see Krig in the back of the store at the glass cooler, contemplating his beer choices. Why couldn't he be Krig? Why couldn't he be satisfied with *Krigness*? Who knows if the guy actually saw Bigfoot? Did it really matter? The guy believed. Or he wanted to believe. That's what mattered. And what was the deal with that waitress? Why did she have to do Krig like that? It was obvious the guy had a thing for her. He wished he could get Krig laid.

After considerable deliberation, Krig grabbed a twelve-pack of IPA and was on his way to the register when the thought of a Butterfinger stopped him in his tracks. He backed down toward the candy, where he found an Indian kid standing perfectly still in the middle of the aisle, clutching a bag of peanut M&Ms and a dead fish — was that a fucking shark? When it became apparent that the kid wasn't going to move, Krig leaned over in front of him and grabbed two Butterfingers. It was then he recognized his job shadow, Rita's kid, Curtis.

"What up?" said Krig.

The kid said nothing. He was baked out of his gourd. It was like he was frozen there in suspended animation, except for his lips, which were silently at work.

"Dude, what's with the fish?"

The kid wouldn't answer. Bending closer to get a look at the fish, Krig saw the burns running up the kid's arms.

"You okay?" Krig looked down the aisle to the guy behind the counter. "Is he okay?" The guy at the counter shrugged. Shrugging back, Krig strode down the aisle to the register and set his beer on the counter.

"'Bout to kick his ass out of here in a minute, if he don't buy somethin'," said the counter guy. "This town's gettin' weirder by the day."

Upon his return to the Goat, Krig lobbed a Butterfinger to Jared, which careened off Jared's wrist and landed on the floor.

"Butterfingers," said Krig.

They crawled straight through town on Front and picked up Route 101 at Lincoln.

"Where are we — *hic* — going?" Jared wanted to know as they passed Gertie's.

"You'll see. Better eat that Butterfinger."

As soon as Krig took the sharp left onto Elwha River Road, Jared knew they were headed for the dam. He wrestled an IPA out of the paper bag between his feet and tried to twist off the cap. Krig produced a church key from the glove box and flipped it to Jared. "Pop me one, too," said Krig.

Jared cracked the beers and looked out the window at the blackness. Now and again he caught a silvery flash of moonlight on the river. Both men lowered their beers as they passed a ranger at the Altair entrance, where, through the alders, Jared glimpsed the glow of a lone campfire along the bank.

"Park rangers can't do shit," Krig observed, swilling his IPA.

He killed his headlights as they pulled into the parking slab. He fished his headlamp out of the glove box. Jared grabbed the rest of the beers, and they walked down the gravel path to the viewing area. The dam was bathed in moonlight. The roar of the spillway, the low, bone-rattling hum of the turbines, the vertiginous dropoff from the lip of the gorge — all of it was dreadful and thrilling to Jared as he gripped the chain-link fence.

"Damn," he said, draining his beer. "Loud as ever." Backpedaling a few steps, he hurled the empty bottle over the fence into the abyss, waiting for a distant shatter of glass, which never came. He grabbed a fresh beer from the box and opened it.

If the dam was a source of dread to Jared, to Krig, the thought of leaving it was dreadful; the thought of walking down the road alone toward the very trailhead where he'd had his recent encounter was nothing less than terrifying. And yet, he was compelled to do so, for his own sake, and for Jared's. Give the guy a few minutes to himself. Let him put things in perspective.

"I'm gonna walk up the road a bit," he said, snapping on his headlamp.

Looking back after a hundred or so steps, Krig could no longer discern Jared's figure in the moonlight. The closer he drew to the trailhead, the darker the night seemed to get. He sat on a big cement block half covered with moss and stared at the dark hulking form of the mountains beyond the clearing, frisking the night with the beam of his headlamp. What was he afraid of out there?

Jared listened to Krig's receding footsteps in the gravel until the spillway drowned them out. After a long pull, he set his fresh beer down by his feet and squatted. Clutching the chain-link fence, he peered down beyond the spillway into the chasm, where he could see the powerhouse partially obscured by undergrowth. How many times had he stood in this very spot, awed as a toddler, curious as a boy, proud as an adolescent? But never had he stood there like this, frightened and ashamed of the thing. How many times had he been reminded of the dam in the years since he started avoiding it? Only to find that there was no avoiding it, that he forever lived in the shadow of this obsolete dam, his fortune linked inextricably to its hulking existence, its legacy of ecological menace. Though he had no vested interest in its fate, no real interest at all, still its presence was inescapable. And why? Because it bore his name. Such were the trappings of history.

"Tear the damn thing down," said Jared Thornburgh aloud to nobody. "See if I care."

'bout fuckin' time

The first night Curtis failed to come home Rita managed to convince herself that he was probably at a friend's house. But had Rita really wanted to be honest with herself (and later she would), she would've had to admit that there was absolutely no evidence — no phone calls (he didn't event *want* a cell phone), no instant messaging, no mention of so-and-so to suggest that Curtis had any friends at all. Never a ride home from school, never the whispers of a conspirator from behind his locked door, always two eyes, never four, peering into the empty refrigerator. Aside from Dan, and to some lesser degree herself, Curtis had scarcely ever connected with anyone in any substantial way. He was a loner, he'd always been a loner. Only in recent years, though, had he become a brooding loner. As a boy, he was content in his aloneness, deep into his distance. He could sit for hours with little occupation. He could literally watch the grass grow. For a time, Rita thought he might be developmentally impaired. Now, he was anything but calm; now, it seemed he was perpetually agitated.

More than Curtis's whereabouts, Randy was concerned with the whereabouts of his "hundred bucks." Settling comfortably back into civilian life, in spite of the fact that he was down to $180 with no foreseeable employment (the muffler shop had been a bust), Randy would have just as soon been without the kid anyway. Christ, even if the little shit stole a few bucks, it was worth it to have him gone. But he knew the kid would be back soon enough, glaring at him from behind those greasy bangs, filching his Salems, basically just being a little shithead all the time.

"He'll come back when he's hungry," Randy insisted.

Rita was more than ready to accept this proposition and did so for the better part of two days. By the third night, however, she required a bottle of Chablis and three beers to ward off her mounting uneasiness, until she finally fell asleep watching an infomercial.

The police phoned at 8:00 a.m. The instant the officer identified himself, Rita felt the unexpected weight of panic like a bowling ball in her stomach, and his voice came to her as though from some great distance. The more the voice explained, the less she understood.

"Found your boy last night in Circle K clutching a bag of M&Ms and some kind of dead fish with no eyes. Stunk to high hell. Wouldn't let go of the damn M&Ms. Got burns on his arms, blood on his shirt. Pupils like saucers."

"But how — what happened? Is he . . . ?"

"He won't say a word. Found a half sheet of Barney Rubble in his coat pocket. Must've been selling the stuff. That's probably at the root of our problem here. Sending him to Olympic Medical Center for psych evaluation . . . Tell me, does he normally, you know, talk? Any kind of verbal communication at all? . . . Hello? Are you there?"

"Yes. Yes, I'm here. He talks. But not a lot. Is there something wrong? Did something happen to him?"

"We don't know anything. He won't talk. It's like he . . . well, like he *can't*. Moves his lips to beat the band, but nothing comes out. Best get down here, ma'am."

By the time Rita hung up the phone, all the warmth had drained out of her.

Randy could see something was wrong. "What the fuck was that all about?"

"The police picked him up."

"Pfff. Figures."

"They've taken him for some kind of psychological evaluation."

Randy burped. "Yeah, well, 'bout fuckin' time."

the leap

As she watched him square the tab, Hillary willfully ignored an ambivalence that extended far beyond Franklin Bell. What was this impulse to act? Why, when it was crystal clear that she and Franklin had no future, when she felt little attraction toward him sexually, was she compelled to prove something? It was the sum of these nagging uncertainties, and her inability to silence them, that finally drove Hillary to the edge. Not two steps into the gravel parking lot, she took the leap.

"How about your place?" she said.

Abandoning the Silverado — along with all contingencies — in the Bushwhacker parking lot, Hillary accompanied Franklin in his green '88 Taurus wagon. The car looked new in spite of its age. The interior smelled like a rental. Hillary liked the car immediately for its sheer lack of pretense. It was quiet and smooth — a gazelle trapped in the body of a warthog.

Having relinquished all preconceived notions the moment he popped in a Neil Sedaka CD, Hillary tried to imagine what it would be like to be with Franklin. He seemed totally at ease at the wheel in spite of the fact he could barely see over it. Piloting the Taurus past Circle K, Murray Motors, and KFC, he hummed along quietly and unashamedly to "King of the Clowns."

From the passenger seat, Hillary scanned Franklin's profile, her eyes straying down to the jelly roll beneath his green-shirted belly.

Feeling her eyes on him, Franklin smiled. "That's my twelve-pack," he said.

That's another thing she liked about him: he was unapologetic. There was so much to like about him, really. She appreciated all the things he *didn't* say, all the sage male wisdom he *didn't* dispense, all the tiresome opinions he *didn't* solicit, even when she tried to draw him out. She liked his short answers. There was nothing ambivalent about Franklin, it seemed. As the Taurus crested Hogback to reveal the panorama of Port Bonita, all lit up from the tip of Ediz Hook to the mouth of the Elwha, Hillary wondered at the futility of her actions. Why did she persist? Why make poor Franklin an accomplice?

"Do you think people are born a certain way?" she said, looking out the window. "I mean, like the people you work with — criminals? Or do you think people are made?"

"People are habits," said Franklin, without hesitation.

"That's it?"

"Way I see it, that's all that matters at the end of the day. What does a person *do*? That's the thing that affects everybody else. Thoughts and intentions sure don't go far, we know that much."

"What if people develop habits that aren't true to their nature?"

"So be it. As long as they keep their noses clean."

"What about people who aren't criminals?"

"Not my jurisdiction," he said flatly.

"Couldn't a person become enslaved by the wrong habits?"

"Hell, happens every day. Look at the way we live. Sometimes wrong is right, though. Sometimes people gotta think outside themselves for the benefit of other folks."

Franklin got surer and more decisive by the minute. Yet, as much as Hillary longed to lean into his self-assurance, as much as she yearned to feel some electrical attraction toward Franklin, she only grew less sure as his apartment drew nearer. She was determined, however, to forge ahead against her better instincts.

Franklin's apartment was a step down from the clean, aromatic roominess of the Taurus. A big step down: soiled furniture and dusty Levolors, a murky fishbowl, casino carpet. The fact that Franklin was unapologetic about any of it was almost enough to redeem the place.

"That's Rupert," he said as the dog nosed Hillary's crotch when she sat on the bile-colored sofa. "Make yourself at home." Franklin took inventory of the fridge. "You thirsty? Beer? I got some Chinese in here if you're hungry."

"I'm not hungry, thanks. But you might want to let those Chinese out. They're probably cold."

Franklin guffawed. "That's baaaad." He snatched two cans of beer from the fridge. "Looks like Rupert is really takin' a shine to you," he said, setting the beers on the smoked glass coffee table.

Gliding to the entertainment center, Franklin began rifling through CDs — pausing briefly to meditate on Steve Forbert's *Jackrabbit Slim* before he found the album that best suited the mood he was going for: Bob Seger's *Night Moves*. Classic.

Franklin seated himself on the sofa, draping an awkward arm around Hillary. She could smell his spicy aftershave, and the rum on his breath, and she thought for an instant that maybe things would be different with Franklin. But even as she leaned in to meet his full lips, and he ran a strong hand down the small of her back, Hillary doubted it.

on your back

Tobin was even more impatient than usual the night he began to suspect Gertie's betrayal.

"What's got into you, whore?" he said, pulling out of her and pushing her into the headboard. "You've been skulking for a week." He grabbed her shoulder and whipped her over on her back. "What's this all about? Gotta case of the clap you're not telling me about?"

Gertie got up on her elbows, and when she offered no reply, Tobin made as if to strike her but stopped himself short and smiled. "Now, why don't you tell me what's on that feeble little mind of yours."

"Well," said Gertie, casting her eyes aside. "Who's to say I'm not nervous about Peaches workin' me out of a job?"

Tobin smiled again, although not as cruelly as usual.

"Ha! Is that it?" He laughed.

Gertie looked up at him hopefully.

"Well, I must say, this news comes as some relief to me, Gertrude. Considering the kind of subterfuge I've come to expect from ungrateful whores."

He leaned down and took her chin in his hand and squeezed it, peering at her through slitted eyes, as his smile wilted.

"Just mind the fact that I hate to lose a whore, one way or another," he said. "Even if she is used up."

WHEN ADAM RETURNED to Port Bonita on his rounds, checking into his regular hotel room at the Olympic, among the messages awaiting him at the front desk were directives from Cal Pellen to proceed directly to Skokomish, Puyallup, and all the way onto Colville in the eastern part of what Adam still conceived as a territory, not a state.

Adam received this news grimly, knowing that it could be months before he returned to Port Bonita. He should have checked on the boy.

"Bad news, sir?" said the clerk.

"Nothing catastrophic, Tom. And none of your business, besides. Is that it for messages?"

"Well, officially speaking, sir."

"Nothing from Jamestown?"

"No sir. But some whore's been asking after you."

Adam shot him a look. "Is that an attempt at humor?"

"No, sir. See, I couldn't rightly tell her as to when you'd be back, so she's been in here nearly every afternoon asking after you."

"How do you know she's a whore?"

"Well, with all due respect, Mr. Gunderson — "

"*How* did you know she was a whore?"

"Well, sir, aside from the fact that I gave her a throw as recently as last month, there was the fact she had a black eye, and of course there was just the plain fact that she dressed frilly like a whore, and if there's one thing about whores in general that gives them away, it's the fact that — "

"Enough. What was she after?"

"She wouldn't say, sir."

"What was her mood?"

"Jumpy."

Adam figured on it, and came up with nothing. "If she comes again, don't send her up, you understand? Just send for me."

"Yes, sir, Mr. Gunderson."

Retiring to his room, Adam dropped his bag at the foot of the bed and moved to the new mirror above the basin, where he was displeased with the unshaven state of his reflection, and the crows feet creeping downward toward his temples. He thought about cleaning up, but found himself lacking the energy. He plopped down on the bed instead, hoping that a short nap might improve his prospects. But his conscience wouldn't allow him to rest. He should have made the stop at Jamestown and checked on the boy. He'd blamed his fatigue this time, along with the late hour, as his carriage rattled past the settlement at dusk. But what of the last three times he'd neglected to make the stop? As ever, he failed the boy, and though it shamed him, he still did not act upon it, which made him exactly what his father had always accused him of being: a coward. For the first time, it occurred to Adam that in spite of his father's intolerance of Indians, he might actually have respected him *more* if he'd owned the truth all those years ago, a realization that washed over Adam like a wave of nausea.

Two hours later, Adam crossed the mucky street and strode tall into the Belvedere with business on his mind. He was not feeling patient, nor a bit rested, and his guilt over the boy still festered to the point of distraction. The blue haze and drunken discord of the Belvedere did little to improve his mood.

"I see not much has changed around here," said Adam, approaching the bar. Though he neglected to remove his hat, he observed his custom of standing at the bar.

"Ah," said Tobin, without looking up from his bar rag. "The White Knight returns. Might I interest you in something in the way of a refreshment — a sarsaparilla, perhaps?"

"Whiskey," said Adam.

Tobin looked up from his rag and stopped his restless scrubbing. He straightened up, and smiled as he poured out two shots, and slid one across the bar.

Adam tossed his shot off in a single throw. "One of your whores has been looking for me, John."

"Is that a fact?" said Tobin. "Whores, too. By God, there's hope for you after all, Gunderson."

"I'm assuming you sent her, John. Is there something you want to tell me?"

Splayed casually against the upstairs banister, making an effort to laugh at the vulgar musings of a butcher from Tacoma, Gertie snuck glances at Tobin and Adam talking. The more she observed of their conversation, the more she sensed with a chill that behind Tobin's chattiness and nervous scrubbing, a dark realization had taken root. She needed to get to Adam before Tobin got to her. Breaking away from the butcher, Gertie slunk into her room and rifled through the drawers of her secretary for a pencil and paper. Her heart was racing when at last she scrawled, *Under the back steps nightly.*

Gertie folded the note and tucked it away in her bust. Quickly, she checked her mascara in the lamplight and smoothed her hair around the edges before returning to the mezzanine and proceeding down the stairs, where she hovered in the general vicinity of the bar. When Adam made to leave, Gertie made her move across the room toward him. No sooner did Tobin register this movement than he broke from behind the bar and intercepted Gertie in the crowd. Seizing her by the wrist, he led her to the corridor and through to the back of the house, while Adam made his exit, unaware of the interference.

When they reached the end of the darkened hallway, Tobin pinned her to the wall, forcing his knee up into her pelvis until her eyes began to water.

"What did you tell him, whore?"

She tried to shake herself loose.

"I asked you a question!"

Stiff-arming him in the face, Gertie eluded his grasp and darted toward the back door. Tobin got a hold of her dress long enough to spin her around and slug her squarely in the face, but when the fabric tore loose in his hand, Gertie scrambled out the back door and down the steps, and Tobin gave chase.

the devil's backbone

Onward Mather and his men trudged toward the Devil's Backbone; ragged, but well fed, filthy, but organized, dragging what they could not shoulder across the hard snowpack. The ancient path promised by the natives was either a fiction or had fallen into such disuse that it was invisible, and so they blazed their own trail, and as always, the Elwha acted as their guide. Upward along the Elwha they traveled through the middle weeks of February, over saddlebacks, across creeks, through wooded canyons, naming all that they passed: Cat Creek; Goblin Creek; Dodger Point; Mounts Carrie, Fitzhenry, and Eldridge. They had put range after range of foothills behind them, and still they had yet to penetrate the alpine interior of the peninsula. However, the delays caused by the boat and the weather were probably a blessing. The weather had turned cold and brutal in recent days and could only get better. Haywood was increasingly of the opinion that had the party managed to penetrate the alpine country on schedule, it was quite probable that they would have found survival nearly impossible.

One evening around the fire, after Cunningham, to the amusement of Reese and Runnells, had just finished his third retelling of a certain medical calamity involving a set of crushed eyeglasses and the derriere of a prominent industrialist's wife from Portland (whose name Cunningham would not divulge, though he spared no detail in describing the glorious attributes of the derriere in question), Haywood suddenly looked up from his journal.

"It is entirely possible, gentleman, that we've been purposefully lulled into this doltish condition of luxury," Haywood said. The remark seemed to be pointed at Mather, who was sitting at some distance from the fire, at once alert and preoccupied.

"And what is that intended to mean?" said Mather.

"That perhaps we're underestimating our adversary. We may find that whatever lies beyond this Devil's Backbone is something entirely unanticipated."

"Like sunshine?" said Reese, eliciting a guffaw from Runnells.

"I'm serious," said Haywood. "I think what we ought to do is expect to be challenged. To go forward diligently. Orderly. Not like a band of ruffians."

Mather knew that he'd been an uninspiring leader in recent days, had not projected his characteristic vim and vigor, had not encouraged his men forward with his unwavering spirit of adventure, had led, in fact, only insomuch that he walked in front of them. He suspected that Haywood's intention was less of a challenge to his leadership than an attempt to rouse the party's enthusiasm for the journey ahead. But the fact remained that Mather's thoughts were far from the future. He was still walking mentally backward through his life, trying to devise a way of thinking by which he could make the past big again.

"Yes," said Mather. "Diligence is exactly what we'll need."

"See here," said Haywood, rising to his feet and leaning toward the fire, illuminating that which had formerly been occupying him, a map in progress. He beckoned the men to gather round the map, and all but Mather gathered around.

"Here is where we've come from, you see?" said Haywood, tracing their path. "And here is where we've been. But you see, *this*, gentleman, *this* is where we're headed. It's blank. The trail ends. The river ends. I haven't the slightest idea what goes here. Not the slightest. Should I venture a guess, I can guarantee you beyond all reasonable doubt that it shan't be anywhere close to what we will actually find there."

25 February 1890

While the mood of the party has been generally good as of late, with Runnells bagging a pair of elk just two days prior, our spirited leader has been more aloof than ever. His appetites cannot be roused. He does not seem to be hungry for the challenge before us. He's even lost the wild-eyed nervous energy that has marked so much of our recent progress. He has been more measured with his steps and with his words. He is, in a word, deflated. I suspect this has mostly to do with something left behind, rather than something ahead, although I am certainly no expert on matters amorous. In any case, I now fear less for Jim's competence or judgment and more for his vigor and strength. The terrain promises, at the very best, more of the same. It remains to be seen if our leader will be up for the task, and I'm hoping that he will soon dispel my doubts.

Runnells's good fortune in bagging the elk did not come without a cost. Heading the bull off as it thundered up the hill, Timber, the big dog, was struck by the beast's forefoot, killing him instantly and leaving his body badly mangled. They buried the dog in the softest ground they could find.

Having traversed some six hundred vertical feet up the scantily timbered face of the Devil's Backbone, the party's hopes of discovering Eden on the far side were soon liquidated by the sighting of another precipitous valley below, bordered by yet another spiny ridge of bald shale.

"The Dark Prince is apparently in possession of two backbones," Mather commented sardonically.

Beyond the second ridge lay two magnificent timbered ranges intercepted by creeks and valleys, and beyond that, a third range in the shape of a crescent surrounding a single hulking mountain of epic proportions, laden with blue glaciers, and cut through with crevasses. It was not a graceful mountain but rather a broad-shouldered one. It did not taper to a shapely peak but formed a wide oval face punctuated by a hard and angular set of extremities, like a sculptured face glowering at heaven.

26 February 1890

It was truly a magnificent site to behold, this behemoth, and yet it too was terrifying, for standing there on the Devil's Backbone each of us knew in our hearts that without the grace of God, we might well perish in these mountains.

Jim, in a rare moment of inspiration, and dare I say ignorance, promptly christened the giant Mount Eva, and somehow I was loath to inform him that the mountain already had a name, and that name was Mount Olympus.

the grace of god

On the first leg of his journey, Timmon had covered nearly seven miles of backcountry; trudging purposefully through the bottom-lands and wending his way into the foothills along the rutty switch-backs, fording streams and crossing gullies, huffing and puffing all the way to the foot of the big canyon, a distance that had taken the cumbersome Mather party weeks to navigate through dense foliage and inclement weather. But it was not winter when Timmon set off from Crooked Thumb, and his long strides had carried him swiftly over the clear path. A single thought sustained him all the way: On-ward. Onward, past the fat-fried stink of civilization, beyond the de-moralizing effects of his plebian existence, safely sheltered from the cesspool of society.

As he drank himself into a torpor that first evening, exorcising his demons by the glow of the fire, he felt at last free of his shackles, adventuresome in his new autonomy. There was nothing left to prove to anyone, nothing owing; he was on his path.

When he passed out four feet from his tent, his withering dingus still moist in the clutches of his right hand, Timmon was nothing if not confident that his trek had taken him safely beyond the reach of humanity. Thus, it was with some confusion (and a whopper of a headache) that he awoke the following morning to the patter of voices from the trail. Slowly, he climbed to his feet and panned the sur-rounding understory with a periscopic gaze. A rustling in the nearby brush froze him. His heart set to racing. Stealthily — on his toes like some Indian tracker — he inched his way toward the rustling. After a half-dozen steps, he was frozen in his tracks by a sustained and hair-raising shriek.

Through a tangle of huckleberry boughs, the source of this deafening wail was revealed in the person of a pudgy little blue-haired lady with her pants around her ankles in the act of squatting. The force of her scream had sent her tumbling backward where she was grounded like a capsized tortoise, dog-paddling in thin air, a fountain of urine saturating the elastic waistband of her jeans. Timmon rushed to her aid. The old lady's caterwaul reached its bloodcurdling crescendo just as Timmon leaned down to extend a helping hand, whereupon the helmeted head of his dingus grazed her chin. Here, her terror met an abrupt end when she passed out cold.

This wasn't happening. No fucking way was this happening.

Now the rest of her group came scrambling (or hobbling, as it were), through the underbrush, arriving just as Timmon was wrestling his manhood back into his pants.

There were five of them, all of them in their seventies at least. In fact, the blue-hair on the ground might well have been the youngest of the lot. They all had matching green pullover sweatshirts with a little patch on the breast announcing their affiliation with the Sequim Seniors Sierra Club. A spindle-legged old sport in a safari hat and high-pocket shorts pushed to the forefront immediately.

"Mildred!" he screamed, rushing to her prostrate form and kneeling on those spindly legs. He began groping for a pulse. "Oh, dear God. What is the meaning of this?" he demanded of Timmon. "Who are you, what are you doing out here?"

"I . . . I was just . . . I was camped over there and I heard . . . and then I . . . I was just. . . and then she was . . . and . . ."

"Somebody go for a doctor!" said High Pockets. "I've got a pulse!"

The four old people looked at one another. They all had walking sticks. The lady with the enormous sunglasses might have been blind. One old guy was still panting from the trail.

"You!" demanded High Pockets, indicating Timmon. "Go for a doctor!"

"But . . ."

"But nothing! Go!"

Timmon jumped into action, breaking toward his campsite.

"Where are you going?" demanded High Pockets. "*That way!* The trail's *that way!*"

"Just a sec." In a whirlwind of activity, Timmon struck his tent, rolled it up, and stuffed the remaining gear into his GoLite. As he strode through the brush toward the trail, he could hear High Pockets shout after him.

"Hurry up!"

Timmon hurried until he reached the trail, at which point he was paralyzed by indecision.

Was she dead? Was it too late? What if somebody wanted him to make some kind of statement, a ranger or a cop or something? He'd be fucked seven ways till Sunday. He couldn't risk it. But what if it were his own grandmother unconscious over there? Certainly that would have made a difference, right? What the hell were these dinosaurs doing way up here in the first place? This was the middle of nowhere. But they got up there by themselves, right? It's not like they were helpless. It's not like they were gonna freeze to death out there waiting for him to come back with a doctor. Were they? But then if he ran, wouldn't he look guilty? What if she croaked and they thought he had something to do with it? What if they found his dick print on her chin or something? Forensics were a bitch these days. And it's not like he could afford a decent lawyer. He'd get stuck with some asshole in Dacron slacks and mustard on his tie, some schlub from a crappy college like EWU or Boise State. Strike three. He'd be a sacrificial lamb. Are you kidding, they'd eat him alive; two-time loser, history of theft, not to mention that other thing with the waitress at the Olive Garden in Silverdale back in '96. No way. Couldn't risk it.

But what if they came after him? Sure, he'd get a good head start, but what if they launched one of those manhunts with the dogs? How long would they search for him before they gave up? How long until a sketch artist's charcoal rendering of him started flashing on TV screens across western Washington? How long before "*police identified the suspect as Timmon Tillman of Port Bonita*"?

Here he was, a free man, still planning his escape.

If Timmon had made quick work of the first seven miles, he tore through the next seven, harried by the thought that eventually somebody would come looking for him. So he beat a path toward the interior as fast as his legs would take him, stopping only twice to draw water from the river. Was he overreacting? He hadn't done anything wrong, not where the old lady was concerned. Besides, she just fainted. A few minutes on her back and she'd be fine. But then, wasn't he just rationalizing his own cowardice and selfishness? What harm would it have done him to go for help? So what, he loses a day? And really, what were the chances that anyone was going to question him? Deep down, wasn't he just saying, who gives a shit? Hadn't he always been saying, who gives a shit? Isn't that what he said at age eleven when he nabbed his grandmother's wedding ring off of the bathroom counter, only to wing it carelessly into the Chicago River two hours later when Fred Catalanotto told him it was shit? Did he give a shit when his grandmother crawled around on her hands and arthritic knees on the bathroom floor, beside herself with anxiety and grief, bonking her head on the bottom of the basin, groping around the sticky perimeter of the toilet, cursing herself as she peered helplessly down the hair-choked shower drain? Did he really give a shit that the old warhorse grieved the loss of that stupid ring for two solid weeks as though she'd lost her husband all over again? The answer was no, he didn't give a shit. He had no reason to begrudge the old woman and every reason to be grateful for her. She practically raised him. Sure, she gave him the occasional beating when she was blackout drunk, but he usually had it coming, and besides, wasn't that her right? She fed him, she housed him, she stuck by him long after his mother died and his old man flew the coop. Yet he still didn't give a shit about his grandmother's loss at the end of the day. Moreover, he felt no remorse for having stolen the last precious vestige of the only man she ever loved and discarding it for shit. All these years he'd figured it was Frank Catalanotto's fault.

That he didn't give a shit about anybody but himself, Timmon came to realize, was the one great truth of his life. His sole motive was self-preservation; it was both his engine and his fuel, the driving force that propelled him ever forward. And how had he ever profited by this selfishness? It wasn't even a big selfishness, the kind that got a guy ahead. Timmon's was a small kind of selfishness, the kind that got a guy just enough to scrape by.

For all his self-improvement in the joint, all of his Walt Whitman and Emerson and Thoreau, for all of his cell-bound forays into religion and philosophy and self-help, for all that lying awake at night and resolving himself to a new life, new patterns, a new way of thinking, it occurred to Timmon, as he switchbacked up the steep ridge, that he hadn't improved his instincts one bit in the past eighteen months or even eighteen years, for that matter. He hadn't *corrected* anything. He was still the same selfish eleven-year-old kid, still looking for an angle, still turning his back on the people that cared the most, still stealing his grandmother's ring. But none of it meant anything where he was going now, and this thought alone heartened Timmon. Self-preservation was the name of the game out here. A guy had better be selfish, or he was dead meat.

By afternoon, Timmon had gained a thousand feet of elevation, arriving at the base of a steep, partially wooded ridge running north to south like a spine. The path switched back at twenty-degree angles up the incline. Now and again as he ascended, Timmon glimpsed the top of the bald, jagged ridge through the treetops. His quads burned. His blister stung. He was thirsty. But he did not slacken his pace.

The nearer Timmon drew to the top of the ridge, the more he was able to put the Sequim Seniors Sierra Club and everybody else behind him, the more certain he became that nobody would come after him. He would be forgotten, even by the state. His whole life had led up to this conclusion — to be forgotten. All the energy he'd spent marginalizing himself, pushing himself ever toward the ragged fringes of society, was not in vain. He would be forgotten. He snuggled up in this thought like the warm shelter of a cocoon and leveled his interior gaze on the future: the nameless creek, the sun-dappled meadow, the days of solitude.

When he arrived at the top of the ridge, Timmon was awestruck by the vista. Beyond the wedge-shaped valley below lay another spiny ridge and beyond that a solitary mountain of massive proportions, snow-clad and laden with glaciers. It was not so much the mountain's height but its breadth that was so impressive. There was no getting around this one, all valleys seemed to lead there. It stood in the middle of Timmon's path like some huge bald-headed bouncer.

And gazing at Olympus, for, surely this was Olympus, Timmon felt the cold reality of death lurking somewhere beneath his skin.

the ghost called memory

It didn't matter how much you moved your lips — nobody seemed to hear you. The man in the white coat was uncomfortably close. You winced in the fog of his aftershave. You could smell the little minty green snake tongue working nervously about in his mouth. Peering inside your ears with a light, down your throat, into your pupils, he kept asking you questions.

How'd you get the burns?

What are you on?

How much?

When?

Where?

But never why.

You tried frantically to tell him about things to come that had already happened, things that were happening even now beneath the thin fabric. You tried to explain to him that you were being chased by a death you had already lived, tried to explain the bone white shark and the hot wind blowing out from the center of the flames. You tried to explain that you were not yourself.

And finally, sensing your urgency, he said, "What is it, son?"

But when you tried to explain about Stone Face, about the sickness, about the death you were determined to outrun, he only badgered you with more questions.

Does this hurt?

Can you see this?

How many fingers am I holding up?

THE BOY WASN'T lucid, by any means. Alert, yes — in fits, anyway. His heart rate was too fast. His reflexes were relatively good. He responded to most directives — *open your mouth, hold out your arm, watch my finger* — so apparently he was hearing all right. His lips were moving like crazy, but it was all gibberish. Kid was out of his gourd. Eventually, he'd return to his senses. Maybe then he'd explain just why in the hell he was walking around town with a dead shark and first-degree burns up and down his arms. Maybe then he'd explain why he stood stone still for forty-five minutes in the candy aisle, clutching a bag of peanut M&Ms until the cops finally rousted him.

The mother was apparently on her way. Single mom, go figure. It's always the single moms. The kid's permit said that he was sixteen. The doctor would have guessed much younger. Cute kid, in a scrubby sort of way. Small and round-faced. When his lips weren't moving, he scowled. Probably led a disappointing life. The kid's shirt said: WHAT THE HELL ARE YOU LOOKING AT? Poor little runt. Now and again, the boy's pupils dilated rapidly, and his legs twitched like a dog dreaming of a rabbit. And when he slipped into a sort of momentary trance, the boy finally uttered his first sound.

Doon-doon, doon-doon, he said.

flight

Catching a heel on the last step, Gertie nearly tumbled face first into the mud but managed not to break stride as she darted off down the alley. Tobin was less fortunate in pursuit. Clearing the steps in a single bound, his boot heels hit the mud and immediately skidded out from under him. Rearing backward, his head struck the bottom step with such force that the world flashed white for an instant. By the time he regained his feet, dazedly, Gertie was well on her way. To where, he couldn't say, but at least she wasn't running toward the Olympic. Maybe to that bothersome whore in the colony. There was still time to nip this thing in the bud, and he knew he'd have the opportunity to nip it. One thing about whores, they always came back. Then again, Gertie McGrew was not your run of the mill whore.

Gertie had no intention of returning as she kicked off her heels and dashed barefoot through the darkened alley in the direction of Hogback. She could not tell whether Tobin was pursuing her. Briefly it occurred to her that she might change her course and backtrack to the Olympic, but that would be as good as suicide if Tobin was waiting for her. But for the frantic beating of her life force, she was deaf to the world as breathlessly she crested the hill at a trot, looking vainly back over her shoulder into the darkness. Below her, the lights of the colony bounced about wildly as they drew nearer. She didn't slow her pace until she was well past the boat shed and on the the path to the cottages, where she pulled up briefly to catch her breath. Not until then could she feel the throbbing of her battered face, or the stinging of her shredded feet in the mud. Not until then did Gertie think she heard footfalls giving chase down the hill, and then she hurried her pace once more.

When Eva, clutching a sleeping Minerva in her arms, answered the frantic knocks with a gasp, Gertie practically fell into the house.

"Dear God, what's happened to you? Who did this?"

"Blow out the lamp," Gertie said breathlessly.

"Whatever for? We've got to —"

"Blow out the lamp!"

Gertie saw the color leave Eva's face as she straightened up and crossed the room hurriedly to blow out the lamp. In an instant the room was awash in darkness, and the world was so quiet that even the beating in Gertie's ears fell silent. Sensing no movement, she was startled to feel the cold flesh of Eva's hand on her elbow and nearly jumped. Minerva stirred in Eva's clutches, and she settled the child. "Shhhh," she said. "Come."

Eva led her by the elbow through the darkness, into the cluttered little sitting room, which she navigated carefully. Groping her way to the corner without upsetting anything, Eva quietly slid the top door of the dresser open and removed the little single-barreled Derringer. It was hardly more than a pencil gun according to Ethan, but persuasive nonetheless. Shepherding Gertie to the rear of the cottage and out the back door, Eva lifted the root cellar hatch and disappeared down the wooden steps. Soon Gertie saw a flash of light from below, the striking of a match, and Eva's stooping candlelit figure filled the jaws of the cellar, beckoning Gertie down the steps.

Once they settled in with their backs against the earthen wall, Eva blew out the candle, and they sat in complete darkness, Eva cradling the sleeping child in one arm while clutching the Derringer in front of her.

"What is this about?" whispered Eva.

"Making a difference," Gertie said. "Or maybe just getting killed."

"Shhhh."

From above came dully the sound of the front door swinging open, followed by heavy footsteps proceeding slowly toward the rear of the cottage.

Gertie clutched Eva's arm, and Eva clutched the Derringer still harder in the darkness, so hard that when she heard the sound of the back door closing, and the footfalls descending the back steps, and finally, the sickly creak of the cellar door as it swung back on its hinges, she could no longer tell whether she was holding the pistol at all.

knowing your place

APRIL 1890

Pulling the cellar hatch back, Tobin was greeted at once by a rush of cold earthen air that set his hair on end. What if the crazy whore was waiting for him with an ax down there? Feeling his way down the steps into the stillness of the cavity, he smelled something else — candle wax? He sensed no movement whatsoever in the tiny space. Arms outstretched, he blindly frisked the emptiness in front of him. He patted around his pockets for a matchstick.

Gertie heard the *switch* of the match and felt the quick acid sting of sulfur in her nostrils, before the flare of the light illuminated Tobin's face unevenly, his eyes black and glossy as obsidians. When he saw the little Derringer pointed squarely at his chest, he sneered.

"You might aim a mosquito at me," he said. But he was frightened, Gertie could tell. His black eyes were alert.

"While sleek in appearance, Mr. . . ?"

"John C. Tobin," said Gertie. "And he ain't a mister. He's a no good sonofabitch."

"While sleek in appearance, Mr. Tobin, I'm told that this mosquito stings quite hard at close range."

"For them that can shoot it," said Tobin. "What about you? You ever shot that pistol?" His match was burning low.

"Ask me again in ten seconds, if you you don't back off."

Suddenly, the match flared and the cellar went dark.

"Still got a bead on me, have you?" said Tobin.

Eva kept her pistol trained straight ahead in the darkness. "Try me, Mr. Tobin."

An abrupt scraping of feet on the dirt floor betrayed Tobin's offensive, as he rushed them blindly, tripping headlong into the dirt wall.

When he recovered, he lit the second match and discovered that the women were on either side of him, Eva still training the gun on his chest, with Minerva in her arms.

"The shovel," she said.

Gertie took hold of the nearby clam shovel and raised it.

"Back out slowly, Mr. Tobin, or I won't hesitate to shoot you."

"John, he doesn't know nothin'," blurted Gertie. "He may suspect, but it's not my doin', I swear! I'm sorry, John."

"Quit apologizing," said Eva, her eyes locked on Tobin's. "You just keep right on moving, Mr. Tobin."

Even as he backed out at gunpoint, Tobin was smiling his cruel smile, first at Eva, then at Gertie, his black eyes laughing. He'd kill her one way or another. If not this moment, soon. And he wouldn't even give it a thought. He'd kill her with no more ceremony than a possum or a rat. That hurt most of all. She raised the head of the shovel still further.

"You're a cruel sonofabitch, John."

"You're a dead whore," said Tobin.

Gertie swung the shovel with an old rage, clipping Tobin on the shoulder. The blow glanced off the side of his face. Dropping the match, he went careening backward into the steps, just as Eva's errant shot rang out, splintering the ceiling above the steps. Minerva began to wail. Eva leveled the pistol once more in the darkness, though the chamber was empty.

Just as he heard the whistle of the shovel inches from his ear, Tobin scrambled to his feet, taking the blow in the back of the leg, as hurried up the steps into the night.

Eva soothed the child, even as Tobin's footsteps grew faint, leaving only a dense silence.

"He's right. I'm a dead whore."

"Come," said Eva. She led Gertie back up the steps and into the house to the sitting room, where she lit the lamp and rifled through the dresser drawer for another round of ammunition, fumbling in the quavering light to reload the pistol as Ethan taught her. It was still a mystery to her how Ethan knew such things. Where did he learn to handle a gun or build a cabin? Where did he learn to believe he could tame the wilds or master his own destiny?

Eva set Minerva in the bassinet. When she succeeded in reloading the pistol, she pressed it firmly into Gertie's palm, then retired to the bedroom with the lamp. Gertie stayed put, still trembling in the darkness with the pistol in her grip. Maybe it would've been better to get it over with in the cellar. Better to be dead already than to deal with the chilling certainty of death. Maybe she ought to turn the pistol on herself.

Eva returned with a full length camel hair coat, a man's from the look of it. She clutched two short stacks of bills fastened smartly with paper bands. Setting the lamp on the dresser, she draped the coat over Gertie's shoulders, where it hung nearly to the floor. Eva stuffed half the money in the coat pocket, then blew out the lamp.

"Come," was all she said.

Gathering the baby in her arms, she led Gertie out the front door, and down the path toward the heart of the colony. They said nothing as they hurried along. The gaping sky was uncharacteristically clear. The stars burned cold, and somewhere in the distance a donkey brayed.

At the Colony Hotel, they circled around the back to the livery, where a half-breed stable-hand was asleep on his pallet with a pitchfork in his clutches. Only when Eva shook his feet did the young man stir.

"Up," she said. "I'll need a horse and a man to go as far Port Townsend, and I've got money." Eva felt the thrill of decision as never before. She waved the stack of money at the stable hand, who jumped immediately into action. "And boots for the lady," she called after him.

Gertie could not help but notice the change in Eva. "What are we doing?" she said.

"You're leaving."

"To where?"

"To wherever that money will get you. At Port Townsend you can catch a steamer to Seattle. Or San Francisco, or the Yukon, if you get the notion."

Suddenly Gertie was paralyzed by a different kind of fear, not the fear of certainty, but the fear of the unknown — it ran cold through her from the roots of her hair to the bottom of her bare feet. But circumstances left her little occasion to ponder. Within moments she was mounting a dark red mare with the assistance of the stable hand, and she found herself clutching the thick waist of a bearded stranger who smelled of campfire, and all of this Gertie acted out mechanically, without a single notion as to her deliverance.

Rapidly, Eva issued the rider further instructions, which washed dully over Gertie's ears. By the time Eva turned her attention to Gertie, she found herself at a rare loss of words.

"Go," she said, as much to the rider as to Gertie.

And as the horse set off at a canter, Gertie McGrew offered only the slow, stunned wave of a hand as she looked back over her shoulder at Eva for the last time.

Thirty-six hours later, upon a chill dawn blanketed with fog, Gertie left Port Townsend on the *Colonel Thomas T. Aldwell,* bound for San Francisco, wearing a new blue dress of a modest cut, a pair of sensible shoes, and a yellow and blue checked floppy bow. On her hip, tucked securely in a square felt clutch, was ninety-six dollars, two hairpins, and a single-barrel pistol.

here

←───────────────────────────────────

the shadow of olympus

JULY 2006

Standing on the narrow ridge with all that he owned strapped to his back, looking over the wedge-shaped valley toward the humbling spectacle of Mount Olympus, Timmon knew, despite the cold reality of death lurking in his bones, that he must cross that threshold to seize his destiny, his nameless creek, his sun-dappled valley, his solitude. Yet standing there in the shadow of Olympus, Timmon was conflicted about his destiny for the first time since he marched out of High Tide Seafood.

For starters, he was out of Snickers bars. Moreover, his crossbow might have been a particle accelerator in terms of his proficiency in operating the damn thing. But worse than the bare bones survival stuff was Timmon's lingering uncertainty regarding the fate of the octogenarian hiking party, particularly that little prune-faced lady who pissed herself. His fate now rested on her. If she was fine — say, a little dehydrated, or exhausted, or even down with a little myocardiopathy (whatever the hell that was), well then, chances were, Timmon was safe. But *if* she had a stroke and her face went all paralyzed, or even worse, she keeled over, then Timmon could be up shit creek with a turd for a paddle. He had a bad feeling about High Pockets, too, the spindle-legged little fucker. He knew the type — Mr. Take Control of the Situation. Mr. Do-Gooder. Mr. Fourth of Fucking July. Timmon saw the way the old man looked at his ink, as though Timmon were some type of common . . . well, criminal. No doubt, the old buzzard would tell the authorities everything, embellishing details to suit his whimsy.

Timmon might have stood ruminating on the ridge for the remainder of the afternoon had something not flashed silver from down in the valley. Scanning the basin, he could find no reflective surface to account for such a beacon — only trees, spurs of craggy rock, and the precipitous shale face of the western ridge. But then, just above the tree line, he picked up the broken ribbon of the trail halfway down the ridge, where he soon intimated two tiny figures wending their way up the bald face of the incline some five hundred feet below him. Once again, the silver point gleamed, and Timmon traced its point of origin to the lead hiker. A wristwatch perhaps. Carabiner, maybe. Possibly an aluminum canteen.

Instinctively, Timmon squatted for cover. Surely, this approaching tandem were no more than recreational hikers crossing the divide from Sol Duc on their way to the trail's terminus at Crooked Thumb. But they were people. That was the problem. Hadn't he had his fill of hikers already?

Prairie-dogging over the ridge, he followed the slow, steady progress of the two hikers up the switchback and guessed that they would be upon him in fifteen minutes, maybe less. He hunkered in the brush thirty feet off of the trail until they finally came trudging through his midst. They were an oddly paired couple of dudes, that much was apparent at first glance. Timmon guessed them both to be in their late twenties or early thirties. One of them — the lanky one with the feral beard and the unmanageable hair — looked homeless. He was hiking in tennis shoes. He had an ancient olive drab external-frame backpack that had seen better days and an army-issue canteen that looked like someone had kicked it there from Fort Bragg. The other guy was a pantywaist, a real yuppie: fancy hiking gear, head to toe. A lot of Velcro, a lot of zippers, a lot of gadgets strapped to his person with carabiners. His wristwatch probably had an altimeter. Timmon caught a brief snippet of their conversation as they passed.

"I don't know," the dirty one was saying. "I guess I just figure there ought to be some sort of like, you know, quality-of-life index or something, you know?"

"What a load of crap," Fancy Pants said, checking his watch impatiently. "Either you play the game to win, or you're grist for the mill. Christ, is that the type of shit they taught you at Evergreen? It's a wonder you don't *live* in a tent."

The Dirty One laughed.

Timmon followed the hikers a quarter mile down trail, where they set up camp in a hollow below the ridge. Fancy Pants had a bivouac tent which would have served Sir Edmund Hillary well at eight thousand meters. The Dirty One simply laid out a tarp.

"Pu-*leease*," said Fancy Pants, beginning to unpack his shiny things and situate them on the ground. "Don't be a boob. There are no nations. It's all about money."

"For some people."

"Yeah. The smart ones."

The Dirty One didn't say anything to that. He just lay on his back, with his arms behind his head, and looked up at the treetops.

"It's the same old game," said Fancy Pants. "Get with the program, Woody Guthrie. War is business, face the facts. We need it. You gotta look at the big picture. Seriously, if Grandpa's generation, or even Dad's had been like you, we probably wouldn't even *be* here. You don't like it, go stand somewhere else." Fancy Pants started repacking his shiny things. "That's the problem with you people," he pursued. "Your ideas. Heh. This country was founded on one idea, and one idea only."

"What about the Boston Tea Party?"

"My point exactly."

Timmon hated that smug little fucker with his fucking gadgets. Mr. All the Answers. Mr. Climb Everything Like It's a Fucking Mountain. Guy like that will lie, cheat, and steal his way to the top. Meanwhile, a guy like Timmon had to lie, cheat, and steal just to stay afloat. All because of the fucking system. Any reservations he had about turning his back on civilization fled while listening to Fancy Pants. Satisfied that the two hikers posed no threat to the pursuit of his destiny, Timmon was just about ready to forge ahead, up and over the ridge, when the Dirty One suggested that they do a little collateral exploration and maybe look for a natural hot spring.

"Shit, you never know. I totally keep smelling sulfur. C'mon. We can just leave our shit here."

"I'm not leaving my shit here," said Fancy Pants. "My BlackBerry and all my shit's in my pack."

The Dirty One was incredulous. "What, Bigfoot's going to steal your shit?"

"No," said Fancy Pants, annoyed. "Animals could get into it or something — bears got my iPod at Whitney last year."

"So, duh, we'll tie the shit up."

Timmon decided in advance, even as the mismatched pair hoisted their packs up and over a nearby fir bough, that he would take nothing from the Dirty One. The Dirty One was okay. He didn't play life like a game and he didn't whine about his stuff. For these reasons, Timmon did not even rifle through the ancient green backpack but turned his attention straight to the fancy pack, which still looked brand new, nicer than anything Timmon had seen at Big Five. Bonded construction, urethane mix, external compression straps, binary hip-belt components. Even a load transfer disc. Fucker must've paid five hundred bucks for the thing. This guy wasn't interested in climbing mountains or communing with nature, thought Timmon. This guy was here to conquer. It even occurred to Timmon that he was doing Fancy Pants a favor, doing the whole world a favor, by stealing his propane stove, his carbon-filtered water system, his *Camp Cook's Companion Guide* (featuring over 150 recipes, made from both fresh and dehydrated ingredients — from simple one-pan offerings, to creative Dutch oven repasts!), not to mention his Enertia Trails dehydrated meals — Switchback Spaghetti, Pinnacle Pasta, and Teton Teriyaki.

Timmon would teach that little fucker about real survival.

In a kangaroo pocket, Timmon found Fancy Pants's wallet. Thirty-six bucks. A couple of credit cards. A fucking Starbucks gift card — a lot of good that would do him out there. He scattered it all on the forest floor, except the thirty-six bucks. He took the thirty-six bucks. Later, he would ask himself why he took the money if he had no intention of ever returning to civilization.

Just before he took flight, Timmon briefly considered just one peek into the old green backpack, just for the sake of curiosity. But he decided against it, he supposed, because he felt something of an affinity for the Dirty One, maybe the last affinity he would ever feel for anyone. Besides, there was probably nothing decent in there anyway.

At the top of the ridge, Timmon paused for one last look at mighty Olympus. But this time a shiver didn't run through him as he stood on the Devil's Backbone — this time he swelled with courage and conviction. His new fancy pack rested comfortably on his back, so that neither his shoulders nor his lumbar were forced to bear the burden alone. There was still two hours of light left. Not a cloud in the sky. Everywhere the warm smell of fir needles, birdsong, the burbling of nameless streams. Somewhere out there in that big country was his destiny. In between, who knew? Timmon began wending his way down the bald face of the ridge toward the tree line, three hundred feet below.

the wisdom of water

Even as the men stood on the ridge looking over the steep valleys toward Mount Olympus, the weather was threatening to take a grim turn. Rolling gray cloudbanks tumbled over the sawtooth range that would soon be christened the Baileys. Mather could not help but wonder at the party's fortunes had they wisely embarked upon this journey in spring rather than winter. But spring was too late. Destiny could not wait until spring.

"Best be getting on," said Mather. "Before our friend Thunderbird comes calling."

And without further pause, the Mather party and their one remaining mule, Dolly, packed tight to the tune of 250 pounds, began trudging through the chest-deep snow, down the bald wayward face of the Devil's Backbone toward the tree line, three hundred feet below.

With the wet wind stinging his face, Mather could not help but wonder where this mythical valley of wide prairies and lush grasses lay. Might they be buried in the snow beneath their feet? Where was this place where the wind stopped howling and the sun nested in a bowl of green goodness? Would this be the place that would awaken in Mather the yearning to pause, to stop, to settle even? He doubted it, as he was beginning to doubt that such a place even existed. The lay of the land was only getting rougher and more precipitous. Between the ridge and Olympus, Mather counted no less than three steep valleys. And none of them appeared to offer easy passage. More disquieting than the terrain was the sleeping wilderness of his spirit, which nothing could seem to stir. While he had little doubt that the passage ahead was to be the greatest and most perilous physical challenge of his life, he could not summon the same thrilling intensity he had experienced along the Mackenzie. He was alert, his senses were sharp, but his steps did not spring with aliveness, the cold air did not excite his lungs. Driven not by his customary restlessness, nor by any crowning sense of anticipation, Mather led his men into the heart of the Olympics mechanically.

For a day and a half the party battled their way through wet, heavy snow, over rugged spurs, switchbacking up and down heavily timbered inclines — valleys within valleys. This terrain had a strange quality that did not speak to its natural formation the way the Yukon, the Rockies, or the Cascades had.

Haywood was also moved to note the odd topography of the Olympic interior.

27 February 1890
There is an observable lack of uniformity to this rugged terrain that suggests great chaos and upheaval in its past. These mountains do not seem to rise up, so much as explode out of the earth, colliding, as though they were competing for room, all crowding in on Olympus as though huddling around her for warmth.

On those increasingly rare occasions when his thoughts turned to Eva, something bitter began to rise in Mather's throat, not because he would never possess her, and not because he could no longer summon her smell or the touch of her delicate hand, but because, like everything else, the thought of Eva did not arouse him; not even the thought of her swollen belly stirred him. Love may abide in some quieter form, Mather thought, but nothing was more transitory than passion.

Upon the second morning following their departure from the Devil's Backbone, the party broke camp from the narrow wooded bottomlands of the first hollow. The steep valley was bitter cold, receiving only scant hours of sunlight each day. Ahead lay a convergence of ranges, a sort of eruption in their path resulting in two giant clefts running west and southwest respectively.

Reese, who in recent days had become quite friendly with his former nemesis, the mule, was pulling up the rear with Dolly's lead firmly in his clutch, as the party ascended the rise past the tree line, past the last stunted firs, and onward toward the next ridge.

"Hope you know where you're going," Reese shouted. "Because I sure as hell don't!"

Gathering all the spirit he could muster, Mather looked over his shoulder and, raising a fist, broke into a bearded grin. "Straight down the gullet of Thunderbird, gentleman!"

Only Runnells laughed.

The truth was that Mather did *not* know where he was going. Throughout the previous afternoon, he had been pondering the two massive clefts that lay ahead and knew that within two days' time a decision would have to be made as to which direction to cast their fates. In spite of the levity he projected for the benefit of the party, Mather understood all too well the gravity of this decision. The stakes did not get higher. Stores were dangerously low. The weather and the terrain were growing increasingly hostile. The decision could well mean the difference between success for the expedition or the death of the entire party. Never along the Mackenzie had Mather agonized thus over his course. With the Mackenzie, decisions had been rather clear. The river had been his guide in most cases. In this case, the Elwha seemed to offer no clear guidance; this was not the wide river they'd come to know but rather a narrow and circuitous channel dashing their expectations at every turn. Neither did the mountainous terrain suggest a logical route through the high country.

The very morning of the impasse, while eating his cold stack of gillettes by the weak fire — the last gillettes he would eat for the remainder of the journey — Mather pondered the decision still.

"You ain't said two words all morning," observed Reese, on his haunches by the fire.

"Just putting some coal in my belly," he said, producing a half smile.

Indeed, there was coal in Mather's belly, and it was a slow burning panic. Was it fear that had him leaning toward the west? Fear that the southwest route would be the longer crossing and that food scarcity was more likely to catch up with him and his men? Or was it recklessness that drove him west? The courage to lower his shoulder and charge straight at Olympus, just as he'd charged up the gut of the Elwha. An honest accounting of himself that morning by the fire yielded the unsettling suspicion in Mather that it was the former. And had he given his own doubts the power, had he been able to summon any passionate response whatsoever to the journey ahead, it might have been one of mortal fear.

After an hour march up a pristine snowfield — the last visible thing approximating a gentle rise — the party arrived at the base of the wedge-shaped collision of mountains that formed the junction of the two valleys, one running southwest to the head of the Elwha, the other due west toward Olympus. Mather stopped in his snowy path until the others pulled nearly even with him. The wind was whistling on the plateau, swirling with snowflakes, stinging the men's faces.

To be heard over the blow, Mather was forced to project his voice. "Well then, here we are," he said.

"And just where the devil is here?" said Cunningham, uneasily.

"In the thick of it," was Mather's reply.

Reese was scratching Dolly's neck, though the beast was disconsolate. The skin of her legs was scraped clean below the knee. Her forelegs festered. She wheezed for breath in the thinning air and did not bother to narrow her eyes against the windblown snow, as Reese tried to give her comfort.

"What have you got in mind?" said Haywood.

Mather had both options in mind. "I suspect west will get us where we're going more directly," he said. "Does anybody reckon differently?"

Nobody reckoned differently — at least, not out loud — that the westward route was not the right choice.

1 March 1890

I fear that leaving the Elwha, rather than rejoining her on her southwest journey, will prove to be a fatal mistake. Given the state of our fortifications, it is madness to proceed due west. I held my tongue only for fear of dividing the party, and I strongly suspect I shall regret not saying my piece. We'd be infinitely wiser to follow the Elwha as originally planned. All things considered, this broad valley has been good to us, and I suspect she would offer more of the same eventually. There is a wisdom to water, and I would sooner follow this wisdom than put my trust in the instincts of men. Especially not the James Mather we've come to know in recent months. Though perhaps it bears mentioning that I have doubted Jim's judgment in the past, and he has proven me wrong. For this reason, alone, I consent to go west.

ONE HUNDRED SIXTEEN years later, even with the benefit of Haywood's grim accounting of the fateful decision, Timmon Tillman, standing tall upon the same gentle incline — though it was bare of snowpack in high summer — would make the exact same decision as Mather and head due west straight at Olympus.

looking back

JULY 2006

Already, Hillary could feel the full force of her hangover approaching, a beating of blood in her temples, a fog of juniper rising up out of her throat. Beside her on the bed, flat on his back with the sheet pulled back, exposing the springy gray hairs of his chest, Franklin snored calmly in long, even measure. With her head propped on two pillows, Hillary stared straight ahead at the window, where the flashing neon of Bonita Lanes played upon the Levolors. Maybe it had been a little different with Franklin, maybe Franklin was gentler than most, a little more generous and attendant with his physical offerings, but now that it was over, she only felt dull and remote, like a stranger in her own body.

Hillary crept from beneath the covers and padded to her heap of clothing at the foot of the bed, where she dressed in darkness. When Rupert began to whimper, she stroked his big square head to settle him down. Franklin sputtered briefly, rolled over onto one shoulder, but didn't awaken. Tiptoeing out of the bedroom, she closed the door behind her without latching it, crossed the living room, and slunk into the night, clutching her high heels.

The night was unseasonably cool. A thick marine layer was rolling off the strait. At the bottom of the steps, she fastened her heels, wobbled a few steps across the parking lot, and nearly tripped in a pothole. Wrestling the shoes off, she threw them aside disgustedly and proceeded barefoot across the lot. She never was comfortable in heels. Heels were frivolous. So much of being a woman seemed frivolous to Hillary. By tenth grade, she'd stopped cultivating her feminine mystique altogether. She started wearing shirts instead of blouses, chose wood shop over home ec. When she double-lettered in soccer and volleyball, a few of the boys started calling her Lesbo.

But her crowning moment of humiliation came junior year, when

Kip Tobin asked her to the prom. For about eleven minutes, she was foolish enough to believe that Kip actually saw something in her, until she intercepted a hushed confidence in front of Dave Gubb's locker. That was the end of innocence for Hillary.

Going to that prom was probably the last courageous thing she ever did. She drank rum and root beers in the parking lot by herself beforehand, and showed up a half hour late. Kip and his friends seemed surprised to see her at all. Kip was not complicit at first. The punch line had already been delivered, as far as he was concerned. But Hillary grabbed Kip's hand and dragged him onto the dance floor, where, finally, after a little encouragement from his wrestling buddies — Lauridson, Gubb, and Gasper, mostly — Kip began playing his role to full effect. And all night long, Hillary obliged, playing the fat oblivious Cinderella to Tobin's leading man, as he spun her in circles on the dance floor, winking not so covertly at the jeering student body gathered round them. Hillary smiled through it all, until, finally, the joke got old, and apparently it no longer felt like sport to Kip. He was actually contrite by the end of the evening, or at least willing to let Hillary suck his dick in the parking lot after a half-baked apology. Of course, it didn't hurt that Hillary had been pushing her breasts up against him on the dance floor all night, while the Lonesome City Kings maligned everything from "Space Cowboy" to "Thriller."

But she showed Kip Tobin, didn't she? She brought him to the knee-buckling edge of climax, and right when the flash pots were due to explode, right when his eyes started rolling back in his head, she bit into him as though he were a celery stick. Sure, he gave her a lump on the head, and a shiner, and rekindled his campaign of humiliation with a new fervor in the coming weeks. But who got the last laugh that night? And who got the last laugh the night of their ten-year reunion at the Seven Cedars Casino, when everybody was still calling Kip "Happy Meal"?

Somehow, though, that last laugh never redeemed her. Even now, twenty years later, barefoot and fogbound in the parking lot of Bonita Lanes, the sting of humiliation couldn't have been fresher had Franklin Bell delivered it an hour ago.

nothing personal

AUGUST 2006

When his nine o'clock still hadn't arrived at ten after the hour, Franklin anxiously checked and rechecked his schedule. Randall Hobart: assault with a deadly weapon, two counts aggravated assault, resisting arrest, a string of drunk and disorderlies, and a history of domestic calls. The thought of losing another one made Franklin momentarily queasy. After a final glance at his watch, he was relieved to discover a lean tattooed figure standing defiantly in the doorway.

"Hobart?"

Hobart nodded his shaved head, just barely.

"Step inside. Take a seat."

Hobart took a seat, sitting low in his chair.

Franklin snatched the file off the desktop, and scanning it momentarily, began absently humming "Night Moves." "Okay, Randall," he said, at length.

"Nobody calls me Randall but my mama. It's Randy."

"Well, you're ten minutes late, Randy."

Randy narrowed a snake-eyed gaze at Franklin. "Yeah, well what can I say? Shit happens."

"Not on my clock. And just what shit would that be, anyway, Hobart? What could possibly be more important than your parole status? You like it on the inside, is that it?"

"Hell no. My shit is all fucked up."

"What's that supposed to mean?"

"For starters, it means my old lady's kid got himself locked up in psych ward. Cops picked him up high on acid or some shit. But not before he jacked a hundred bucks from my wallet."

"This happened this morning?"

"A couple days ago. But she was supposed give me a ride. Instead she's down there at the loony bin. So I had to take the shame train. Fuckin' thing was twenty minutes late."

"Always somebody else's problem, ain't it, Hobart?"

"Fuckin' a."

"Always somebody else fuckin' things up for you, ain't that right? Somebody always makin' your road tougher, right, Hobart? Isn't that how it goes?"

"Just a-fuckin'-bout."

"Let me ask you something, Hobart. What do you do for fun now that you're sprung? No, wait, let me guess. I'll bet you like to go down to the bar and have a few beers with your old lady, or maybe just solo. I'll bet you like to feed a few crisp dollar bills into the jukebox and play some pool. And I'll bet you're pretty decent. Bet you run a table now and then. Bet you hardly ever lose — at pool, anyway. And I'll bet you're feelin' okay for the first three beers or so. But maybe as the night wears on, you start feelin' a little restless, like you been there before. Sorta stuck, am I right?"

"You ain't wrong."

"I know how it is, Hobart. You think I don't know how it is? It's cold out there. You find a little comfort, you stick. That's human. We like that. We like to stick. Let me tell you about stuck, Hobart."

But even as he began telling Hobart about stuck, Franklin knew two things: (A) that he already had this kid dead to rights and (B) that he couldn't care less what became of Hobart as long as he didn't break parole. There was no light in Hobart's eyes. Hobart wasn't the kind you inspired — too lazy and unimaginative. And dumb. Hobart was the type you cajoled into submission by dotting his *i*'s for him. You facilitated Hobart's dependence by scaring him with paperwork, by convincing him, finally, that keeping your nose clean and following a few simple rules was easier than negotiating the intricacies of the state, should he fail to comply. Hobart was one of the ugly victories you ground out in the fourth quarter from the stripe, not the harrowing victories that distinguished the sterling record above all else. The kind of victory Timmon Tillman might've been. Tillman had potential. Tillman wanted something better for himself. The guy read a lot of books — obviously, he was looking for answers. Maybe Franklin had asked the wrong questions. Maybe his pep talks had sounded disingenuous in the end. Where had he lost Tillman? Was it the second meeting, when Franklin had decided against his better judgment to keep Tillman on a steady diet of optimism?

"So you're sayin' it doesn't matter shit about my past?" Tillman had said.

"Hell, no. That was then. All you gotta do is take the initiative, son."

Why had he called him son? He'd never in a million years call a guy like Hobart son. So why Tillman?

"Bullshit," Tillman said, halfheartedly.

That's why, the halfheartedness. Because somewhere in him, Tillman wanted to believe in something, wanted his glass half full. Franklin could see in Tillman's eyes the potential for decisive action, the determination to make some great leap in the face of lousy odds, the sort of reckless heroism that could drive a man to extraordinary acts.

"Look, we both know I'm stuck with the record," Tillman had pursued. "Which means I've got shit for opportunities on the outside. It doesn't matter what kind of high-minded bullshit I fill my head with — trust me, I've read books, hundreds of them in the klink: poets, philosophers, you name it. None of it means shit on the outside when it comes to getting ahead. The only thing that means shit out here is my record."

"That's where you're wrong, Tillman. But first things first: Stop sayin' 'shit' every other word. Because the man who says 'shit' every other word ain't the man that's gonna get ahead."

"Ain't's not a word."

"I ain't ahead," said Franklin, pausing to sip reflectively from his eggnog container. "Ever think maybe I'm just talkin' to myself here, Tillman? Maybe you and me, we're not so different. What you need, son, is a plan."

"Yeah, and what plan is that?"

Franklin narrowed a steady gaze at him. "Got me. And it wouldn't do you a damn bit of good if I told you. It's gotta be your plan, on your terms. And plans you don't talk about. Any fool can talk about 'em. I reckon you could go down to any bar on Front Street and find somebody willing to give you an earful of plans. I'll bet you heard all kinds of plans in the joint. I'll bet you've heard the same plans three, four times from the same guys. Real plans ain't like that — and damn it you're right, I gotta stop sayin' 'ain't.' Plans you decide. Plans you act out, Tillman. Slowly. Steadily. Plans ain't — *aren't* — gonna happen overnight. Rome wasn't built in a day."

"Burned down awfully quick," observed Tillman.

"True enough, son. Takes longer to build a life than destroy it."

Tillman was a smart kid. A few warts on his personality, but nothing like Hobart. Kid like Tillman just needed a break. When the second session with Tillman wound down, Franklin had walked the boy to the door, and they'd talked about hobbies and interests with the sort of familiarity Franklin never shared with his parolees, because familiarity undermined his authority and sent the wrong message to guys who were always looking for access, particularly when it was easily gained. But with Tillman, Franklin had been familiar. He'd set the tone himself. He'd elicited familiarity. Tillman had said he liked camping. He'd said that it nearly drove him crazy in the joint not being able to camp. He said at night he would sometimes lie in his cell and stare up into the darkness, trying to summon the smell of a wood fire, a smattering of stars through the treetops, the grit of fish skin on a cast-iron skillet. Timmon was a poet when he talked about camping. And he didn't say "shit" once.

"What about you?" Tillman wanted to know.

"Oh, no. Not much of a camper myself."

"How come you never see black people camping?" Tillman wanted to know. "I've been camping two hundred times at least, and I don't think I've ever seen a black person camping."

Franklin laughed, and gave Tillman a warm, almost fatherly pat on the back. "Son," he said, "we been campin' our whole lives."

"SO, WHAT'S THE deal?" Hobart wanted to know. "Can I leave now, or what?"

"Yeah, you're free to go. And you best be on time next time, got it?"

"Yeah, I got it."

Watching Hobart leave the office, with a sneer and a nod of his blue shaven head, Franklin knew Hobart would be back. Probably even on time. Guy like Hobart wouldn't have the balls or the ambition to jump parole. Guy like Hobart would keep fucking up time and again but never on purpose.

no handmaid

The bumpy progress of the carriage inspired giddiness in the child. The world was brimming with endless quantities of sunshine—indeed, it tickled her face around every corner, set her eyelashes to fluttering. All around her were the stirrings of possibility, darting spritelike in and out of the shadows beneath the sunlit canopy. Whether or not she was coming or going anywhere in particular did not occur to the child. She had no thought of the future, no thought of the past. She was simply afloat in the sun-drenched forest.

Hoko stroked the child's forehead in a way she had never stroked Thomas as a baby—gently with the backs of her fingers. Minerva gave a coo and a giggle and flashed a wealth of pink gums. Her front teeth had broken through at last.

As though the child's mirth were some cue, Eva set aside her notebook—in which she'd been distractedly scratching out another false start on her story-to-be—and reached across the narrow aisle to scoop Minerva out of Hoko's lap. Holding the girl aloft like a mirror, Eva felt the tears welling up once more and promptly manufactured the smile of a young mother. This was just temporary, she told herself, a few weeks at most.

"And how is Mommy's big girl? Does Mommy's big girl like carriage rides?"

As the child began to fidget in her arms, Eva quickly exhausted her store of placative measures: the tummy tickle, the nose rub, even the aching promise of the nipple, from which she'd recently weaned the child. But Minerva would have none of it.

Something hardened in Eva's stomach as she passed the infant back to Hoko, and the child calmed down immediately. Retrieving her notebook from the berth beside her, she set it in her lap but did not resume her writing. Instead, she looked distractedly up at the wooded hillside, as the valley unfurled behind them. One cannot provide what one does not have to give, she reminded herself.

They came to the wide-plank bridge spanning the swamp. A single winter — the crossing of perhaps three hundred ox teams dragging a thousand chains, countless lengths of timber, a seemingly endless procession of carriages heaping with fortifications — had taken a toll on the crude structure. In a year's time, the bridge would be replaced by a much larger bridge, one built of concrete. In a year's time, steam would come to the forest, and the ox would become all but obsolete.

The clearing at the head of the canyon had grown exponentially since Eva's last visit, exposing stubbled hillside all around. The far bank of the chasm had been blown open well below the lip, and the canyon was now a good deal wider at the top. A huge timber scaffold was being erected up the canyon wall. The little valley was filled with voices. From a distance, Eva spotted Ethan among a small gathering of men. He seemed to be drawing elaborate plans in the air in front of them.

The chaotic crisscross of furrows carved into the soft terrain by wheel and hoof and heel had hardened into gullies in the flat expanse of dirt that had once been the meadow. As it now stood, the clearing had the look of a battlefield, right down to the pitted earth and the smoldering stumps strewn along the edges.

Taking the baby back from Hoko, Eva navigated the rutty terrain carefully on foot, clutching Minerva tightly against her chest in spite of the child's protestations. Ethan was apparently unaware of their approach, standing near the edge of the chasm like a general, pointing this way and that, issuing directives, outlining stratagems, mobilizing his troops. But Eva knew the truth. He wasn't really mobilizing anything anymore. *They* were, from a boardroom in Chicago, cigar smoking men, leaning back in their chairs with their bellies pushed tight against the waistline of their suit pants, men like her father, fat with prosperity, not babies, saddled with destinies, not diapers. And this, Eva was taught her whole life to believe, was her destiny: to marry right and bear children, to be a loyal unquestioning daughter, sister, mother, and wife. To subordinate her every whim and ambition. All of this strengethened Eva's resolve as she marched toward Ethan.

TO HOKO, THE little cabin on the bluff seemed small and homely amid the ravaged valley. The huge timber scaffold straddling the gorge made her uneasy. It did not belong there. The very proportions of it were troubling. That the white man believed himself the master of the river was no small conceit. Hoko knew that eventually he would learn otherwise.

She found Indian George on the stoop of the cabin. His yellow scarf was filthy, his small-brimmed hat misshapen. He did not seem his usual self, the way he sat with slumping shoulders and his calloused hands at rest in his lap, as though they'd given up on something. He nodded but did not smile upon Hoko's approach. Never had Hoko seen George in such low spirits. She took a seat beside him on the stoop, where they sat in silence. Hoko took a slow panoramic inventory of the busy valley, fraught with tiny workers. They scurried around like ants — thoughtlessly, yet purposefully — bearing burdens bigger than themselves.

"If the river were meant to be stopped," she said, "then it would not be a river."

George nodded his affirmation. "That is true," he said. "But a river is easier to stop than a white man."

They both fell to silently watching Eva cross the rutted clearing toward Ethan.

"How is the boy?" George said, at last.

"The boy is in Jamestown."

"Abe Charles thinks the boy is a prophet."

"Abe Charles believes what he wants to believe."

THE INSTANT HE spotted Eva approaching with the baby, Ethan broke into a broad grin and abandoned his work. Eva knew in advance for whom the smile was intended, a fact that was confirmed instantly, when Ethan snatched the child from her arms. He swung her once about in a circle and held her above his head and looked up into her cherubic face before cradling her in his arms.

"You ought to have sent word you were coming," he said. "Just look at me, I'm a mess."

"I won't be long, Ethan. I've come with a purpose."

Ethan smiled at her. "You always do, my love. I can only hope that you've finally seen clear to — "

"I'm leaving Minerva," she said.

Ethan went cold. "What do you mean, you're leaving her?"

"I'm leaving her with you."

"But — what — for how long?"

Eva could not bear to look at him. Swinging around to avoid his perplexity, her voice faltered. "Indefinitely," she said. "However long it takes."

"It? What are you talking about?"

"I need time to work unmolested. Perhaps a week, perhaps two."

"For heaven's sake, Eva, look around you! What are you saying? You can't possibly — "

"I've contracted a woman."

"Certainly not that whore you've been keeping company with?"

"That 'whore' was my friend. You should be so lucky. I've provided a woman to see to Minerva's needs until such time that — "

"A woman?" Ethan peered over her shoulder. "You mean to say that Indian on the steps there? She's to be the mother of my daughter?"

Eva strangled her grief and swung around to face him. "I'm the mother of your daughter! What's more, you're the father of your daughter, and I daresay you haven't been acting it."

"Eva, this is no place for a child! Not yet!"

"Then you'd best make it one," she said. "If you can build a dam, then I should think a nursery wouldn't be too much trouble."

business

SEPTEMBER 1890

Eight days after she'd left Minerva, Eva was back at the construction site. Upon her arrival shortly before dusk, she proceeded across the muddy flat toward the office, at which point she was directed rather vaguely by a man with a broom to a location outside, where Ethan was most likely to be found. Eva set out to find him, her notebook clutched tightly against her cotton blouse and her chin thrust out above her collar and tie like the prow of a steamship. She resolved herself once more not to cave in to weakness, not to let her affections for Ethan or the child get the best of her. She must stay true to her course. She must bear in mind at all times the burden of responsibility placed upon her shoulders by the public interest. She must not waver in her beliefs, because beliefs were bigger than individuals, bigger than babies and husbands. Beliefs could do anything with enough steam. The evidence surrounded her. The unconditional surrender of the valley, once wooded and remote, now seemed complete. What remained was a ravaged landscape, scarred and splintered and blasted.

Ethan stood with the baby in his arms on the near side of what was once a narrow gorge, gazing down at the dry riverbed, where day and night men hammered lengths of steel into the earth, and the great dredgers heaved and grunted ceaselessly, coughing out clouds of bitter steam. High-scalers worked the scaffold on the far edge of the canyon, now straddled by a great wooden bridge like a train trestle. One day, in the not so distant future, they could begin pouring concrete into the box molds, setting them in place. Soon the water would begin to rise on the upriver side, and Lake Thornburgh would begin to be a reality.

When Ethan registered Eva's approach, he bolted upright in a rush of gratitude and relief. Eva stopped well short of him, but Ethan soon bridged this gap, planting a kiss on her forehead, which she received with the magnanimity of a queen. The child did not stir.

"Oh, Eva, thank heavens you're back. I knew you'd come to your senses."

Looking at the baby, all wrapped up like something precious and delicate, Eva felt herself weaken. She ached to hold the child. She ached too for Ethan's embrace. For all his rough edges, he looked handsome. But she fought the aching. "I did not leave my senses, Ethan. I merely left you."

"*And* your child, lest you've forgotten."

"*Our* child," she said, brushing a maverick hair out of her face. "To whom I've devoted the lion's share of my time and energy ever since the day you decided to build an empire in the middle of nowhere. *Our* child, I might add, who appears to be doing quite well asleep on your lapel."

Ethan could not disguise a certain pride in this fact, and a smile played again at the corners of his mouth. "At any rate, thank heavens you're back."

Eva turned from Ethan and the baby. In that moment she very nearly caved in. The only thought that sustained her was that she needed just a little more time, and it would be better for everybody. "I'm not back, Ethan. I'm here on business."

"Business?"

"Yes, business. That's what you run here, isn't it?"

"See here, what is this all about, Eva?"

"That's what I'm here to find out. For starters, I — *we* — should like to know just who you and Jacob are forging partnerships with. Honestly, Ethan, what became of 'bringing hydroelectric power to the people'? What happened to 'completely revolutionizing the economical industrial conditions'? I'm here for an accounting."

"You're here to do a *story*? Surely, you've got to be joking."

Eva crossed her arms. "I'm quite serious."

"What happened to birthing cows and bridle paths?"

"And I quote, Ethan: 'Who do you think is going to roll up their sleeves and put this place on the map? Men like your father? Stodgy old capitalists with no vision, the bed partners of senators and — '"

"That's not fair, Eva, and you know it."

"Isn't it?"

"This dam can't be built without money from the east. It's just not possible, and all the Utopian rhetoric in the world is not going to *make* it possible. It's simply a financial reality."

"Whose financial reality?"

"Report what you want, Eva, but know that my hands are tied. If it's a lamb for the altar you're looking for, well, look no further. But why stop there? Why not sacrifice your daughter's future while you're at it?"

"Sacrificial lamb. Ha! You've lost all sense of proportion, Ethan."

"Have I? This from a woman who abandons her child to write stories for a—"

"Don't be evasive, Ethan. You've been selling your dream to the people of Port Bonita since day one, selling them on *equitable* returns and convenience for all, as if they had some vested interest in—"

"They *do* have a vested interest! How can we have growth with—"

"With what, Ethan? With . . . with migrating capital? So that men like my father can—"

"The resources are endless, Eva! Goodness, woman, look around you!"

Looking around, Eva thought she saw the future.

"It's a wasteland, Ethan."

"Think of the future, I beg you."

"Whose future?"

"All our futures. The future of Port Bonita—and yes, even your commonwealth. The future has already begun. Don't you see, Eva—I don't want to surrender control, but I can't stop the momentum. And it's actually a good thing, this outside money. It shows confidence in our economy. A hundred years from now this dam will still be the engine of Port Bonita."

Eva looked him squarely in the eye, and what she saw in his unwavering gaze was the very same determination that had driven him to this place, and nothing less. He still believes, she thought, he sincerely believes: in progress, in destiny, in his own place in history.

chill waters

Minerva came to know the caress of rough hands, and the deafening crack of mortar blasts from dawn until dusk. She came to know the yellow light of late summer slanting through the window and how the dust turned somersaults in its radiance. She slept always with the orange pulse of candlelight behind her eyelids and the soft murmur of gruff voices beneath her dreams. And she slept well. And each time she woke, it was as though she had done so for the first time, and the newness of life was a thing to crawl up inside of, a thing to savor on her tongue, a thing to grasp with chubby fingers at every opportunity and not let go. She came to know a sea of voices and a sea of faces, and a thousand different smells, from the sweet spice of rough-hewn cedar to the chalky itch of basalt dust. And her favorite smell of all would become the acrid odor of her father's neck, her favorite touch, his calloused hand. There were days in the waning summer and early autumn when he took her far from the clatter of the canyon, to the chill waters upstream, where she lolled on the riverbank beneath his delicious gaze, sharing it with no one, and she watched the endless stream of silver fish fighting their way upriver as though their lives depended on it, little knowing that they did. The silver fish were a miracle in the sunlight, a river running inside the river, a leaping, wriggling ribbon of life. And it felt to the child as though the whole world existed in the shade of an alder, on the bank of a river, beneath the gaze of her father.

kaw mix bux

They kept calling you Curtis. They wouldn't stop calling you Curtis. They thought you were me. *How are we today, Curtis? Are we ready to talk today, Curtis? Curtis, this is so and so, he'd like to ask you a few questions.*

When they weren't calling you Curtis, they were asking their endless questions:

Does this hurt?

Can you feel this?

How many fingers?

How many fingers now?

And the woman. She always cried. Every time they brought her in and sat her down in a chair in front of you, she would smile her brave smile, but then she would begin to cry. *My baby,* she would say. *What happened to my baby? What have they done with my baby?*

You tried to tell the woman that you didn't have her baby. You tried to tell her in your silent way that you would help her look for her baby. If she could only get you out of this place.

And she would cry again. And blame herself for losing her baby.

Do you remember the day she came with the picture books? And how, at first, you just looked at the pictures, but then you began to read the talking white spaces, and you recognized the white spaces because you, too, talked in white spaces. At great length, you tried to explain that to the woman, but like everybody else in that place, she could not understand white spaces. She only looked at the pictures.

Everywhere there were shiny things, and colorful things, hard and smooth as bone. Things with no straight lines, which you liked. You picked them up and ran your hands over them, and tried to ask the people questions about the things.

Does this hurt? they would answer.

Can you feel this?

How many fingers?

They would not let you wander. They followed you where you went. They followed you to the window, where they watched you look out. They led you outside the window and walked you around in circles on the yellow-striped ground. You liked that. You wanted to go farther, but they would not let you.

The food they brought you had strange flavors. It was always too hot. They encouraged you to eat with a fork. The fork was strange and flexible and white. You would turn it over and over in your fingers and bend it this way and that and snap its long white teeth off. You would wave it at them, laughing in white spaces about funny teeth. They would smile, but not really. Mostly they just watched the fork very carefully.

Curtis, they would say. *This is doctor so-and-so, he'd like to ask you some questions, Curtis.*

When the woman came you managed to communicate your desire for more picture books, and for the first time she seemed to understand you. They all seemed to understand you.

He really responds to the kaw mix bux, they would observe among themselves. They brought you others, but they were not the same. They had white spaces, but no John Proudstar, no Thunderbird. When you tossed them aside, they shook their heads in disappointment. The woman began to cry again.

My baby. What happened to my baby?

you never know

With her apron strings still dangling, Rita wrestled her hair into a net, just as she noticed Krig upstairs standing at the smudged Plexiglas window looking down at her. He glanced at his watch and, with a wince, scratched his shaggy neck.

Rita pretended she didn't see him and took her place on the line next to Hoffstetter who, pausing with a handful of entrails to wipe his mustache on a shirtsleeve, also checked his watch.

Twenty minutes later, Rita found herself seated in Krig's dingy cubicle, gazing at the mottled brown carpet. She could feel Krig's eyes upon her as he sprinkled nondairy creamer into his Styrofoam cup and gave it a pensive stir. How long had she been at High Tide? Seven years? Eight? Could it be eight? Jesus.

Though Rita knew it was highly unlikely, part of her hoped Krig would just cut her loose. Part of her wanted her whole world to go up in flames.

"Everything all right at home?" said Krig, finally. How long had Rita been there, he wondered — five, six years? Until three weeks ago, he didn't even know she had a kid. He hated this managerial bullshit. He hated being the man. The truth is, he liked his years on the line a lot better than the front office, except for the crappy paycheck. He liked the camaraderie of the line. He could remember the late eighties, when they were moving ten, twelve million pounds a year through this place. They'd stack up a lot of overtime in those days. And go to the bars after: Kip Tobin, Williams, the whole bunch of them. Life felt like a Bob Seger song back then. Krig felt like part of something. Port Bonita ruled.

"Everything's fine," said Rita.

Krig stifled a sigh and was about to scratch his neck but went for his coffee instead. Rita could tell that the whole line of questioning was uncomfortable for Krig, and she felt a little sorry for putting him in this position.

"Then, uh, I guess my next question would be . . . uh . . ."

"Okay," she said. "Everything's not all right at home. Actually, if you want to know — nothing's all right at home. Not one single thing in my life is all right — it's all wrong."

"Ah," said Krig.

"My son is having serious mental problems . . . he's . . . they're not even sure if . . ." Rita pulled up short, fighting back a wave of emotion.

She remembered the night she first brought Curtis home from the hospital. He was a happy baby, calm and curious. He slept through his first night and well into his first morning. Rita watched him sleep most of the night and awoke in the morning curled on the love seat next to the bassinet, clutching her grandmother's quilt. Where did everything go so wrong? Where did their lives jump track and become so hopelessly derailed? What happened to the calmness, the curiosity? She didn't even know where her grandma's quilt was anymore.

"I'm sorry," she said. "I just . . . it's been a . . . the last couple weeks have . . ."

Krig scratched his neck yet again. "No, no. Not a problem. You, uh, need some time off. Or . . . ?"

"No," she sniffled. "Look, I can't afford to. I need this job. I'm barely making it as it is. I don't know what's going to happen with Curtis, I just . . . everything is . . ." Cursing her weakness, she succumbed finally to hoarse sobs.

Krig felt like a gorilla trying to comfort a canary as he rested his big hand between her shoulder blades. He could feel her spine through her cotton sweatshirt. "We can juggle some stuff around," he said. "Figure out some kind of arrangement."

Back when Mullen was GM, and Krig, gooned on Rumplemintz and Old English, had broken his collarbone trying to tackle a weaner pig down at Tobin's dad's place, Mullen had worked out a special arrangement for Krig. You had to take care of your people. That's just what you did at High Tide. That's what you did in Port Bonita, USA. If that made him old-fashioned, so be it.

"Look, I'll talk to Jared," he said.

Rita sniffled.

"How much time do you need? Two weeks do it?"

Rita nodded, wiping her eyes.

"Let me talk to J-man. Thornburgh and I are drinking buddies."

Rita daubed her smeared mascara and looked at Krig hopefully for the first time. "You drink?"

Krig smiled. "Does the pope shit in the woods?"

SITTING SHOTGUN IN the Goat, Rita was ashamed of herself for feeling better, but the shame was a lot easier to swallow than the cold hard facts: that her son was likely brain-damaged, her relationship was a powder keg, and she was likely to spin in the same circles the rest of her days — unless she took the initiative to change her orbit. Why risk the heartache, the loss, and all the attending mess? Why confront the naked truth if you couldn't change it? Why not just feel better? Her thoughts turned reflexively to Randy, and she tried to chase them off, with little success. He was doubtless at home on the sofa, four beers deep into a six-pack, offering up his signature brand of wry commentary aloud to various television advertisements. *Ford, my ass . . . Pff, NAPA, yeah right, Never Any Parts Available.* Midway through beer six, Randy would begin to wonder where the hell Rita was with dinner. She'd have to tell him she'd been at the clinic with Curtis all evening. He'd grumble about it, but what could he do? She'd pick up a BBQ beef and some Jo Jos from Circle K to placate him. Him. It was always about him. Another guilty finger prodded her at the thought of Curtis. She was using him as a happy hour excuse. Suddenly, she had half a mind to ask Krig to turn back toward the plant. If the Monte Carlo would start, she could still squeeze in a half hour of visiting time.

Last Thursday, Curtis had showed marked improvement. The burns were healing nicely. He'd finally issued his first sound. Baby talk, sure, but the specialist was heartened. He said there was light in the boy's eyes, that he seemed to want to communicate something.

The Bushwhacker was slammed when Krig and Rita arrived. Molly was working the bar and the floor, circling the room like a frantic mud shark. Krig spotted an empty stool next to Jerry Rhinehalter and figured if Rita sat in it and Krig loomed like a buzzard, they could probably chase Rhinehalter off in ten minutes flat. The guy was probably supposed to be at a little league game or something anyway. He had a whole gaggle of kids. But as Krig was considering this course of action, a two-top opened up in the far corner, and he ushered Rita across the crowded bar, even as Molly began busing the table. Krig was hoping for a little familiarity from Molly to help him break the ice with Rita. *Hear about the Wal-Mart fire? Guess it was arson.* Something like that — some little piece of news. Something that engendered familiarity or confidence, something that said Krig belonged here.

"I'm out of Kilt Lifter," she said, promptly sashaying off with a loaded bus tray.

"That's Molly," explained Krig.

"Yeah, I know. I used to work with her at Gertie's."

"Small world."

"Mine sure is," said Rita.

After two PBRs, Rita was able to put Curtis and Randy out of her mind. She found that she liked listening to Krig talk. He was pretty smart. His mind had scope. A lot more scope than Randy. Mostly, Krig was a good distraction. He talked about all kinds of weird shit — Bigfoot, Atlantis, something called the Bimini Road. She hoped he was picking up the tab but kept ordering two-dollar PBRs just in case.

"You never know," he was saying. "There's a lot of unexplained phenomena out there. You know anything about string theory?"

"No."

"Me neither, really. Google it — it's some pretty tripped-out shit, I know that much. Parallel universes and that kind of thing. Wormholes. Dark matter. I saw it on the Science Channel — not that I put too much stock in the Science Channel. Their Bigfoot coverage is crap."

"Mm," said Rita.

"Sorry, if I'm talking too much," said Krig.

"No, no."

"I have boundary issues."

"It's okay," said Rita. "It quiets my head."

"You sure?"

"Positive."

Thus encouraged, Krig proceeded to enlighten Rita on — among other subjects — the musculature and carriage of the female Sasquatch featured in the Patterson footage. *You couldn't fake something like that. You have to look at the muscle groups. Watch the flexation in the legs and the butt. The bending of the knee joints and stuff.* Krig talked about the cultural tracks of Sasquatch through centuries of Salish and Klallam cultures, hoping Rita might have some unique Native American insight to offer — something along the lines of what Meriwether Lewis Charles Running Elk had offered him at the Seven Cedars Casino. But Rita just nodded all the while, sipping her PBR at a pretty good clip. Krig talked about the Gaussian curve of the footprints. *Believe me, a hoaxer just isn't going to understand the weight distribution of a biped that size enough to fake something like that. He'd have to be some kind of expert on the mountain gorilla — there's no way Patterson knew all that stuff.* But never did Krig broach the subject of his own experiences along the shore of Lake Thornburgh. That's one boundary he wouldn't allow himself to cross.

The more Rita listened to Krig, the more she leaned into his curiosity, the more she liked that Krig didn't profess to have all the answers. Krig was willing to speculate, willing to wait and see. This seemed healthy. Rita had decided long ago that she already knew all the answers. Stunted. That's how she felt. Like a frost-damaged tree — as if no amount of warmth could ever undo the damage. And yet she seemed to be thawing with each PBR. Until finally it wasn't enough to listen.

"Do you think people can change?" she said.

Krig very nearly broached the subject of his encounter on Lake Thornburgh. Certainly that experience had changed him. "Yeah, sure."

But it was as though Rita could hear him thinking. "I mean change themselves."

Krig gazed into his beer, spun it in his grip, and finally took a big gulp. "Well," he said. "After my dad left, and my mom was . . . well, she went a little nuts . . . I was sort of forced to be the — "

"I don't mean adapt. I mean *change*. Completely reverse everything that's come before. Obliterate it. Because you decide to, not because something else decides for you."

Krig was pensive once more. All these questions made him thirsty. Why the sudden turnabout in Rita? Why did it seem that the boundaries were always shifting? Krig had no idea where the line was anymore. "Hmm, okay," he said. "How about this? Back in my JV days, I was a point guard — I distributed the ball, I tried to make everyone around me better. It was my instinct to pass, see? But Gasper and the rest of those clowns just couldn't finish. I mean, not even a damn layup. It was like throwing perfectly good passes into the abyss. And none of them could shoot from the perimeter, so we couldn't beat a zone. So after sophomore year, I decided I could help the team more by shooting. So I developed a wicked — "

"You're talking about your role on a team. In high school. I'm talking about you. Me. Without roles." Rita gazed out the window. "Can we really be whoever we want to be, now that we've collected all that we are?"

Krig knew the answer was no — for all the mysterious possibilities and unexplained phenomena in the world, the trappings of identity wouldn't seem to budge. The whole process of becoming was reductive; each choice was like another bar in the prison of self. Everything got smaller. This from a guy whose name had been reduced to a single syllable.

"I think it's an uphill battle," he said, at last. "You'd need a lot of momentum."

"But you still think it's possible?"

"I do," he lied. "Maybe the key is to let the person you want to be make your choices."

Choices, ha! Krig knew about choices. Krig knew that you didn't always choose for yourself, no matter who you were. Sometimes other people chose for you. Who passed up a hoops scholarship to Eastern Oregon to stay with his mother? Really, didn't she make that choice for him? He could've been a biologist, a primatologist, an anthropologist, instead of some half-baked cryptozoologist bullshit artist. Maybe then, somebody would believe him about the upper Elwha, maybe then somebody would take him seriously. Maybe if he'd drawn different boundaries for himself in the first place. But he didn't, did he? Because he was scared shitless, that was the real reason. That's why he never left P.B. — he was afraid. Exhibit A: his trip to New York for his twenty-first birthday. He was gonna see Ewing at the Garden. He was gonna check out the Chrysler Building, see the Museum of Natural History (he even read books back then). He was gonna drink beer in Times Square, eat a steak at the 21 Club, maybe even take in that dumb *Miss Saigon* on Broadway.

And what happened?

He flew into LaGuardia and totally wussed out on taking a bus to the subway, like he'd promised himself. He took a cab straight to the front door of the hostel on 103rd and Amsterdam, where he checked into a room with six farting Dutchmen. He was too intimidated by it all. He felt vulnerable. Once he finally quit procrastinating with his toiletries and ventured out into the Manhattan night, he didn't make it far. He almost walked into Oscar and Tony's, around the corner, and almost ordered a beer. But peering in the window, he paused, got indecisive, made a false start toward the door, made another, but stopped himself. When he felt he was being watched through the window, he felt like a total pussy and fled to the corner store, where he bought three Foster's oil cans and a pint-sized plastic Statue of Liberty coffee cup to drink them out of.

Where did he go with his coffee cup and his beers? To the pulsing variegated madness of Times Square? Did he stroll along the edge of Central Park? Did he sit on a bench and watch the rich pageantry of the Big Apple as it passed him by?

Not quite. He went straight back to the hostel, where he spent the evening playing bumper pool by himself, listening to Sinatra on the old phonograph. He hated Sinatra. What a cheese-dick.

The next day, he ventured as far as Sal's Pizza, twice. He returned to the corner store to stock up on oil cans for his Statue of Liberty cup. He got pretty proficient at bumper pool. Even old blue eyes started growing on him. Gotham was never the same after Krig's barnstorming birthday weekend. They're still talking about him in Times Square.

He never went back to New York. He never went anywhere. After that, he stayed right in Port Bonita, where he was once a double letter in hoops and wrestling. Port Bonita, where he could curl up in the familiar security of his one-syllable name. Yeah, okay, maybe people do change. Maybe they get more afraid the fewer choices they make.

"I'm sorry," said Rita. "God, I'm a wet blanket. Let's play darts."

They played 301 and two games of cricket. Krig tried to let her win every time, but she sucked too bad. They talked about movies, and Krig resisted the urge to bring up *Sasquatch: Legend Meets Science*. They talked about music, and Krig was willing to forgive her for hating Jethro Tull, even willing to forgive her for saying she hated "him" instead of "them." They talked about some of the crazy shit they did in their youth. Krig told her about wrestling weaner pigs, about locker-room shenanigans — neglecting to mention that he was invariably on the ass-end of these shenanigans. Of course, he avoided his adventures in New York.

As the evening progressed, Rita made up a whole new youth for herself, one without the creepy stepdad and the couch surfing. She painted the rez of her youth as the person she wanted to be might have experienced it. She painted an adolescence that might have been Marcia Brady's. She even invented siblings. A brother Joe and a sister Gail. A household of rank-and-file orderliness. A silver tiara on prom night. And each fiction was more thrilling and liberating than the last.

Rita was giggling in the passenger seat as Krig pulled off of Marine and into the back lot of High Tide. Her laughter ended abruptly when she noticed a shadowy figure sitting on the hood of the Monte Carlo.

"Oh shit."

"What?"

"Turn around — no, it's too late, just let me out here."

"What is it?"

"Randy."

"So what's the big deal?" said Krig, pulling up next to the Monte Carlo. But hardly had he uttered the words, before the big deal became perfectly clear. In a flash, Randy was wrenching Krig out of the driver's seat, even as Rita tried desperately to pull him back into the idling car. But Randy won the tug-of-war, and Krig soon found himself facedown in the gravel lot, breathless, the right side of his torso burning like fire and ice.

Rita leapt out of the car and tried to pull Randy off, but she was no match, never was.

"Shouldn't have crossed the line, douchehammer!" Randy observed, delivering a crisp right foot to the kidney. "How does it feel now, fuckstick?"

Krig would remember thinking if he could only get to his feet, he could take this shrimp. And he could have. He could have rolled to the left and popped up — Christ, shouldn't that have been his fucking instinct? Once he got on his feet, he could have had his way with the little ferret. He had the size, the reach, the superior strength. He could've rolled, popped, and bing-bang, he'd have been on his feet. Done a quick duck under, and got him low. Pretty soon he'd have had all that weight on top of him. If he rushed Krig, Krig could've got him in a body lock and shook him around like a rag doll. Better yet, got him in a head shuck, and start twisting that skinny little neck. Either way, he could've had him. But where was Mr. Double Letter? Mr. Double Letter was flat on his beer belly, wincing at each blow, saying to himself, *Just get this over with.*

Krig watched dazedly as Randy forced Rita into the Monte Carlo through the driver's side, kicking and screaming — at least *she* was putting up a fight.

With one arm on the wheel and the other fighting her off, Randy whipped the car in reverse, swung a 180, and immediately stalled.

Krig had a window there. A chance to turn the tides. A chance to revise his history. All he had to do was get his fat ass off the ground and rush the car as Randy turned it over — once, twice, *three times,* with no success. Krig could have ripped that little weasel right out of driver's seat and pummeled him.

But he didn't, did he? Worse, he distinctly remembered thinking — after Randy's third failed attempt at turning the car over — *C'mon, start, start, damn it!* He remembered thinking, *Don't flood it, you idiot, you're gonna drain the battery.*

And even more vividly than Krig remembered the shame and humiliation, he remembered the relief that washed over him when the engine caught on the fifth try, and Randy and Rita tore out of the gravel lot.

AN HOUR LATER, Rita collided with the edge of the bathroom door but only after Randy called her a whore and struck her with a backhand across the face that sent her careening across the hallway into said bathroom door. After much shouting, and more shoving, Randy cried like a baby for forty-five minutes, apologizing profusely for his very existence. *I can't help it,* he whimpered over and over. *I just love you so much.* And before she even realized it, her eye had swollen half shut, and Rita found herself comforting an inconsolable Randy on the bed until two in the morning, eventually succumbing to his sexual advances. For ten minutes, he fucked her even harder than usual and, having spent himself inside of her, rolled over and fell quickly to sleep.

Rita lay awake half the night, worrying. Why did she have to get poor Krig involved? What if he was badly injured — what if he was dying in that parking lot right now? She had his cell number, what was she waiting for? After two six-packs and all the excitement, Randy was out cold. When Rita couldn't stand it anymore, she stole out from under the covers and across the darkened room. The floor was still strewn with Curtis's laundry. She tiptoed out into the creaky hallway and quietly closed the bedroom door behind her.

In the darkness, she located her purse on the kitchen counter, fished out her cigarettes, her cell phone, and a lighter. In only a nightshirt, she snuck out the back door and down the steps. The night was considerably colder than she had imagined, clear and moonless. The stars were spattered brightly in a wide brushstroke across the sky. Rita padded in bare feet through a dew that was turning to frost, around the back corner of the house to a single lawn chair on a buckled slab of concrete overgrown with long grass. She pulled her knees up under her nightshirt for warmth and lit a Merit. Clutching her cell phone, she looked briefly up at the sky and shivered. How was it possible that the stars burned cold? How was it possible that they burned at all? The sight of them caused Rita to shiver once more. She pulled her legs in tighter under her nightshirt and smoked her Merit down to the filter and snubbed it out on the concrete. She lit another before dialing.

"Krig?" she said, just above a whisper.

"What up?" he said groggily. "Who is this?"

"It's me, Rita."

Krig sat up in bed in the glow of the television. "Hey."

"Are you . . . are you okay?" she said.

Locating the remote on the pillow beside him, Krig turned off the TV and settled into the darkness. "Yeah. A little sore, I guess. What time is it?"

"I don't know," said Rita, exhaling. "Late. Or really early."

"What about you?" he asked. "Are you okay?"

"I'm fine. Everything is fine. I just . . . I'm sorry that I . . ."

"No worries. I needed my ass kicked, I think."

"Are you sure you're okay?"

"It's *you* I'm worried about."

"I can handle myself," she said. "But thanks."

They lapsed into silence. Krig could hear Rita smoking.

"Krig, I . . . all that . . . tonight, when I was . . . look, I . . . I better go."

"Say it."

Silence again. The sound of Rita smoking.

"All that stuff I told you tonight, that stuff about me growing up —
none of it was true. I don't know why, I just . . . I guess I just wanted
to step outside of my life, you know? I was having fun."

"I think I get it," he said. "I've made up stuff before."

"I wasn't lying to you because I . . . I don't want you to think . . ."

"Really," said Krig. "It's okay. I don't think anything. I think your
boyfriend is a dick, but other than that . . ."

"Thanks. I mean for, you know, defending me, I guess."

"Defending you? That's a laugh. I didn't even defend *myself*. Jesus,
I may as well have been a piñata."

Rita stopped her giggle short when a light snapped on in the trailer.
"Shit."

"What is it? You okay?"

Rita snubbed out her cigarette. "I gotta go," she said.

the specialist

AUGUST 2006

Doubtful, that's the vibe Rita got from the specialist. She saw it in the first cursory blue-eyed glance he bestowed upon her when they met in the corridor. He didn't inquire about the black eye; in fact, he hardly seemed to notice it. Still, Rita could feel the force of his doubt as he leafed through his clipboard distractedly, his golden brows scrunched upon his tanned forehead: doubtful of her qualifications as a mother, as a woman, as a human being. Rita could tell that he blamed her for Curtis.

"We think he understands us," the specialist said, not looking at Rita's black eye. "And we know for certain he can hear us. The tests show he can hear us." Here he heaved a sigh and shook his head doubtfully. "Frankly, I'm at a loss; we're all at a loss. There's no edema, no clotting — nothing to suggest trauma. Nothing in the EEG points to neurodegeneration. In short, we're finding nothing to account for the deficits. The tests have told us all they can tell us, I think. I'd like to send him to a specialist."

"I thought you were the specialist."

"A different specialist," said the specialist. "Someone nontraditional." For the first time, he looked at Rita's black eye, and Rita looked back at him defiantly, but the specialist did not shrink from her gaze; he merely shook his head doubtfully and made a notation on his clipboard.

It was raining pitchforks when Rita emerged from the clinic. She sat in the driver's seat of the Monte Carlo in a desolate stupor, listening to the rain assault the roof with a clattering both sharp and dull. She had no notion of where to go from there. Mechanically, she fired up the Monte Carlo and found herself heading in the direction of home.

Rita tried to remember a time when home was not at the very least an ambiguous proposition. She had to go all the way back to the summer of her eleventh year, when her parents were experiencing "difficulties," and Rita lived with her grandparents two miles off of the rez, near town. Only then, in the absence of her mother's bitter silence, relieved of the eggshell uneasiness inspired by her stepfather, did Rita come to know something other than cold comfort. Only by subtraction had she ever experienced the ease and succor of domesticity. With her grandmother, Rita spent her days making lavender cakes, and mending clothing, and folding laundry with one eye on the television set, while her grandfather was at work canning. In the afternoons, Rita and her grandmother would drive to town on errands, with Rita's grandmother sitting rigidly in the driver's seat of the old red truck, all five feet of her, clutching the wheel fiercely. She looked like a potato doll, though she couldn't have been fifty. That was 1979. Poco was all over the charts. Chic, Anita Ward, the Little River Band. Every afternoon in the truck, on the drive to Swains, or the grocery, or Coast to Coast, Rita hummed along with the radio. Her grandmother chimed in with smiling eyes for Eddie Rabbitt and Shalamar. Sometimes they drove as far as Jamestown, past the spit, beyond Happy Valley, around Sequim Bay, to the tribal center. Rita loved these drives. The world felt big and full of possibilities.

Her grandfather never came home tired; he arrived smiling, an hour before sunset. Over dinner he talked of his day — whether or not it was full of adventure — and always, in his playful manner, he asked Rita about her day.

"How many marriage proposals did my girl get today in town?" he'd say.

"Only four," Rita would say.

"Four? Is that all?"

"Okay, maybe five."

Her grandfather grinned at her, spearing a steamed carrot off his plate. "When am I going to meet these young men?"

"I said no."

"All four times?"

"Five."

"Good girl."

Every evening, while her grandmother tended to the dishes and made her grandfather's lunch for the following day, Rita retired with her grandfather to the den, where they sat side by side on the green sofa and watched one television show together. Rita always got to pick the show — it didn't matter to her grandfather what they watched. All of it seemed to amuse him.

"You come down to Forks, sometime," he'd say. "I'll show you real dukes of Hazzard." Or "Three is a crowd, and eight is more than enough, if you ask me. But . . . different strokes for different folks, I guess."

Other than those two and a half months with her grandparents, when had Rita ever known life to be reliable, predictable, comforting, something to sink into like a green sofa? The refrigerator was always deliciously full at her grandparents' house. There existed in the lives of her grandparents a sense of the imperturbable, a sense that nothing could jeopardize the foundation on which their house was built — indeed, it *had* a foundation, it was a real house, not a metal box. Even the rain didn't matter in the summer of '79. The ten weeks went by in an instant, though Rita tried to preserve them for a lifetime. But the ruinous effects of time were stronger than nostalgia in the end.

After that summer at her grandparents', things only got worse at home. Rita's presence made things tougher on everybody. Her mother seemed to resent her and did little to buffer her from her stepfather's fury, which needed no impetus. There was no youth center on the rez in those days, no library, no bus to town, and soft-spoken Rita had few friends to offer her distraction. And like Curtis after her, she spent long hours in her tiny room, yearning for invisibility. Her stepfather could not be avoided, though, and as Rita approached womanhood, even her bedroom fell under his dominion. The doorknob was removed, so that Rita could not so much as dress without fear of intrusion. And as she blossomed into maturity, she took to wearing baggy sweatshirts and did not bother with cosmetic frivolities. Her voice had grown willowy soft. Some nights her stepfather would burst through the knobless door in his underwear and order Rita to make him a sandwich or fetch something from the carport, and always when she obeyed she could feel his eyes upon her.

Finally, Rita left home at fifteen, following three months of sexual humiliation that, though it never evolved past the touch of a calloused hand upon a thigh or beer-stinking breath upon the back of her neck, was all the more humiliating because it made her feel ultimately unworthy of such attention.

The decision to flee that afternoon in 1983 — following a particularly humiliating episode involving a tampon — had proved to be neither for better nor for worse in hindsight. Rita could not help but wonder how things might have turned out had she sought the safe haven of her grandparents' instead of the patchwork support system of marginal personalities she'd woven together while planning her escape. Sometimes she slept in Trish Groves's garage. Sometimes at Mal's, a forty-year-old woodworker she'd befriended at Traylor's Diner, where she often whiled away the late-night hours drinking coffee in a booth farthest from the window. Mal never laid a hand on her, but Rita often felt the force of his gaze. His desire was palpable from the sofa across the room, and though she slept, she never slept easily at Mal's. She should have never dropped out of school. That decision, perhaps more than anything else, sealed her isolation. It forced her underground. Throughout her fifteenth year, Rita's invisibility, like her survival, became a matter of guile. She avoided the rez altogether. But even two long miles away, avoiding authority in its many guises proved to be an unrelenting challenge in a town the size of P.B. She kept odd hours, avoided downtown, she walked down the least trafficked streets. The worst part of it all, though, was the fact that she was frightened to leave Port Bonita. What held her there?

Rita's meditations on the past were rudely interrupted when on the edge of town, the Monte Carlo stalled in front of Murray Motors, where Jerry Rhinehalter was standing in the showroom window with a Styrofoam cup of coffee gazing wall-eyed at the rain. The car stubbornly resisted numerous attempts at restarting, but there was nothing unusual about that. The old heap always started back up eventually. After applying a little finesse — a butterfly fluttering of the gas pedal, a pat of encouragement on the dashboard, a breathless willing for ignition — invariably it coughed and sputtered back to life with a cloud of black exhaust. But not this time. This time the Monte Carlo wouldn't start.

"YOU'RE WHERE?" SAID Krig into his cell, releasing his Kilt Lifter long enough to check his wristwatch.

"In front of Murray Motors. Across from Beehive Odor Control."

"Yeah, okay, I know where you're at. I'll be there in five."

"Thank you sooo much, Dave. Seriously, you don't know how much I appreciate this."

Dave? *Dave?* His ears rang. Had she really said it? That had to mean something. A boundary had been crossed there, no doubt. "Not a prob," he said. "See you in a sec."

An hour later, after Krig had called AAA and the Monte Carlo was well on its way to Rita's, after they'd sat in the Goat for a half hour waiting for the tow truck, with the heat on so high that the furry dashboard was warm to the touch, listening quietly to Steve Winwood's first solo album as the rain rolled down the windshield in sheets, Krig and Rita sipped weak coffee at Traylor's, of all places, in one of the back booths of Rita's teenage exile, a fact that Rita did not mention.

It was dark now. Out the window, Rita watched the rain falling diagonally, illuminated by the purplish wavering light of the parking lot.

"I honestly don't know why," she said. "Why do I keep making the same mistakes over and over? It's all right there in front of me — or behind me. I can see it. But still I keep rushing blindly at it. And I make every possible excuse for myself. Habit. Laziness. Fear. I'm never ready to own the consequences. Oh, I'm sorry, Dave."

She liked that Dave always listened. He didn't pretend to have all the answers; he didn't feel like he had to offer commentary on every single thing. He just listened like he was interested; listened to her wax on about a thousand small fears, and a few very big ones; listened silently to her litany of regrets, her inventory of woes. Now and again — if she gave him the chance — Dave would emerge from all that silent nodding and say something unexpectedly sage. Again, on this occasion, he did not disappoint.

"It sounds like the stuff you're scared of already happened."

scoop

Eva marched through the weak light of the warehouse clutching the *Commonwealth Register* like a baton, liberating her frazzled hair from a bun and shaking it loose as she came.

Griffin was hunched over his desk, scratching out notes on a legal pad. He didn't look up as Eva approached, but he'd been expecting her.

"Yes, Miss Lambert?"

"Where's my story?"

"I didn't run it," he said.

Eva slapped her newspaper on the desktop, where it remained furled. "I can see that. When do you intend to?"

Dotting an *i* with gusto, Griffin looked up from his work impatiently. "Frankly, I don't."

"What do you mean?"

He busied himself writing once more. "Simply put, I'm not interested."

"How can you say that? You told me to bring you a cause! You told me —"

"Not a lost one, Miss Lambert. You're six months too late."

"How is this a lost cause?"

Griffin paused in his writing and looked up. His lips were bloodless. His eyes were rimmed with thin blue crescents.

"It's an avalanche," he said. "It can't be stopped. And besides, I'd no sooner stop it than —"

"It can be regulated!" Eva said. "It can be altered! The structure is not even built yet! They've hardly begun! How can you call it a lost cause? You're talking about the future of this place. You're talking about the very corporate plundering that inspired you to start this newspaper in the first place! And there's other things at stake here besides equity. How can you fail to consider the fish? What happens to those fish when they can no longer propagate? What happens to the natives who depend on them? What happens to our *economy,* which could well depend on fishing. Don't you see? The designs don't even allow for — "

"I'm not interested in fish!" bellowed Griffin. "I'm interested in people. I'm interested in what benefits society. And before you go admonishing the editorial decisions of this newspaper, consider that I've been in this business longer than you've been alive — long enough to know that you've got to choose your battles wisely if you wish to be an instrument of reform."

"So you're backing down?"

"I'm doing nothing of the sort! This is not my battle, Miss Lambert. It seems to me that this particular battle belongs to you and your husband."

"He's not my husband. And that's ridiculous! I'm not the one confusing the issues here. The public has a great stake in all of this — and you know it! It's all spelled out right there in a thousand words."

"A thousand sensational words of speculation and innuendo."

"I've seen the designs, and there's no passage for the fish! I know the investors, I've seen the contractors — and they're not from around here!"

"You said all that in your story."

"And what about the workers? They're not from around here either!"

"At least they're not coolies."

Eva turned and faced the high windows. There was dust swimming in the light. She felt a quavering in her chest and the bitter sting of bile in her throat. "I gave up my daughter to write this story," she said.

"Well then, perhaps you owe your daughter an apology, Miss Lambert. That's beyond my jurisdiction. Whatever the case, I simply cannot allow you to grind your personal axes in my newspaper. I'm concerned with more pressing issues."

Eva swung around to face him once more. "This is a labor issue! This is an economic issue! This is a conservation issue!"

"Conservation?" Straightening up, Griffin looked almost amused. "You can't be serious," he said. "Look around you. How do you convince the public to conserve what they cannot even see the end of? You're taking a narrow view of this issue, Miss Lambert."

"I most certainly am not. You know as surely as I do that no resource is unlimited — or none of these people would have come west to begin with. There would be no land rush if land were unlimited! There would be no — "

"I know that sometimes the benefits of a thing outweigh the unpleasant necessities," Griffin interjected. "Sometimes the end justifies the means."

"You don't expect to sway me by resorting to cliché?"

"I don't care to persuade you one way or another. The decision has already been made."

"But the decision defies reason! It defies every intention of this newspaper. The decision is unacceptable!"

"Well, you'd better start accepting it!" snapped Griffin.

Eva could see the veins of his forehead standing out. She looked for the truth in his eyes, and no sooner did Griffin divert them than Eva experienced a plummeting sensation and the vacuum effect of sudden and unexpected recognition. For a moment she was struck dumb. When she finally spoke it was as though her voice were coming from outside of herself. "He paid you, didn't he? He *paid* you not to run the story!"

Griffin's eyes sought occupation on the desk top. "Nonsense. Had I received payment, Miss Lambert, I should think I'd invest in a rotary press or at the very least buy a lamp for my desk."

Eva felt a numbness washing over her. "I can't believe he actually paid you." This time she said it as though to herself.

shadows and white spaces

Your days ran together as one long day, and you took to pacing back and forth down the sterile corridor, speaking in white spaces to nobody, bobbing and dodging the punches as the many worlds shadowboxed inside your head. Sometimes the light inside your mental room was too bright. Dimly, you knew you were not yourself. But how could you recognize me?

The white coats were pleased with your appetite, satisfied with your reflexes and the rhythms of your heartbeat. But clearly you vexed them with your behavior. They talked about you as if you were not there, shaking their heads in disappointment.

If anything, he's regressing.

The one with the bad breath became short with you. His curiosity gave way to impatience. His grip became firmer and more forceful as he poked and prodded you, jostled you around on the crinkly paper sheet, held your eyes open and blinded you with sharp pointy lights. Sometimes you tried to slow down the many worlds, tried to pin them in columns on the wall like charts for him to see.

Take it easy, he would say. *Just hold still.*

How could you trust them when they could not see?

time

OCTOBER 1890

When at last Thomas felt the sickness welling up in him, tasted the blood rising in his throat, he understood that his time was near. The Siwash were beckoning him home. Shortly before dawn, wrapped in a goatskin rug, Thomas crept out the back door of Lord Jim's and into the chill darkness. The air was heavy with moisture, and the ground was not quite frozen beneath his feet. An icy moon still clung to the western horizon. In spite of the chill, Thomas sweated profusely. His body rang with the spirit; it vibrated inside of his bones, it pushed at the back of his eyeballs, it spit at the fire burning in his belly with a hiss. And even before he took his first steps toward the Siwash, Thomas felt the spirit grab hold of his lungs and squeeze. He feared that the spirit would overpower him but resolved himself to fight it. Trudging west along the muddy road, the boy began to hear whispers, voices both human and not human. They circled the inside his head, faster and faster, until they were but a blur, and still they spun faster until they swallowed time, and the world turned to spots and finally to black.

The boy awoke eighteen miles away at the mouth of the Elwha, where he waded into the icy riffle up to his hips and bathed his feverish body until he could no longer feel himself. He scrubbed his skin until it was raw. Then he huddled on the bank beneath his goatskin and waited, his body racked with shivering.

The sky turned to snow in the afternoon; giant flakes floated through the air like ashes, dissolving as they touched the damp earth. The trees moaned as the wind rolled up through the valley. The spirit began to vibrate in the boy's jaw as if it were trying to sing through his clattering teeth. The boy tightened his chest and gritted his teeth in an effort to contain the spirit. Then he saw what he was waiting for:

a shadowy figure along the bank beckoning him from upriver. His father had come back for him at last. When he stood to greet his father, the world turned to spots, until gradually a black curtain descended, and a warmth expanded inside of him, and the only sound was the thump of a heartbeat from the center of the earth.

SUDDENLY, THOMAS AWOKE to a world he did not recognize. He discovered himself amid an abandoned sea of concrete, spreading in all directions atop a treeless plateau. He recognized at once that he was not himself. His body was a strange and cumbersome thing that moved of its own will yet with a purpose dimly familiar to Thomas. His shoes were odd and also cumbersome, slapping on the hard, black ground. His denim pants hung in tatters, and his baggy shirt smelled of tobacco and sweat.

Near the center of the empty expanse stood, or rather squatted, the largest structure Thomas had ever laid eyes on; slate gray, unadorned, its smooth surface broken by neither window nor door. Squinting through unfamiliar eyes, he now saw beyond the great structure — all the more minuscule in its massive shadow — dozens of tiny, driverless carriages of every shape and color, a few of them moving restlessly about, while the others huddled in rows.

Thomas could not help but marvel at the great structure, at how and why and where it came to be. It was ten times bigger than the Olympic Hotel, at least. Twenty times bigger than the Belvedere. It was as big as all of Port Bonita. Bigger than Jamestown. Bigger than Hollywood Beach. Its breadth might run the length of Hogback from the livery to the boathouse. Such was its scale that even as his oversized shoes piloted Thomas toward the structure, it did not seem to draw closer.

At last, after 184 steps, he arrived at what he presumed to be the back of the building and found himself creeping in the shadow of the great gray thing toward a line of heaping metal containers. The building was alive, monstrous, humming from the inside out.

There were seven heaping containers in all, slick midnight blue like the wing feathers of an eagle, streaked and spattered down their steel fronts with the hardened liquid refuse oozing from their open mouths. Their breath stunk of fish and moldering fruit. Suddenly, his heart was beating out of his chest, and his shivering was such that his teeth set to clacking mechanically. Thomas felt the part of himself that was not himself ease like liquid pressure from behind his eye sockets and slide down the back of his throat with a shiver. Then, the world turned to spots again, and the darkness descended.

THIS TIME, THOMAS awoke in a place so strange that he was not sure if it was even a place at all, a place suffused with a light that was not the light of the sun but a light just as bright. It burned in even rows running the length of the room. The space was broken into colorful cluttered rows. And at the head of the place stood a glass door that talked when people passed through it, and it always said the same thing:

doon-doon, doon-doon
doon-doon, doon-doon
doon-doon, doon-doon

All but hypnotized by the talking glass door, Thomas stood before a confusion of small colorful things. The things came in various shapes and sizes and were arranged haphazardly in five long rows. None of the items was smaller than two fingers and none of them bigger than the boy's fist.

A large man with curly hair and a stomach pressed tight against his shirt leaned in front of Thomas, snatching two orange sticks from the middle row.

"Curtis?" the man with the belly said. "Dude, what's with the fish? Is that a *shark*?"

The boy said nothing. The belly man looked at him strangely, as though he were from another world.

sons and daughters

Hoko stood all but invisibly in the light of the doorway, with Minerva silent in her arms. Inside, the room buzzed with electric tension. Cigar smoke hovered in flat blue clouds amid the rafters. Ethan presided over the assembly from the head of the table.

From Chicago and Seattle and Peoria they came, men of consequence, restless all, checking their pocket watches, shifting in their seats, daubing their brows, fidgeting with their tight collars. Even as Ethan addressed them, they murmured among themselves.

"Now, I'm not suggesting that the outside firm is in any way incompetent, incapable, or otherwise. And the same applies to any other outside firm that wants this or any other contract. What I'm suggesting is — and Jake and I have figured and refigured the numbers — that the expense of moving all this equipment from the outside is going to result not only in delays but cost overruns, too. Maybe as high as fifty percent. Which is why I'm strongly of the opinion that —" Ethan, unable to ignore Hoko in the doorway any longer, cut himself short. "One moment, gentlemen." Leaving his station at the head of the table, he met Hoko in the doorway and pulled her aside.

"What is it?" he said.

"I have to go," said Hoko.

Ethan stole a quick glance over his shoulder, and lowered his voice. "What do you mean 'go'?"

"I have to leave now," Hoko said flatly. She passed him the child, and he opened his arms tentatively to receive her, clutching the bundled girl in front of him like a vase. He stole another look over his shoulder. "For heaven's sake, can this wait twenty minutes?"

Hoko shook her head. The color began to drain from Ethan's face. Minerva began to wriggle, and issued a plaintive whimper. He bounced the child gently in his arms a few times for good measure, and she reached up to tug upon his wilting mustache. "And when can I expect you back?"

"There's no saying."

"Come again?" he said, liberating his seahorse from Minerva's clutches.

"I don't know if I'll come back."

Ethan felt himself go cold. It was happening again. Had he not built the nursery? Had he not rocked the child to sleep for thirty nights or more? Had he not sat Minerva on his knee, cradled her in his flannel embrace through meeting upon meeting with engineers and contractors and shareholders? He had, in fact, run himself to the ragged edges of exhaustion, walking her to sleep at dusk each day, circling and recircling the entire perimeter of the compound until his very being begged for rest, with still more candlelit hours of labor left in front of him. Was it too much to ask for a little help? "But you've been contracted," he said lamely. "You can't simply leave and not come back."

"It's my son. He's ill. I must go to him."

"But you can't just . . . What on earth am I supposed to do about . . . ?"

"Good-bye," said Hoko, turning on her heels.

Watching Hoko go, Ethan nearly gave in to pessimism but turned instead to greet the future.

Even as Minerva slumped in his arms, alternately giggling, whining, and fouling herself, Ethan tried to quell the mutinous whispers of his stockholders.

"Don't misunderstand me. It's not that I'm questioning the fiscal wisdom of Chicago — though I'd be lying if said I didn't have a few misgivings. My primary concern is local. I put my faith right here in Port Bonita, where it belongs."

Ultimately, Ethan found his associates disagreeable and was forced to concede to Chicago, because Chicago had the grease that kept the wheels spinning, Chicago had money — and only money, Ethan came to realize, offered total control.

"I don't like this one bit," he said upon his concession. "The whole idea was to invigorate our own economy, put our own contractors to work, not bring in outside help. This dam was supposed to be for Port Bonita *by* Port Bonita."

After the meeting had adjourned, and the men had filed out of the office, heading for town by carriage, then onward by water and rail to their great cities, Ethan slumped in his chair at the head of the table and sat Minerva on the tabletop before him as the empty room cooled down and the pale blue smoke began to dissipate. The girl dangled her feet over the edge of the table, sitting upright by her own strength, though Ethan's hands were there to guide her. A smile played at the corners of his mouth. The child smiled back at him.

"What are we to do, you and I? What is written in our future, child?"

Minerva reached out for one of his seahorses and gave it a playful tug. Looking at the girl, her wonder-eyed, expectant face, Ethan tried to see her future written there. He ran a coarse thumb down Minerva's face, and she batted her eyelids and kicked her legs.

"We shall see," he said with a sigh. "We shall see."

After the blasting had ceased for the day, Ethan walked Minerva about the little valley as the dust settled, and the afternoon air surrendered its warmth. He walked until the child fell asleep in his arms. Circling back in the direction of the office, Ethan took a detour and cut through the camp that had sprung up along the western fringe of the compound. The workforce had outgrown the bunkhouses, erecting shacks and lean-tos willy-nilly beyond the mess hall. All of it would be thirty feet under water one day. Workers were milling about in doorways and in the road as Ethan walked with Minerva through their midst. *Evenin', Mr. Thornburgh. Howdy, Mr. Thornburgh. Comin' right along, Mr. Thornburgh.* The smell of cooking hung everywhere in the air. A single staccato laugh cut through the evening. And even with his daughter in his arms, Ethan felt a pang of loneliness.

He came upon Indian George squatting on his haunches in front of the bunkhouse. He was packing a bag.

"What's this?"

George rose to his feet and dusted off his backside. "I'm leaving."

Ethan was less shocked than disappointed by the news. "Leaving? You, too?" Indeed, it was an exodus: first his woman, then his helper, now his loyal companion.

Indian George tied off his bag and heaved it on his shoulder. "The boy is back among the Siwash," he explained. "And the people are saying he's changed."

shit happens

AUGUST 2006

With summer winding down, Hillary lowered her shoulder and charged at her work with renewed diligence. She spent long afternoons on the river mapping fish holes and riffles, kneeling along the banks in her baggy pants to measure flow and velocity, scurrying up and down embankments, collecting silt and gravel and detritus. But she knew in her bones that her labors were futile. A dozen flow hydrographs, a gazillion velocity plots — none of it would save the salmon, who would continue to suffocate with mucus-coated gills in the light flows and tepid waters of the lower Elwha until the day they shunted the headwaters and started building the dam in reverse, draining Lake Thornburgh, liberating countless tons of silt, creating dozens, perhaps hundreds of jobs directly and indirectly. The day was coming. Hillary was certain that the politicos would quit stalling, face the music, and finally succumb to pressure, pushing the restoration through. Once again, the dam would be the engine of Port Bonita, only this time in reverse. And what would be left to power? What was Port Bonita without the Thornburgh Dam?

Some afternoons, Hillary took her lunch up to the dam and lingered in the rainbow-colored mist near the foot of the spillway, while the great turbines rumbled up through her bones. Eating her lunch, Hillary watched the futile plight of the fish, leaping time and again at the dam to be rebuffed at each pass. She admired and despised their determination. She figured that after a hundred years they'd get it. After generation upon generation of beating their heads against the same concrete wall, the fish would figure it out at some point, the people of Port Bonita would figure it out. For five generations, Port Bonita was an orgy of consumption that seemed like it would never end. Every day was Dam Day. But now it was time to clean up the mess.

Hillary had put all thoughts of Franklin Bell behind her, until one morning in late August, collecting silt samples up near the rubble diversion at river mile 3.4, a numbness washed over her as she forced herself to consider the distinct possibility that she was pregnant. It wasn't enough that at thirty-eight years old she was sexually conflicted and willfully single, that she had no equity, and was essentially working herself out of a job in a dying town. No, she had to go and get pregnant by the only black guy in three counties. Her numbness broke suddenly like a fever, and Hillary began to cry for the first time in ages, and it felt good. The tears gushed for the better part of an hour, and when she was all cried out, she squatted on the bank of the river, where the fast eddies swirled, and contemplated various futures.

On her way home, she stopped at Fred Meyer for a chocolate cake and an EPT. She never ate the cake.

black

Having left the Elwha behind nearly two weeks prior, Mather had unwittingly led the expedition into the most rugged and precipitous terrain they had yet to encounter. Ascending far past the timberline, out of the wooded valleys and canyon country they trudged, starving and beleaguered, straight into the jaws of the alpine wilderness. They soon found themselves besieged by a jumble of jagged peaks, their steep faces scarred by slides and avalanches. Down the hulking shoulders of the mountains ran great yawning crevasses cut through with veins of glacial ice. The thin air burned icy hot in their lungs. The absence of anything as small as a frost-stunted tree or a shrub or even a bare patch of earth in this vast white world, distorted all sense of scale. Carving wide switchbacks up snowfields in their ragged single file, the men seemed even to themselves insignificant. Their progress — so hard won — seemed infinitesimal. For days on end, they marched silently but for their own labored breaths and the plodding progress of their snowshoes, toward the broad face of Olympus. The brittle wind chapped their faces, burned their eyes, whistled past their ears with a ghostly howl. Hunger would not be ignored, nor was it content to simply gnaw at their bellies; by the middle of March, it began to work upon their minds. Trudging forward, they were as five strangers — together yet alone — imprisoned by their thoughts.

Nobody's determination was less dogged, or progress more mechanical, than Cunningham, who plowed forward listlessly, pulling up the rear. The thoughts that crowded in upon the doctor were not welcome thoughts, or even sensible thoughts, but stray flashes of memory — crisp and vivid — the significance of which he could not comprehend: concrete steps, the hem of a coat sleeve, a leather-upholstered ottoman. An ink blotter, a flagpole, the pale flame of a streetlamp. These benign images more than anything else were the source of the tears freezing upon Cunningham's wind-stung face, not because they stirred his sensual appetites, or filled him with longing, but precisely because of what the images *didn't* evoke, the meaning they didn't possess.

Reese, owing not to his own depleted vitality, but to Dolly's, was never far in front of the doctor. He coaxed Dolly forward on a short lead, encouraging her vocally on occasion with a pat on the rump. The beast was in poor shape, her ribs protruding, her breathing shallow and tattered.

Perhaps the heartiest member of the expedition by this time, Runnells remained right on Haywood's heels throughout the ascent, pushing his compatriot forward. Runnells alone was not bothered by his thoughts or troubled by the future. His mind was fixed only on his next step.

13 March 1890

This afternoon, having traversed a saddleback and struggled up the face of a mountain we might well have named Exhaustion, the altimeter read 2,850 meters. I do not know if this number is accurate; I'm highly suspicious of it. Surely, we are at a higher elevation. I must confess that as I set my pen to paper, shivering in the dusky light of our fireless camp, with a sickening hunger gnawing at my insides and a chill in my limbs which cannot be thawed, I fear that other eyes may never look upon any of us again. It is now readily apparent to me that leaving the Elwha was a grave miscalculation and that I should have spoken my piece. For this, I cannot blame James Mather. That in some strange way he seems to be enjoying the catastrophe, that he continues to exude confidence in the face of disaster, nay, even a certain mocking good humor, is reckless and unforgivable. My patience has been exhausted, and I feel my wick burning low. I've half a mind to turn around, with or without them. But I haven't the vigor. I am also of the mind that the remaining mule should be dressed while it still has something besides sinew on its bones.

On a morning in mid-March, as the men snowshoed up a thick bank toward the crest of another rise, Dolly finally gave out—tottering once, with a ragged wheeze, she toppled onto her side beneath her load. After numerous attempts, she could not be persuaded to rise again. For several minutes the party gathered wordlessly around Dolly and watched her languish, dull-eyed and senseless, in the snow. Reese squatted on his haunches and stroked the mule's head. Looking up into the hungry faces of the men, he felt an unfamiliar shame and appealed to Mather with uncertain eyes.

Recognizing the naked hunger in Haywood's eyes, along with an unsettling glimmer akin to madness, Mather spoke gravely. "No. Let's move on."

Reese stayed behind, kneeling in the snow. He watched as the other men crested the snow-covered rise. He stroked the beast one final time, and spoke her name softly, before setting the muzzle of his rifle between her eyes.

WITH ONE EYE, Dolly watched the sky, dully, contentedly. It was a mottled shifting sky, many shades of gray. She breathed easily once more, as the clouds tumbled lazily on their way past. She could no longer feel the sting of the ice or the burning in her belly. She felt only a throbbing from the center of the earth. There was warmth still in the hand atop her head, comfort in the soft voice which uttered her name. When the hand was lifted, she felt a slight pressure between her eyes, heard a deafening ring in her ears. Then she saw black.

Now forced to bear their own burdens, the men dragged as never before beneath the weight of their loads. Throughout the morning, Mather could feel the piercing eyes of Haywood between his shoulder blades. Something was at work on Haywood, gnawing away at his good sense. Mather had never known this sort of weakness in his companion. If only Mather could give Haywood some of his own strength.

As afternoon approached, the terrain leveled out in a narrow white-washed valley running east to west. Perhaps a mile ahead—though such short distances had become nearly impossible to gauge — the valley doglegged to the south, beyond which point the lay of the land was invisible. It was the dogleg that spurred Mather on through the deep snow. The gentle curve amid a landscape otherwise sudden and brutal suggested to Mather that something forgiving lay ahead, a wide river valley descending into the tree line, perhaps. So tight did Mather cling to this hope that his pace quickened as he plowed through the waist-deep snow toward the bend. Shortly before sunset, they reached the wide arc of the valley, and Mather pushed harder than ever through the snow until he had almost managed a trot. By the time he reached the far end of the bend, he'd put a distance of a hundred yards between himself and Haywood. And when at last Mather rounded the bend, he stopped dead in his tracks and fell to his knees.

28 March 1890
When I saw Mather drop to his knees, all that was not broken in my spirit rose in a flash of warmth. I ran toward the bend with a heart full of contrition, an apology taking shape upon my wasted lips.

betwixt green hills

Having renounced Mather's upland route and rejoined the upper
Elwha at the foot of the Press Valley, Timmon Tillman came upon a
small creek a half mile southwest of river mile 19. It was shortly before
noon, and already his feet were itching when he decided to stop and
catch his breath. The clouds had burned off and the thrushes were
sounding their otherworldly whistle. Timmon stood on the edge of
the burbling stream, which ran a meandering downhill course for
a half mile, where it fed into the Elwha at the head of a wide channel. Not only was the spot idyllic with its nearby grassy glade and its
dramatic vistas of the rugged interior, but surely, Timmon reasoned,
there were plenty of fish in the upper Elwha to sustain a hundred men
through fall. By winter he'd have a grasp on bow hunting — hell, if Ted
Nugent could do it, an Irish setter could probably do it. Everything he
would ever need was right there. The fast little creek would provide
fresh water, the dense canopy would shelter him from the elements,
and the isolation of the place — twenty-odd unihabited miles from
Port Bonita and fifty or more from anywhere else — would ensure
Timmon a life of unmolested solitude.

What had really distinguished this little creek from two dozen
other lovely little creeks was the fact that Timmon was tired — tired of
plodding ever onward, tired of packing and unpacking his fancy backpack, tired of sweat pooling in his socks and the insatiable itch of ath-
lete's foot. He was tired of starting all over again every morning with
the unzipping and zipping of zippers and the clicking and unclicking
of carabiners, tired of the multitude of tedious chores — wrestling his
tent into its sheath, folding his damp clothes, shaking the needles off
his tarp — tired of the endless details. In spite of what he'd told the
parole board, Timmon came to realize that he really didn't want to

live his life one day at a time after all—he wanted to live it like one long day, without all the packing and unpacking. The more still you sat, the fewer problems you seemed to attract. The less you moved, the fewer obstacles you were bound to encounter. Hadn't he adapted quite easily to prison life for these very reasons?

He christened the place Whiskey Creek but soon decided that it sounded too much like a steakhouse and redubbed it Lost Creek, Clear Creek, Fish Creek, and Little River, before settling finally on the frank and unpretentious the Creek. In the warmth of early afternoon, he scrupulously cleared and graded a flat expanse between three giant cedars. He dug a circular fire pit and ringed it with rocks he hauled from the creek. He shed layer upon layer of clothing as the hours unfolded, until he was shirtless, pale and skinny and tattooed, limbing fir trees with his Felco in the afternoon sunlight. He sawed limbs in six foot lengths, two to three inches in diameter, until it seemed he'd amputated every reachable limb of that description for a half acre in all directions. He dragged them two by two through the forest and staged them in a clearing at the edge of the glade. Late in the afternoon, he began to construct a shelter between the three cedars—part lean-to, part cabin, part teepee. And as the structure took shape, Timmon was fully engaged in his task and outside of time. Now and again, he stepped back to clear the sweat from his forehead and scratch his beard, and to admire his work in all its confused glory. Sure, it wasn't Hearst Castle—it looked more like an upside-down bird's nest than anything else. But it was a hell of a lot homier than a tent, and hell of a lot roomier. Though the doorway might have served a hobbit quite comfortably, Timmon was forced to bend his lanky frame almost in half to gain entry. Once inside, the structure had all the charm of a fox den.

In the waning hours of day, as Timmon was shoring up his patchwork roof, he was alerted by a nearby trilling and looked up to find a chipmunk watching him from a high crook in a cedar. Cute little guy. Huge cheeks. Funny little buck teeth.

"Hey, there, little buddy. You live around here?"

The chipmunk trilled.

"Guess I'm you're new neighbor then. Make yourself at home."

Locking in on the chipmunk, Timmon slowly backpedaled toward his equipment, crouching as he went, groping blindly behind his back for the bow. Running his hand down the riser, he found the grip and began to pat around for his quiver with the other hand.

The chipmunk trilled.

"That's right, little buddy. Just stay right there and make yourself comfortable."

Timmon fitted the arrow into place and lifted the bow. Steadying himself, he angled the bow up and steadied his aim at the chipmunk, who trilled once more with a playful singsong. Slowly Timmon drew the bow string back tauter and tauter until he hit the wall. Holding his breath, he let the arrow fly. The bow kicked back unexpectedly hard, and Timmon faltered backward a step as the arrow disappeared with a whiz into the canopy. The chipmunk never moved a muscle. The arrow never came down.

Timmon dined not on chipmunk that evening but on a small handful of pumpkin seeds and the last of the shriveled huckleberries he'd collected two days prior. He did his best to quiet his grumbling stomach with water as he hunched over the fire. Tomorrow he would fish. He'd catch an even dozen and cure them in a salt brine and smoke them just like he'd read online at the library. He'd pan-fry a couple, too. In the afternoon, he'd practice with the bow. He'd find that arrow that never came down. He'd make a few improvements on his shelter.

Late in the evening it began to drizzle. Abandoning the fire, Timmon gathered his things and took cover beneath his shelter. As he lay in his sleeping bag, he listened to the hiss of the rain and stared up at the thatch ceiling. He had a mind to talk out loud but resisted the temptation. Outside he thought he heard something scratching around by the fire pit but decided it was only the rain playing tricks on his ears. For no apparent reason, with his mind set free to wander, Timmon recalled his elementary school gym teacher, Mr. Black, and his knee-high tube socks and his hairy arms and his whistle. He recalled playing crab-soccer with that huge canvas ball. He'd actually been decent at the game. He could move fast like a crab. He remembered stealing Fudgsicles from the walk-in freezer in the kitchen adjacent to the gym. He remembered those big buttery rolls they served on the yellow plastic trays next to the already cut-up spaghetti. He remembered Sloppy Joe Thursdays. Corn Dog Fridays. A green lunch ticket. Glowing casseroles crisp around the edges and cheesy in the center. The abundance of school lunch. Often, those lunches held him over until the next day. Once in a while, his father's heavy footsteps clomping up the wooden steps would wake him in the middle of the night, and he knew what was coming, and was powerless to stop it. His father would clomp right to Timmon's bedside and turn on the light. Smelling of whiskey, arms loaded with white boxes of cold Chinese takeout, he would rouse the boy out of bed. This was the closest his father ever came to being gregarious.

"Up! Get up!" he'd say.

He'd tear the covers off the boy and march him to the sickly light of the kitchen and set him down at the table and foist the boxes on him.

"Eat! Go on, eat!"

And when the boy continued rubbing his eyes in sleepy bewilderment, his father's temper would rise.

"I said eat! What are you waiting for? I got chink food!"

He'd clomp to the bedroom and rouse Timmon's mother, too, and march her to the kitchen, and the two of them would silently eat cold Chinese food under the watchful gaze of his father, standing magnanimously over them with his arms folded.

Timmon thought he heard the scratching again, and when he thought he heard something large disturbing the brush, he bolted upright and listened intently. But all he could hear was rain. Rain, and the beating of his own heart. He lay back down and resumed staring at the thatch roof and tried to empty his head. But one recollection crowded in on him: eight years old and the disappointment of a rainy afternoon at old Comiskey Park as the tarp was rolled out even before the first pitch. If anything, his old man had seemed pleased about the rainout.

"We would've lost anyway."

Even as they filed out of the stadium — his old man hurrying him along with two fingers pressed to his shoulder — the rain began to subside. It was hardly raining at all as they emerged on West Thirty-fourth and cut through the dispersing crowd toward the old Dart. They could've played that game, Timmon was sure of it.

"Quit your sulking," his old man said. "It ain't the end of the world."

"But it's hardly raining."

"It's always raining. Get used to it."

They didn't even need the windshield wipers, a fact that Timmon was quick to note but afraid to mention. Neither did they get on the expressway toward home, another fact Timmon was afraid to mention. Instead, his father piloted the Dart south down Wentworth, producing a pint-sized paper bag from under the seat, and uncapping it at the first stoplight, where he hunkered down slightly and snuck a few quick draws before restashing the bottle under the seat. He fiddled with the radio reception until he found the Cubs game. The Cubbies were in St. Louis, down 6–0.

"There. There's your ball game, okay, you satisfied?"

Timmon pressed his face to the window. The afternoon sun was trying to peek out from behind the clouds.

"I thought I told you to quit sulking," his father said.

"I don't care about the stupid Cubs."

His old man's arm shot across the seat in a flash and grabbed him by the coat collar. "Snap out of it, God damn it! Quit sniveling."

Timmon felt all the blood drain out of him as his father released his grip. He stared straight ahead with his jaw trembling, pretending to listen to the Cubbies as his father guided them still farther south through the fifties and into sixties streets, where he began to circle unfamiliar blocks. Finally, they parked in front of a crumbling brick apartment building. His father fished out the bottle and took a few more quick hits before stuffing the pint in his coat pocket.

"Keep the doors locked," he said. "And don't drain the battery listening to the radio."

Timmon watched him walk away down the sidewalk, bobbing between people as he went, past a drugstore, past a liquor store, and around the corner. The terror was still palpable all these years later. How long had his father been gone? How long had Timmon sat locked in that car as the strange dark faces passed by? And worse, the group of young men gathered on the stoop, looking right in at him. He could feel their eyes on him. He knew they were talking about him. He knew they had guns and knives. He knew they were not to be trusted. The city was full of them. Everything was going to hell.

Timmon took comfort in the old black man who emerged from the apartment across the street and seated himself on a piece of cardboard on the top step, where he leaned slightly forward on his cane, looking out over the street through a rain so light that Timmon could barely hear it tapping on the roof of the Dart. The man was graying at the temples. He wore orange plaid pants and an old-fashioned porkpie hat and brownish red shoes so shiny he could see them shining all the way across the street. A young woman in pink hair barrettes walked by and said something to the old man and smiled, and the old man smiled and said something in return, then went back to leaning on his cane. Timmon began to feel that he was safe as long as the old man remained. With the old man watching, he could almost forget the men on the stoop. He scooted over into the driver's seat to be closer to the old man. Once, he went so far as to wave, and the old man nodded his head and raised a finger without letting go of his cane, and Timmon could've sworn that he'd winked. That's when he felt certain that the old man was watching out for him. This certainty was short-lived, for at the first clap of thunder, the old man took up his cardboard and his cane and went inside, and Timmon was once more alone with the men on the stoop. The men on the stoop didn't seem to care that it was raining. They made no effort to huddle in the broad entryway at the top of the steps. They weren't afraid of getting wet. They were laughing. And smoking. And talking too loud. They weren't afraid of anything. Like animals, they could smell fear. Timmon tried to will his father back to the car. He thought about turning on the radio, just for a minute, just to check the score, but was afraid of wearing down the battery. After a few minutes, he curled up on the floor in the foot well of the backseat and closed his eyes.

Two months later, his mother took her own life. Two months after that, on yet another rainy day, his old man dropped him off at his grandmother's house with a flower-spotted canvas suitcase and never came back. It'd been raining ever since.

A cold stream of water slithering down his neck awoke Timmon suddenly. He sat up in the darkness, and groped for his headlamp. Outside it was pouring. Rainwater streamed in through the boughs of the ceiling directly above his head. From all corners came the sound of dripping water.

"Fuck me," said Timmon.

Strapping on his headlamp, he wiggled out of his bag, wrestled his wet boots and jacket on, and procured his tent from beneath the tarp. For fifteen cursing minutes in the downpour, Timmon struggled with the tent by the light of his head lamp. By the time he commenced draping the rain tarp, the fabric was already wet through. He fetched his sleeping bag from the abandoned shelter and slipped inside the tent. The bag was damp when he wiggled inside of it. The rain was rat-tat-tatting on the tent with machine-gun rapidity, but even as the tarp began to sag beneath the weight of it, Timmon remained reasonably dry inside his sleeping bag. Mercifully, sleep was quick to claim him once more.

crazy fucking indian

"Another specialist? I thought he *was* the fuckin' specialist," said Randy, firing up a Salem and kicking his bare feet up on the kitchen table. "What the fuck kind of specialist are they talking about? And how you gonna pay for it? Crazy fuckin' kid."

For weeks Rita had been teetering on the edge of Randy as though she were teetering on the edge of a cliff. Now she could feel her narrow purchase giving way. Gripping the skillet tighter, she did her best to ignore him.

"State ought to pay for this shit," he pursued. "I sure as shit ain't payin' for it, I'll tell you that much. The hell if I'm gonna bust my ass so that kid can sleep in a better bed than me."

Rita dropped the skillet on the burner and whipped around to face Randy. She couldn't believe she was actually going to say it. But now that the words were on her lips, she was fearless of the consequences. "Get out," she said, calmly.

Randy smiled stupidly. "What the fuck?"

"Out."

His smile wilted. "Whaddaya mean, *out*? Is this some kind of joke?"

Rita dropped her spatula in the sink. Seizing his boots off of the kitchen floor, she swung the back door open and winged them out onto the dead lawn.

"No joke," she said. The surface of her calm threatened to shatter.

Randy's face was a prairie of blankness. "What the hell crawled up your ass? I'm just sitting here minding my shit. Is this about your kid? Because that ain't got nothin' to do with me. I've put up with a lot of shit around here. I didn't sign on to be no daddy to your screwy kid. You should be thankin' me."

Later, Rita would wonder how she managed to hold out so long. "You know what," she said. "You're right."

"Fuckin' a right, I'm right. Hey, you're burnin' that shit — watch what the fuck you're doin'."

Rita snapped the front burner off, pushed the sizzling skillet aside carelessly, tore the fire extinguisher off of the wall, unclamped the hose, clasped the trigger, and began firing it with a spate of forced air directly into Randy's face. He jumped up from the table and began backpedaling. His feet got tangled in the chair legs.

"What the fuck?" he said, shielding his face.

"Thank you," she said. As he tried to right himself, Rita moved in closer. "And Curtis thanks you."

"Holy shit, you crazy fucking Indian! I'm gonna . . ."

"What, Randy? You gonna bounce me off the walls? Bust my lip open?" Grasping at her blindly, he got hold of her sleeve and went for her neck with his other arm. The instant she felt his fingers around her neck, a lightning bolt ran up her back, and Rita snapped. Later, she would remember this instant as a hot suffusion of joy, a blinding red flash, and a flood of adrenaline. The very thought of it would cause her knees to weaken. Famished for violence, she swung the tank at Randy with all her might. The canister offered a sickly thud and the faintest of reverberations as it connected with the side of his head. Rita would remember thinking Randy's head felt a lot softer than she might have guessed. Randy reeled backward into the refrigerator and almost lost his footing. He didn't look angry anymore. He looked stunned. Too stunned even to cover his head for the next blow.

"Fuuuck, babe," he said groggily.

Had Rita's rage allowed her to see him clearly, Randy might have looked pitiable with his dull eyes and wounded expression. She saw only confusion on his face — and the fact that any of this should confuse him drove her rage to new places. She swung the canister again, grazing his shoulder, only to connect with his cheekbone. She paused long enough to watch him slump to the floor and reel around on the linoleum trying to get his bearings. He managed to prop himself up with his back against the fridge, deliriously. He started bleeding from the nose and tried to dab at the blood, but his fingers missed his face completely on the first pass. When he managed to bloody his fingers, he stared stupidly at them, then, swooning, looked up at Rita just in time to see black.

When Randy slumped to the floor and stopped moving altogether, Rita set aside the canister and instinctively stepped away from his body. But almost immediately, she was on her knees, nudging his arm, tentatively at first, then earnestly. His eyes were as lifeless as a mannequin. He was still bleeding from the nose. Looking upon her work, the cold crippling reality of it spread through Rita like numbness from her chest to her fingertips, until she was frozen in place, unable to move. It was the slowest panic she would ever know. She knelt there on the warped linoleum, watching through her haze of panic, as the blood pooled. Finally, she noticed, ever-so-faintly, the rise and fall of his chest.

Rita would later wonder what she might have done if she'd actually killed Randy that evening in the kitchen. God knows, a couple more shots to the head, a few more delirious seconds of hot red joy might have done the trick. She might have staved his skull in had she managed to land a square shot. In retrospect, it was terrifying to think how close she had come to that reality, bewildering to think how many things had conspired to save Randy, how many velocities and angles and height differentials figured in his favor. If she hadn't killed him, it wasn't for lack of intent. And that was the most difficult thing for Rita to reconcile.

What would she have done if Randy hadn't regained consciousness after the third or fourth nudge, if she hadn't called the cops and the paramedics, if reality had taken that hard left turn? Would she have turned herself in? Disposed of the body? Dug a grave in the back yard in the middle of the night? Bewitched by the dumb luck that had prevented her from murdering Randy, Rita was nonetheless grateful that reality hadn't taken that hard left turn. This time.

a reunion

While Dalton Krigstadt recognized the man behind the desk by his formidable mustache and his silver eyes, he was also quick to notice certain changes in Ethan's manner since the day he met him nearly a year ago in the Belvedere, when Ethan was still just an idea man with moth-eaten trousers and a thirst for conversation. The man behind the desk looked tense and distracted. He seemed to have no idea that Dalton even stood before him.

Indeed, Ethan was distracted and tense, not himself, and he had become increasingly so in the weeks since Eva left the child, weeks in which the days grew shorter and shorter and pressure from Chicago continued to mount. Fussing absently with his crooked thumb, Ethan scanned the *Commonwealth Register* spread out on the desk before him. Shipping news from Port Townsend, a scathing editorial on railroad promoters, but still no byline reading Lambert, a fact Ethan noted with both disappointment and relief.

Finally, Dalton cleared his throat. "Mr. Thornburgh, sir?"

Looking up, Ethan did not recognize the dough-faced man with the shabby work clothes — garb that seemed all the more tired from having apparently submitted to laundering recently. "Yes, what is it?"

"Krigstadt's the name, sir. Dalton. We met the day you came to Port Bonita."

Ethan was drawing a blank.

"At the Belvedere," Dalton pursued. "You thought it should be called something else. We drank whiskeys. You said I was the first person you'd met."

"Ah, yes, the mason."

"Nope."

"The woodsman."

"Nope.

"Railroad man?"

"Nope. I haul things, sir."

"Yes, yes. The hauler, that's right." Ethan turned his attention back to the *Register*. "What is it I can do for you, Mr. Dalton?"

"Well, sir, I came because of an idea."

Looking up from his paper, Ethan made another skeptical appraisal of Mr. Dalton, whom he reasoned to be a brute of a man — hewn from the raw materials of flesh and bone with little attention to detail. This Dalton was not a man of angles. Framed in a rectangle of sunlight, his very silhouette was amorphous. His shadow on the dusty floor may well have been the shadow of a whiskey keg. "I thought you were a hauler, not an idea man."

"So did I, sir."

Ethan did nothing to disguise his impatience. "Very well, then. What sort of idea, Mr. Dalton? Briefly."

"You see, Mr. Thornburgh, it's about ice."

"Ice."

"Yes, sir."

"And how is that?"

"Well now, first let me explain how I came upon the idea, sir. See, I started thinking how you had all this work going on up here, and all these workers to house, and so forth. Then I was thinkin' how you've got that road extending way up the mountain, well past the clearing and into the high country."

"And?"

"And there's bound to be mountains of ice up there."

"One would presume, Mr. Dalton. And no shortage of snow either. What good is it to me?"

"Well now, if you had you a great big icehouse up here, I'd say you could lay yourself into a pretty good store of ice."

"I see, Mr. Dalton." Ethan turned his attention back to the *Register*. "And now that I've harvested *mountains of ice* and stacked it neatly in my warehouse, what then? What am I to do with it? Build igloos?"

"Well now, sir, for starters you could sell it to cold storage houses in San Francisco."

Ethan left off rubbing his thumb and looked up from his paper, a little stunned. For an instant he felt in his bones that Dalton had hit upon a great idea. But another look at the man and his overall lack of detail was enough to convince Ethan firmly otherwise.

"Perhaps you should stick to hauling furniture, Mr. Dalton."

Jacob mounted the steps and filled the open doorway behind Dalton, blotting out his squat shadow.

"I'm afraid I don't follow, sir," said Dalton.

"Jacob, come in, come in. Meet Mr. Dalton. Mr. Dalton has devised an ingenious plan by which mountains of ice can be transported right here to our little outpost, then on to San Francisco, a thousand miles away. Tell us, Mr. Dalton, the length of the western coast aside, just how do you propose to haul that ice thirty miles down the mountain? Float it? Haul it by the wagon load?"

"Wooden flume, sir."

"Ha! The world's grandest wooden flume! And how, Mr. Dalton—"

"It's Krigstadt."

"How, Mr. Krigstadt, do you propose to get it to San Francisco? Another flume, perhaps?"

"Ship it, sir. Or send it out from Port Townsend by rail—that is, when the railroad's finished."

"Possibly viable," said Jacob, nodding his head and looking slightly impressed.

Ethan scoffed. "Ridiculous. The whole plan is ridiculous."

"This from the man who conceived of the electric stairs?"

"The electric stairs will be a reality, Jake, wait and see."

"And what of *Will-o'-the-Wisp*, your delightful comedy of manners?"

"Fair enough, Jake, though I've seen worse at the Lyceum Theater. Perhaps best to leave literary pretensions aside. However, I really should've got a patent on the electric stairs, Jake, because somebody is bound to beat me to them. On the other hand, this scheme with the ice is nothing short of preposterous. A thirty-mile flume wider than the Elwha? Whoever heard of such a thing?"

"Mr. Thornburgh, if I may say so, when I first heard how you was scheming to dam up the Elwha with all that concrete, I thought that was the damnedest thing I ever heard."

Jacob smiled. "He's got a point, Ethan."

Ethan narrowed his silver eyes. "Mr. Krigstadt, I hardly think our plans are the least bit comparable. As you can see, mine is becoming a reality before your eyes. Whereas this daydream you've hatched up is doomed from the start. In your naive optimism, you've completely overlooked the fundamental problem with this operation of yours. Hauling ice is all well and good. But how do you turn a glacier into slabs of ice? Certainly not manpower, because this is ice we're talking about, not gold. There's not enough ice in the world to sustain the labor force it would take to chop up those glaciers. So then, dynamite, is it? Liable to be an ungodly mess, don't you think?"

Dalton straightened up slightly and could not suppress a grin both bashful and proud. "Heated electric wires, Mr. Thornburgh. Me and another fellow has got a patent." Silence. For the second time in the conversation, Ethan was certain that Krigstadt had stumbled onto a grand design. Glancing at Jacob, he could see that his partner was also struck. But the moment that Ethan ran his tongue over the words "heated electric wires," he saw more clearly than ever the plan was ridiculous.

"Ha! Heated electric wires. Giant flumes. Cold storage in San Francisco. Jacob, if you wish to indulge this man further, I'll ask that you take the conversation elsewhere. I haven't time for daydreams. Goodbye, Mr. Krigstadt. Good luck with your scheme. I'd warn you to look before you leap, though. Take a good hard look at your future. I suspect you'll see yourself hauling furniture there. Perhaps that's your destiny, Mr. Krigstadt. We're not all made to move mountains."

Dalton's doughy face reddened. He was stuck in place momentarily, as though he didn't know how to proceed.

Jacob shot Ethan a look.

Silently, Krigstadt turned. Jacob stepped aside to accommodate his passing, and watched him cross pitifully over the threshold and down the steps.

Jacob turned his critical gaze back at Ethan, who met him with icy determination.

"There was no call to treat the fellow like that, Ethan."

"Like what?"

"You've developed a mean streak."

"Nonsense. Jacob, as my business partner, I should think you would understand better than anybody the demands on my time. Look around you. I clearly haven't got time to hear the scatter-brained contrivances of every laborer that passes through my door. You know that! And yet you encourage him. Is it not crueler to give the man hope?"

"You've changed," said Jacob.

"I've adapted, Jacob. There's a difference."

EARLY IN THE EVENING, when the dredging had ceased for the day, and the hammers were silent, and the dust was still settling, Ethan strode across the empty clearing to the makeshift nursery, where he stomped his boots clean on the doorstep before entering. The young nursemaid was seated on the rug with Minerva, a line of wooden ducklings between them. The young woman stood to greet him, straightening her skirts, but Ethan paid her no mind and went straight for Minerva, scooping the child off of the ground with steam-shovel hands. Immediately, his whole manner slackened, and he did not feel at odds with the world, at least for a moment. The girl squealed and giggled in his arms. Ethan noted the dark crescents under her eyes with a nagging concern.

"Has she napped?"

"For two hours, sir."

Ethan playfully pinched the girl's distended belly. The child squealed with delight and immediately went for his mustache with her fingers.

"How is the rash?" said Ethan.

"Almost gone, sir."

"Good."

Ethan carried Minerva in his arms to the edge of the canyon, as he did every evening. The child was asleep before he was halfway there. Jacob was right. He had changed, along with the playing field. The impatience that had once stirred his dreams, pushing him ever onward into the arms of his destiny, had hardened into a different sort of impatience. For the first time, he felt the world owed him something. The tightness returned to his shoulders as he peered down into the gorge, beneath the bridge, where the scaffolding on the far side spiderwebbed its way up the cliff face. Gazing down farther, a hundred feet to where the dredging continued below the riverbed, Ethan felt his stomach roll. He could practically see the dam as it would look finished; its completeness was now strongly suggested by the shape of its surroundings, from the tapering depths of the channel to the broad expanse at the lip. Yet Ethan found himself unable to revel in accomplishment. The world seemed to be pulling him in different directions. From all quarters he felt the tug of opposition. From Eva, who was no longer content to merely vex him but seemed intent upon ruining him. From Chicago, who defied his every advice, resisted his every judgment, and finally usurped his executive power and undermined his vision. And now resistance from Jacob, whose opinions grew stronger every day, whose judgments of Ethan seemed to grow harsher by the hour.

The only person in the world who didn't seem to oppose Ethan's very existence anymore, the only person who seemed to accept him unconditionally, to trust his every judgment and consent to his every decision faithfully, was his daughter, now asleep in his arms with her downy hair swept sideways over her face.

still port bonita

AUGUST 2006

"Happy hour's over," said Krig as Jared plopped down in the adjacent stool. A flotilla of appetizer boats lined the bar in front of Krig: artichoke dip, buffalo wings, shooters in the half shell, all of them half eaten — *exactly* half eaten.

"Sorry, bro. I had to drop by the house first. Janis made Thai. She's convinced it's my favorite. You know how it is."

"Yeah," said Krig, harassed by the knowledge that he should be happy for J-man, heartened by the recent turnabout in the Thornburgh home, and above all, gladdened by the news of Janis's pregnancy. "I know how it is."

Molly arrived immediately for Jared's order, something she never did for Krig.

"Kilt Lifter, J-man?" she said.

J-man? Did she call him J-man? WTF? Krig couldn't suppress a little burp, that is, he couldn't resist not suppressing it. It smelled like roasted garlic. Molly nearly gagged.

"Another for me, too," said Krig. "And could you box up this crap? J-man already ate with his *wife*."

Watching Molly gather up the boats without bestowing so much as a glance at Krig, Jared felt — as he'd often had occasion to feel in recent days — more than a little sorry for Krig. The guy just wasn't good with signals. His intentions were golden, but . . . but what? Was it his complete lack of self-awareness? His inability to step back? Or step forward, for that matter? In so many ways, Krig seemed completely undetermined. And yet, there he was, as constant as the tides. His attendance was perfect. The problem was, he just stood there at the starting line, apparently unaware that the gun had sounded. What if

Jared could light a fire under Krig's ass, offer him some incentive, a promotion, or something?

"You see what Texas did to Cleveland today?" Jared ventured.

"Yeah."

"Damn. Talk about a beating."

Both men cast their eyes vaguely on *SportsCenter*. Stuart Scott looked smarter in glasses. Felix Hernandez left the M's game in the fifth with a sore shoulder. WNBA news started scrolling along the bottom of the screen.

"So, I'm gonna do it," Jared said.

"Do what?"

"Write that stupid speech for Dam Days."

"What are you supposed to do — apologize or something? Little late, don't you think?"

"Jesus, I have no idea of what I'm supposed to say. Who the heck am I, anyway? Why do they even want me to speak? It's not like I'm some pillar of the P.B. community or anything. I don't even have a library card. We shop at freaking Wal-Mart most of the time — which makes me a big fat traitor as far as half this town is concerned. My dad, I can understand, my grandfather, sure — but *me*?"

"Beats me," said Krig.

They fell silent for a long moment, turning their attention back to the TV, where a Powerade commercial was unfolding. Krig drained his beer.

"So, I watched that Manitoba video last night," said Jared.

"And?"

"Meh. I'm just not convinced. The footage was sorta lame. It was just kind of a blob moving along the shoreline. It could've been any- thing — a fisherman in dark clothes. And why is the video always blurry? Always. Don't most cameras these days have some sort of auto focus or whatever?"

"The footage is totally bunk," said Krig, draining the last of his Kilt Lifter, even as Molly approached with their pints. "I could've told you that. That's why I wanted you to watch it."

Molly was all business when she delivered the beers. She didn't even look at Jared this time. Krig didn't look at Molly, either, which Jared supposed was a good sign. At least maybe Krig knew *how* to give up.

"First of all, the gait is all wrong," Krig said, once Molly was out of earshot. "If you watch the Patterson-Gimlin footage, you'll see the carriage is lower. That blob in Manitoba isn't bending its knees. The anatomical proportions are all wrong."

"How can you even tell from that crappy footage?"

"Dude, I've been studying Cryptoids — specifically Bigfoot — for twelve years. The P.-G. footage is the real deal, I'm telling you."

"But they already proved it was a hoax."

"The *hoax* was a hoax. If you're talking about that BBC baloney — everyone knows that's crap. There's been a busload of guys over the years who claimed to be the guy in the suit. So where's the suit? Tell me that."

"I still think that shiny thing is a zipper."

"That's just reflected sunlight. They proved the bell was a load of crap. Dude, did you watch *Sasquatch: Legend Meets Science,* or what?"

"Not yet."

"I gave that to you two weeks ago."

"Janis won't watch it, Krig. You've gotta understand. We're on a steady diet of *Steel Magnolias* and *Fried Green Tomatoes.* I'm lucky if I get to choose one movie a month, and I'm not going to pick *Sasquatch: Legend Meets Science.* I just can't do that. She's still giving me shit about *Behind Enemy Lines,* and freakin' Owen *Wilson* was in that. What is she going to say when I put in a video — a *video,* no less, not even a DVD — where they keep playing the Patterson-Gimlit foot — "

"Gimlin."

"*Gimlin* footage over and over and — "

"So you *did* watch it, then?"

"Just a couple seconds. Look, the only reason I could watch the Manitoba thing was that it was sixteen seconds long."

Krig gave his beer a little swish. "I'm glad I'm not married. That would suck."

"You're lucky," lied Jared.

Both men took a couple of silent pulls off their beers, and gave *SportsCenter* a glance. It was the debacle in Cleveland.

Nursing his Kilt Lifter, Krig felt the heat of a familiar shame. "You think I'm full of shit," he said. "Admit it. You don't actually believe me about what happened. You think I'm just making it up to get attention."

"I never said that."

"You've been totally skeptical all along."

"You yourself said it was pitch black. You even thought you might have dreamed the whole thing. What am I supposed to think? I totally believe something happened to you up there."

"Something?"

"It's all so unclear to me, Krig — to *you*. I just think whatever. People see what they want to see. And I'm not saying you didn't see anything."

"Why would I want to see Bigfoot? I mean, if I can see anything I want to, why don't I see Gwyneth Paltrow rubbing my feet every night after dinner? Why don't I see myself playing two-guard for the Spurs? What, I want to see myself damn near shitting my pants in the woods in the dead of night, cowering like a fucking rabbit under a bush, clutching an aluminum bat?"

"Well, admit it, Krig. You *want* Bigfoot to exist, right?"

"Yeah, okay, fine. So what? What's wrong with that? I think all kinds of stuff exists that we haven't discovered yet. Look at the panda bear — for hundreds of years everybody thought they were a myth. Look at dark matter, or black holes, or all those weird-ass glowing jellyfish and stuff they're discovering at the bottom of the ocean. It's not like I'm fooling myself by thinking that there's still stuff to be discovered. Even if they do have Wi-Fi in Papua New Guinea."

"I'm just saying — shit, I don't really even know *what* I'm saying, Krig. You probably did have an encounter. Let's just say that I'm not overwhelmed by the Peterson — "

"Patterson."

"The Patterson footage, that's all. That big clump of fur on his face — "

"Her."

"It looks fake. It looks like a novelty beard. And he's got — "

"*She.*"

"She's got a weird mouth. Those lips look like hot dogs. And there's no hair in that one little strip around the eyes."

"Duh."

"It's just too boxy. The hair would thin out or whatever. It wouldn't just stop in a perfectly rectangular strip. It looks silly to me. And isn't six foot seven kind of short for a Bigfoot? I thought they were like eight feet tall."

"Just watch *Legend Meets Science,* dude. The *whole* thing. They address all that stuff."

"All right, okay, I'll watch it in my office on Monday." Jared checked his watch and downed the rest of his beer in a single long gulp. "Shit, gotta go."

"You just got here."

"I know, I'm supposed to be at the video store. Fucking *Jane Eyre* or some shit. I just popped in for a beer. Sorry, man, you know how it is."

"Yeah," said Krig. "I know how it is."

"See you Monday."

"What about the M's game on Sunday?"

"No can do. We've got a baby shower." Jared fished out his wallet and dropped two twenties on the bar. "I got this one," he said. "Sorry about bailing."

Once Jared made his exit, Krig finished his beer and fidgeted restlessly with the glass for a few minutes, half watching *SportsCenter,* which had rolled over and begun repeating the same highlights from the five o'clock hour. Molly had disappeared into the kitchen a good ten minutes ago to box his food. Probably out back smoking. The Bushwhacker felt dead. Even Jerry Rhinehalter wasn't around. Just as Molly reappeared with Krig's boxed appetizers, Krig dropped an additional twenty on the bar and walked out without a word or glance at Molly. Who the hell wants leftover oysters anyway?

The stars popped cold and white, but Krig paid them little notice as he ambled across the parking lot toward the Goat. The crisp bite of fall infused the air, but Krig hardly noticed that either. When he guided the Goat north onto Route 101, without the accompaniment of Van Halen, or the Stones, or even Billy Squier — indeed, it felt as though his life no longer had a sound track — Krig didn't leave any rubber in his wake. The traffic was light. All of Port Bonita was dead. Krig slumped lower than usual in his seat as he proceeded over the hump past KFC and Taco Bell. To his own surprise, he crawled right by the hallowed lights of Circle K without getting his customary six-pack for the bluff. His senses were dull enough already.

As always, the park gate was closed after dusk, so Krig parked on Kitchen-Dick Road, hopped the bar, and hiked the quarter mile through the grassy meadow to the bluff. The wind knifing in off the strait was so sharp that Krig couldn't ignore it, and he walked with his arms folded for warmth. At the first turnout, he didn't proceed to the high spot overlooking the slide cleft, as he normally would. Instead, he just stood at the split-rail fence in front of the darkened picnic area and stuffed his hands in his pockets, gazing west. The lights of Port Bonita — from the newly developed stretch east of town, to the hills west of Ediz Hook — burned cold and clear along the strait. The little lights filled the bottomlands: purple and yellow and green and white. They spilled over into the hollows, where they began a gentle rise up the foothills below Hurricane Ridge. There was even a smattering of lights on the ridge itself. Dead and still spreading.

For nearly a half hour, Krig turned his face to the wind and endeavored to see the lights of Port Bonita as though for the first time, presuming by the sheer force of will to see in the distant winking lights an unfamiliar city, a whole new set of possibilities. But try as he might, Port Bonita was still Port Bonita.

the river giveth

The child grew to trust her chubby legs, though they failed her when she gave the slightest pause, and pitching backward on her rump, she knew not frustration but only a fleeting impatience to move forward. She grew to understand that the scented breeze and the light of day were things outside of herself. She began to see the world as the world. Tiny birds flitted in and out of the brush, and the swishing treetops painted invisible circles in the sky, and the silver and white flashing miracle in front of her, with its rumbling and roaring, its hissing and tinkling, gave off a cool breeze all its own. All that fell under her gaze or touch, it seemed, was a revelation to the watchful eyes of her father, too, as he sprawled out on the bank with his papers and his pipe. With each discovery grew the irrepressible impulse to master all that was outside of herself. And so she touched and smelled and tasted the world, paused to inspect it, and spin it within her tiny fingers — the brittle husk of a pinecone, the peeling red length of a madrona limb, a flat rock worn as smooth as the skin of her belly. Things that sat still, and things that crawled, things that skittered across the sandy bar in the breeze.

FROM CHICAGO CAME improbable deadlines and a three-page letter from the board voicing their disapproval of the very cost overruns that Ethan had not only predicted and forewarned against but publicly condemned as well. The board even had the gall to insinuate that Ethan was not the man for the job — not *committed to the job*, were the words they used. What did they know of commitment? Ethan breathed the chalky dust of his commitment hourly, felt it drilling and blasting and hammering at his bones, while they sat in leather chairs, smoking. What did they know about unforeseen logistical hurdles, conflicted engineers, and squabbling contractors? What did they know of dredging a riverbed that refused to yield rock, shearing off cliff faces given to crumbling, taming a raging river that rose by the hour?

Sprawled on the bank in his shirtsleeves, with his back propped against the mossy ledge, Ethan read the board's letter for the third time with a bitterness rising in his throat.

> It occurs to the board that administrative and technical misman-agement may well have accounted for costly scheduling delays. Having taken the matter up with Mr. Lambert, the board is of the opinion that certain changes in administration may be in order.

So, that was it? Jacob was to take charge? By what turn of events, behind which closed doors, by what plotting means had this decision come about? Why had Ethan not heard of these matters being taken up with Jacob?

Irritably, Ethan looked up from the letter to check on Minerva and saw her lolling on the sandy bar, a safe distance from the bank.

"I knew you were capable of a lot of things, Ethan Thornburgh," came a voice from behind him. "But not this."

Ethan spun around to discover Eva, standing arms folded at a distance of ten feet. "Darling," he said, climbing to his feet. "How did you find me?"

Eva folded her arms tighter, as though fighting a chill. "Don't you dare."

"What is it?"

"How could you?"

Ethan set his papers on the mossy ledge and approached her, smiling tentatively. "What are you talking about?"

No sooner had he said it than he felt the sting of her outrage across his cheek. He didn't flinch at the blow.

"How could you pay them, knowing how hard I've worked on that story, knowing all that I've sacrificed in the name of . . . of—how could you?"

He grasped her by the shoulders. "Who? What are you talking about?"

She shook free of his hold, and turned her face from his. "Quit pretending," she hissed.

"My God, Eva, you have to believe me. I haven't a clue what you're talking about. Pay whom? What story?"

His silver eyes seemed to hide nothing. His slightly parted lips seemed to express only confusion. Eva believed him.

"Then it wasn't you?"

"I still don't know what you're talking about."

"Somebody bought Griffin."

"I don't follow."

"*The Register* pulled my story."

Ethan still did not comprehend the implications. The fact was, he'd hardly given a thought to Eva's story in the weeks since she last stormed down the mountain intent on ruining him. As if a newspaper story could stop progress. Ethan himself could not stop it, and he'd put it in motion. If anything, he'd hoped her writing would come to something, so that she could feel whatever sense of accomplishment necessary to remedy her wrongheadedness. Gradually, the light of recognition shone in his eyes, even as his face darkened. "The scoundrel," he said. "He threw *me* under the train, why should I be surprised that he'd trample his own sister underfoot."

"Jacob? You think it was Jacob?"

"Of course, it was Jacob. Apparently, there's no end to his subterfuge."

It struck Eva as ironic that her brother, he who by his very arrival in this place had threatened to tear her and Ethan apart, had become the force that now unified them. Eva felt herself pulling in two directions, tethered between the disillusion of her brother's betrayal and the relief — considerable and unexpected — that Ethan had acquitted himself of the charge, that he had not proved himself unworthy. A third consideration presented itself with chilling suddenness.

"Minerva!" she shouted, breathlessly.

Ethan spun around, the hair on his neck bristling, as frantically he scanned the riverbank. One black thought eclipsed all others, ringing in his ears, as he scrambled madly up and down the bank searching for his daughter. He took a grim inventory of the current as it moved swiftly toward the bend like a dark mass. *My God, what if the river took her?* Suddenly, something flashed among a cluster of mossy rocks jutting from the shallows upstream, and Ethan took off running.

With her heart beating in her ears, Eva desperately ransacked the wooded hillside, fighting her way madly through the brush, giving no thought to the limbs slashing and stinging her face as she called the child's name. Neither could she escape the blackest of thoughts: *This is my fault. I've done this. I've killed her.* Eva froze when she heard Ethan's shouts from upriver. She could not decipher them. Holding her skirts aloft, she scrambled down the hillside to the bank and moved desperately over the rocks toward Ethan's shouts, running the length of an upended cedar, where she caught her first glimpse of Ethan, just upriver, knee deep in the riffle along the right bank. He turned to face her, wading toward the bank with the child's body cradled in his clutches, her wet hair cascading down his arm. She was not moving.

Eva fell to her knees.

Ethan looked to the heavens. "Noooooooo!"

From across the gorge, his own voice echoed back at him.

something else

Mather was still kneeling in the snow when a heavily panting Haywood staggered up beside him. What Haywood beheld upon his arrival was not some paradisiacal view of their deliverance but an impassable wall of rock rising some four or five hundred feet directly in their path. Haywood, too, fell to his knees, and for an interminable moment the two men kneeled side by side in a deafening silence, the only sound that of Haywood's labored breaths hacking away at the thin air like a dull saw blade. When the others straggled in behind, their own uneven breaths sullying the silence still further, Mather did not allow them to linger in blighted hope.

"We're losing light," he said. "We'd best make camp before we freeze."

And like the walking dead, they collectively set about making camp.

With nothing to burn, the best they could hope to do was break the wind with tattered canvas, hunker down beneath their blankets, and hope that sleep would carry them through the worst of it.

They awoke, stiff to a man, covered in snow. To add further insult, Mather soon discovered that the dog had gotten to the lion's share of the jerked elk, which, beyond a bit of bacon grease, represented the last of their protein. Haywood, in an uncharacteristic outburst, got ahold of the dog and might've killed her, had Mather and Runnells not subdued him. Mather, for his part, found it difficult to blame the poor beast in her bony state of degradation. Following her beating, as the men broke camp, Sitka paced nervous half circles in the snow at a safe distance from the party, whimpering on occasion. When the party set off and began retracing their path, Mather was uncertain whether the dog would follow.

After nearly three months in the backcountry, only Reese had managed to preserve the dignity of a hat. As for the rest of the party, a piece of cloth knotted at the back sufficed. They were down to a single blanket per man. By the slimmest of estimates, they had enough food remaining to sustain the party for a week. Shouldering sixty pounds each, Mather and his men backtracked through the narrow valley. In spite of flagging spirits, they made steady progress with the hard snowpack and the wind blowing at their backs. By early afternoon, they had ascended into the wide windless basin they'd left two days earlier. They skirted the edge of the valley until they found what Mather reckoned to be a suitable route for western passage, a deep saddleback bridging two snow-covered peaks. With the better part of the day still in front of them, they struck up the side of the mountain, if not with a nose for the Quinault watershed, then at the very least with the hope of finding some way out of the wilderness. The steep incline forced them to attack the rise hillside fashion, painfully and deliberately kicking footholds in the deep snow. They were nearly three hours in reaching the narrow shelf that ran several hundred feet below the crest of the ridge. The prevailing western winds had formed snow cornices on the leeward side of the crest, a fact that made the men more than a little uneasy, particularly as afternoon approached, and they began to hear the distant rumble of avalanches.

By late afternoon the party had crested the ridge, and they spread out to disperse their weight across the narrow passage, which was little more than a catwalk. The vista was humbling. To the northwest loomed Olympus, with its broad face and, to the east, in a string of tattered clouds, the steep studded range whose peaks bore the names Mather, Haywood, Reese, and Runnells. Before them, up a gentle rise to the southwest hung an outcrop from which point, according to Mather's calculations, they might catch a glimpse of the Quinault watershed at last.

When they reached the lookout and peered down over the broad green river valley spread out thousands of feet below them, Mather's look of triumph shortly gave way to bewilderment.

"What is it?" said Haywood.

Mather gazed down at the river in stony silence, taking hold of his long hair with both hands, as the color drained from his face.

Haywood, too, stared down at the river, looking for the source of Mather's discomfiture.

"It runs north," Mather intoned.

Haywood felt the blood drain from his face in the moment of recognition. "Then it . . . ?"

"Yes."

"No," said Haywood. "Good God, no."

"What?" demanded Cunningham. "What is it?"

"It's the Elwha," said Mather.

windows

The Reverend Sheldon was even paler than usual in black, his jowls tucked into his white collar. He stood with his robed stomach pressed firmly against the pulpit, a Bible open before him. The chapel was cleaved crosswise in half by a swathe of early morning sunlight slanting through the window.

But the new day was lost on Ethan, numb and bewildered in the front pew, with Eva beside him like a perfect stranger, her hands folded in her lap. All the days of Ethan's life seemed lost.

When Reverend Sheldon spoke, he delivered his message in uncharacteristically soft tones.

"The chosen are called unto to him even before they've come to be. And so this child was chosen by him, bathed in the blood of Jesus Christ."

The words washed over Eva. Engrossed by the sunlight, teeming with dust as it angled through the window beyond the pulpit, she permitted her thoughts to bask momentarily in the light of a different window, in a different room, on a different morning, so long ago, it seemed. Chicago. The sun-drenched kitchen late in spring. Their first morning in the lake flat, the window ajar, with the gentlest of breezes blowing in off the water. A bounty of biscuits and eggs. An afternoon to look forward to, a notebook to be filled. Ethan sitting across from her at the table in his new brown suit, poring over the financials in which he had no stake, only a prayer. There was hope at that table. Still shades of youth. Optimism. And possibly even something as durable as love. Two years out of fashion, and in desperate need of mending, only the suit survived. The suit Ethan wore to meet her father. The suit he wore to dinner when she rebuked his marriage proposal — twice. The suit he wore on the train west. The same suit in which Ethan had arrived at Morse Dock, a little worse for wear, his silver-eyed gaze leveled squarely on the future. And now he was wearing it to his daughter's funeral.

"Saith the Lord God: that my Kingdom belongs to the children. And today he calls this child into his Kingdom."

destinies

Eva was among the first to file out of the little church after the service. Wrapping her black shawl about herself against the autumnal chill, she did not linger but set out alone down the muddy path toward the colony. She neither turned nor slowed her pace when she heard Ethan's squishy footsteps hurrying to catch her. He was impervious to defeat. Nothing, it seemed, could deter his will, or break his spirit. These thoughts embittered Eva as she hastened her own pace, squinting into sunlight. But when Ethan overtook her and stood in her path, breathing heavily, she could see plainly that she was mistaken, that his silver eyes were brimming with doubt. And for an instant, she yearned for his embrace.

"Don't blame yourself for this," he said.

Eva stiffened at the words, and her yearning took flight along with all warmth from her body. Wrapping the shawl still tighter about herself, she said nothing as she pushed her way past him. Immediately, he fell into step beside her, as she knew he would.

"Stay," he said.

She ignored him and kept walking.

Ethan stepped in front of her once more, and set his hands upon her narrow shoulders. "Eva, darling, listen to me: I love you."

"Impossible," she said, breaking free and pushing past him.

Again, he fell into stride with her, worrying his gloveless hands one inside the other for warmth. "We can start again. From the ground up, Eva. We can still build the life we set out to build."

Eva stopped and looked him in the eye. There was bitterness in the lines of her face. "You talk about life as though it were some kind of construction project, Ethan — like your dam, something that will adhere to your designs. Well, mine amounts to just the opposite — mine is a demolition. Don't you see, Ethan? While destiny bends to your will at every turn, it hammers me to dust. If there's any hope for me, it lies in the fact that there's nothing left of me."

Ethan took her firmly by the elbow and turned her so that she was facing him. When she tried to elude his grasp, he gripped her harder. "Was it my will that the woman I loved would not have me? Was it my will to see my dreams commandeered by the very men I sought to overcome? Was it my destiny to outlive my daughter?"

"Perhaps not. But your destiny is still here, Ethan," she said flatly. "Mine never was." This time Eva managed to break free of his clutches. This time, when she pushed past him, Ethan did not follow her but stood on the muddy path and watched her go for the last time, her black-clad figure bathed in sunlight.

into the sunrise

Pulling her knees up under the wool blanket and clutching them tightly against her, Eva was only vaguely aware of the clacking rails beneath her, hardly mindful of her forehead pressed against the icy glass. Gazing dully out the window, she wished only that her eyelids were heavy as the boundless prairie unfolded, somewhat less than golden in the predawn.

For eleven months she would mark her days in Chicago in the shadow of her father's wealth, and she would not write a word. In a year's time, she would settle in a cottage of her own, midway between Fort Wayne and Chicago and begin to write again, looking west out her office window in the hours approaching dusk.

In June of 1894, the news of Ethan's marriage would reach her, and Port Bonita would seem like another lifetime. Two months later, Eva would receive the news of the dam's completion and, seven months after that, the news of Ethan's son, Eben Allen Thornburgh.

But rattling east into the sunrise, Eva's thoughts were somewhere outside of time. She felt her past curling like smoke into the distance and knew, even before the light of day washed out the gray dawn, that night would surely come again, and perhaps on its heels, a new dawn would follow.

the trail

"Sure, I remember him," said Krig, handing Timmon's mug shot back to Franklin.

Franklin looked around for somewhere to set his Styrofoam coffee cup. Damn cubicle was too crowded.

"When's the last time you saw him?"

"Gotta be three weeks," said Krig. "At least."

"You fire him?"

"Walked out."

Franklin nodded, as if he saw how it was. "What kind of worker would you characterize Tillman as?"

"Decent. As far as I could tell from a couple of weeks."

Franklin scratched out a note in his tiny spiral notepad. "Talk to him at all during that time?"

"Sure, we had a few beers one night at the Bushwhacker. Or I did. Tillman wasn't drinking."

"Bushwhacker, huh?"

"Yeah. Actually, didn't I see *you* in there one night? I know I did — you had a green shirt on. You were with Hillary Burch."

"Could've been."

"Yeah, okay, I thought you looked familiar. Not like P.B.'s crawlin' with black dudes, right? How is Hillary? I haven't talked to her since — " Sensing Franklin's impatience, Krig yielded.

"What did you and Tillman talk about?"

"Hell, I don't remember. Guy stuff, I guess."

"He seemed depressed to you?"

"Quiet, maybe."

"You say he wasn't drinking?"

"Nope. Not a drop."

Frankled scribbled a note. "He didn't mention any plans for the future, anything like that?"

"Not that I can remember."

"Did he say *anything*?"

Krig shrugged. "Said he hated basketball."

"Yeah? What else?"

"Said he liked camping."

"Hmph. Said that to me too. Any idea where he was staying?"

"The Wharf Rat."

"Wharf Rat?"

"The Wharf Side. Down on 101. Right by KFC, across from the Dollar Store. Why, what'd he do?"

"He mention any family or friends in town?"

"Nah," said Krig, swiveling and plopping his feet down on a disheveled foot-high stack of invoices and manila folders. "Wait, yeah. Don Gasper."

"Gasper, you say?"

"Yeah. Two-guard back in the day. Couldn't create shit off the dribble."

Franklin took down Gasper's name. "What did he say about this Gasper?"

"Just said Gasper told him P.B. was a kick-ass town."

"Know where he lives?"

"Still in the clink, last I heard. Tried to rob his grandmother. He left his wallet and an empty ice-cream bowl on the kitchen counter is how I heard it. Gasper always was dumb as a stump. What did Tillman do, anyway?"

"Skipped town, most likely."

"No, I mean what did he do originally?"

"That'd be confidential, son, sorry." Franklin finally set the coffee cup down at the foot of his chair. "Well, thanks for the coffee." He stood to leave. "That's some shiner you got there."

Krig smiled. "Yeah. You should see the other guy."

Standing to leave, Franklin kicked his coffee cup and it toppled over, emptying its contents on the mottled carpet.

"No worries," said Krig.

SURVEYING THE WHARF RAT lobby, Franklin felt a pang of sorrow for Tillman. Hard to resolve pep talks with this dump. No wonder he skipped.

"I don't interview them," the Dragon Lady said, tapping her ash. "I just rent them rooms. As long as they don't steal my coat hangers or burn holes in my carpet, I don't ask questions."

"How long was he here?"

"I don't remember."

"Could you check your records, then? When did he check in? What kind of hours did he keep? Did he have any company?"

The Dragon Lady gave Franklin a long snake-eyed look, exhaling through her nose. "Maybe two weeks," she croaked. "Normal hours. No company. Who did you say you were?"

"His parole officer."

"Does that mean you're a cop?"

"Not exactly."

"What do you want with him?"

"I want to help him."

The Dragon Lady drew from her cigarette until the cherry crackled. She gave Franklin a long hard look, trying to get a read on him. "Hmph. Well, he seemed okay to me. Kind of quiet. Didn't steal any hangers."

"Paid up?"

She exhaled a cloud of smoke in Franklin's face. "In full."

"Did he happen to mention any plans for the future?"

"What do I look like, his grandmother? Beats the heck out of me. Looked to me like he was going hiking."

"What makes you say that?"

"Could barely see him underneath all those packs and gadgets."

A hopeful thought flitted suddenly into Franklin's mind. What if Tillman hadn't skipped at all? What if he'd just gone hiking and got in trouble, got lost or injured? He could still be out there somewhere.

"We done here?" the Dragon Lady wanted to know. "I got a motel to run."

"We're done. Thanks for the cooperation." Franklin turned and crossed the cramped little lobby in three strides.

"What'd he do, anyway?" the Dragon Lady called after him.

Franklin paused in the threshold and looked back over his shoulder. "It's like you said. He took a hike."

SUPPOSING — THAT is, if he ever tracked him down — Franklin was able to land Tillman a better job than gutting fish. Something where the kid could use his brain. Supposing Franklin could pull a few bureaucratic strings, and the state could stake Tillman to two months in a decent apartment. Not some halfway house. Something he could call a home. Supposing Tillman got a break. Supposing he was given some tools to carve out a life. That's correctional, giving a guy a shot. But first, he had to find him. These were Franklin's thoughts as he guided the Taurus west of town and up River Road to the ranger station.

"Nothing here in the way of permits for Tillman," said the bearded clerk, scanning the list a second time. "Nothing at Sol Duc either. You try Dosewallips?"

"Not yet," said Franklin. "Too far. See, he ain't — er, he *don't* got — *ahem* — he *doesn't own* a car. Far as I know."

In spite of the beard, Franklin was beginning to suspect the clerk might be a woman. The voice. The bearing. The posture. The suggestion of two flattened lumps beneath her khaki shirt. Alex was the name on the tag. This town was getting weirder every year.

"Friend of yours?" she said.

"I'm his parole officer."

A light of recognition showed suddenly on the clerk's face. "Hold on a sec." She waddled over to the counter opposite and snatched a clipboard. "This the guy you're looking for?"

Franklin thumbed the sketch. It was Tillman, all right: Caucasian male, approximately six foot six, replete with the distinguishing tattoo (whatever it was) peeking over the shirt collar. The sketch artist had gotten the eyes all wrong, though. The eyes in the sketch were flat, lifeless; they made the guy in the sketch look dumb and mean. Why did that bother Franklin?

"Report filed last week by a group of elderly hikers. Said the man in the sketch harassed them. Can't go into details. It's under investigation. But one old lady had a heart attack."

"Heart attack?"

"Couple days later, guy from Kirkland — kind of a jerk, if you wanna know the truth — reported a theft up near Whiskey Bend. Over a thousand bucks worth of gear. But that could've been bears. 'Course, we notified the sheriff's department. They sent a couple fellas up there, but they didn't turn anything up. Guy could be long gone by now. If they'd have known he was jumping parole, they'd have probably —"

"Now let's not get ahead of ourselves. What's that mean, harassed them?"

"Can't go into it," said the clerk.

"Listen, I ain't — I'm not just anybody, here. I'm his parole officer."

The clerk looked around and seemed to consider. "Well, I suppose in that case — okay, look: I don't know the whole story. Apparently, he's some sort of"— here, the clerk leaned in close, and Franklin thought she smelled like a man, like liver and onions — "some sort of sexual predator."

"Say what?"

"Old lady says"— the clerk leaned in even closer, and Franklin thought he saw an Adam's apple — "this fella assaulted her with his penis. They got a name for it — I heard the young one from the sheriff's department call it a"— now, the clerk leaned in so close that Franklin caught the full force of her breath. Definitely onions — "a *cock-slap*, he called it."

Franklin knew criminal behavior. He knew more criminals than most men would ever care to meet, from his father on down. Most of them were pretty consistent at the end of the day, and none more so than the repeat offender. But this was straight out of left field. What the hell was Tillman — breaking-and-entering, criminal-trespassing, drunk-and-disorderly Tillman — doing cock-slapping old women? It just didn't add up. Nothing in his profile about predatory behavior, sexual deviancy, Catholicism. Nothing about the man himself to suggest anything of this nature — and Franklin knew there was a big difference between robbing a pharmacy and cock-slapping an old lady.

"As for the theft complaint," pursued the clerk, interrupting Franklin's meditations, "like I say, could've been bears. Wouldn't be the first time. We had a female black bear two summers ago up by the hot springs kept stealing people's skivvies. Took one woman's purse. She tried to pin it on a couple of gay guys — hot springs are full of them — but we found the purse a quarter mile down trail, stuff scattered all over the place, lipstick half eaten."

"Listen," said Franklin. "A few things about all of this don't add up. I gotta get that boy back in here."

"I'm no cop," said the clerk, "but if this fella's a parole jumper, I'd say — "

"Easy now. No need getting the law involved again. I can handle this guy."

port townsend

Adam dropped his nine-page report, months overdue, on the white tablecloth just in front of Cal Pellen's heaping plate.

"Sit," Pellen insisted, gesturing with a forkful of steak.

Reluctantly, Adam took a seat across from his supervisor and cast a look around the gilded interior of Delmonico's — airy and soft around the edges, lamplit, even by day. The dining room, half empty, redolent with cooking smells, had no trace of the oily smoke that hung in the air at most of the establishments where Adam took his meals. Delmonico's was brass and polished wood, sturdy high-backed chairs and large immaculate windows. The two men could have been sitting in Chicago or New York or San Francisco. But Adam preferred rugged Port Bonita with its splintered wood and lack of airs to the cosmopolitan charms of Port Townsend. He preferred men who worked with their hands to men like Pellen, who worked with their guile.

"And how goes it with our squatters along the Elwha?" Pellen inquired.

"It's in the report."

Pellen smiled and raised his fork. "Not a chatterer are you, Adam? Not like your father. Now, there was a man who understood the benefits of conversation."

"Well, I'm not him."

Raising a brow, Pellen masticated for a moment before wiping his gray mustache with a cloth napkin. "No, I suppose not. Eat, eat," he said.

"I'm not hungry, thanks."

"You look pale, Adam. Hard to trust a man without appetites."

"Hard to trust a man either way," Adam said.

Outside, behind the glass, the bustle of Water Street unfolded in silence. Pellen called for the waiter. "A steak for my associate." Then, to Adam: "What are you drinking?"

"I'm not. And hold the steak."

Pellen sawed off another mouthful of steak. "Suit yourself then. Have you been to Point Hudson?"

"I just came from there."

"And what did you see?"

"Natives dressed up as whites. None of them fishing."

"Sober natives, I hope."

"As far as I can tell, they've got that going for them."

"They've integrated rather nicely over the years, haven't they? We can all thank the Duke of York for that. Your Chet-Ze-Moka left us quite a legacy, Adam. He was indeed a friend to the white man. Too bad about the drink. It made a great man small."

"Not so small that they haven't built him a statue, I see."

"That's true. Lovely, isn't it?"

"I suppose." It finally occurred to Adam to take off his hat, which he set on the table in front of him. Never had the hat looked so filthy as on the white tablecloth. "The Siwash are drowning," he said.

"Pity they wouldn't relocate. We — *your father* — did everything within his power."

Adam did not disagree. He checked his pocket watch, though he had nowhere to be. It did not occur to Adam that the watch had been his father's.

"Now, if we could only teach these Celestials how to blend," his supervisor pursued.

"Don't hold your breath, Pellen. There's a reason people hold on to things."

"And there's a convincing reason why people let go of them. It's called progress, Adam. Of course, the Chinese are beyond the agency's influence, but is it any wonder that their storefronts are vandalized and their children pelted with vegetables, when they refuse to conform? Look around you. This isn't some wild outpost like Port Bonita. We've got cobbled streets and masonry, streetcars and electricity. We've got six banks in Port Townsend. We've got the railroad."

"And who's building it?"

Pellen smiled. "You've got an answer for everything, haven't you?"

"Ask enough questions and that's what happens."

"And what about Jamestown?"

Adam tensed at the reference but relaxed once he put the question in context. "That's in the report, too."

"Indulge me," said Pellen, with a mouthful of steak. "Really, Adam, you've got to learn to be a little more forthcoming."

Adam narrowed his gaze. "Jamestown is completely stable. Economically viable. No whites, no liquor, and no federal recognition."

Pellen grinned again but could not belie his annoyance. "You know the score on that count. Our hands are tied. Jim Balch and his people knew exactly what they were getting into when they bought that land."

"Did they?"

"They knew enough, Adam. I admire their initiative, I do. But there are laws."

"The Great White Father."

Pellen stopped chewing and looked at Adam critically for the first time. "Nobody's taking sides, Adam, in spite of what you may think. The census, the agency — all of it was put in place for the benefit of the natives. Frankly, I don't know where you get the gall to question that. Your father spent twenty years among the Indians, from Puyallup to Port Bonita. He dined with them, prayed with them, he did everything but conceive with them. And yet you continue to doubt him. What does it take to earn your respect?"

Adam had no answer. He lifted his dirty hat off the table and set it in his lap, and glanced out the window. The streetcar rattled by, bound for Kah-Tai Valley. He could feel it rumbling up through the floorboards. "I'm just trying to do my job," he said. "I don't mean to ruffle feathers."

"I suppose it's just in your nature, then." Liberating a string of steak from between his teeth, before clearing his mustache once more, Pellen suddenly remembered something. "Ah, and speaking of Jamestown, what of Lord Jim's health? It comes to me from the Indians that he's fallen ill recently."

"This is the first I've heard of it. How ill?"

"That, I can't say, though quite ill I'm taken to understand. I assumed you'd be able to tell *me*."

Plucking his hat from his lap, Adam replaced it on his head. "I ought to go," he said.

"Adam," said Pellen, adopting a somewhat graver tone. "If you don't mind me saying so, you ought to start a family. That's what you ought to do. Quit eating in hotels. Settle down in one place. You seem to fancy them so much, you ought to find yourself a native woman."

Adam felt his face color.

"My apologies, son. But a man is no different from a tree. He needs to lay down roots. All this moving around, it just isn't healthy."

"Did you learn that from the natives, Pellen?"

"If I've learned anything from the natives, Adam, it's that one must adapt."

IN LESS THAN two years, the boom had transformed Port Townsend from a rugged little outpost scarcely bigger than Port Bonita or New Dungeness to a hive of industry, a bustling city of seven thousand, with all the hum and rattle of Tacoma or Portland. The landmarks of the Pioneers — those modest framed homes and quaint houses of commerce — had seen the coming of the demolition crews. Three- and four-story structures, no fewer than twenty in number — buildings of stone and brick and mortar — lined Water Street from Pierce to Jackson. To Adam, as he elbowed his way down a crowded Water Street, past the Columbia Saloon toward Union Wharf, Port Townsend was hardly recognizable. Sea walls had been constructed. The wharves had been extended to allow for further construction while grades had been cut through the high clay bluff that hemmed in downtown. Everywhere, it seemed, money was changing hands, deals were being cut, the future was being paved. Port Townsend had become everything Port Bonita ever aspired to be.

Chief upon Adam's mind, as he drifted along Water Street, was the health of his friend Lord Jim and, specifically, how it affected the boy's fate. He knew he must pay Jamestown a visit immediately, yet he could not stop himself from wandering farther, as though something compelled him to do so. At Union Wharf, Adam came upon a group of black-hatted Chinese squatting around a game of fantan, and even as he approached, they scurried to pocket their beans and buttons and stood to disperse. But as soon as Adam passed, they settled back on their haunches and fished the pieces from their coat pockets. Adam found himself fascinated rather than repulsed by the Celestials, drawn toward the green grocers and spice dealers of Washington Street. It was here, before an open storefront brimming with delicate, exotic wares of staggering variety, that Adam chanced upon the only Chinaman he had ever had occasion to know personally, the very doctor with whom he and the reverend had once shared a carriage to New Dungeness. Was it fate that led him to the Chinese doctor? Among the throng of Chinese on Washington Street, only Haw wore his hair braided in a queue, a fact that distinguished him in Adam's mind as a man of importance. Only later would Adam learn that the queue symbolized a three-hundred-year-old defeat. Curious to Adam was the fact that the Celestial touched nothing with his right hand, which hung at his side as though it were lame. His movements were methodical, measured; he functioned gracefully in spite of his apparent handicap, inspecting roots and vegetables with his good hand, fishing coins from his leather purse.

Haw did not recognize the white man but could feel his eyes upon him as he fingered the goji berries and inspected the rhubarb, could feel them still as he paid for the goods. Weaving his way through the crowd toward Madison, Haw's heart quickened — though not his pace — when he sensed that the white man was pursuing him. Turning the corner, Haw's relief was short-lived, as the white followed close on his heels. Finally, Haw turned to face his pursuer.

"Why you follow?"

"We've met," said Adam, drawing a step closer. "The reverend? The carriage?"

Haw inspected Adam scrupulously. Though he remained perfectly straight-faced, Adam could see the Chinaman's eyes smile in recognition. "Reverend get sleepy."

Adam smiled. "Yes. As a matter of fact he did. I owe you one for that."

"No owing."

"You're a doctor?"

"Not like white doctor."

At Hudson Point, Adam secured the two-man canoe passage to Jamestown from a flat-nosed Indian in a rumpled top hat.

"Buchanan is my name," their pilot informed them, pushing off.

The cedar dugout was perhaps twenty feet, bow to stern, sharp-ended and wide in the middle.

To Adam's surprise, the strait was uncharacteristically calm and windless around the point. In spite of its weight, the canoe cut like a wedge through the flat water, much quicker than any skiff. The boat was far more stable than its shape would suggest. Unperturbed by the breakers, they glided west along the peninsula, several hundred feet off shore, past the mouth of Discovery Bay, where the green foothills reared up out of bottomlands and the tiny outpost of Gardiner revealed itself by a thin plume of smoke.

They proceeded silently but for an occasional, and invariably short, observation on the part of Buchanan, who spoke with all the tonality of a foghorn.

"Protection Island," he would say. "Good hunting, once."

"Smells like burned fish," he observed on another occasion, sniffing the air.

As the journey progressed, Adam's thoughts revolved around Thomas.

Even before Buchanan set the canoe ashore at Jamestown, the faint ringing of a dozen bells floated toward them from across the bay, accompanied by the chaos of seagulls feeding along the shoreline. Other than the bells — chiming no doubt from within the windowless church — and a few chickens pecking away lazily in the street, scarcely anything in the little town stirred.

Buchanan could not be persuaded to stay ashore. The tides were in his favor, and dusk was approaching, and his wife was cooking hamburger steaks and fried potatoes.

As Adam approached the little red house with the willy-nilly shingles, Lord Jim's wife emerged on the step to greet them. Her eyes did not question Adam's Chinese companion.

Ida Balch cut an imposing figure for a woman five feet tall, for she was nearly as wide, and peered up at the world without deference. When not decidedly grim in facial expression, Ida was poker-faced. Not unlike Buchanan, she bore a flat nose, which she was not afraid to stick into things. In spite of her imposing veneer, Ida Balch was gentle of spirit and disarming by nature.

"I knew you would come," she said, taking Adam's hand between her own. "Jim said you would come." She then lowered her voice in confidence. "The Shakers cannot cure my husband. He says that the healing is outside of himself, and that is the problem. The bells only give him a headache. I wanted to call for the white doctor in Port Bonita, the one with the funny smell, but Jim would not have it. He says that the white doctor is not fit for horses."

"I brought a different kind of doctor," Adam said, indicating Haw, who gave the slightest of bows. "This man once cured the Reverend Sheldon of talking."

Much to Adam's surprise, Haw soon called his right hand into action. Shushing the old Indian, he read Lord Jim's pulse at the wrist and at the temple. Though confined to the bed, Lord Jim's irrepressible voice was strong and steady as ever.

"What ails me, *cayci*, is a sickness of the spirit. The bottle has followed us to Jamestown at last. Two weeks ago I found Horatio Groves sick with the drink in a potato field. When I tried to take his hand, he spat in my face. He said, 'Leave me. I am already dead, old man.'" Lord Jim turned his eyes toward the window.

Haw, his right hand having resumed its state of dangling inactivity, began laying out his herbs on the dresser with his left hand, as Adam pulled up a chair and sat across from Lord Jim, cursing himself inwardly for having not monitored the situation. He knew all along that temperance in Jamestown was too good to be true. In spite of sovereignty, security, and religion, somebody was bound to weaken in the end. Somebody always did.

"Two days after Horatio Groves," the old man continued, "John Johnson gave his wife and boy a beating in the street outside of the church. He was sick with whiskey, too. And the sickness has spread to his wife."

Adam ran his calloused hands over his unshaven face, and stifled a sigh. "Where? Where is it coming from, Jim?"

"If I knew that, *cayci*, maybe I could stop it. But maybe not. Maybe Horatio Groves was right, and we're already dead."

"Horatio Groves was drunk. A drunk has already surrendered."

"Perhaps."

Haw pulled the blankets back and set his right hand lightly upon Lord Jim's chest.

"Is the boy about?" said Adam.

Lord Jim closed his eyes momentarily. When he reopened them, he turned toward Adam, nodding grimly.

"You must not be angry, *cayci*. I wouldn't have stopped him, even if I could have. He fled over a week ago. Back to the Siwash."

Adam rose to his feet immediately.

"They tell me his time has come," the old man pursued. "And that he has begun to talk. They say he speaks at Hollywood Beach, night after night. They say his words are strange and that they have a strange effect on the people who hear them."

"Nonsense," said Adam impatiently.

"That's what some of the people who have heard him speak say. They say he speaks nonsense. But I don't think so, *cayci*."

"The boy's never uttered a word in his life."

"Then you must hear for yourself to believe. I'm too weak, or I'd seek him out myself and hear these strange words. Find the boy, *cayci*. Find your son. Hear what he says."

"I'll need a horse."

"You will take mine."

Shortly before dusk, Adam readied himself to leave for Port Bonita, just as Haw was beginning to rub a poultice of herbs into the old man's chest.

"You're not going to cook me, are you?" Lord Jim said.

"No cooking," said Haw. "Make better."

As Adam mounted Lord Jim's mare, a pale moon was just rising in the east.

time again

It is said that Storm King remained upriver for five days and that he appeared on Ediz Hook on the sixth day, next to a white shark with hollowed-out eyes. It is said that the boy spoke to no one in particular, that he merely spoke aloud; that he walked the length of Hollywood Beach for three days speaking softly in a voice that was too deep to be his own and that his words were as puzzles. But nowhere does it say that his first words were not numbered among the English and Salish dialects that streamed from his mouth, nowhere does it say that among all of that language there existed no word or meaning to subscribe to the one utterance he would come to favor most, always at the end of sentences, like the word *amen* — the anomalous singsong *doon-doon, doon-doon.*

It is said that he stood on a drift log, gazing out past Ediz Hook until the fires burned low and dawn appeared as a thin gray sliver on the horizon. It is said that during the night he had carved strange symbols in the sand, and it is said that the tide would not wash them away for six days. Nobody among the Klallam had thought to write these symbols down. But it is said that among them were the letter *K*, the letter *F*, and the letter *C*.

awakenings

OCTOBER 1890

Far out on Ediz Hook, Hoko spotted a tiny solitary figure standing on the inside edge of the natural jetty. She was certain it was Thomas.

When she was within shouting distance, Hoko called out his name and waved her arms in the air, but Thomas paid her no notice. He did not so much as glance in her direction as she approached

"I've been worried for you," she said, when she was upon him. "They told me you fled Jamestown. They told me you were back at Hollywood Beach." She rested her hand on Thomas's shoulder, knowing that he did not like to be touched. Oddly, the boy did not pull away from her. His skin was hot to the touch. He was sweating, in spite of the chill. His lips were not moving. In his eyes, she could read only confusion.

"They said you were talking. I didn't believe them."

Thomas offered no indication that he could even hear her voice.

"We won't go back," she said. "You'll stay with me. Things will be as they used to be."

Hoko looked him right in the eye, knowing he did not like to be looked in the eye. The boy gazed steadily back at her without the slightest light of recognition. Behind his steely blue eyes, Hoko thought she caught a glimpse of what George Sampson called the Invisible Storm, and it sent cold fingers running down the back of her neck.

"First, we must make you well again," she said.

To her further surprise, the boy allowed Hoko to take his hand, and she began leading him down Ediz Hook toward Hollywood Beach. The clouds on the horizon were draining of color. Darkness began to settle over Hoko and Thomas as they walked, and the lanterns of Port Bonita began to alight, along with the fires of Hollywood Beach.

"You must not listen to what they say about you," Hoko told him.

"They want so badly to see you as something else; they cannot see you for who you are."

The boy could summon only flashes of a recent past. A desolate beach, not so different from this one, the pounding surf, the urgent crowing of a dozen seagulls swirling above. The eyeless, bone-white carcass of a dogfish and its unaccountable significance. Apples and cigarettes and the cold metallic stink of armpits. Dry throat, and aching spine. Stinking rags, hatred, and the sting of fire and ice.

He could only understand the woman when she spoke English. He did not know if he was inside of his head or outside in the world. He did not know whether he was talking or thinking. He did not know whether he was deciding what happened next or whether what happened next was deciding him.

When he felt the simmering in the pit of his stomach rise up through him like a shiver, he began to vibrate, and he wrenched his hand away from the woman.

HOKO HAD SEEN the boy shake, but never like this, never with his eyes rolling back inside his head, and his teeth clattering together, never until he collapsed on the ground, and began flopping about like a fish in the bottom of a canoe. Rushing to his side, Hoko tried to contain him. He was whipping his head side to side, and it was as though he had no eyes at all; they were all white. At the sight of them, Hoko scrambled to her feet and started running toward the fires of Hollywood Beach.

She returned, panting, several minutes later, Abe Charles in tow. The boy was lying still when Abe squatted down beside him. His eyes opened just as Abe looked down into his face.

"Little Storm King has awakened," said Abe Charles.

"Don't call him that," said Hoko.

Abe looked up at her. "You should hear him speak."

"He will not speak."

"But he *has,* he *will.*"

"He's sick. He needs to be cured."

"You see him as weak instead of strong. Like a white sees him."

"I'm his mother."

The boy remained on his back, looking up at the moon.

Abe allowed the boy to get his bearings before he sat him up and helped him to his feet. The boy did not refuse his help.

"We'll take him to my place," Abe said. "He can rest there."

The boy walked between them down Hollywood Beach. Hoko held his hand.

"He will be fine," Abe assured her. "You'll see."

On the outside, he seemed fine to Hoko. His eyes were clear now, if not distant, and he appeared to be physically none the worse. But he was still not himself, still not moving his lips, still not tilting his head at the world like usual. She liked that the boy let her hold his hand as they walked, yet she felt she did not know whose hand she was holding.

They passed three fires before they got to Abe's shack, where Abe immediately began stoking the fire and rearranging the clutter of his camp.

"There's fish on the rack behind you," he said. "And elk, too."

"I've already eaten," lied Hoko. "But maybe Thomas."

Squatting on his haunches, the boy was transfixed by the fire. When the woman offered him salmon, he would not take it. When the man offered him a blanket, he would not take that. Finally, they let him stare into the fire. And though nobody noticed, there were soon tears streaming down his face.

After several more minutes busying himself, Abe sat down beside Hoko and offered her part of his blanket, which she refused. "He's been shaking like that ever since he came back," he explained.

"He's ill."

"It's the spirits," Abe said, scooting closer to Hoko, until their shoulders were grazing. He draped the blanket over her knees, and she accepted it. "Eight days ago, he carved strange figures in the sand. The tide didn't wash them away for six days."

Hoko looked into the fire. "He always carves figures in the sand."

"Six days, woman. The tides ran right over the symbols — in and out, twenty times over — and the symbols would not go away."

"Then he must have carved them deep," she said.

"He knows things," observed Abe.

"He hardly knows we're here."

Indeed, the boy seemed to pay no attention to them.

"I'm glad you've come back," said Abe, leaning a tiny bit closer to Hoko. "Things are not the same without you."

"I should never have let him take the boy," she said, as though to herself.

"All of that is done, now. He is a man. Everything is just as it should be."

Hoko shifted her weight away from Abe, and leaned into the fire. "He is a boy, and he will always be a boy."

With a cold heart, Abe stood up to busy himself once more, and Hoko leaned back and pulled the blanket up higher, tucking her knees in tighter and watching her son from across the fire, perfectly placid, unaware of the tears drying on his cheeks as he stared into the flames. She did not remember falling asleep, only the instant before sleep washed over her, when she saw the boy rocking gently back and forth on his haunches.

When she awoke, the fire was dying and there was a slight breeze. The moon was nearly straight overhead flanked by towering clouds. Both Abe and the boy were gone. Down beach, one fire was burning larger than the others, and there were voices on the wind.

Hoko scooted in closer to the coals of her own fire and gave them a stir.

what is

For nearly an hour that night, Storm King rocked silently back and forth on his heels in the glow of the fire as the Siwash gathered all around him. Stirred by the faint breeze, the flames lapped at the air in front of the boy while dark forms danced with a ghostly waver behind him. In the distance, the lights of Port Bonita were strung out east to west, with a smattering of new cabins aglow on the stubbled hillside and beyond. Behind the town, the mountains reared up in darkness.

The people began to grow restless. Each night the silence grew longer, they said. Each night the words that followed were stranger. George saw many familiar faces among the assembled: Abe Charles was among them, and Abe's cousins Tilly Houghton and Lyle Groves. Even the Makah was there, the drunk with the dark-pitted face, standing near the back in his sullen manner. As always, his tiny companion was beside him, shifting about restlessly. Near the outer edge of the crowd, just inside the ring of firelight, the boy's grandfather swayed side to side as though the breeze were stirring him. He looked ghoulish in the firelight, with his hollowed-out eye sockets.

When it seemed that his silence would never end, Storm King stopped his rocking back and forth, and his eyes grew wild in the firelight, and he spoke at last.

"I have seen the many worlds," he said. "And they are here."

And the Siwash looked around at one another, puzzled and frightened.

"Aya hosca d' ayahos," Storm King sang.

But they could not be made to sing in their confusion.

"There is no there," said Storm King. "All paths lead here."

"Are we here?" said George.

"We are here," Storm King said.

"Where will we go from here?" said Abe Charles.

"We will go here. Always."

"And the spirits, where will the spirits go?"

"They will be here always."

"What if we cannot see them?" someone said. "How will we see them?"

"By believing," Storm King said.

Now the Siwash mumbled among themselves some more. And when they fell silent, and the popping of the fire was audible once more, the boy held a finger aloft.

And the people looked at his finger.

"How many fingers is this?"

"One," somebody said.

The boy opened his hand. "Now how many?"

George saw three fingers. "How many do you see?" he whispered to Tilly Houghton, next to him.

"Three," she said.

Suddenly the boy went stiff as a board and began to tremble in the firelight. When his shaking ceased, his whole manner changed. He folded his arms and tapped his foot impatiently, then heaved a sigh. "Look," he said, in a different voice. "You can't just stand there holding shit, Little Chief. You gotta move."

The Siwash looked at one another in confusion. They looked at their hands to see what they were holding, but they were holding nothing.

"What does it mean?" Tilly whispered to George.

"He wants us to move," said George, uncertainly.

"Move where?"

"Move like he moves," George said, straightening his posture like the boy's.

The boy looked straight up at the sky, and George looked up at the sky, and Tilly Houghton, too, looked up at the sky with her near-sighted gaze. The moon was high on the horizon, washing out the stars with its purple light.

"*Doon-doon, doon-doon,*" the boy said. "*Doon-doon, doon-doon.*"

"Doon-doon, doon-doon," said George, dropping to his knees.

"Doon-doon, doon-doon," came another.

And another. They were all looking at the sky.

From down the beach, Hoko saw them all gathered around Thomas in the firelight, and squatting by the light of her own dying fire, she felt alone. Gathering her shawl around her for warmth, Hoko moved toward them in the darkness. When she was within several hundred feet, the hypnotic chant reached Hoko's ears, and she found herself drawn toward it. It was the sound of the Siwash speaking in one voice. When she stepped inside the ring of firelight, Hoko dropped to her knees, like the rest of them had dropped to their knees, and looked to the sky.

"Doon-doon, doon-doon," she said.

And kneeling before the fire, Storm King listened to the sound of the Siwash singing in one voice. The moment had arrived to act. Entranced, the Siwash watched as Storm King reached into the fire and pulled out a burning bough. He stood tall before them and held the burning branch aloft like a torch.

"Ceqwewc! Ceqwewc!" he said.

traveler

The new specialist pulled up in a white Cadillac Escalade. Rita and Dr. Kardashian watched his arrival through the window.

"Ah, here he is now," said Kardashian.

The first thing that struck Rita about the specialist was his age: he looked to be about two hundred — a little raisin of an Indian in a white suit, white vest, and a white ten-gallon hat. He wore his hair in a long white braid. He couldn't have been three inches over five feet tall. When he sprung down out of the Escalade, the top of his hat settled a foot below the roof of the vehicle. He was agile for an old guy, and there was a catlike springiness in his step. His posture was that of a much younger man. When he passed under the window, only the top of his white hat was visible.

Rita wanted to be hopeful, she really did. All around her there was reason for hope: Randy was out of her life — a minimum of five hundred feet out of her life. On top of that, he was no more damaged (well, except for a broken jaw, two black eyes, and a fractured orbital socket) than he had been before she nearly staved his head in with a fire extinguisher two weeks prior. Furthermore, the Monte Carlo was up and running. It wasn't even stalling. Krig installed a CD player. And Curtis did seem to be making *some* sort of headway. He had, after all, taken to the comics as though he'd recognized them, even if he did lose interest. The fact that Curtis was responding to anything was reason to hope according to Drs. Lilith, Broderson, Meachem, Fortnoy, and Kardashian. The fact that he'd made the funny little bell sound, the fact that he smiled at his own revelation. These were all reasons for hope. Still, Rita couldn't rally much hope of her own. And the sudden appearance of a pint-sized Indian with a face like an old russet potato did little to rouse her optimism, even if he was dressed in white.

YOU DID NOT register the arrival of the new specialist. Nor did you recognize my mother. How could you? You stared straight ahead at the letters hanging on the wall. You tilted your head sideways to the left, then sideways to the right, then straight up again. You covered one eye, then the other. There was a letter *f,* and a letter *c,* but no matter how you looked, you could find no letter *k* pinned to the wall. The letter *k* seemed like the key to something. If you could find a letter *k,* perhaps you could order the universe once more, put everything back as it was supposed to be, make everything not quite perfect again.

When the specialist walked into the room, you finally abandoned your letters and looked at the strange little man in white — so different from the other men in white. Do you remember how the old man seemed instantly familiar? Was it the smell of him, like lavender and fir needles and something burned? Was it the little skin tags flowering all around his eyes? Or was it the smiling eyes themselves, which seemed to share your secret right from the start? You knew immediately he spoke in white spaces, knew that he would hear your voice where the others had failed. He spoke directly to you — without looking at the others. It was as though the others were not there.

"Hello, son. My name is Meriwether Lewis Charles. But you can call me Lew if you want. That's what they call me at the casino. Or you can call me Running Elk. Nobody calls me that anymore, though." The old man pulled up a metal stool and set it directly in front of you, and when he hopped up onto the seat, his white shoes did not quite reach the ground.

"They tell me you aren't talking."

"They aren't listening," you said.

"Ah, yes, the age old story. But I can hear you."

"Who is he talking to?" demanded Rita. "Who are you talking to?"

Kardashian smiled uneasily. His eye twitched.

"Shush," snapped the old man.

The woman and the doctor exchanged glances, then promptly turned their attention to you.

"They told me you had a dogfish," said Meriwether.

"The shark is the truth," you said, just like George told you. You reached for your shark-tooth necklace and it was still gone.

"They told me you've been shaking. When they told me that, I knew I had to meet you. I hope you were clean for the *tamanamis*. *'Qway ya?nenict.'*"

"What's that?" said Rita. "What's he talking about?"

"Shush," said the old man. *"Aya hosca d' ayahos,"* he sang. *"Aya hosca d' ayahos."*

"Is this some kind of joke?" demanded Rita. "What is he saying?"

"Silence," said the old man. "How did you burn yourself?"

"I don't want to talk about it," you said.

"It's better if you do. Trust me."

"I don't remember. It was a long time ago."

"How long?"

"Too long to remember."

"I see. Are you sure you can't remember anything?"

"I don't want to."

"Was it a fire?"

"I don't remember."

"It was a fire, wasn't it?"

"It was nothing."

"Tell me."

You covered your ears, my ears, and closed your eyes, and gritted your teeth, and began to swing your dangling legs and sway side to side in your stool.

"Tell me."

"Stop," said the woman. "Leave him be." She reached out for you.

"Ceqwewc! Ceqwewc!" you shouted. You pointed to your arms. Your heart was beating in your ears. You smelled the burning flesh and creosote, heard the dull groan of the planks as the ceiling collapsed.

"Ceqwewc! Ceqwewc! Ceqwewc! Ceqwewc!" you shouted. You pounded your fists in your lap like hammers.

But the woman didn't understand. She only looked frightened.

"Ceqwewc!" you shouted as they tried to calm you. *"Ceqwewc! Ceqwewc!"* as you watched the woman's hope turn to fear and then to tears and finally to revulsion. You fought the white-coats when they came for you, clawing and lashing out at them with a fire in your belly and a fire on your tongue and the flames of an older fire consuming your memory.

RITA WAS SOBBING inconsolably as the attendants wrestled Curtis out of the exam room.

"What happened to my baby?"

"It's okay," assured Dr. Kardashian. "It's okay. This is good, we're making progress."

"What's wrong with him?" Rita choked. "What did you say to him?" she demanded of Meriwether.

"Just part of an old song I thought he might know."

"What song? Why would he know an old song?"

"He's a traveler," said Meriwether.

"What does that mean? What are you saying?"

Kardashian's expression seemed to ask the same questions.

"He walks between worlds," observed Meriwether. "I don't know what that means to you. We do not see things the way they are, we see things the way we are."

"What was he carrying on about?" said Kardashian.

"A fire."

"The burns?"

"That's where things are complicated. His burns are fresh. The fire was much older."

"None of this makes any sense," groaned Rita.

Kardashian concurred with a furrowed brow.

"Many things do not make sense in my experience," said Meriwether.

"Sense cannot explain everything. Why are the sharks dying? Why are the chinook changing sexes? How does a pigeon find its way home? I once met a man in Peru who knew everything. I was on a twelve-day Andean trail tour with my cousin, until her phlebitis started acting up. I met this man in a small village. He was not a clean man. He frequently walked about with food on his shirt, and often throw-up. His feet were caked with mud, his clothes were ragged. He smelled like a goat. Every night he drank rum until he was spinning stupidly in circles and slurring his words and spitting up on himself. His own family would not let him into their house."

"What does this have to do with my son?"

"I'm getting to that. You see, this man had never even left his village. He had no education. And yet he knew everything there was to know. He knew how far Anacortes was from São Paulo. He knew the train schedule for Laramie, Wyoming, in 1869. The elevation of Albuquerque, the population of Dover, the name of every mosque in Pakistan. This man had dined on betel nuts in a thatch hut in the Solomon Islands, and beer nuts in a sports bar in Milwaukee. He spoke Klallam perfectly. He spoke Mandarin, Portuguese, English, Arabic. He knew the name of my cousin, the location of my house, the mayor of Nome, Alaska. He could recite the *Iliad*, count backward in Gaelic, tell you who won Super Bowl XII. And this is not hyperbole, what I am telling you. This was a real man in Peru. And this man knew everything there was to know, saw everything there was to see. Now, how is it possible to know everything and see everything without ever having set foot out of a mountain village? Can you tell me how this is possible, how this makes any sense? Wouldn't you like to know?"

"How?" asked Kardashian.

Meriwether shrugged, and took a coffee nip out of his coat pocket, unwrapped it, and popped it in his mouth. "Beats the heck out of me," he said. "Darndest thing I ever saw, though."

"*What* does this have to do with my *son*?"

"He's been places he's never been."

"So you're saying he's delusional?" said Kardashian.

"He has a better memory than most."

"How can he remember what didn't happen?"

"It did happen. Just not to him, exactly."

"That makes no sense," said Rita.

"As I said, everything does not make sense. Our memories are not ours alone. Our experience belongs to all that is living, and all that has ever lived. It even belongs to that which is not yet born and may never be born."

what's what

For nearly two weeks, Jared Thornburgh agonized over his Dam Days speech. Where was he supposed to begin? What the hell was he supposed to say? To christen something was one thing, sure, but to usher it out of existence? After all, it was official now. The feds had finally pulled the trigger. The news was all over town. The dam would slowly be undone. So was this spiel supposed to be hopeful like a toast or somber like a eulogy? And how do you shoehorn 150 years of history into a four-minute speech? And whose story do you tell, anyway? What about the Indians — should he talk about the Indians? What about those weirdos with the colony? Weren't they socialists or something? Didn't they put up a stink about the dam way back when?

In an effort to bring all this history into focus, Jared decided to pay a visit to the North Olympic Library, which he did one unseasonably dreary Wednesday on his lunch hour. Although Krig had done his best to tag along, hemming Jared in between Dee Dee's cubicle and the Xerox machine on the way out, Jared was able, by the tactful employment of the word *we* on several occasions, to insinuate Janis's presence in the afternoon's affairs, at which point Krig bolted.

Aided by a flabby-armed woman in a corduroy dress, Jared located no less than eleven volumes in the 979.79s — ranging from slim to elephantine, hardback to tapebound — devoted to various histories of Port Bonita and Clallam County. One by one, the librarian pulled them out and handed them to Jared, never failing to comment.

"The Gorseline accounts in this one are splendid," she assured him. "This one has the most comprehensive coverage of the mills," she informed him with a tap on the dust cover causing the flab of her arm to jiggle. "This one has the most dam and fishery coverage. This one here is about the Klallam tribe — both the Elwha and the Jamestown.

Lots of interesting stuff about Shakerism. This here is probably the most comprehensive coverage of the fire of October 1890. But this one also covers the fire. This little one here is the first enviromental impact study done on the dam from 1931. Dry but informative. We have a much more comprehensive environmental coverage in Dr. Phillip Fenner's *Historical Assessment of the Elwha River,* which, if I recall, is still out to that short-haired gal from Fish and Wildlife, but if you'd like to put a hold on it . . ."

"I'm good," said Jared. "Thanks."

"You'll probably want something on the Mather expedition," she said.

"That's cool," he said. "I think I'm good with these."

"Oh, no, you'll definitely want something on the Mather expedition."

"Uh, okay."

"Come, come." Trailing in her wax-scented wake, Jared followed the librarian down the aisle to the 917s, where, expertly scanning the chaos of spines, she soon degenerated into a mild state of agitation upon discovering *The Olympic Journals of Charles Haywood* to be absent from their designated post at 917.9794 — absent, in fact, from the entire vicinity of of the 917s.

"This is not good," she intoned.

"Oh well, that's cool," said Jared. "I'll just get started with these."

"No, I insist. Let me look into this. Come, come."

A wax-scented stroll past the computer cubbies to the information desk, followed by a cursory check of the database, yielded a status of lost or absconded, causing Flabby Arms to frown and knit her brow.

"Another one lost or stolen," she said with a sigh. "And they're actually cutting our budget next year, if you can believe that."

WHEN JARED RETURNED to High Tide, minus *The Olympic Journals of Charles Haywood,* he ducked past Krig's cubicle, told Dee Dee to hold his calls, and locked himself in his wainscoted office for the remainder of the afternoon, poring over *Shadows of Our Ancestors: Readings in the History of Klallam–White Relations, Taming the Elwha: The Story of the Thornburgh Dam,* along with *Port Bonita:*

From Steam to Electric and Beyond. Far from putting things into focus, or providing any kind of context whatsoever in which to couch
his presentation, the information made Jared's head spin. Still, he
soldiered on — through Quimper's early reports of the Klallam vil-
lages, past the establishment of the Customs House and the National
Reserve, to the platting of Port Bonita, to the erection of the dam,
to the fire of 1890, through five decades of booming mills and the
harvesting of the greatest stands of Douglas fir on the face of the
earth. He finally left the office around five forty-five, stack of books in
arms. After a brief stop at Siam Palace to pick up dinner upon Janis's
request, Jared resumed his studies at the dining room table between
bites of pineapple curry, perusing George C. McGurdy's *Port Bonita
Days: Conquering the Last Frontier; A Photographic History,* which, as
promised by Flabby Arms, provided excellent photo collateral.

"Man, what a dump," Jared commented aloud in reference to a tintype taken from the crest of Hogback in 1889, looking west down a
muddy Front Street. "It looks like Dodge City after a tsunami. What
were these people thinking?"

Below this, another photograph offered virtually the same vantage
a year later, shortly after Front Street had been gutted by fire.

"That's more like it," Jared said.

On the page opposite, two tiny mustachioed figures in suspend-
ers, clutching one giant whipsaw between them, stood upon a massive butt log at the base of a rubble-strewn hillside. Little plumes of
smoke unfurled here and there behind them. The sky was a slate gray
wash. "What a mess," Jared said, flipping the page, where he was immediately confronted by the proud personage of his ancestor, Ethan
Thornburgh. "There he is," he announced, sliding the open book
across the table for Janis's inspection.

With a spring roll in one hand, and her other hand just below the
tabletop resting firmly upon the imperceptible bulge of her abdomen,
Janis peered down at the picture until a smile played at the corners
of her mouth.

The photo in question, an 1891 tintype studio portrait, was faded ghostly around the edges. Ethan was snug in waistcoat, morning coat, wing-collar shirt, and Burberry necktie, his thin mouth hard and straight beneath his mustache, his silver-eyed gaze pointed like a challenge directly at the camera.

"I think he looks like you," said Janis.

west of here

a talk

Beverly was fifteen minutes late already, a fact that neither surprised nor perturbed Hillary. Nor was it any surprise that the Bushwhacker was dead on a Tuesday at three fifteen. The dining room wasn't even open until five. The kitchen help was still tying their aprons and turning on the lights. Hillary sat alone nursing her flat Diet Pepsi, as the waitress circled the room with a tray, dispensing dimpled red candle holders. Quietly, Huey Lewis was "Workin' for a Livin'," and Hillary couldn't help but think of Franklin Bell for an instant. It was a song he'd listen to.

Hillary fought the impulse to stand up and leave before Beverly arrived. Anxiously, she buttoned up her puffy jacket to hide the evidence, though at six weeks it was hardly visible at all. She looked for something else to do with her hands but, finding no purpose for them, began tearing little pieces off the edge of her napkin and rolling them into balls between her fingers and dropping them on the carpet by her feet.

Her mother finally showed up at three twenty, festooned from shoulder to wrist with shopping bags from the mall — Victoria's Secret, T.J. Maxx, Alley Cat Boutique. She was sporting a pair of equestrian boots (though to Hillary's knowledge she'd never been within thirty feet of a horse) and a freshly dyed Rachel cut that was way too young for her (not to mention ten years out of style). Tethered like a pair of water buoys beneath a tight brown sweater, her tits were riding high. Her lips looked puffier than ever. They were stuck open. Coupled with the tight skin around her cheeks and forehead (which lent her a saucer-eyed look), the overall effect was that of a blow-up doll.

"Congratulations," said Bev.

Hillary blushed.

"I mean about the dam coming down. I heard on the radio last week."

"Oh. Right. Why didn't you leave that stuff in the car?" Hillary said.

Beverly snuck a glance over her shoulder at the empty bar. "Here?" she half whispered. "Are you kidding me?" Staging her bags around the foot of the chair, she smoothed her black pencil skirt over her bony butt and sat down. "Incidentally, why on earth are you wearing that jacket, Hill? You look like the Michelin Man."

"Thanks a lot."

"Honey, I didn't mean — "

"What *did* you mean? How am I supposed to take a comment like that?"

"Well, dear, I just meant that — well, it's so warm in here and . . ."

"And what?"

"Well, it's not the most flattering jacket in the world. There, I've said it. I'm sorry I care about these things, Hillary. I know you think I'm shallow. I just think a person ought to give a little thought to how they present themselves. You look pale. Are you getting enough iron?"

"I'm fine."

"You look thin."

"There's one I never thought I'd hear from you."

"I'm concerned, dear, that's all. Now, what's good here?" she said, flipping her menu open.

To Hillary's surprise, her mother didn't say anything when Hillary changed her order at the last minute from the chef salad to the Reuben. Beverly ordered the bacon bleu burger with home fries and a Manhattan. She could eat anything she damn well pleased and stay thin.

"Still dating the thirty-year-old?" she said.

"Twenty-eight, dear. No need to be bitter." Beverly pushed her Manhattan aside. "Why can't we just get past all this?" She reached over the table and set her hands atop Hillary's. "I've always wanted the best for you, dear. I'm sorry things didn't work out with your father. I know you blame me for that, and I truly am sorry. But it's time to forgive and forget." She straightened up and hoisted her tits.

"Mom, I'm pregnant."

It was as though the air suddenly went out of the blow-up doll. Beverly's mouth folded in on itself. For once, there seemed to be general alarm in those saucer eyes. "Hill, honey, I . . . what . . . when did this . . . with . . . ? I'm just, I'm . . . honey, congratu—this is a good thing, right? I mean, you're keeping the . . . this is good, right?" Beverly gave her daughter's hand a squeeze and smiled sadly. Hillary glimpsed something genuine beneath all that surgery. She forgave her mother in that instant. She thought she even saw a tear in Bev's eye and no sooner did she feel her own eyes begin to burn. "Yeah, Mom, I guess it's a good thing, yeah."

"How far along are you, sweetie?"

"About six weeks."

Bev got a glimmer in her eye. "We need to start shopping."

"Mom, I think we should just wait until—"

"What we *need* to do is gut that second bedroom of yours and get to work on the nursery. Now, aren't you glad you didn't buy that dumpy trailer? Everything happens for a reason."

"Mom, seriously, I just—"

"Think neutral colors for now. We can add the appropriate highlights later when we know. You are going to find out, right? Surprises are overrated, honey, trust me."

"But Mom, don't you even care who the—?"

"Have you still got that white dresser that used to be in the bedroom? Because that would be perfect for—"

"The baby is mixed, Mom."

"Mixed how? What are you talking about? Listen, what about the vanity that used to be in the downstairs bedroom at home . . . you know, the one with the—"

"The baby is half black."

". . . the polished brass fi—*half black*?"

Molly arrived just then with the bacon bleu and the Reuben. "Can I get you two anything else? Another Manhattan?"

"Yes, please."

"Anything for you?"

"Nothing for me," said Hillary.

Beverly looked pale and bewildered. She slumped perceptibly as the waitress took leave.

"The father's name is Franklin Bell," Hillary explained. "He's a parole officer here in Port Bonita. He's black, Mom, okay? Black as the ace of spades."

"Hill, honey, I don't . . . I'm just a little, well . . . a little shocked. You don't see too many African Americans here in — "

"Mom, he's not an African American, he's just black."

"Oh. Well, still, you don't see a lot of — "

"I'm not even with him, Mom. I just slept with him. I was drunk."

"He didn't . . . did he rape you?"

"No, of course not. Look, the point is I'm not going to marry him."

"Does he know?"

"No."

"Are you going to tell him?"

"No."

"Why not? You'd be eligible for child support. You really need to think of the child, honey. Whether or not you plan on raising this — "

"I'm going to do it my way, okay, Mom. I'm going to wait and see."

Beverly patted her daughter's hand once more. "Of course you are, honey, I'm sorry. I won't interfere, I promise. But there's no reason we couldn't strip that paint from the — "

"Mom, please," Hillary pleaded, but really she was grateful for her mother's attention.

Throughout Bev's second Manhattan, and her third, they talked almost like friends. Bev was unnervingly candid after her second Manhattan, divulging at one point that she'd twice had sexual relations with black men back in the 1960s.

"Not at the same time, of course," she said. "I was never that wild." Leaning forward, Bev lowered her voice to a half whisper. "For the record, it's not true what they say."

"Can we change the subject?" said Hillary.

"Okay, dear. I didn't mean to upset you. I just want you to know that your old mom still has a few surprises up her sleeve."

"Mom, I'm gay."

Bev nearly choked on her Manhattan. She cleared her throat and blotted her lips with a napkin, and generally composed herself, smoothing out a sleeve, and straightening her posture.

"Did you hear what I just said, Mom?"

"Yes . . . yes, I heard, darling."

How could she possibly be this calm? "And?"

"And . . . well, Hill, honey, it's an awful lot to process. In light of everything else. As you might expect, I'm not entirely comfortable with the idea. But I'm proud of you."

"Proud?"

"It took courage to tell me. And you're sure, Hill?"

"I'm sure, Mom. I like women."

"No, I mean about being pregnant."

"Positive."

Bev opened her purse and started fishing around for her lipstick. "Oh, honey, it's so exciting."

Hillary was stunned by her mother's reaction. So that was it? Everything was hunky-dory? She was gay and pregnant with a black man's child, and her mother was proud of her? Had Port Bonita come that far since the day Kip Tobin started calling her Lesbo?

KRIG TOOK HIS stool at the end of the bar opposite Jerry Rhinehalter, who was slumping even more than usual.

Molly soon emerged from the kitchen, glancing in turn at Jerry, then Krig. "Bookends," she said.

Jerry Rhinehalter gave her the finger.

"No more Kilt Lifter, Dave," said Molly. "You were the only one drinking it. Bonnie switched it out with Alaskan Amber."

"Ech," said Krig. "What are my other choices?"

Molly heaved a little shark sigh and cocked a hip. "Sierra, Bud, Bud Light, Manny's, Hale's Pale, and Port Townsend IPA."

"So, nothing dark?"

Molly rolled her eyes and cocked her other hip. "Alaskan Amber's the darkest."

"Yeah, okay," said Krig.

Krig scanned the bar for a sports page or an auto trader but found only the business section and the technology section. "Workin' for a Livin'" was playing in the background. It reminded Krig of the 1980s. He found himself tapping his foot, and thinking about that first summer after high school. Good times. Tobin and the gang. Parties at the icehouse. Life was like a highway leading in every direction back then.

Krig took a chug of his Alaskan. Too rich but in a dull way — not enough umph. The thought of no more Kilt Lifter pissed him off, and soon he was shining this bitter light backward into the past. *Highway leading in every direction* — ha! When had Krig ever done anything but spin his wheels? Tobin and them had always made him feel like an outsider, plus the icehouse was a dump. And hadn't the eighties actually sucked? Sure, he had youth on his side, and while the future may have been elusive, at least it seemed far away back then. But with twenty years and an unsentimental gaze, Krig could see now that it actually sucked. Without the benefit of nostalgia, Huey Lewis sucked. The summer of '84 sucked. Krig's prospects sucked hard after he passed up the scholarship. Isn't that when Krig started cashing in his dreams and *workin' for a livin'*? Isn't that when Krig's life jumped the shark? Peering across the bar at Jerry Rhinehalter, Krig couldn't help but wonder when Jerry's life jumped the shark. Probably when he started squirting out kids and selling cars. And hanging out at this place. But somehow the knowledge that Jerry Rhinehalter endured was both comforting and disturbing. Who was he kidding feeling sorry for a guy like Rhinehalter? At least Rhinehalter had a wife and family. At least Rhinehalter had a purpose.

Krig could see Rita was losing interest in recent days. The more she trained her focus on the future, the less she seemed to notice him. Daily, that focus seemed to sharpen, and the more it sharpened, the blurrier Krig became. Sooner or later they'd have the *friends* talk.

There would be boundaries. And the more he tried to cross those boundaries, the further away Rita would move them. Looking around the bar distractedly, Krig's eyes landed on Hillary Burch. Second time he'd seen her in here. He nodded at her, but she didn't see him. He remembered how everyone had started calling Tobin Happy Meal after she'd almost bit his dick off after that fiasco at the dance. Guys were afraid of her after that. Whoa, was that her mom? Damn, kind of a cougar. Rhinehalter was checking her out, too.

When Beverly felt Krig's eyes upon her, she gave her tits a hoist and cocked a questioning eyebrow at him.

Krig turned away immediately and could feel himself blushing. He glanced at the television, then the window, and finally across the bar at Rhinehalter. "How's the family, Jerry," he said.

"Fuck off," said Rhinehalter.

everything

The old man was patient with you. Even when you refused to listen, or hammered your fists in your lap, or hurled your mashed potatoes against the wall, the old man was unperturbed. When you flung the checkerboard across the room with such force that checkers rained down in every corner, he waited out your fury, nodding his head ever so slightly beneath the weight of his big white hat, as the checkers tinkled and rolled and settled to rest all about him. Sometimes he smiled at your outbursts. Sometimes he hoisted a playful eyebrow. When you refused to speak, he made you draw what was inside of your head. But you could not draw the many worlds, even with my hand. You could only scratch out erratic lines and bubbles of white space, and you scratched so hard that sometimes you tore through the paper. And as you scratched and scribbled your chaos, the man in white talked and talked, and you let his voice wash over our senses like the burbling of a stream.

the ragged edge

Mather's overland route had led the expedition through some twenty miles of the roughest country the Olympic interior had to offer, at the cost of their last mule, the morale of the party, and three weeks of precious stores. Mather's decision to leave the Elwha had delivered them to the brink of starvation, four thousand feet above the very river they thought they'd left behind. For, indeed, the overland route had merely rejoined the Elwha, intersecting eight miles from where they left the river, a distance they might have snowshoed in three days.

The party retreated into a chilly state of silence as they set off from what would later be named Deception Divide and began the steep descent back into the depths of Press Valley. Plunging in a ragged single file through the soft snow toward the Elwha below, Mather's nerves were set further on edge by the fact that he could often hear water running beneath the crust. A half-dozen times in the afternoon, the men were stopped in their tracks by the rumble of avalanches, and on each occasion Mather could do nothing to prevent himself from looking back at the unstable ridge looming in their wake. With each footfall came the certainty of a slide. Mather was afraid to stop and let his weight settle and afraid to move forward lest the ground disappear from under him. He would have welcomed cloud cover, even driving snow and ice but for a little stability.

Falling to the rear in favor of his customary post behind Mather, Haywood kept a considerable distance from Cunningham, who never seemed to master his snowshoes — plodding forward as though each step were an assault on the mountain.

Slowly and irrepressibly, like a lava flow, a searing hatred was welling up in Haywood.

30 March 1890

He has led us in circles and in doing so led us straight to ruin.
I could just as well blame myself for permitting it to happen.
Cursed am I for being loyal, for never voicing my dissent. I fear
we shall not live to see the Quinault.

With every agonizing step, with each rumble from the bowels of
the earth, Haywood cursed himself for being a follower.

Cunningham did not associate the distant rumblings with his
own predicament, as he pushed forward dazedly, his sights locked
between Reese's shoulder blades. The present moment was as distant and elusive as a dream. Indeed, he no longer knew whether he
was asleep or awake, whether he was moving himself or being pulled
along by Reese.

Outwardly, Reese's set jaw and squinting eyes projected the same
dogged determination as ever, but his steps, unlike Cunningham's,
were tempered by extreme caution as he negotiated the steep terrain. With his squinted eyes alternating between his footsteps and
the lofty ridge across the valley, where a stiff wind was kicking up
snow flurries and blowing them sideways off the peaks like streamers,
Reese longed for the shadowlike presence of a confidant, the sturdy
guileless companionship of a mule.

Late in the afternoon, without mishap, the party arrived with a
palpable but unspoken relief at the timberline, where the slope began
to ease into the wide valley floor and the roar of the Elwha could be
heard in the distance. They trudged through snow five feet deep in
places, wending between trees that increased in size as they drew
nearer to the bottomlands. At last they met the Elwha where she was
running wide near the head of the valley. On the right bank, with a
clear view upriver into the gap, they shoveled a flat swathe clear of
snow and began to set up camp. Mather could not ignore the tension
as the men went separately about their tasks.

"We've been here before," Mather said to Haywood, setting a canvas aside and turning his attention to Haywood. "Recall the Liard in

the dead of winter. Or the Yukon in 'eighty-six, right smack in the middle of—"

"Damn it, it was never like this!" snapped Haywood. "Not on the Liard, not on the Mackenzie, not anywhere! This ceased being an expedition sometime back and became a fight for survival. And we're losing, Jim, we're losing." Immediately, Haywood regretted the reckless impulse to give his desperation voice. So much so that he was almost relieved when Mather met him with contempt.

"Is that what you think, Charlie? If that's the case, then I've sorely misjudged you for a lot of years, my friend. This *remains* an expedition, not some whimpering fight for survival. These are the lessons explorers must learn, the perils explorers must face, so that the rest of the world can enjoy free passage. I suggest you get to mapping this wilderness instead of surrendering to it, Charlie, or I'll have to set my own unskilled hand to the task. There's an hour of good light left, and I've got a mind to fish. Anyone else who's hungry ought to strongly consider doing the same." With that, Mather seized his whipsaw and his tackle off of the ground and proceeded on an upriver course along the bank. Runnells was the first to follow.

Ironically, it was Haywood who enjoyed the most success fishing, albeit grudgingly, pulling in a sizable rainbow and a pair of early spring chinook before dusk. Mather added a small rainbow, and Runnells, fishing a dark gray channel along the far bank, added a pair of steelhead.

They ate silently by the fire, except for the dog, who enjoyed but a few precious morsels of fatty skin before traversing the circle, whimpering in an attempt to ingratiate herself. Finally, they were forced to tether her to a tree, where she lay wide-eyed and disconsolate as the men ate slowly in spite of their ravenous hunger. Only quietly did they lick their fingers, as Sitka began to whimper once more from her prone position in the shadows, where Mather could sometimes see her hungry eyes flash in the firelight. When the last greasy skin had been consumed, and the fire settled at last into a slow burn, the men crept off to their bedrolls one by one, and rousing herself in the darkness,

Sitka got to her feet and pulled vainly at her tether for the better part of an hour, if only to nose around the coals or discover some discarded morsel in the snow.

Morning broke crisp and clear and found the party refreshed. Even Sitka, who still did not begrudge the men their neglect, harbored a renewed optimism, sniffing furiously about the dead fire the moment she was unleashed. In spite of all appearances, the bedraggled expedition assumed an air of business as they readied themselves for the day's journey. They traded their moccasins and snowshoes for boots as they were forced to kick steps into the snow up the steep incline heading into the gap. The dog exhausted herself in frantic bursts getting up the hillside, often slipping back as she pedaled furiously to gain purchase. There was still determination in her, but it was grim at its center.

By midday, the party had ascended nearly twelve hundred feet, from which vantage they could see almost to the foot of Press Valley, where everything had begun to unravel and continued to unravel until they arrived here, two weeks later, clinging to a crust of thawing snow high above the Elwha. And lest they forget their precarious plight, the warmth of afternoon brought a procession of rumbling reminders that they did their best to disregard as they trudged onward and upward. By three o'clock they had reached the pass. According to the aneroid, they had ascended just over seventeen hundred feet from the valley floor. From this vista they could see beyond the narrow curve at the foot of the valley to the very cleft that had first deceived them. To the northeast, the peaks of Mounts Mather, Haywood, and Runnells were visible in a cloud-broken line.

"It's all downhill from here, gentlemen," quipped Mather. "Home free."

Scarcely had the words left Mather's mouth before Haywood pounced upon him furiously and without warning, tackling the bigger man and pinning him to the ground. Before the others could pull him off, Haywood had his hands around Mather's neck and bore down with all his might. But he was no match for Mather's superior strength. Mather threw Haywood off and was about to launch his own offensive when a deafening rumble like rolling thunder stopped them in their tracks. Dumbstruck, the men gaped across the valley to the northwest at the face of the very ridge that they had only yesterday descended.

"Good God," said Haywood beneath his breath. "Look at the size of it."

Each man stood frozen in place.

The whole face of the mountain seemed to be in motion, sliding in a great crust toward the timberline, its descent almost perpendicular. Snowballs the size of houses bounded down the mountain in advance of the plunging mass — sputtering, as Haywood would later describe it, like drops of oil on a heated surface. The timberline began to shiver well in advance of the descending mass. Within seconds the breath of the beast hit the tree line with a tremendous rush of air, rolling up the forest like a rug before it, uprooting a swathe of timber a thousand feet wide, snapping the mighty trees like matchsticks and hurling them hundreds of feet down the mountain. The slide gathered mass as it thundered toward the basin, pouring a dirty flow of snow and timber and rocks into the canyon, until the canyon was virtually no more, filled to the brim with hundreds of feet of rubble. When the rumbling ceased and the last of the rubble had sifted down the canyon, the ensuing quiet was almost as deafening. The men stood stupefied, gazing upon all that was left in the wake of the slide: splintered trees and great patches of bare earth and naked rock. And in his heart, every one of the men knew that it was only by some whim of fate they'd been spared.

"Thunderbird," said Mather at last, breathlessly. "Of course!" He began to laugh. "Why didn't I think of it before?" He laughed, and laughed heartily, as though the realization tickled his fancy to the very core. But nobody laughed with him.

been campin'

When, after nearly eleven years in Port Bonita, Franklin Bell snuck his first look at the Thornburgh Dam, he refused to stray within four feet of the chain-link fence. Craning his neck tentatively for a peek, he straightened up immediately upon glimpsing the vertiginous drop. Everything about the place made him uneasy. The rumble beneath his feet seemed to suggest that the dam might give way at any second. Trudging back up the gravel path to the Taurus, Franklin opened the hatch. Rupert bounded out immediately, thrusting his square head to the wet ground and sniffing all around the car as Franklin unloaded his big blue gym bag with VICTORIA CLIPPER emblazoned on both sides in flaky white letters. He never did take that cruise. Passed up a week of his paid vacation that year and spent the other week looking for a hobby, unsuccessfully. Got a free bag, though.

Franklin wasn't treating this like any vacation. The bag was stuffed to the gills with trail and topo maps, six cans of Chunky soup, two pairs of tan corduroys, three sweaters, a knife, a fork, a spoon, a plate, a tiny skillet, a pair of comfortable loafers, and four pairs of socks. The bag weighed roughly thirty pounds, distributed unevenly toward one side where all the soup cans nested. The second and larger bag, a hulkish black affair with many superfluous straps, contained a gallon of water, three Pres-to-Logs, eight books of matches, and the world's biggest flashlight. This bag weighed roughly forty-five pounds and presented the additional obstacle of excessive lumpiness. To make matters more cumbersome, a two-man tent, an orange sleeping bag, and a foam cooler stuffed with turkey franks, spicy mustard, and two pints of eggnog were lashed to the bag with lengths of yellow nylon rope. As Rupert nosed around the parking lot, pausing to lift his leg on the back tire of a Silverado, Franklin fished the trail map out of the big bag and spread it out in front of him on the hood of the Taurus for final review.

All evidence suggested that Tillman had picked up the Crooked Thumb trailhead. The alleged cock-slap had occurred between trail miles 6 and 7 and was marked accordingly by Franklin with a red *X*. The "theft" had occurred just shy of mile 16. Tillman was heading in a southwesterly direction. He was probably not far off trail — probably somewhere in the vicinity of mile 20. On paper the plan looked feasible — a twisted line from point A to point B, but glancing at the endless green expanse spreading out beyond Lake Thornburgh, it occurred to Franklin, with a shiver, that he probably should have brought a few extra cans of soup. Maybe another pack of turkey dogs.

Who the hell was he kidding? He'd never find Tillman out there. And what if he did? What if the injury scenario Franklin had concocted was true, and Tillman was on the side of the trail with a busted kneecap? How the hell would he get him out of there — carry him? And what if Tillman didn't want to be found at all? What if Tillman really was dodging the law? Why was Franklin convinced of his innocence in the first place? If Tillman was injured or innocent, why not get the law involved? Franklin tucked the map in a side pocket and hefted the smaller bag, slinging its thirty pounds over his shoulder, where instantly the edge of a soup can dug into the tender fat roll below his rib cage. The moment he tried to heft the second bag, he knew he'd badly miscalculated.

The Pres-to-Logs were first to go — plenty of logs where he was going, and he had plenty of matches to light them with. Next to go was the plate. He could eat out of the skillet, just like at home. He even opted to leave the spoon — since you could eat Chunky soup with a fork. He left two pairs of socks and one of the sweaters in the backseat. He drank one of the eggnogs and left the empty carton on the passenger seat. By the time he was finished consolidating, Franklin slung but a single bag and the foam cooler over his shoulder, then crossed the slab to the trailhead, where he began his journey up the squelchy trail. The midmorning sun slanted through the dripping trees. The mosquitoes were in hiding. Rupert sniffed along at Franklin's heels, as he trudged up the incline, his quads already beginning to burn, the foam cooler squeaking incessantly in its halter, the rolled up sleeping bag bonking him on the back of the head with each step.

Shortly before noon, Franklin reached mile marker 4, huffing and puffing. He'd gained nearly a thousand feet in elevation, leaving the last vestiges of Lake Thornburgh behind. The mosquitoes were out in full force now. A blister had formed on the little toe of his right foot. He was sweating like Buster Douglas. Worst of all, he had a bad case of swamp ass further complicated by the leaking cooler, upside down in its rope halter. The lid had snapped like a saltine cracker just shy of mile marker one, and begun to crumble shortly thereafter. Stopping along a high crest overlooking the river, Franklin sat on a moldering evergreen beside the trail and fished a turkey dog out of the cooler, snapping off a bite as he loosened his shoelaces. For all his ailments, this outdoor stuff wasn't so bad once you stopped to soak it up. A hot dog really did taste better outside. Even cold. Not until Rupert started mooching did Franklin realize he'd forgotten the dog food.

"Doggonit, Rupe." A quick mental inventory of the food stores — six cans of Chunky soup, fifteen jumbo turkey dogs, and a bag of Funyuns — eased Franklin's mind somewhat. Hell, he could probably stand to lose a few pounds anyway. That jellyroll had really slowed him down coming up the steep parts. His tits had gone soft, too. Lobbing the last half of his turkey dog to Rupert, Franklin fished out the map again and traced his path in red pen from the head of the trail through mile marker 3.

"Damn if it don't look like a straight line on the map, Rupe."

But Rupert was busy rooting around a rotten stump. Once Franklin retightened his laces, got to his feet, hefted his gear, and began plodding onward, Rupert abandoned his stump and loped into stride behind Franklin, nose to the ground. The second leg of the hike proved considerably less grueling. The trail leveled out for several miles along the ridge before descending into the dark bottomlands, where Franklin could hear the river once more. While the ridge had smelled of summer, of warm cedar and dry air, the shady lowlands smelled to Franklin like a flooded basement or a wet carpet. The ground softened beneath his feet. Rainwater gathered in footprints along the path, collected in puddles along the edges of the trail. The squeaking cooler continued to crumble, dropping little foam pebbles in Franklin's wake. Marked with a rough wooden sign depicting a triangle, he soon came upon a little side trail wending its way through a patch of gold-leafed trees to the riverbank, where the sunlight flooded in, and the Elwha ran fast in silver ropes. Here he found a raised dirt clearing, a crude fire pit, and a notched log bench with initials carved into it. Franklin plopped his bags down on the tent pad and sat heavily upon the bench, where he ran a hand over the surface as he surveyed the initials looking for T. T. And though Tillman's initials were not to be found, he had left what Franklin imagined to be his his mark in other ways: a pair of crumpled Snickers wrappers in the brush, an empty pint of Smirnoff along the riverbank.

"I'll be damned, Rupe. Looks like we've got a scent."

For fifteen minutes, Franklin walked along the riverbank collecting firewood. Pausing on the gravel bank drenched in sunlight, with the river rushing by and the mountains looming in the distance, he told himself he could get used to this camping business. It was quiet out here in nature. A guy could experience a different kind of aloneness than the loneliness of a dateless Saturday night spent on his bile-colored sofa or the loneliness of strolling the aisles of Safeway late at night with a heaping cart of Chunky soup and four gallons of eggnog.

The problems began back at camp when Franklin burned through three books of matches trying to set fire to a sizable log without the aid of paper or kindling. How hard could this be if a caveman could do it? Finally, he got the splintered edge to take, and spent the next forty-five minutes blowing on the flame until he became so lightheaded that spots threatened to blot out his vision. When, an hour later, he'd finally succeeded in starting a cooking fire that actually crackled, he unpacked the skillet and a can of soup.

"Mm-mm, Rupe. You're eatin' like a king tonight, old boy."

Rummaging through the bags, an unsettling realization began to take hold: he'd forgotten the can opener. He spent ten desperate minutes stabbing at the top of the can with a table knife before he finally staved it in with a river rock on the edge of the fire pit in an explosion of brown goop. Rupert lapped the lion's share of it off the ground in a frenzy. Franklin forked out the few remaining chunks and ate them straight from the can. To top the meal off, he inhaled a cold jumbo dog with a snake of mustard running down its spine and washed it down with a pint of eggnog.

Even as evening fell, and the light drained from the forest, Franklin found himself surprisingly at ease in the darkness. What was he afraid of in the first place? The wilderness was so expansive, so big and serene and passive, it didn't seem to notice he was there. Where was the threat in that? It wasn't until he awoke from a dreamless sleep that Franklin realized he'd nodded off by the fire. The log pulsed orange in the fire pit. Rupert slept curled at his feet. There was a chill in the mountain air and the buzzing of crickets from as far as the ear could hear. The river roared in the darkness. Through the treetops a smattering of stars winked down on Franklin. He sat soaking it all up with a great satisfied yawn welling up in him. Not too shabby.

"What say we hit the sack?" he said, patting Rupert's ample rump.

In his sleeping bag, on his back, with Rupert smacking his lips and breathing sleepily at his side, Franklin savored his final waking moments staring up through the mosquito net at the treetops and the stars. The next time Franklin awoke, he awoke to sounds — a can skittering across hard ground, followed closely by the familiar squeak of foam rubber. Some snorting, some sniffing, then the violent scattering of ice. Finally, a deep guttural growl — a growl with saliva clinging to the edges. Franklin shot upright in his sleeping bag. *Sweet Jesus, what the —!* Rupert began to whimper and got to his feet as Franklin tried to settle him. The intruder rummaged about the fire pit, chortling and sniffing at the air. As the beast drew nearer to the tent, Franklin felt his scalp tightening, felt the blood beating behind his eyes. A dark snorting form began circling the tent just below the mosquito dome. Suddenly it stopped in its tracks and began sniffing. Even the crickets fell silent. When the snorting nose pushed at the fabric of the tent,

Franklin swooned with a rush of fear. The instant the beast reared up on its hind legs, something in Franklin snapped.

"AAAAAAAAAAAAAAAAAAAAHHHHHHHHHHH!"

Rupert began to bark wildly.

Franklin rolled to his left, snapped on the flashlight, and aimed it right up into the shining eyes of the beast, which let loose a roar that seemed to come from the center of the earth. Scrambling for the entrance, Franklin fought with the snagged zipper. Rupert squirmed out before him and charged straight at the intruder with such rabid intent that the beast seemed confused as Rupert lunged snarling at it, driving it back. Franklin hit the bear again with the beam of the flashlight, and it irritably tried to shield its eyes from the light. Finally, it swung around on all fours and charged off into the woods. Franklin's relief turned to panic as Rupert took off after it, hurtling through the darkness full speed ahead, howling, crashing through the underbrush on the heels of the bear. His trumpeting grew fainter and fainter until the night swallowed it up altogether. Weak in the knees, with the river ringing in his ears, Franklin pointed his flashlight out into the impentetrable wooded darkness. The smart thing to do was to stay put. Stir those coals up. Find himself a big stick. Rupe was probably already on his way back. Prodding the embers until their orange bellies were up, Franklin scattered some twigs on top and blew into the center, and the flames flared up in his face, casting a pale glow all around the clearing.

drip, drip, drip

It was still raining when Timmon awoke at dawn. Inertia was his instinct. Sneezing, he forced himself upright, where he soon discovered that groundwater had leached into the tent from the corner nearest his head and ran a channel down the length of the tent, gathering in an elliptical puddle near his feet.

"Fucking shit on a stick," he said.

After a hissing fire and a cup of hot water, Timmon readied his tackle and made the half-mile trek downstream to the Elwha, where he chose a level stretch of low bank from which to cast. Though he didn't have his bow, he was heartened almost immediately by the appearance of a buck on the far shore. Watching the beast saunter off into the brush, Timmon felt certain his luck was changing. The rain was sure to stop. Nature would surrender its bounty yet.

He fished until late in the afternoon and caught nothing. He hunted until dusk and succeeded only in getting wetter. In the evening he sat shivering by the fire, cursing his misfortune. But things only went from bad to worse. By the next afternoon, the hunger expanding like a balloon in his stomach could no longer be ignored. In a moment of weakness, knee deep in the riffle with another snagged lure at the end of the line, Timmon, cold and hungry and sleepy, wept like a child.

For the better part of three interminable rainy days he fished and fished — from the bank, in the riffle, up to his waist in deep, dark pools. He pulled nothing out of the Elwha, did not enjoy so much as a bite. In the crepuscular hours, Timmon stalked the forest all around the creek, wild-eyed with hunger, clutching his bow so tight his knuckles were white, crouching in the brush, lurking in the shadows, scanning the understory with his desperate gaze. He did not encounter so much as a doe or a chipmunk in all his scouting.

After dark, he busied himself to avoid the hunger. He dug a pit and fashioned a smoker around it with river rocks and fir boughs, though he had nothing to smoke. He constructed a gangly bed frame four inches high, lashed with salal vines, and crossed with thin green cedar boughs to combat the groundwater. He hung the rain tarp inside the shelter above his bed. He washed his socks and hung them over the fire to dry. He nested and renested his pans. He organized his fishing tackle. He emptied every pocket of his fancy pack of pennies and lint and burs. His fingernails were down to nothing. But in the end there was still the hunger, black and eclipsing. As a last resort, he consumed creek water by the quart to fill the hunger balloon and was awakened in the night by explosive diarrhea.

Though the rain finally let up by morning, Timmon's fortunes only worsened. Further weakened by dysentery and fever, he could not summon the will to mobilize himself. He could not bear to face the barren Elwha another day, could scarcely bear the thought of gathering wood for a fire, or boiling water, or least of all tramping around in the wet foliage looking for movement. Instead, he lay on his back and stared up at the rain tarp until his eyes felt heavy, though not with sleep. In his feverish apathy, he could scarcely even rally his self-contempt. So he was a big fat bust in the wilderness, same as he was in civilian life, so what? None of it seemed to matter. He wasn't even hungry anymore. If he died there in the middle of nowhere — or in a room at the Wharf Side for that matter — who would really care? He wouldn't even miss *himself*—if *that* wasn't a good measure for the value of his life, what then?

The urgent and burning chill of dysentery finally stirred Timmon into action early in the afternoon. Scrambling free of his sleeping bag, he scurried out of the shelter, clipping the doorway on his way, thus caving in a small portion of ceiling. He couldn't make it halfway to the creek before he was forced to drop his pants not three feet from the smoker, where he squatted gurgling for fifteen minutes in his own sweet stench, bathed in a film of sweat, too weak and miserable to even swat at the cloud of mosquitoes enveloping him. When it seemed he was empty of everything he'd ever eaten plus half of his stomach lining, Timmon staggered back to his shelter, stepped over the collapsed portion of ceiling, and fought his way stupidly into his sleeping bag. There, he lay on his side staring at the small square of light that was his doorway, unable to think of anything at all until sleep came for him.

He was awakened by a trilling. He opened his eyes to find a chipmunk standing in the doorway. "Tweeeel tweeeel," it said.

"Get lost," groaned Timmon.

The chipmunk was doing funny things, things Timmon didn't know chipmunks could do, making its head bigger and smaller.

"Don't fuck with me," Timmon said.

The chipmunk was definitely fucking with him. "Tweeeel tweeeel," it said, its head the size of a grapefruit.

Pulling himself upright, Timmon's world began to spin. Inky black shapes played at the corners of his vision. The chipmunk trilled once more, its distended head about to burst.

"Fuck me," Timmon said as he felt himself slipping down a dark hole.

And for the better part of untold hours, he flashed in and out of this feverish state of semiconsciousness, dreaming in nonsensical fits, staring open-mouthed at the caving thatch ceiling with no thought in his head. Twice, he rolled over in his sleeping bag and pissed himself. At times, the world upended itself, and Timmon looked down at his prone figure from the ceiling without recognizing the gaunt grizzled face staring back up at him. And though he felt on those occasions the faint stirrings of something between pity and disgust, these impulses were fleeting, soon blotted out by a swelling of vertiginous blurry space, which popped like a bubble full of black spots and swallowed his consciousness. There was no telling how long the delirium lasted. There was no telling at first whether it was morning or evening when the world broke like a fever, and his senses awakened this time to the trilling of a thrush and a weak gray light slanting in through the doorway. Outside, the rain was little more than a mist. The awful churning in his stomach had given way to a raw emptiness that seemed to feed upon itself. With a ragged and prolonged moan, he tried to undo the knot of panic in his chest. Working his way into a sitting position, he perched on the edge of his makeshift bed, buried his face in his hands, and began to weep. He wept slowly at first, with the dim hope that tears might somehow bring comfort, that some benevolent force in the universe might hear his plea and respond soothingly. But when he found no comfort, his crying came fast and pinched and desperately uneven, punctuated now and again by falsetto whimpers, not unlike those of a child in distress. Finally, his grief reached such a pitch that it drove him to his feet, and he paced the muddy floor in circles, alternately balling his fists and pulling his hair. He spoke in snatches, unable to finish a sentence, not knowing what he was trying to say.

I didn't think . . . But what about? . . It's not supposed . . .

His breathing came faster and shallower, his pacing grew progressively more erratic, until he was dancing a desperate stooping jig around the inside of the shelter. And when he wound himself so tight that he could get no tighter, he snapped, scattering in every direction at once. Swinging his arms about wildly, he tore and kicked and raged at the walls all around him, pulling apart all that was lashed together, yanking anything that resisted his force. And indeed, the entire structure fought back, turning his own strength back on him, seizing his lean arms as he assaulted it, blinding him with its needled fingers, hopelessly entangling his legs as it toppled, limb by limb, all around him. Though he made quick work of the demolition, he did not tear his house to the ground; he wrestled it into submission. And when at last his blind rage had played itself out, Timmon collapsed in the heap of wet branches that remained. Wiping his burning eyes with a tattooed wrist, he began to laugh. And he laughed so hard that he began to cry again.

"Tweeeeeeeel tweeeeeeel," said the chipmunk from his perch overhead.

"Trooooooooool," said the thrush.

Drip, drip, drip, came the forest.

By the time the laughter and tears subsided, Timmon felt shucked, as though everything had been scooped out of him, and in the absence of everything, a calm soon washed over him as he set to building a fire. And when the fire burned hot, he leaned into it and slowly began to wind himself back up until he felt something like a man again.

Half-starved and better than half-beaten, he passed several hours in front of the fire, plumbing the very depths of his being for a persuasive reason to go on living, groping for any incentive to stay or any inducement to go. If not to be left alone, what did he want, then? Maybe the opposite — *not* to be left alone; whether locked alone in a car on a rainy Chicago street; or locked alone in a cell, a ward of the state; or merely locked in the prison of his own selfish design. What if, at the risk of betrayal, at the risk of being forsaken, he had the balls to be penetrable again; the balls to connect with someone, or something, or some otherness instead of being tough or repellent? What if he had the balls to give a shit, to decide *not* to know better? Could he free himself from the burden of experience, could he ignore the overwhelming evidence and convince himself that somebody actually cared or something actually mattered? If so, then maybe, just maybe, he'd have the balls to be innocent again.

In the end, after all the plumbing and searching, it was the thought of two cheeseburgers and some dry socks that prevailed. Timmon began his preparations with grim determination — nesting his pans, folding his tarp, winding his ropes, scrupulously avoiding any speculation as to what sort of fresh start thirty-six bucks might actually stake a man to in Port Bonita, or anywhere else.

four-cans-of-chunky-soup-and-a-half-bag-of-funyuns fast

The wind was starting to pick up and Franklin folded his arms for warmth, rocking ever so gently back and forth. Here and there a tree creaked in the darkness. And high above Franklin's head, the treetops swished restlessly. He stared into the fire, as he had for hours, distractedly at first but then fixedly. Franklin worried little for his own safety anymore. The fear was gone. Even the thought of another bear was not at the forefront of his anxieties. Tillman's whereabouts was a matter of even less concern. His sole concern now was Rupert, alone out there in the wilderness. He'd happily spend the rest of his days in bachelordom living in that crappy apartment behind Bonita Lanes, if only to have old Rupe back — no girlfriend, no Tillman, no sterling record, and definitely no more camping. Just he and Rupe, like always. The M's on UPN 11. Takeout from Ming's Royal Garden. Evening walks around the parking lot beneath the flickering streetlights, Franklin humming Joe Walsh, Rupert lifting his leg at every tire. He'd taken it all for granted. Now the thought of life without Rupert was too desolate to contemplate. But worse was the thought of the old boy suffering somewhere in the darkness, dying some slow, agonizing death, wondering, even as he heaved his last ragged breaths, where his keeper was. How lonely that river would sound to old Rupert.

It was impossible to say how much time passed. Franklin hardly budged from his place except to stir the coals. He'd grown so accustomed to the roar of the river that it no longer registered. The wind had died down again by the time a stirring in the underbrush demanded his attention. Clutching his big stick, he looked up just in time to see Rupert amble out of the brush and into the firelight, panting heavily, exhausted, but apparently unharmed. He set his square head on Franklin's knee and looked up at him, his jowls dangling saliva, his big sad eyes looking grateful, and Franklin's heart all but took flight.

The next day, following a breakfast of Funyuns and cold Chunky soup (the jagged edge of a basalt wedge having cleaved the can open quite handily), Franklin and Rupert broke camp and set out in search of the second red X, the site of the alleged theft near mile 16. If, in fact, Tillman was responsible for the theft (and it was certainly more plausible than the cock-slap scenario), then the second red X represented the last signpost on Tillman's trail. That's where things got sticky. From there, it was anybody's guess which way Tillman fled. But knowing what he knew about Tillman — that he was a runner — Franklin knew that Tillman would never turn back on his own tracks unless he had to. Tillman would keep moving forward.

Franklin figured that he'd better move fast — *four-cans-of-Chunky-soup-and-a-half-bag-of-Funyuns* fast — if he wanted to catch up with Tillman. He hiked with renewed vigor in spite of his blister as Rupert bounded along in front of him, nosing around and lifting his leg and wagging his nubby tail. Like Rupert, Franklin was awake to the world, at once enamored and suspicious of the mysteries surrounding him. Never had his senses been quite so alert. Nothing escaped his notice. He glimpsed every bird flitting in the understory, noted the trickle of every water source, the slightest temperature drop when the trail dipped into a gulley or the sun ducked behind a cloud. On several occasions he even paused to sniff the air like Rupert. Once he thought he smelled grape jelly.

Early in the afternoon, midway across a wooded bluff some five hundred feet above the river, Franklin and Rupert arrived in the vicinity of mile 16. Two hundred yards up trail, Franklin located the scene of the crime, marked by a tattered remnant of yellow tape; a small clearing just off trail in a hollow. A crude fire pit. A tent slab. A rope strung between trees. And there, tossed aside in the ferns just outside the clearing, having either been overlooked or simply ignored by the investigation, Franklin discovered a GoLite frameless backpack and a cheap aluminum skillet.

They proceeded south along the ridge, switchbacking up the steep incline over rutty terrain, until the trail emerged above the treeline on a bald narrow crest facing west. Nothing had prepared Franklin for the terrifying splendor that greeted him there. Across the wedge-shaped valley below him, beyond yet another narrow green valley, a jagged row of snowcapped peaks were strung out in a crescent, surrounding one mountain so broad and massive that its craggy white face dwarfed the others. A shiver ran up Franklin's neck at the sight of it all. Suddenly the middle of nowhere seemed boundless. Somewhere out there was Timmon Tillman, and the odds of finding him suddenly seemed impossibly slim. Still, Franklin was determined to search as long as the Chunky soup held out. Without further pause, he began wending his way down the bald face of the ridge toward the tree line, three hundred feet below.

Late in the afternoon, Franklin and Rupert reached the bottomlands once more. So narrow was the valley that the sun could not find an angle in, and an autumnal chill settled into the still air. On a high bank overlooking the Elwha, the trail forked, with paths heading upriver and downriver respectively. The downriver course offered the wider passage, snaking along the bank toward the foot of the long valley. The upriver trail was clearly the more rugged course, switchbacking down into the rocky canyon a hundred feet to the river. Franklin felt in his bones that Tillman would have taken the rugged path.

At the bottom of the canyon the trail met with the river at a fast-running slough, where a wide tree had been felled and notched, bridging the rapids. Rupert made the crossing jauntily, pausing midway to lift his leg on a gigantic knot, and waited at the trailhead, wagging his nub. Franklin crossed the gigantic log like a tightrope walker, arms outstretched, holding his breath, looking straight ahead at all costs, as he tried desperately to ignore the roar of the boiling rapids. He sped up the last five or six steps, and upon reaching the far side, stopped to pee, while Rupert rooted around in a clump of ferns. Just as Franklin concluded with a delicious shiver, Rupert lit out of the brush clutching something in his jaw: the remnants of a paperboard package. Zipping his fly up, Franklin liberated the package from Rupert's slobbery jaws.

PINNACLE PASTA, the wrapper said.

legend meets science

AUGUST 2006

"See, now look at the similarities," said Krig, leaning forward on the burnt orange sofa, slowing the frames manually with a furious clicking of the remote. "See how the shoulders rotate? See how the arms swing when he walks?"

"Yeah, okay," said Rita.

"That's a mountain gorilla — silverback."

"Ah."

"See, that's the mistake a lot of people make — they use the bear comparison. It's like comparing apples and wolverines. Well, of course, it doesn't look like a bear. But it just might be a North Amercian gorilla we're talking about, here."

"Why do you suppose he evolved so tall? I mean, there'd have to be a reason for something to evolve so tall, right?"

"Hmph. Interesting question."

"And the white Bigfoot in Texas," Rita pursued. "Why would that one be white? I mean, an abominable snowman, yeah, I can see that. But a white Bigfoot in Texas?"

"The white Bigfoot is a complete hoax. *Sasquatch: Legend Meets Science* is concerned with the hard evidence. The P.-G. footage, the Skookum Cast. There's thousands of hoaxes every year. In fact, *most* Bigfoot sightings are hoaxes. Show me a sighting report and I can tell you right away whether it's a hoax."

"How is that?"

"They almost always use the bear comparison, for starters. They always say the same things: 'It had long brownish red fur, but it wasn't a bear.' 'It smelled like a skunk.' 'It walked away slowly.' "

"What's hokey about that?"

"First of all, I didn't smell any skunk. And those things weren't walking slowly. But what's really hokey about the fake ones is that there are no *details*. The fact that they say the same old things just tells me they're making it up. It's all about the specific details. That's how you know it's the truth. It doesn't always make sense, I guess, but it isn't vague." Krig paused the video and avoided Rita's eyes, surprised by the sickly rush of emotion welling up in him. "My encounter on the Elwha was at night." He shifted his weight ever so slightly away from Rita on the sofa. "So I didn't actually see anything — *no reddish brown hair, no big feet* — and that's not good enough for some people. But I can tell you what the strange, deep whispering sounded like — it sounded like it was circling the inside of my head. And I can tell you how it all made me feel."

"How?"

"Terrified. But more alive than I knew possible. It was the only time in my entire life that I felt like anything was possible."

"I've never felt that," said Rita, fishing out a Merit. "Mind?"

"Go for it," he said.

"Dave," she said, firing up her Bic. "We need to talk. I just . . . I guess I . . ." She hesitated.

"What's wrong?"

"It's just that right now my life is . . . I don't . . ."

"Do you need more time off?"

Softly, she began to sob. Krig moved in closer and pulled her head to his shoulder and stroked her hair. She straightened up almost immediately and wiped her eyes and gathered herself and puffed on her cigarette. "I just want to thank you for being such a good friend the last month. Really, Krig, I don't know how I would've made through all this stuff with Curtis, and Randy, and the rest of it, if it weren't for you."

"You don't have to thank me. I love doing it. You're the coolest girl I've ever met — the coolest *woman*."

"Oh, Dave, but I'm not. Look at me, look at my life. I'm damaged. I'm almost forty and I'm about to start my life over."

"So? So, that's a good thing, right?"

She swiped once more at her runny mascara and drew deeply from her Merit until the cherry crackled. "I don't want to hurt you, Dave."

Krig felt the ache immediately. It was as though her voice came from somewhere else. His eyes sought refuge on the television screen, where the P.-G. footage was frozen. Why *did* they evolve so tall?

"If I were in a different place in my life," Rita pursued, "things might be different. The timing is all wrong. I feel like I'm using you as it is."

"How?"

"To get over things."

"But I *want you* to get over things."

"Nobody should be a springboard, Krig."

"It's okay."

"It's not. It's not right for anybody." She receded into smoking silence.

Krig set aside the remote and scratched his neck. How was it that he actually believed her? "I get it," he said.

"I don't think you do, Dave. It's really not about you."

"I get that, I really do. Maybe we should just be friends for now. You know, until you feel like you're ready or whatever. There's no hurry. I'm not going anywhere."

"I'm moving to Seattle," she said.

"When?"

"As soon as I can afford to."

"How soon is that?"

"Probably not soon enough. But it's gotta happen as soon as I can afford to. There's better resources for Curtis in the city. Better opportunities for me."

"Why don't I go with you?" Krig said, startling himself. "I've got money. I've got almost six — "

"It's something I need to do alone. With Curtis. I owe him that. But that doesn't mean that you couldn't come visit us," she said brightly. She set a hand on Krig's knee, and that was a first. He put his hand atop hers as though to trap it there like a butterfly.

"I'll definitely come visit you," he said, knowing that he would never visit her and knowing that it would not be the failure of good intentions or the gradual withering of desire that prevented him from doing so but an act of will, mostly for her sake.

When Rita left that night, she kissed Krig in the doorway in a way she'd never kissed him before, not awkwardly, not recklessly, not defiantly, not desperately — but sweetly, softly, carefully, like something meant to last.

THE FOLLOWING MORNING, Friday, when Rita arrived at High Tide with a hard-won sleep still tingling in her bones and her hair in a jumble, she found a crisp white envelope in her work locker. *Rita,* it read in a masculine hand. Hesitantly, she opened the envelope, with a mounting certainty that it contained bad news, at best a lovesick plea from Krig to feed her ambivalence. Rita swooned upon revealing the envelope's contents. Inside was a check signed by David Dalton Krigstadt for the amount of fifty-seven hundred dollars.

There was a note:

Rita,
I Googled your question. One paleontologist I found said gigantism is typical of cold climates, and *Gigantopithecus* was a form of the Ice Age megafauna. Another dude said it was probably an endocrine imbalance.

Krig

P.S. I'm taking off for a few days, so if I don't see you before you leave, good luck.

P.P.S. You can take as long as you need to pay this back, seriously. It's just sitting there anyway.

After Krig left the note at High Tide that morning, he drove east toward Sequim, without really knowing why. Maybe he'd go out to the spit. Or maybe drive up to Hurricane Ridge. For now, he just felt like driving. The traffic was light on Route 101. The Goat was hitting on all cylinders. Maybe he really should take off for a few days. He'd only told Rita that he was leaving so she wouldn't confront him about the check and talk herself out of cashing it. The thought of changing a life with one gesture left Krig giddy. Maybe he should go to Seattle and hunt for an apartment for Rita and Curtis. Surprise them by doing all the footwork and research, maybe even put down a deposit. Nah — that might be kinda weird. Boundaries, Krig reminded himself. Boundaries.

Surprising himself, Krig drove right past the Dungeness spit, clear to Discovery Bay, where he ate a six-egg omelet and drained an espresso milkshake at Fat Smitty's. With his distended belly pressed fast against the counter, Krig stared down at his empty plate. Somehow he wasn't upset about Rita leaving. By breaking his heart, she'd actually sort of inspired him in a way. What the hell was he doing all the way out in Discovery Bay? Something about this breakup had a butterscotchy taste.

After breakfast, Krig navigated the Goat in a wide arc out of the gravel lot and surprised himself once again by hanging a right onto Route 10. With his stereo uncharacteristically silent, he drove the hundred-odd miles south down the peninsula to Olympia, where he walked around the farmers market, bought a star fruit, a Chinese lantern, and a pair of wrought-iron candleholders for J-man and Janis. After dropping his bags off at the Goat and feeding the meter, he browsed a few antiques malls, took a tour of the capitol building, and ate Mongolian stir-fry.

remembering

Throughout work that Thursday, as she spooned and gutted chum by the dozens, pausing only to itch her nose on the shoulder strap of her rubber apron, never speaking to Hoffstetter as he slit bellies mechanically beside her, Rita struggled with the question of Krig's check. How was not accepting the loan the right thing? Why the heck was she morally obligated to return the check — why? Why couldn't the check just be an answered prayer, a stroke of good fortune, or simply a huge favor? Fifty-seven hundred bucks could change everything. She and Curtis could move to Seattle as soon as next week and get an apartment. She could buy two or three months with the remainder if she scrimped, three months to coordinate the best care for Curtis, three months to navigate the labyrinth of social services, three months to get a job (something better than waitressing or processing — maybe something administrative), three months to begin a life that didn't start in a big fat hole. The mere thought of fifty-seven hundred dollars strengthened Rita's resolve to the point that she actually felt hopeful about the future for the first time she could remember. But take away the fifty-seven hundred dollars now and suddenly all her plans seemed impossible, suddenly the thought of a future was exhausting. The thankless drudgery that she'd be forced to undertake in the name of incremental progress seemed unendurable. Didn't she deserve a break? Didn't everybody get some kind of break eventually?

When she took her ten o'clock break, Rita retired to her locker. Even before she fished out her smokes, she seized the envelope from her purse and looked at the check long and hard, until the slant of Krig's handwriting looked like an old friend. As lunchtime approached, she convinced herself to tear the check up on her next break and be done with it. When she went to her locker again and clutched the check firmly in her fingertips, she couldn't go through with it. Instead she folded the check and put it in her back pocket. Throughout lunch, Rita smoked cigarettes on the loading dock. Occasionally, she pulled the check out and unfolded it and pondered the possibilities anew. Maybe the thing to do was wait until next week, talk it over with Krig when he got back: make it legit, put it on paper, design a payment plan, even add a little interest — maybe then, taking the check would feel right. But it still wouldn't be right — why? Krig was trying to buy her freedom, right? Like maybe her freedom to love him at some later date? Is that what this loan was for Krig — a way of holding out hope? A string attaching the two of them even after she left? Oh, but what a small price, one little string — especially one attached to a heart as reliable as Krig's. Maybe Krig really didn't need the money. Maybe he gained something bigger by his sacrifice.

When Rita arrived back at the trailer after work, she skipped dinner and began cleaning the kitchen. On her hands and knees, she scrubbed the buckled linoleum, cleaned the grease-spattered oven, douched out the sticky fridge, and washed the windows until she could no longer see the glass. Next, she attacked the monstrous carpet, with its green tentacles, running the old Oreck over it until it lay in one direction like new-mown grass. In Curtis's room, Rita slowed her pace to gather from every corner, from under every carelessly strewn T-shirt and pair of jeans, his discarded drawings, which she paused to consider as she scrupulously stacked them. The proportions were a little off, but they were the work of a talented sixteen-year-old boy — maybe not a prodigy but a boy who, with the right opportunities, with enough encouragement, might make something of his abilities. Straightening the tattered edges, Rita set the stack of drawings carefully aside and resumed her work folding Curtis's sweatshirts, stripping his bedding, correcting the upended lamp, and vainly scrubbing at the spreading mold blotches along the back wall. The little room shamed her more than the rest of the trailer. It didn't seem to matter how much she scrubbed or straightened the boy's room, it remained as cold and squalid as a cell.

In Seattle, they'd have a real home, Curtis would have a real room —

she'd get him a bed with a frame, a desk, a computer, a chest of drawers. They'd get an apartment with good light, lots of windows, wood
floors. The refrigerator would be full. She'd keep the place neat and
orderly. They'd shop together like they used to, confide in one another as never before. Curtis was going to snap out of all this — he was
improving daily: no more twitching, no more screaming, no more
clamping his eyes shut and covering his ears. Any day now, Curtis
would begin to recognize all that was once familiar — and just in time
to forget it. Because everything was going to be different once they
got out from under the cloud of hopelessness that forever hung over
this trailer, this rez, this entire town.

Krig's folded check was dog-eared and tired at the crease by the
time Rita arrived at the clinic ten minutes early for visitation on Friday. Meriwether, in his signature white suit and white ten-gallon hat,
his braided ponytail dangling halfway down his back, was already in
the waiting room, perched in a straight-backed chair, his feet barely
touching the carpet, so intent on *Jeopardy* that he did not look up as
Rita entered.

"What is Mount Rushmore," he deadpanned.

"What is Mount Rushmore," echoed a toothsome, gravelly voiced
contestant, as Rita lowered herself into a seat beside Meriwether.

"Drinker," the old man said, with perfect conviction. "Look at the
nose."

"He's improving isn't he?"

"Yes. But the red-haired woman has the momentum. She's at
twenty-five hundred right now."

"My *son. Curtis.* He's getting better, isn't he? You said he was improving," Rita said. "Dr. Kardashian said you were making progress.
He said you were having breakthroughs. You said yourself he was
remembering things. He's going to be all right, isn't he? He's going to
come back?"

"How can I know these things?" Meriwether said, his eyes fixed on
the television. "Who is Helen of Troy?"

"Who is Helen of Troy?" echoed the red-haired contestant.

"Last time, when I was watching you through the window, I actually felt like you were getting through to him — like you actually could communicate with him. Two weeks ago, I thought you were crazy talking to him like that. But the other day, I saw it — I did. And toward the end of the session, it looked like he was drawing, *really* drawing — *pictures*, like he used to."

"What is Antarctica?" said Meriwether. "They cut your boy's hair — over the ears. It looks good."

"The drawings — they're a good sign, aren't they?"

"Could be," said Meriwether. "Oh, goodie, Double Jeopardy. This should be good." Eyes glued to the screen, Meriwether fished two coffee nips out of his white coat pocket. "Nip?" he said.

bushwhacking

Twenty minutes after Rupert had unearthed the Pinnacle Pasta wrapper, Franklin began ascending the steep face of a narrow wooded ridge, keeping his eyes peeled on the periphery of the trail, looking for movement or any sign of Tillman's passing. Low clouds had moved in during the morning hours. The wooded hillside was shrouded in mist, and visibility was less than a hundred yards. In the early afternoon it began to rain so lightly that it collected like dew on Franklin's sleeves and didn't penetrate the fabric of his sweater. It clung to his face like perspiration.

Midway up the face of the ridge, Franklin paused to reposition the lone remaining can of Chunky soup within his blue bag, which was digging into the small of his back. Bracing himself unsteadily against a mossy outcrop the size of a VW Beetle, he switched from his tennis shoes to his easy breathing loafers, which accommodated his swollen feet more comfortably. Once inside of them, he wiggled his toes and hiked up his socks, then trudged onward somewhat refreshed.

Was he crazy to continue under these circumstances? Was it crazy to think that in this vast and seemingly endless wilderness he could actually find Tillman? Was it crazy to believe that it was actually his *destiny* to find Tillman? Was it naive to think that Tillman *wanted* to be found in the first place? Franklin granted himself one more day. If his search yielded nothing by morning, he'd have no choice but to turn back.

As Franklin approached the ridge, the clouds broke, and he found himself walking above the clouds. The sensation was indescribable. *Ethereal* — was that the word he was looking for? It was sort of heavenly up there above the clouds. The air was lighter, sweeter, with just the slightest hint of underarm deodorant. Even his footsteps felt effortless above the clouds. The sun shone down, gloriously unobstructed, and Franklin paused to close his eyes and turn his face upward and soak in some of its goodness. He opened them again to a sky impossibly blue, so blue it was hard to look at. Gazing back across the valley, the eastern ridge was visible in the distance like a dimpled pie crust running in a crescent around a creamy cloud filling.

"Holy Toledo. Would you look at that, Rupe?"

But Rupert was already descending the ridge on the far side, nose to the ground. The bald shale face of the ridge was the trickiest terrain Franklin had negotiated yet. The ground skittered out from beneath his feet with nearly every step. He descended the steepest portions crab-wise, descending back into the clouds to the tree line until the grade of the trail leveled out somewhat, whereupon Franklin and Rupert assumed a steady pace, the former with his gaze ever scanning the forest all around them and the latter with his butthole puckered and his nose to the ground intently. Within the hour, they reached the bottom of the narrow valley where the trail jogged south, and somewhere in the distance the river roared dully, shielded by the trees. Though Franklin tried to avoid his thoughts, the creeping fear of finding his way back out of this wilderness, trail or no trail, was inescapable. They must've covered six miles since the Pinnacle Pasta wrapper. Tillman could have proceeded anywhere from there. Hell, he could be on a bus for Jackson Hole. He could be eating lobster right now at Dupree's. Or rib-eye. Or jumbo prawns. Or garlic mashed potatoes slathered au jus. The thought of it was almost enough to make him hate Tillman.

The next mile offered relatively flat terrain through the woodlands. The cloud cover lifted and the mist let up, though the forest all about continued dripping. Puddles riddled the trail, and Franklin's shoes were soon soaked through. Sunset was still two hours off, and that Chunky soup was more enticing by the minute. The trail was about to jog around a corner to the south when Rupert caught a scent and began to pick up speed. Before Franklin could stop him, the dog went bounding toward the bend and out of sight. Franklin took after him at a jog, then turned on the afterburner as Rupert rounded the corner.

"Rupert!"

By the time Franklin cleared the bend he was winded, and Rupert was nowhere to be seen. Stopping in his tracks, he did his best to quiet his breathing, and he listened intently, scanning the forest with a slow panoramic sweep of his narrowed eyes.

"Ru-peeeeeeert!"

Suddenly, something flitted out from beneath the brush to his right, and Franklin spun his head around just in time to see a bird shooting off into the canopy. Deliberately, he resumed his inventory, tracing no further movement beyond a gentle swaying of treetops. Somewhere to the east — if the sun could be trusted — the river was just barely audible, a low steady hiss, and from here and there in the canopy came birdsong. Beyond that, a deafening silence. Franklin held his breath and felt the panic rising in him. Suddenly there came three staccato barks in the distance up ahead. Franklin took after the barks for forty or fifty yards and then stopped once more to listen, his heart beating out of his chest.

"Ru-peert!"

Rupert loosed another series of clipped barks, farther off this time, in the direction of the river. In spite of the panic, Franklin kept his wits about him. He scurried to a nearby tree, where a broken limb jutted out seven or eight feet above the ground. Just as Rupert barked once more, Franklin rose on his tiptoes, slung his bag strap-wise from the limb as a marker, and began tromping through the underbrush. Creeping vines entangled his shins, low limbs whipped his face and arms and he plowed forward, a hundred yards, two hundred yards, until he stopped to listen and gather his breath. Looking back he could not discern his own path. He strained to locate his marker, but the harder he looked, the harder it was make out anything distinct in the shadowy forest. As a precaution, he wrestled his striped sweater off, and dangled it over a limb, reasoning that the cobalt blue and orange stripes would be more visible than the dark bag.

"Ru-peeeeert!"

A few birds twittered.

Franklin could no longer hear the river. But he knew it was dead ahead — just as surely as the trail was directly behind him. He was at a sudden loss as to which way to proceed. Perhaps the wise choice was to backtrack and find the trail and await Rupert's return. But what if Rupert was hot on Tillman's trail?

"Ru-peeeeeeert!"

Not even a bird twittered on this occasion, though Franklin heard the faint trail of his own echo calling back from across the valley. He stood perfectly still in the calm of the forest for a minute or more, waiting for Rupert to betray his whereabouts. But Rupert was silent. Finally, he gave up, yanked his sweater down off the limb with a sigh, and decided to proceed back to the trail to await Rupert's return. Turning back, he retraced his steps for fifty or sixty yards, until they ceased to look familiar. Or maybe they were familiar. It all started to look familiar. He forged ahead for thirty or forty more yards, until he could hear the river faintly, once more. But something was wrong. The river seemed to be coming from in front of him now, which made no sense at all. That would mean the trail was the other way, when clearly he'd come from this way, right? Wait a minute. But then — hold on a sec. Shit. He scanned the forest desperately for his marker, for any sign of the trail, but the more he tried to gather his bearings, the more disorienting were his surroundings. Somewhere out there, Rupert maintained his deathly silence, as an icicle of fear ran down Franklin's neck.

This was bad. This was real bad. Franklin told himself to stay calm. Think this thing out. Take a deep breath, close your eyes, and reassess your surroundings. He couldn't be *that* lost, because he hadn't trekked more than a couple hundred yards off trail. The thing to do, Franklin decided, was to climb a tree — get a better look. Maybe he could see the river from up there, or maybe the trail. Couldn't hurt. With that, Franklin selected a nearby tree whose fluted trunk seemed to offer good footing and began climbing the first tree he'd climbed in thirty-nine years.

moxie

Wet, bedraggled, half starved, but above all else resolved to procure a cheeseburger and a pair of dry socks at almost any cost, Timmon Tillman set out from his lost paradise having enjoyed a breakfast comprising hot water and the peanut husks he'd managed to scrape from an inseam of his backpack. God, how they'd melted on his tongue. To think of the countless times he'd scattered husks carelessly at his feet at old Comiskey. To think of that curlicue of mustard on a hot pretzel, with that little dapple at the end, like an exclamation point. And the fucking hot dogs. Oh, the hot dogs. Maybe he should give sauerkraut another try. His old man had sure loved the stuff. The bastard.

Timmon's long strides carried him fast on a downhill course through clustered ferns and thickets of salal, until he could hear the Elwha raging in the distance. He traveled light, having cut bait on the useless fishing tackle, abandoned his nest of skillets, and closed his books for the last time. A mile into his journey, he nearly went back for the crossbow, which might've fetched a decent dollar in hock — maybe even a hundred bucks. But coasting on forward momentum, he didn't have the strength to turn back for anything.

Timmon was willing to forgive himself for his most recent failure, on the grounds of false pretense. His unmolested solitude had, after all, been molested — molested by old ladies peeing themselves, by neofascist yuppies in Gore-Tex socks, by dead industrialists, and finally, by a gnawing hunger and the irrepressible thought of a cheeseburger. Timmon was forced to concede that his fate was inextricably linked in the most arbitrary ways to things and people and events he'd never given a thought to.

The mist had burned off in the highlands, though a ghostly ribbon of clouds still clung to the valley floor below. As he switchbacked his way down the wooded ridge, a weak sunlight was beginning to filter through the canopy, and his thoughts warmed along with his muscles. Though he had nothing to buoy his optimism, Timmon felt it creeping into his step and decided he liked it there. What if it were true, that a decision—as much as any person or event or thing—could change a life, really change it?

Timmon's path met the Elwha running fast at the head of a wide channel. After the next gap he knew he would descend into Press Valley—a half day of easy traveling. Moving still at a brisk pace, he trained his eyes always upon the rutty trail and its perimeter. It wasn't until he quit whistling that he heard the first shout and stopped in his tracks. There came another. They seemed to be coming from the northeast, but the echo made it difficult to tell. One thing for certain, the shouts were earnest, though something in their tone could not belie to Timmon's ears a certain hopelessness.

Proceeding slowly, ears alert, Timmon came upon a blue gym bag hanging from a tree limb on the side of the trail. *What sort of dumb-fuck packs a gym bag for the backwoods?* Timmon yanked the bag down, snapping the limb, and instinctively began the business of unzipping it and rifling through its contents: an ugly sweater, a map, three books of matches, two pairs of filthy socks, and a lot of little Styrofoam crumbles. And lo and behold, in a corner of the bag behind some wet corduroys, bingo—a can of Chunky soup! Timmon could scarcely believe his good fortune.

Even as the ragged pleas continued in the distance, Timmon swung his fancy pack off his back and fumbled around in the pockets for his Swiss Army knife and, squatting on his haunches, opened the can furiously with trembling hands. No sooner had he pried the top loose than he brought the can to his lips like a pint of beer, where he discovered that Chunky soup was too thick to consume in such a manner. He dug into the brown gravy with three fingers, furiously shoveling the mess into his mouth. When the can was scraped clean but for a pair of marooned peas refusing to be dislodged, Timmon nearly tossed it aside but checked himself and stuffed the can in a plastic grocery bag, which he replaced inside the gym bag.

That's when Timmon noticed that the shouting had stopped. A wave of nausea washed over him like a chill. What if his selfishness had cost a life? What if destiny had offered him a choice, a shot at redemption, and he'd chosen Chunky soup?

He listened intently, hopefully, for another shout. When it didn't come, he called out into the valley:

"Hello?"

"—*ello-ellooo?*" came his echo.

He waited a few seconds, and called again. And this time, as his echo reverberated, Timmon's scalp tightened as he heard a reply from the thick of the woods, perhaps a quarter mile to the north.

"Hold on!" he shouted. "I'm coming for you! Keep shouting! Do you hear me? Keep shouting!"

Stepping lightly, Timmon wended his way intently through the dense undergrowth toward the shouts, traveling several hundred yards, until he was nearly upon the voice. Fighting his way through a tangle of dead thimbleberries, he stepped out in the clearing, and there, on his ass, leaning against the furry bark of a heavily buttressed cedar, looking sheepish with a weak grin and clenched teeth, was Frank Bell.

Franklin hardly recognized Tillman, gaunt and bearded, wild-eyed with hunger and who knew what else. It was his tattoos and his height that finally betrayed him.

"Tillman?"

Timmon narrowed his gaze. "What the fuck are you doing here?"

"Looking for you," said Franklin, struggling to his feet with a groan.

Tillman's face darkened.

"No, no, it's nothing like that." Straightening up, Franklin groaned again, and his legs nearly gave out.

"What's wrong with you?"

"Threw out my back tryin' to shinny up that damn tree."

"What for?"

"So I could see my bag," he said, indicating Timmon's right hand. "I lost sight of it."

Instinctively, Tillman clutched the straps of the bag a little tighter but then caught himself and loosened his grip. He tossed the bag at Franklin's feet.

"Here's your shit."

"You eat the soup?"

"Hell, yes. You got more?"

Franklin cast his eyes down and shook his head gravely.

"Shit on a stick," said Timmon. "Well, get up, then. We gotta get out of here before I run out of steam."

"Er, no can do, I'm afraid," said Franklin meekly. "My back."

Timmon had a bitter taste on his tongue. He wished he hadn't come. He should've ignored the shouts and kept moving. This could cost him a lot of time. He didn't have a lot of time. But looking at the pathetic figure Bell cut, slumped against the tree, Timmon soon chased away his regret and drew a deep breath. "All right," he said, exhaling. "We gotta think this thing out. We gotta sit down and fig—"

Suddenly, both men were startled by a great thrashing in the nearby underbrush. Timmon put a hand on his holstered buck knife. Franklin sat up stiffly as though bracing himself. Something was charging straight for them through the brush. Before Timmon could even unsheathe his knife, a brown blur leapt out into the clearing, clutching something furry in its jaws

"Rupert!" cried Franklin, wincing in pain.

Rupert dropped the dismembered animal at Franklin's feet, panting and smiling, wagging his nub.

"What the fuck?" said Timmon.

"Looks like ole Rupe just saved the day," Franklin said.

The carcass was shaggy and fat, stiff and matted with blood.

"Holy Toledo," said Franklin, patting Rupert's square head. "Would you look at the size of that chipmunk!"

"Marmot," said Tillman.

Damn if it didn't look like a great big gopher or a chipmunk to Franklin. Looked awful meaty, whatever it was.

"Marmot, huh? Ever cook one?"

"Ask me again in ten minutes." And with that, Timmon wiggled out from under his fancy pack and unsheathed his knife. "How about starting a fire, Cochise," he said.

LICKING HIS FINGERS, Bell didn't seem to mind the taste of marmot — in fact, he seemed to savor it. As far as Timmon was concerned, it tasted like an old fan belt, but at least it was staying down.

"Let me get this straight," said Timmon. "You're out here looking for me in Bumfuck, Egypt, *not* to run me in for skipping town but because you've taken some kind of *personal* interest in me? What kind of boy scout shit is that?"

Gnawing on a leg (or maybe it was an arm), Franklin paused to wipe his mouth with the sleeve of his sweatshirt. "We've been through this already, Tillman. You and I, we're not so different."

"You're crazy if you think I'd be out here looking for you or anyone else dumb enough to light out into the sticks with nothing but a gym bag and a can of soup."

"Well, you're here right now, ain't you? You found me."

"Ain't's not a word, remember? What did you think you were dealing with out here, Bell? You think this was some kind of garden tour? You think I'm out here playing leapfrog with deer and feeding corn bread to bears? Is that what you think?"

"Didn't give it much thought, Tillman, I really didn't. When you know you gotta do something, you can't afford to give it much thought."

"Yeah, well, if I hadn't happened along to find you, you're one lost, dead sonofabitch, you know that? Man can die of exposure in this wilderness in a few hours after nightfall, if he's not careful. And considering you're walkin' around out here with a gym bag and a polyester sweater, I'd say you're not careful. My guess is you'd have probably been dead meat in two days' time."

"Maybe. But maybe somebody else hears me calling, if you don't. Maybe my back stops spasming, and I find my way back to that trail and hike on out of here."

"Maybe."

Franklin picked some fat from between his teeth and flicked it into the fire. "But you're probably right, Tillman. I got no business out here — heck, even if I *could* handle myself. But damn it, I just . . ." Franklin trailed off and shook his head, gnawing thoughtfully on his marmot for a moment while gazing out into the canopy.

"Maybe I'm old-school, Tillman. That could be. But the way my mama raised me — the way I always felt — was you hate to see another man throw in the towel. Especially not when his life ain't hardly begun."

"Don't fool yourself, Bell. I'm no spring chicken."

"It ain't about — damn it, it *isn't* about — how old you are. It's about what you've been taught and the tools available to you. Sometimes a man just needs the tools for the job. Who knows — somebody gave your daddy the tools, a lot of things might've turned out different."

"You don't know squat about my old man."

"Let's just say I've got a pretty good idea. Point is, sometimes damage gets done and a guy can't see past it. Sometimes maybe he needs a boost, a pair of shoulders to stand on."

"You really believe that shit?" said Timmon. "Tools and shoulders, and second chances, and the rest of that garbage? You're a dope, you know that?"

"Maybe so."

Timmon threw a bone in the fire and wiped his hands on his filthy jeans. "But I like your style, Bell. You're upbeat. Seems like you must lead a pretty good life to fill your head with all that Boy Scout stuff and actually believe it."

Liberating a string of marmot from between bicuspids, Franklin flicked it into the fire with a sizzle. "Depends what you call a good life, Tillman. If you call living behind a bowling alley a good life, well, then, I gotta good life in spades."

"You bowl?"

"Never," said Franklin.

"Too bad."

"Maybe I should start. Anyway, I suppose I got a few things goin' for me. Got my job, got my music, got my college hoops."

"That don't sound too bad. Except for the hoops part."

"I ain't complaining. It's pretty steady, all in all. Ain't nobody looking out for me at the end of the day, though. 'Cept maybe Rupert here."

"Not married, huh?"

"Nope."

"Ever been?"

"Nope."

"Why not?"

"Got no luck with women, Tillman — worse, I've got no skill. I haven't had a second date in three years." Franklin shook his head and looked into the fire. "Hmph. Must have that smell of hopelessness about me, or something."

Timmon waved at the subject. "It's kinda like you said: if you've gotta do something, you don't think about it. Well, I'm here to tell you that women think about it. And *think* and *think* and *think.* We're supposed to be the smart ones, but they're the ones always thinking, trust me. They'll think themselves right into a corner and start scratching. And in the end, they'll almost always, *always,* do the wrong thing. And they'll even do it knowingly. Contrary — that's what women are."

Franklin grimaced suddenly and went rigid.

"What is it?" said Timmon.

"Spasm," said Franklin breathlessly.

Timmon got to his feet. "Here, hold still." With one hand on Franklin's shoulder, and the other between his shoulder blades, Timmon eased Franklin back until he was flat on the ground, staring up in wide-eyed agony.

"Okay now," said Timmon. "Try to relax — take a few deep breaths, think of the Bahamas or whatever. You gotta use your stomach — that's the problem. Take a little pressure off your spine."

"How do you know this shit?" grunted Franklin.

"I did a lot of readin' in the joint, remember? Now quit talking and relax."

Timmon slid Franklin's sweatshirt up, until his bare belly was exposed. Franklin flinched at Tillman's touch. "What're you doin'?"

"Relax — we gotta jump-start those stomach muscles," said Timmon. "I'm gonna guide you through some crunches."

Tillman's touch was gentle and knowing as he guided Franklin through a series of painful contractions while somewhere high in the canopy a thrush whistled its strange song.

a chorus of crinkling

Curtis remembered the Monte Carlo, the smell of it, the film of dust on the heat-cracked dashboard, the half-peeled Bosch sticker in the back window, the soiled and cigarette-burned fake sheepskin seat covers, the one crackly speaker. He kept expecting the Monte Carlo to stall, but it didn't. He recognized his mother now. He kept expecting her to light a cigarette, but she didn't. She looked tired and nervous behind the wheel, dressed up, as though for a job interview, in a gray skirt and tights and a ropy blue sweater. She looked pale and pretty and unhappy all at once, brave and determined and out of gas. He wanted to hold her hand and squeeze it. He wanted to undo whatever had been done. He wanted this other presence to leave him. He wanted it so badly that soon he could feel sentences pushing at the inside of his lips, feel the fluidity of his thoughts begin to harden into something familiar. Looking at his mother, Curtis felt his old life settling into his bones. He ran a hand through his hair. He looked down at his beat-up tennis shoes. He flipped down his sun visor and inspected his own image in the tiny mirror — furrowing his brow and scowling until his face seemed to say, What the hell are you looking at? He flipped and mussed his hair disapprovingly. Dimly, he felt the many worlds receding, spiraling like tepid water down a hole in the back of his brain. He felt the tug of himself like a thousand sinewy strings beneath his rib cage, felt it rising like pinpricks up his ankles. And that is when the other left his body. Spotting the red and white sign, Curtis felt his life force squiggle up his spine. Suddenly, his lungs expanded, and his throat opened up of its own, and in a rush of familiarity, he found his voice.

"KFC," he said.

Stupefied, Rita screeched to a halt in the middle of the intersection, and whipped her head around. Throwing her arms around the boy, she began to laugh and cry at the same time as the Monte Carlo stalled for the first time in weeks.

"Oh, honey," she gasped.

Never had she yearned to hold on to something so tightly and never let it go. A slow calm spread out like ink inside of her, even as she sobbed, and the car horns began to sound behind them.

"Oh, Curtis, I'm so sorry, honey. Please forgive me."

He wriggled free of her embrace.

"Okay, I love you already. Just keep driving,"

This caused Meriwether to grin so wide that his skin tags were almost level with his eyes.

A fat guy clutching a burger in a red F-350 slowed as he passed the stalled Monte Carlo, hollering out the window.

"Move your stupid Indian asses!"

Smiling, Meriwether calmly gave him the finger as though it were a peace offering.

Relinquishing her hold, Rita fired up the Monte Carlo, wiped her eyes with the sleeve of her sweater, and guided the car through the intersection, bestowing one final sidelong glance at her son. Eyeing his raggedy sneakers, she felt ashamed. Monday she could cash Krig's check. They could go to Ross, and Big Five, and the mall. They could do anything they wanted with fifty-seven hundred dollars. Rita turned to look at Meriwether, who nodded his head so that the dome of his big white hat went *scritch-scritch* on the ceiling fabric.

They took a booth facing the street, and spread out the feast with a chorus of crinkling. Curtis dove directly into his Crispy Strips and honey BBQ sauce while Rita sipped her Diet Coke and watched him lovingly as he gorged himself.

Meriwether bit into a drumstick, chewing thoughtfully many times.

"Is this Original Recipe?" he wondered aloud.

"Fuck if I know," Curtis said, attacking a Crispy Strip.

Rita never thought she'd be so glad to hear him talk like that. She never thought sitting in some shitty KFC in Port Bonita could ever be so good.

After the feast, Rita and Curtis drove Meriwether across town to the clinic and dropped him off at the curb in front of his Escalade.

"Thanks again for everything, Lew," said Rita. "I hope you'll take us up on that dinner."

"As long is it's not shellfish," said Meriwether, who doffed his big white cowboy hat, drew his key chain from his pocket, popped his doors with a beep, and climbed up into the Escalade.

Rita whipped a U-turn in front of Sav-On, and she and Curtis began their journey home. Rita gripped the wheel tightly, wishing she still smoked cigarettes. Curtis kept his face to the window, his conscience spinning restless circles as he listened to the thrum of the windshield wipers.

"Mom," he said. "There's something you gotta know. About the burns, about how I got them."

"What is it, honey?"

Curtis was hesitant. He looked out the window, as they passed the Red Lion. "You'll be mad," he said.

"Of course, I won't be. I'm just grateful you're okay."

"It's all right if you're mad. You should be. It was stupid."

"I won't be mad, I promise."

Curtis turned from the window and looked her in the face. "Well, the thing is, when I was . . . I don't know exactly if . . . When's the last time you were at Wal-Mart?"

"Last week."

"And?"

"And I bought a case of Diet Coke. What is this about?"

"So, I mean, Wal-Mart was there?"

"Of course it was there."

"Everything was okay? It wasn't, you know, burned to the ground or anything?"

"Curtis, what are you talking about? Honey, just relax. Whatever happened is over now."

Curtis sank back into his seat, faced the window once more, and fingered the scars running up his arm. They felt cool beneath the surface.

the old men are all dead

The week before school started, Curtis met Coleman in his office. Coleman's ponytail was even longer than Curtis remembered it, held in place with an agate-studded leather band. Even Coleman's face seemed to have taken on an Indian roundness. What was it called? Crowder was always going on about it in biology — osmosis?

There was a new print hanging on his office wall — when you looked at it one way, it was a pack of wild horses running across a prairie, and when you looked at it another way, it was a head and shoulder silhouette of Chief Joseph. There was a name for that, too, the art docent told him — not a palindrome, but something else. Beneath the image there was a Chief Joseph quote: "The old men are all dead. It is the young men who say yes or no."

"Are you writing about your experiences at all?"

"Drawing some."

"Anything you want to share?"

"Nah."

"And what about the home front? How's that going?"

"Good, I guess."

"Your mom?"

"She's working at a new place. She's talking about going back to school or something."

Setting the paper weight down, Coleman fingered its glass edges thoughtfully.

"Can I ask why you changed your mind about the Jamestown position?"

"I don't know. It seems cool. And it would look good on a transcript, maybe, right? Isn't that what you were saying?"

Coleman smiled, nodding his head. "It'll look dynamite on a transcript," he said. "But you understand it's just an internship, right? There's no pay."

"That's fine."

"There's a stipend, though — for lunches and transportation. The casino's got a great buffet. Just stay away from the Swedish meatballs."

Coleman fished a green organizer out of his desk, riffled through some paperwork until he found what he was looking for, and slid a paper across the desk to Curtis. "Fill this out, and I'll submit it with a letter of recommendation."

"Thanks, Mr. Coleman." Curtis took the paper, and turned to leave.

"And Curtis."

Curtis looked over his shoulder.

"Keep it local."

special features

Krig sat alone at a two-top by the window, looking across the lot at Murray Motors, where he thought he saw Rhinehalter out in front of the showroom, cupping a cigarette against the rain. But a glance at the bar revealed Jerry in his usual spot. The guy was a spook. Krig did a double-take out the window nonetheless, half expecting to see Rhinehalter both places at once — but the smoker had fled. Krig couldn't tell if the '89 Seville was $2,450 or $3,450. A rip, either way. Tobin drove a Seville senior year. What a pile.

Checking his watch, Krig saw Rita still wasn't due for another five minutes. He'd been a half hour early. Of course he was early, he was always early for dates! It *was* a date, right? Rita initiated the whole thing, which was particularly surprising in light of the fact that she'd quit High Tide, which Krig viewed at the time as the final nail in the coffin of their romantic possibilities. So was it presumptuous to think this was a date? Maybe things weren't on ice after all. Hadn't she said that bad timing had been the whole problem? So there you go — everything was different now. Curtis was back to normal, better than normal from what she'd said. Randy was out of her life for good. Maybe she'd had a few weeks to reconsider; maybe leaving High Tide had helped her see that she could do worse than spend the rest of her days with Krig. The fact that she hadn't cashed the check yet might suggest a change of heart as well. Maybe she'd decided to stay. Was he foolish to be hopeful — foolish to think that the three of them might share some kind of life together in P.B.? Maybe rent a house west of town, something with a decent yard and a view of the strait, maybe use the six grand to buy an old RV to go camping on weekends, or a boat, or hell, put it toward Curtis's college fund. Why not? Krig made a decent living. J-man had even been hinting about a promotion lately. Hell, maybe they could even buy a place, get a loan and all that.

Rita arrived right on time, clutching a flat colorfully wrapped package in one hand. She looked great, rested, Krig thought. Her hair was up, and one sexy little wisp had escaped the bun and hung down over her face. She was wearing heels and a silky red dress that looked Asian to Krig. As she sat down, she smiled sweetly across the table at him, but a little sadly, he thought. Already, his heart began to sink.

"Here," she said, sliding the package across the table. "I got something for you."

"My birthday's not until October."

"It's not a birthday present, silly. It's just a token of my appreciation. It's from Curtis, too."

The thought that Curtis should appreciate him had never occurred to Krig. If anything, he'd always feared that Curtis would resent him. Probably, she was just saying that — probably, Curtis didn't even know about the gift. Deliberately, Krig began to unwrap it.

"Oh, go on!" she said.

He tore back the wrapping to reveal a DVD: *Sasquatch: Legend Meets Science.*

On the cover, cast in not-so-crisp relief against the Bluff Creek riverbank, was the familiar digitally enhanced female form of the P.-G. Bigfoot: tits sagging, arms swinging, lips like hot dogs.

"The most comprehensive and conclusive inquiry to date into the Bigfoot phenomenon," blurbed *Willamette Weekly.*

"I noticed that videotape of yours is all squiggly from all the pausing you do," she explained. "This one pauses automatically frame by frame throughout the whole clip. It's got all kinds of special features — a whole extra DVD — including a Roger Peterson interview."

"Patterson."

"And a segment on the Skookum thingy."

Krig ran his fingers over the DVD cover. "Thanks," he said, with a forced jauntiness. Why was he disappointed? What did he expect? And really, it wasn't the gift that was disappointing but the presentation, the implication — real or imagined — that the gift belonged to the past, to something they would never share again. But why had she dressed up — simply to torture him? Why wouldn't she wear a baggy sweatshirt? Surely, she'd intended to impress him. The thought of it heartened Krig momentarily.

"I've got something else, too," Rita said, fishing around in her purse, from which she produced Krig's check. She slid it across the table, facedown, the seam fuzzy from all the folding and unfolding. "I think that was the single nicest thing anybody has ever done for me, Dave. But I can't take it."

"Why not?"

"I just can't."

"It's just a loan. You're not taking anything."

Rita sighed and gave Krig something of a pleading look. Suddenly she didn't look so rested. The wisp of hair hanging over her face seemed more tired than sexy. Even her red dress seemed to have lost a little of its shimmer.

"I don't know," she said. "I guess I thought at first that money might be some kind of solution, a ticket out. But now I see that the stuff in my life that needs fixing can't be fixed with money — and it especially can't be fixed by running away."

Krig straightened up in his chair. "So you're staying?"

Rita glanced down at her menu, then up at Krig, then back down at her menu. "Yeah. I think we are."

"Does this mean that maybe you and I . . . ?"

Rita sighed, and looked at him pitiably, with her lower lip pouty. "No. Dave, no. And it's nothing personal. Really. It's like I said before — "

"But the timing is different now."

"It's still wrong. Don't you see? I need to stand on my own two feet. I need to concentrate on supporting Curtis."

"So cash the check. Nobody said you had to leave town to take the money."

"I don't mean support him financially, Dave. I mean be there for him one hundred percent — with no distractions. I owe him that. At least for a year."

Krig slumped slightly in his chair and diverted his eyes.

"Look," Rita said. "I didn't come here to get your hopes up. I just wanted to thank you."

"So why are you all dressed up?" snapped Krig, surprising them both.

Rita cast her eyes back down at the menu. "I'm going dancing with a friend."

"What friend?"

"He's just a friend."

Krig's jaw tightened. His tongue tasted like brass. "No distractions, huh?"

"He's eighty years old, Dave! He's just a *friend*."

"Friends," said Krig. He sharpened the word into a little arrowhead.

"Why are you acting this way?" she said.

"What way?"

Krig thought about saying it. All of it — about the house, and the yard, and the happily ever after. He thought about saying that he loved her, that he wanted to take care of her, that he wouldn't get in the way, he promised.

"You're acting like a jerk," she said.

Couldn't she see how this was hurting him? How could she not see it? She had to see it.

"Go to hell," he said, regretting it immediately.

Rita stood without a word and swiped the stray hair from her face. "I'm sorry, Krig, I really am," she said, and turned and walked away.

Krig didn't watch her go. He looked at his menu intently as if he were really considering the prime-rib dip. Coleslaw or potato salad? He could feel Rhinehalter's eyes on him, he was sure of it. He heard the swinging door close as Rita made her final exit; he kept his eyes glued to the menu, feeling Rhinehalter's curiosity. What fucking business of Rhinehalter's was it, anyway? Krig thought about calling J-man but remembered it was date night. He and Janis were probably out at the Regal Seven seeing some chick flick. He thought about driving out to the bluff, clearing his head, looking at the lights, putting things in perspective, but somehow he couldn't muster the wherewithal to stand up and begin the journey. Hard as it was to believe, the truth was, he didn't even feel like draining his beer.

divided

Bright and early on the morning of April 6, the party broke camp in a businesslike fashion and set out in search of the Quinault. The pale light from the southeast and the waning chill of dawn seemed to promise spring. Spirits were cautiously optimistic as they began their trek up the steep face of a mountainside soon to be known as Barrier Ridge.

Within the hour, the weather took a turn for the worse, as low cloud cover crept in from the leeward side of the Baileys. Mather's men soon had to contend with poor visibility as they crossed the path of yet another recent avalanche. The slide had cut a wide swathe through the timber and left in its wake a rutty snowfield cut through with shallow gulleys and uprooted trees. In single file, they ascended slowly at roughly thirty degrees for the better part of the day, until they reached the slope above the destruction, where they began switchbacking toward the summit.

Leading the way, the filthy length of his ragged headband dangling in tatters, Mather plodded onward, step by crunchy step, even as his thoughts reached backward into the past — thoughts of flagstone hearths, and perfumed women, and that aching restless compulsion for discovery. He made no effort to govern these recollections but let them run their course like windblown clouds. He saw himself, a child, holding his baby brother at the foot of an endless prairie as darkness began to fall, and amber was turning to gray, and he saw himself again at his brother's graveside, where beside him his father clutched a wilting hat as he looked toward the horizon. At night, shadows playing on the wall, and his mother's forgiving face, drawn in the lamplight. And then came the prairie again, suffused with hot light and laughter and, somewhere beyond the flatness, the promise of a future.

By noon they had gained thirteen hundred feet in elevation and paused to look back over the Elwha, which they could barely glimpse through the cloud cover.

"Perhaps we've seen the last of her after all," commented Mather.

The terrain ahead of them, though nearly free of snow, was most formidable, a broken ascent of bare ledges and outcrops, studded and splintered with jagged basalt, riddled with stunted trees struggling to maintain their hold on the cliff face. However, the men did not linger long enough to be daunted but began instead to secure their loads and ready their lines. The dog, now a lusterless bag of bones and a pair of dark pleading eyes, could not be coaxed forward. When confronted with the cliff, she took only a few nervous paces, whimpering twice without looking up before she lay on the ground at the foot of the escarpment, where she lowered her head onto to her forepaws and stared shiftlessly straight ahead.

"Sitka. Up girl!" said Mather.

But the dog did not lift an eye.

"Up!"

This time the dog slowly exhaled, but her black eyes were frozen. When she finally blinked, it was sluggishly.

Mather issued a staccato whistle, and still the dog would not budge. Runnells approached her as though to rouse her, but Mather stopped him with an outstretched arm.

"No. Leave her in peace."

"We could hoist her with ropes," Reese suggested.

Mather shook his head grimly and ran a hand through his shaggy beard. "No. She's out of fight."

Mather almost envied the dog. Looking at her there on the frozen ground, the pale flame of her spirit all but spent, he felt a welling of emotion for which he was grateful. Even in her present condition, she was, by his estimation, a nobler beast than he. He squatted down next to her and ran his hand over the dog's head, past her ears, and she exhaled once more with a wheeze. He could not bear to look at the washboard of her rib cage or look her in the eyes. He could not bear to feel her spine running like a row of gravestones down her back. The best he could do was pat her head.

"Rest now," he whispered.

Rising to his feet, he turned to face the cliff, doing everything in his power not to look back at her as, hand over hand, he began climbing ahead of the party. The going was exceedingly slow and measured, and the rock was given to crumbling under the force of their toeholds. Mather paused at each crevice to lower a cod line. Halfway up, he could not help but look back at the dog and immediately wished he had not. She was lying just as he'd left her, head on forepaws, staring straight ahead, at nothing. Part of him wished he was lying there beside her.

Along with the precarious ascent itself, the jangling of nerves had taken a toll on the men by the time they reached the flat narrow shelf, which hung as though suspended just below the ridge, not a hundred feet above the wispy cloud tops. The sky was deep blue again, though Mather could hardly see it through the blinding sun as he approached the final stretch, where, just below the crest, the face gave way to a series of natural steps, not unlike a ziggurat. A final step brought Mather's head above the sharp wedgelike saddle, and the curtain rose from before the unknown region, and there before them, wide and green and pristine, lay the valley of the Quinault. Mather might have fallen to his knees and wept then and there were it not for his impatience to put it all behind him.

After grueling months in the wilderness, through the most perilous winter on record, having traversed some of the most rugged terrain in North America, ever in the shadow of death, the Mather expedition had reached the central divide at long last. From this vista, they could see to the west, unobstructed, all that lay between them and the Pacific. Beyond the first range lay a wide, handsome valley. The thickly wooded bottomlands gave way gently on either side to a range of mountains that rose gradually, green about the waist and capped with snow. The river, visible some two thousand feet below, where it emerged out of a dark funnel of rock, appeared to run wider and generally straighter than the Elwha.

Bountiful country, there could be no doubt, a generous watershed running right to the very edge of the world. Endless resources. Boundless timber in every direction and a wide, navigable waterway to move it. Yet standing on the divide, with the wind whistling past his ears, Mather could not shake a certain disillusion in knowing that what lay in front of him had already been discovered, had no doubt seen the restless footsteps of other men. Paradise, if it existed, lay somewhere behind them — perhaps they'd trudged right through its midst without recognizing it. Mather would not be the man to discover it. He'd known that this day was coming, or at least sensed it, the day when everything before him had yielded to discovery. Thus, it felt to Mather less like he had arrived here and more like this place had been following him all along.

"We can reach bottom by sundown," he said. "There, we can camp."

"Onward," said Haywood wearily.

Thus the party gave pause but momentarily before they began their zigzagging descent down the wayward side of the divide. And even the fitful past gave way to Mather's footsteps, as he plodded through the thick snow, while behind him, the men strung out in a crooked line, trudging onward one ragged step at a time. Nobody said a word.

In a day's time, they dove into the dense bottomlands and began fighting their way westward. Haywood would describe a high-canopied forest fecund with rot, a brackish cathedral festooned with moss. He would describe the biggest timber he'd ever laid eyes on, spruce wider than train cars, colonnades of hemlock so massive that "the wingspan of three men stretched finger to finger could not match the diameter of these giants." He would describe a soft and yielding forest floor, presenting a crust so brittle with rot that the casual footfall would break through the surface. He would describe the party's perilous crossing of the the raging gray Quinault, whose swift current they forded some fifty yards across. Late in the afternoon, in a sloping valley brimming with maple and spruce, they would come upon the first evidence of human activity in two months — blazes consisting of two sets of slanting lines conjoined at an apex in the manner of a chevron.

Like their own blazes, they were relatively fresh and notched high on the trunks of the great gnarled trees, suggesting deep snowpack in the recent past.

Awash in silence as he trudged through the fertile bottomlands, Mather scarcely paused to observe the wonders he passed, which might have taken his breath away were he still the man he was when he left Port Bonita. Perhaps, with enough rest, he would be that man again. Perhaps a few months spent in the relative ease of society would reawaken that restless urge to discover. But for now, he was no longer that man nor certain what man he might become. Perhaps his days of discovery were not over after all. More than anything else, with each muddy step westward, Mather was eager to get home — wherever that was.

In three days' time, over the foothills and through the bottom-lands, the party would come upon a squat little cabin with a smoking chimney on the wooded edge of a small glen, where, standing beside a woodpile with one leg propped on a chop log, and a rifle slung at his hip, a skinny stooping figure with a long gray beard would finally move Mather to speech.

"God help his plug of tobacco," he said.

make it stop

On the bluff to the northeast came the baying of hounds, maybe a half dozen, maybe more. Even before Adam crested the hogback on Lord Jim's mare, a cloud of black smoke unfurled into the moonlight. He could hear the distant shouting. Already the air was thick with the acrid stink of creosote and burned timber. Ascending the rise, first at a trot, then a canter, Adam felt the frantic heat of panic rising all around him. There was sure to be chaos on the other side. Finding the boy might be impossible under the circumstances.

The mare reared up and whinnied at the first sight of the flames, and Adam held on and eased her back down. Dismounting, he settled the horse with a quiet hand, surveying the scene below as colonists hurried past him down the hill. The flames were fanning out in both directions along the south side of Front Street, though the prevailing wind was doing its best to push them southeasterly. Furious bucket brigades were strung out on all sides, heaving and splashing vainly at the blaze. The Belvedere, its fiery roof caving in on itself, was nearest to the center of the inferno.

The horse balked, worrying her head all around the bit as Adam led her down the hogback slowly toward the center of town, with a hot, ashy wind blowing into his face. Front Street was littered with rubble, burning shingles and scattered brick amid shattered glass. From the back lot of the leather works, a phalanx of fifty or sixty men drove the flames back. Others scurried about madly in the street to no apparent purpose. Dogs skulked in the shadows. Doc Newnham darted across the street in front of Adam, flanked by a pair of teenage boys; he clutched his leather bag in his right hand as he ran. Flames consumed the hardware store, lapping at the roof of P. G. Rhinehalter. Old man Rhinehalter, in spite of the advices of a half-dozen screaming men, scrambled to save his inventory, heaving tack into the street with desperate haste. The mare fought Adam harder and harder as they drew closer to the center of town, continually throwing her head back against the reins. Adam ran a comforting hand down her damp neck and coaxed her along gently.

The muddy street pulsed wildly with shadows. Chaos cut through the night on wings, breathing fire. Suddenly there came a commotion from up the street as the frantic crowd dispersed, and right through their midst with a furious clopping came a pair of frenzied black geldings hitched to a flaming carriage. The mare pitched, landing on stiff forelegs as the carriage shot past like a cannonball. Then, from the east end, came an explosion of plate glass, followed by the staccato cries of a dozen or more voices as a column of flames flared thirty feet into the air, roaring at the center like a great furnace. A tethered mule brayed in earnest before the Olympic Hotel, where luggage of all shapes and sizes was cloistered in the mud nearby. They came upon the gutted Belvedere, a dozen splayed timbers and a collapsed roof and a row of blistered piles still flaming. The boardwalk, too, had collapsed, running like a black shattered spine west down Front Street. In front of a charred splintered section of railing, Adam came upon a human torso, charred blood red and black beyond recognition. The second body was draped with a blanket, but even so, by its very configuration Adam could guess at the brutality of its repose. Up ahead, he could see several other bodies in a line, even as another was being dragged into their midst by a man Adam recognized as the druggist's son. On the west end of town, near the foot of Morse Dock, women and children gathered, their faces at turns stunned and terrified in the firelight. Some of the children were crying. One child, charcoal-streaked and tear-soaked, clung tightly to her mother's waist.

"Make it stop," Adam heard her say.

He cut through the crowd to Hollywood Beach, where up and down the shoreline the Klallam huddled in clusters of five and ten, murmuring. Adam led the mare through their midst, searching for a familiar face. He came upon Abe Charles clutching his rifle as he stood in a small group before his shack. Another rifle was propped against a saw log.

"I'm looking for Hoko King's boy," said Adam.

"They've gone after him," said Abe.

"Who?"

"Tobin and maybe a dozen others. With dogs and rifles. They're headed east along the bluff."

A chill washed over Adam. "Give me your rifle."

No sooner did Abe surrender his rifle than Adam mounted his horse and galloped east down Hollywood Beach.

GEORGE STOOD LIKE a statue in the shadow of Morse Dock, still perplexed by Storm King's puzzling revelations. What did it mean to hold nothing in your hand? What did it mean, this strange song? Even as the flames threw long shadows down the length of Front Street, even as George heard the frantic shouting and the clanging of bells from all quarters, he sang softly under his breath:

doon-doon, doon-doon

doon-doon, doon-doon

A dozen Siwash brothers streaked past him, headed toward the blaze, clutching buckets and hatchets. A dozen horses whinnied crazily in the night. A black and terrible cloud threatened to blot out the moon. And still George puzzled and pondered. What did it mean, the fingers? Why did it matter how many he held up? While others huddled in whispering groups up and down Hollywood Beach, George stood alone and turned toward the shore, with one hand holding nothing and the other holding up three fingers, singing louder now as the flames reared up behind him:

doon-doon, doon-doon

doon-doon, doon-doon

His trance was broken when a young woman, whom he soon recognized as Hoko, wandered dazedly into his midst, moving like a ghost between worlds. Stopping a short distance in front of George, she swayed faintly side to side, wide-eyed like a blind person, open-mouthed but silent like a mute, with one hand out in front of her, reaching toward nothing.

And when it seemed that she was totally without voice, she spoke, not to George, but to no one.

"They," she said. "Them."

MINERVA WAS SCARCELY three days in the ground when Ethan came down the mountain for the first time since the funeral in a rickety old carriage bursting with caged chickens, driven hard by an old white-beard named Lofall who lived just downriver of the gorge. As they began their descent of Homestead Hill, Ethan could see the pale yellow nimbus of fire glowing on the horizon. He wondered if it was already a lost cause. They rattled in on the east end of town, where Ethan jumped from the moving carriage and began fighting his way west down Front Street toward the center of town, through the frenetic crowd of onlookers, through the mad scramble of bucket brigades. He claimed a station squarely in front of the post office, where driven slantwise by the wind, a tongue of flame lapped at its roof and clapboard walls. Wresting a bucket from a confusion of hands, Ethan attacked the fire with furious haste, ducking low under tentacles of flame. Narrowing his silver eyes against the heat, which seemed almost liquid itself, he heaved bucketful upon bucketful of water at the fiery onslaught. The post office must be saved, above all else — it was the address of Port Bonita, the very proof of its existence, its link to the outer world. Without an address, Port Bonita was no longer a destination. Without an address, Port Bonita was not a place. To what purpose would the great twin turbines of Ethan's conception hum without a town to power, without a place to light?

Beside him at the front, where the heat singed and chafed, a squarish, dough-faced man, slick with perspiration and ruddy about the cheeks, called out instructions to the mob.

"Heave!" shouted Dalton Krigstadt. "*To the left, to the left!* Heave!"

Preceded by an ominous creaking, then a great yawn, an interior wall came crashing down, and a burst of flames roared from the center of the blaze, swelling to a forty-foot crescendo. The men in front recoiled breathlessly. From behind them in the muddy street came a collective gasp.

"Heave!" Dalton spurred them on. *"She's jumping the break. Cut her off at the break!* Heave! *You there, shift to the left*! Heave! *To the left, to the left, you!"*

Shifting to the left, Ethan was grateful for the instruction, grateful to be a cog in a machine greater than himself.

RIDING LOW AGAINST the wind, Adam pushed the mare to her limit, and she was responsive to the reins, galloping gracefully on sure hooves through the long grass. Adam's thoughts, however, did not gallop so gracefully but scrambled madly to order themselves. How was this happening? How did this come to be? He was almost upon the hounds now and gaining fast. He could see the shadowy mob strung out behind them in the purple moonlight. Even from a distance, he sensed the danger coursing through them and knew he could not reason with them, though he must try. When it seemed the mare had no more to give, Adam pushed her harder and she obliged in spite of the rutty terrain. He came up fast on the bluff side of the mob, overtaking them at the crest of a gentle grassy slope, where swinging the gray mare around in a half crescent, he stopped them in their tracks.

Sure enough, Tobin was among them with an oil lamp and a rifle. The Makah also had a rifle. He was sneering in the purple moonlight. As always, his tiny companion was there beside him. The tethered dogs were all but pulling over the postmaster's son, who leaned back on his heels. Adam did not recognize the others. He spoke forcefully to be heard over the cacophony of hounds.

"Best leave matters to the law, John."

"We'll have justice, Adam. The boy started this, and I intend to finish it. Now, stand aside."

"I can't do that, John."

Tobin smiled cruelly in the moonlight. The tethered hounds continued pulling at their leads, baying frantically.

"C'mon, boys," said Tobin. "We're losing ground."

Adam leveled his rifle.

Tobin's smile did not budge. "Somehow I don't think you'll be using that," said Tobin. "That would be out of character for you."

"Maybe, maybe not."

"Release the dogs!" Tobin shouted. And with that, the tall boy let go of the leads, and the hounds bounded off furiously down the hill. Adam gave chase on the mare and was soon running abreast of the pack, all but stumbling over themselves in their haste. At the bottom of the hill, the grassland leveled out for several hundred yards before diving into a wooded gulley. Halfway across the flat expanse, Adam caught his first glimpse of the boy bathed in the eerie purple light. Apparently, Tobin saw him, too, for a shot rang out in the night. Adam rode straight for the boy, and when he was beside him, he pulled hard on the reins with his left hand, and when the mare had managed a gait, Adam swung side saddle, sweeping the boy up in his arms. When he heard a terrible yelp, Adam knew he'd crushed one of the hounds, but still the others kept after them. The boy weighed little more than a sack of feed. Adam swung him onto the saddle front, just as another shot rang out. Without looking back, he drove the mare toward the tree line and blindly down into the gulley; to her credit, she didn't balk or falter once. Within ten strides, they hit the creek at a trot and galloped up the far side of the gulley through dense brush. With the cold limbs stinging their faces like razors in the darkness, they thundered up the far side of the ravine and back into the moonlight. The boy could feel his father's heart thumping between his shoulder blades.

SHORTLY BEFORE MIDNIGHT the blaze jumped the break completely, and within minutes thirsty flames were consuming the clapboard walls of the post office, and the tower of flames reared to new heights, and a plume of soot black smoke rippled a hundred feet upward before it began to mushroom. Within minutes the post office was a lost cause, and yet, to Ethan, the defeat proved nothing less than thrilling. That the heaving brigades did not surrender, that they did not step back awestricken into the muddy street and defer to the flames — did not, in fact, so much as break their rhythm — sent a noble chill running up Ethan's spine. That's when he knew all was not lost, that there was something to be gained by the fight itself. And Ethan crept closer still under the fingers of flame, threw himself that much harder into the fiery heart of destruction, as the dough-faced Krigstadt led the charge.

"Heave!"

The heat of the battle was glorious, the glow of the flames cleansing. The machine was unstoppable — feeding, it seemed, on the very flames themselves. Even the gritty spoils of defeat tasted sooty and delicious on Ethan's tongue as he heaved, and heaved, and heaved, untold times, tired but unflagging. The heat melted in his mouth and ran down his throat like fuel.

"Heave!"

As the brigade fought for precious momentum in the early morning hours, a sudden and fortuitous change of winds arrived from the west to push the flames back upon themselves. And emboldened by the wind, the brigades took the offensive, putting their shoulders straight to the flames and heaving, heaving, heaving with the persistence of a steam engine as they drove the flames back, hour after hour after hour, inch by hard-won inch, until shortly after dawn they had managed to contain it. From there, it was only a matter of hours before they had reduced the inferno to a broken patchwork of smoldering heaps.

And as the thinning mob spread out to wander amid the wreckage, Ethan straggled west down Front Street in the full light of day, with the ground smoking and hissing all around him. He gravitated toward Morse Dock, where he propped his weary elbows on the rail and gazed back toward the gutted center of town. All that was left of Port Bonita was a railroad office, long vacated, a sundries store run by an old deaf woman, and two real estate offices — one of them bearing the name LAMBERT AND SON.

With a limp mustache draping over the corners of his thin mouth, and his shirt dangling in blackened tatters, Ethan knew in his bones that something had been born in the fire, though it was hard to pin down what, and harder still to measure. Perhaps Port Bonita was not an address, after all, not even a place, but a spirit, an essence, a pulse — a future still unfolding.

THE SKY WAS the color of oyster shells at daybreak, and it was drizzling, and Thomas was cold, and a lone plume of smoke unfurled from Lord Jim's chimney on the horizon. The mare beneath him was slick with rain and sweat, her gait a tired saunter. The boy's eyes were burning, and a cool aching weariness dripped down the back of his throat. He knew beyond all certainty that his father was dead in the saddle behind him.

In a few minutes time, Thomas would bring the news of Adam's death to Lord Jim, who lay pale and weak on the mattress on what would prove to be the eve of his own death. And Thomas sat with the old man late into the evening, by candlelight, as the wind off the strait rattled the windows, until Lord Jim said unto to Thomas the last words he would ever speak — words that Thomas himself would later say unto the people at Jamestown, as they laid Lord Jim to rest.

"We are born haunted," he said, his voice weak, but still clear. "Haunted by our fathers and mothers and daughters, and by people we don't remember. We are haunted by otherness, by the path not taken, by the life unlived. We are haunted by the changing winds and the ebbing tides of history. And even as our own flame burns brightest, we are haunted by the embers of the first dying fire. But mostly," said Lord Jim, "we are haunted by ourselves."

wooly bully

Silently, Timmon and Franklin broke camp shortly after dawn, amid a fog so thick that it clung to the forest like a cool curtain of mist. A fitful night's sleep and one more night of hunger had left Timmon restless and precariously on edge, a state of affairs further aggravated by the fact that Franklin was forced to proceed cautiously over the bumpy path, lifting his knees ever so slightly with a grimace each step of the way. Progress was so slow that Timmon could hardly contain a frenetic impulse to forge ahead and leave Franklin behind. With a steady pace, he could be out of here in a day and a half tops. But with Bell holding him back, he might never get out of here. Hell, he might starve at this pace.

Two miles in, following a stretch of moguls on a downhill course, Franklin felt the cold tug of a rip cord beneath his lower spine, and progress was halted altogether as Timmon ministered for twenty minutes to Franklin's knotted psoas. When at last they resumed the trail, Franklin was forced to rely heavily on Timmon's shoulder for support, slowing their pace still further. Finally, resigning himself to the futility of his pairing with Bell, Timmon ceased wrestling with hunger and impatience and gave into his better instincts. What was an extra day? Hadn't he decided that he would dare to give a shit? Why not start with Bell? Christ, the guy hauled his ass all the way out here to look for him, right? The guy was a Boy Scout.

Franklin's condition only worsened as the day wore on and the terrain grew rougher. Stops became more frequent. Bell's steps only seemed to get smaller. But Timmon remained steadfast in his patience.

"Hold steady, Bell. We'll get you out of here, man. May take a while, but we'll get you out."

Late in the afternoon, on the backside of Deception Divide,

Timmon was forced to lift Franklin up and over a washout, sidling cautiously over the uneven grade, as he strained under the weight of his companion.

"Looks like I owe you one, Tillman."

"Don't sweat it," grunted Timmon. "Call it even."

In eleven hours, they covered just under eight miles, rejoining the Elwha in early evening at the head of Press Valley, where they set up camp beneath a stand of giant hemlock.

That night, as the chill air of early autumn settled into the moonlit valley, the two men lay on their backs by the glow of the fire, staring up at the treetops while Rupert lay curled between them. Timmon found himself compelled to talk more than usual. Maybe it was the cumulative effect of being alone all those weeks. Maybe he was just warding off the hunger. Or maybe Frank Bell was just disarming — maybe something about his salt-and-pepper hair and his sad, slow-moving eyes inspired candor. Franklin, for his part, was more than content to listen.

"Yeah, well," Timmon said. "Mostly, I was sick of shit comin' down on me, you know? Shit I didn't have any control over — other people's shit — my old man's, that idiot in the White House, some guy in a suit in Minneapolis."

Timmon folded his arms behind his head and gazed harder than ever into the canopy, as though some answer might be waiting for him up there. "But you can't escape it, man. Shit doesn't just roll downhill, it rolls all over the place."

"How's that?"

Timmon shifted over onto one elbow and looked at Franklin. "Well, for starters, let's talk about survival. Used to be that a guy could live off the land out here, just on fishing alone. And I know how to fish, Bell. I've been fishing for twenty years. I fished like hell out here. For weeks on end I fished — from the right bank, from the left bank, from the riffle. And I never caught a goddamn thing. Nothing. Zilch. And it didn't occur to me once — not until maybe twenty minutes before I found your black ass out here in the woods — that it had nothing to do with my luck. It was because of that fucking dam down there. A guy's got about as much chance of catchin' a fish in this river as he does of catchin' Jennifer Lopez."

"That right?"

"You're damn right, that's right. The real question is, why the hell didn't I see that coming? Why didn't I put two and two together in the first place? You see what I'm saying? I didn't make the connection."

"Forest for the trees," said Franklin. "Forest for the trees."

Both men fell silent. The fire was down to coals, now, hissing softly. The trees swayed ever so slightly above, swishing side to side with each breath of wind. Occasionally, a tree trunk issued a plaintive creak in the darkness. And each creak seemed only to make the silence more implacable.

Suddenly, the silence was shattered by an otherworldly howl. Both men felt their scalps tighten.

"What the fuck was that?" said Franklin, breathlessly.

"An owl," said Timmon, unconvincingly.

Rupert began to whimper.

"That's a loud-ass owl, Tillman. And Rupert ain't scared of no bird."

No sooner had they started speculating than another hair-raising series of hoots came from deep in the forest behind them.

"Okay, Tillman. If that's an owl, it must have mated with a hillbilly."

"That ain't no owl. Shhh."

"Well, it ain't a bear," whispered Franklin. "I been face to face with one of those, and he was —"

Before Franklin could finish, there came a series of four very loud whoop-howls from no more than a hundred yards away. Rupert began to pace the campsite nervously, whimpering.

When Timmon looked at Franklin in the darkness, he felt his skin crawl.

There came the slow heavy crunch of underbrush from behind them as the men leaned breathlessly against a tree, their shoulders grazing. When the crunching stopped momentarily, Timmon imagined some dark form on two legs, not four, sniffing the air.

Franklin felt a primal life force beating inside him, something ancient and half remembered. Whispering voices began to circle the inside of Franklin's head. Suddenly he was not frightened. He pushed away from the tree and let out a holler.

"*Whoop-whoop-whoop-whoop!*" he called.

"What the *fuck* are you doing?" Timmon said, wresting him by the arm and pushing him back against the tree.

"*Whoop-whoop!*" said Franklin.

"Shut the fuck up, you dummy."

"Listen, Tillman. Listen to the voices."

Timmon released his grip. "Shhh, you crazy motherfuck. Shut up."

The crunching resumed. It seemed as though the beast had began to backpedal with measured steps.

"I think it's leaving," said Timmon.

"Did you hear the voices?"

"I couldn't hear shit with you whispering in my ear."

When it was apparent the thing had fled, they stoked the fire and huddled close to the flames, resisting the temptation to talk about it. Rupert had stopped his pacing, but not his whimpering, as he sat alertly in the glow of the flames. Finally, Timmon could resist no longer.

"You're bat-shit crazy, you know that, Bell? What the hell were you thinking? Was that a fucking mating call, or what?"

"Truth is, Tillman, I'm not sure what got ahold of me, but I liked it."

"I've been thinkin', and I think that was a bull elk out there, a big one, that's what I think. And I think you're one crazy black sonofabitch hootin' and hollerin' at it like that. Lucky it didn't try and mount you."

That was the last anyone said on the subject. As they set out upon the muddy trail amid a torrent of showers the following morning, neither man spoke of the experience. Nor did either man make mention of what looked like six giant washed-out footprints on the trail.

Aided by the level terrain of Press Valley, and Franklin's miraculous recovery, they made considerable headway through the basin. Stops were few and far between. By the time the clouds broke, both men were in good spirits, and the previous night was at a safe distance.

Nothing more was said about the howling. Their clothing soon dried on their backs in the heat of afternoon. The conversation assumed an airy tone, with Timmon joking about, among other things, the quality of food in the joint.

"Not that I wouldn't give my left nut for a slice of that mystery meat loaf right now," he said. "Or a bowl of lima beans."

"Hell," said Franklin, "I'd give both nuts. I ain't using them."

In the waning hours of daylight, having covered well over ten miles, they reached the foot of the Press Valley and set up camp in a grassy meadow along the right bank, where the river ran wide and shallow. Exhausted, they did not linger around the fire but slept restfully to the steady roar of the Elwha.

They awoke well after dawn to sunny skies. A slight cedar-scented breeze was blowing up the valley, rippling off the surface of the river. Timmon and Franklin idled longer than usual on the riverbank, lacing their shoes, repacking their loads, rinsing their faces in the riffle. With his sore back all but behind him now, and his hunger cramps having inexplicably subsided, Franklin actually felt a little pang of nostalgia — also inexplicable, in light of the circumstances — at the knowledge that their journey would soon meet its end. He felt somehow buoyed by the adventure. Standing lean and feral beside him, Timmon was thinking less about endings and more about beginnings as a little pit was forming in his stomach.

Soon after they hit the trail at a steady pace, they caught their first whiffs of civilization. With the late morning hours came an increase in air traffic, along with a proliferation of park signage. A palpable electricity seemed to waver in the breeze. By early afternoon they began their descent to the head of Lake Thornburgh. Even before the reservoir revealed itself, the distant thrum of syncopated bass drums reached their ears like cannon reports, soon followed by the brassy strains and intermittent honking of what sounded like a high school marching band.

"Is that 'Tequila'?" Timmon wondered aloud.

"'Wooly Bully,'" said Franklin.

dam days

SEPTEMBER 2006

On the main stage — a hastily painted two-foot riser, festooned with star-studded garlands of crepe paper — the Port Bonita High brass band was honking out a spirited rendition of "Wooly Bully" when they were suddenly forced to contend with the incomparable din of two dozen screaming chainsaws as the speed carving competition began in earnest.

With an Indian taco held aloft in each hand, Krig wended his way through the crowd toward the stage, glimpsing familiar faces and nodding his recognition along the way. There was Hoffstetter from second crew. And the dude from Ace Hardware. Was that Principal Ellick? He spotted Kip Tobin in front of the Fraternal Order of Eagles funnel-cake stand. Krig smiled and gave a nod, but Tobin pretended not to see him. Not fifty feet later, he spotted Molly walking toward him past the Speed Pitch, but she dodged him. In front of the blue honey buckets, he spotted Jerry Rhinehalter, floating like a gray ghost in a sea of his kids. His wife was nowhere in sight. Ashing his cigarette, Jerry gave Krig a little nod, and Krig felt redeemed, if only briefly.

He found Jared leaning restlessly on the edge of the stage, sporting an uncomfortably close shave and a blue dress shirt.

"Brought you some grub," said Krig.

"Not hungry," Jared said, a little queasily, glancing at his watch. "But thanks."

Krig looked around for somewhere to set the extra taco. "Nervous, huh?"

"Pretty much."

Krig decided to set the taco down on the stage, right between Jared and a white leather purse. "You'll do great," he said, wrestling the remaining taco into submission. "Just forget they're there. All those people, I mean. They're all total strangers anyway."

"Krig, you're not helping."

"Sorry, bro."

"I know you are." Jared began to pace around distractedly. He daubed some sweat off his brow with the sleeve of his shirt. "Oh, so what about the promotion?" he said, as though he'd just remembered it. "Why don't you just take it, Krig? It won't increase your workload, I swear. Your hours will probably be shorter. You'll get a new office. No more rubber bib. Hell, you can go golfing with Don Buford — *on the clock.*"

"Thinkin' about it," said Krig.

"What's there to think about?"

Emerging from the crowd, Janis registered Krig with a cursory smile.

"Hey," she said.

"Did you find it okay, hon?" said Jared.

Sidling in beside Jared, Janis smoothed the lap of her yellow dress before sitting squarely on top of the open-faced taco.

"Oh shit, watch out," said Krig, way too late.

Janis sprung to her feet, swiping urgently, then pitifully, at her backside, powerless to stop the rush of blood to her face.

Jared scrambled into action looking for a solution.

"Damn," said Krig. "I should've grabbed some napkins. Here," he said, foisting his own taco on Janis. "I'll run and get some."

"Hurry up," said Jared.

Navigating the crowd, Krig berated himself for fucking up J-man's big day, for that matter fucking up everything he ever touched. Here, a missed free throw, a crossed boundary, a blown scholarship. There, a forgotten invoice, a misplaced taco. It didn't matter how small the fuckup, how seemingly insignificant the oversight. The results were always bad. His fuckups defined him. People expected them.

Snatching a fistful of napkins from the frozen banana stand, Krig hurriedly began weaving his way back to the stage, still cursing himself for his failures, when he nearly bowled into Rita outside the logging exhibit. Her hair was pulled back, smooth and dark behind her ears. She was holding three cotton candies. Krig wished one of them was intended for him.

"Oh, hey," he said.

"Dave!"

He felt his scalp tightening. She flashed a smile, weakening his knees.

"Somehow, I knew I'd run into you here," she said.

Krig clutched his napkins tighter. He couldn't look her in the eye.

"Heard you were up for a promotion," she said brightly. "Ran into Hoffstetter."

"Sorta, I guess."

"That's exciting."

"Yeah, I guess so."

"Hey, there's somebody I want you to meet," she said.

"Oh, uh, yeah," Krig said, shifting restlessly on his feet. "The thing is, Janis sat on a taco, and I've got these napkins, and J-man's about to give his speech, and—"

"I understand," she said. "You go. Maybe we'll run into you later."

"Okay, yeah, that'd be cool." Krig peered shiftily over her shoulder toward the stage, into the crowd, up the mountain.

They both stood in place for an awkward moment, as though stuck there. Krig scratched his neck and dug his toe into the dirt. Finally, looking up into his face, Rita managed to meet Krig's eyes.

"You know, Dave, I—" She stopped herself short, casting her eyes down on the cotton candy. "Well, I guess what I'm trying to say—what I tried to say before—is, well, that I never said it was impossible, you and I. I mean, if the time were ever to be right, if I were in a good place, and if Curtis was in the right place, and if, you know, you were in the right place, I mean, in a year or something . . ."

Krig could feel himself blushing. He had no idea where the right place might be, but he knew himself well enough to know that he'd probably be willing to drive in circles until he found it. "Um, okay," he said. "I'll keep that in mind."

"I don't want you to think I'm making any promises, Dave. I'm just saying, you know, *if.*" Rita smiled sweetly, almost apologetically. "Well, you better deliver your napkins," she said.

"Oh. Yeah. Right."

"It was good seeing you."

"Totally."

Leaving Rita behind, Krig felt a surge of immediate relief, along with a nagging wistfulness and a rapid heartbeat. In the thick of all those *ifs*, had Rita just offered him hope? Winding his way back toward the stage, he fought the impulse to look back over his shoulder.

MIDWAY THROUGH THE distant strains of "Wooly Bully," as Timmon and Franklin and Rupert began their final descent into the basin, stooping beneath the weight of their packs, wild-eyed and feral, a sputtering chorus of chainsaws suddenly threatened to drown out the music. Exchanging puzzled glances, they scampered down the rutty incline toward the trailhead. Rounding the last wooded bend, the valley revealed itself in a dramatic sweep, checking both men in their tracks.

"Whoa," said Timmon. "What the — ?"

Spreading out below them like a colorful rash on the butt end of the basin, extending a little ways up the lakeshore on either side of the dam, lay a veritable tent city, cut crosswise by corridors running east to west. Like arteries, the wide channels undulated slowly with the pulse of humanity. A sea of cars extended far beyond the parking slab, to the edge of the valley, where it funneled down River Road toward the strait. Franklin didn't bother trying to spot the Taurus among the confusion. He just hoped it was still out there somewhere. A thin blue haze, redolent with the smell of barbecue and cedar, hung over the entire celebration. It was a feast for the eyes and an assault on the ears. And beneath the chainsaws, beneath the marching band, beneath the collective murmur of a thousand voices, Franklin could hear, just barely, the ominous hum of the turbines.

Tillman's face was a prairie of blankness. He was having doubts.

Franklin could see them stirring beneath the smooth surface. He needed a push.

"Snap out of it, Tillman. I smell ribs."

For the first time on their journey, Franklin took the lead as they wound down the final stretch of trail and eased into the eddying crowd near the back of the main stage. Timmon looked displaced, almost dazed, bumping his way through the crowd. He was still fighting it.

"Ribs," Franklin reminded him. "Think ribs."

Ribs indeed provided Timmon with a welcome focus. Gradually, he relinquished his opposition and eased himself into the flux, seeing the pageantry for what it was — freedom, of a sort. No sooner did he begin to smell the dizzying array of possibilities than he realized they were all right there for the taking. And remembering the thirty-six bucks in his pocket, with Franklin leading the way, Timmon felt strangely secure surrendering to the current.

HAD HILLARY NOTICED Franklin passing with his tattooed companion she might not have recognized him with four days' growth of salt-and-pepper stubble. She might have taken both men for homeless, as indeed Beverly did, clutching her purse tighter at the hip as the two vagrants strode by with presumably all that they owned strapped to their backs and a dirty dog in tow.

"Oh, Hill. Look at this one, this is cute," her mother said, lifting a knit baby cap — an oversized rasta tam in Jamaican stripes. Beverly could feel the stand attendant staring at her tits, and she obligingly gave them a hoist.

Hillary was holding a half-eaten corn dog, for which she'd lost her appetite. A little wave of nausea washed over her as the smell of salmon wafted past on a warm breeze.

"Honey, are you okay?"

"Can we sit somewhere, Mom? Maybe out of the crowd. I just wanna rest."

"Of course, sweetie." Beverly replaced the tam and gave her tits a final hoist before taking Hillary by the elbow and easing them both into the stream of traffic.

They rested on a wooden bench with their backs to the crowd. It was Hillary's usual perch above the sluice gate. Behind them, the band was striking up some patriotic mainstay, which felt to Hillary like the end of something. Maybe Monday she'd get word on the trailer — at the very least a counteroffer. Maybe Genie wanted to go to the new Thai place tonight, although at the moment the very thought of food made her nauseous.

A year from now her days would be filled with the soft warmth of footed fleece onesies and the lily fresh scent of baby's breath. A year from now, though the dam would be incrementally smaller, Dam Days would go on; they'd just be celebrating something a little different. Hillary would be pushing a stroller through this same crowd, and the band would be playing some rousing anthem, and the chainsaws would be ringing, and the colors would be dizzying, and Hillary would see the world through her child's eyes — see it all as though for the first time. Maybe by then, Genie would have the courage to walk beside her. Maybe then, they could reinvent themselves together. But even now, with the cool mist on her face, and the twin turbines — soon to be silenced forever — humming up through the earth, a calm vibrated softly in Hillary's bones.

"IS THIS THING turned on?" *Tap tap.* "Can you hear me out there? Is this — ? It is? Okay — *ahem* — uh, all right, then — *cough cough.* Hello, Port Bonita. And welcome to the fifty-sixth annual Dam Days celebration — *ahem, cough* — *eeeeeeeeeeeerrrrrrr.*"

"Back off the mic!" someone yelled.

Backing off the mic, Jared smiled sheepishly and shrugged to a sprinkling of polite laughter. "Sorry about that. *Ahem. Ahem. Cough.* I was nine weeks old the first time I came to Dam Days, which makes this my thirty-third celebration." With the first sentence behind him, Jared sunk into a comfortable groove. "My father was not yet a senator back then but a Port Bonita councilman, and a proud one. I'm afraid I'm not quite as comfortable as my father in the arena of public speaking. But all the same, I'm proud and honored to be up here today."

And Jared really was proud, profusely and unexpectedly. So much so, that for a brief moment, looking out over the colorful wash of people toward the lip of the dam, he felt himself misting over. Center stage and three rows deep in the assembly, pressed between a fat lady in an Old Navy sweatshirt and skinny guy in a Stihl chainsaw cap, Krig, too, swelled with pride for J-man.

"Proud not only," Jared continued, "to be commemorating our long and rich history but to usher in a whole new chapter in our history — the Elwha River Restoration. The inconceivable has come to pass, the dam is coming down, slowly but surely. And I know everyone isn't happy about it. We've been hanging our hat on this dam for over a hundred years."

A smattering of applause mixed with a few boos rose from the crowd, and when it died back down the hum of the turbines filled the ensuing silence.

"I think it's important to remember, Port Bonitans, that we have a long history of overcoming adversity, stretching all the way back to the Bucket Brigades of 1890."

"Hell yes!" Jared heard someone yell. He thought it sounded like Krig.

"And I might add that most of those men and women who fought to save Port Bonita the first time may not have dams and mills and streets named after them, but they're every bit as much a part of the fabric of our history as the captains of industry."

Meriwether, near the back of the assembly, could feel the first raindrops on the brim of his white cowboy hat, and he nudged Curtis with an elbow.

Krig felt the first drops on his bare forearm.

Jared could hear the rain tapping on the canopy high above his head.

As the showers came harder, Rita's cotton candy began to wilt.

Hillary and her mother began making their way to the car.

Jared forged ahead as the crowd began to disperse. "Once again, Port Bonitans, we've been presented with the opportunity to rewrite our history."

"Hell yes!" yelled Krig, determined to stick it out until the very end, even as puddles formed around him and the vendors began closing their hatches, and the band huddled beneath the canopy at the back of the stage. "Tell it like it is, J-man!"

Looking across the vacant muddy flat, Krig noticed that Jerry Rhinehalter had stuck it out, too, leaning against a light standard at the very edge of what used to be the crowd, cupping his cigarette from the rain. His kids were nowhere to be seen.

"For as long as anybody can remember, this dam has been the heart and soul of Port Bonita. It was the Thornburgh Dam that put us on the map, that brought light to our fledgling town, the Thornburgh Dam that powered the mills that fueled our economy for a hundred years. And even as the twentieth century passed it by, the dam remained an unshakable part of our identity. And with the dawn of a new century, the debate surrounding this dam remained at the forefront of our consciousness as a town and, ironically, put us on the map all over again. But" — here J-man paused for dramatic effect — "sometimes we must leave part of ourselves behind in order to move on. And for Port Bonita that means the Thornburgh Dam. But as my great grandfather Ethan Thornburgh said on christening this dam —even as Port Bonita was rising again from the ashes: Port Bonita is not a place, but a spirit, an essence, a pulse; a future still unfolding. So I say to you, Port Bonita: Onward! There *is* a future, and it begins right now."

WHEN THE RAIN started falling in torrents, Timmon and Franklin aborted their search for ribs and commenced searching for the Taurus among the sea of automobiles. Up and down three aisles they searched the slab until at last Franklin spotted it, a sopping, ink-mottled parking infraction adorning its windshield. Franklin peeled the pink ticket off disgustedly, then fished the keys from his pocket.

Timmon stood at the passenger door, waiting impatiently for Franklin to unlock the car. Tossing his sodden gym bag heavily in the backseat, Franklin climbed behind the wheel and slapped the ticket on the dash, where it clung like a slice of baloney. He reached across and unlocked the passenger door.

Timmon climbed in and fastened his seat belt. "Better pay that," he said, registering Franklin's disgust. "It's the little shit that will catch up with you if you're not careful."

LINGERING AT THE edge of the gorge, Krig let the rain wash over him, feeling strangely as though he'd lived this moment before. Working the fingers of his left hand over the raw knuckle, then over the pale and unfamiliar flesh the ring had covered for twenty-two years, he wondered how long the imprint would last, whether the hair would grow back on his knuckle, whether the P.B. Varsity Boys would ever make it back to state. If they did, Krig hoped they won it all, even if it meant Port Bonita forgot all about that '84 squad. P.B. could use a champion. Crossing the muddy clearing, Krig discovered that already the rain was washing away his footprints.

Wending his way through the muddy fairgrounds past the first-aid station and the Speed Pitch, Krig arrived at the north entrance. It was tough not to feel a little wistful stepping over the rope. How many summers had Krig left behind with this very step? How many autumns has he ushered in? Was this the last?

In the distance, Krig saw J-man and Janis climbing into their Lexus. He could see the stain on Janis's ass from fifty yards. He saw Jerry Rhinehalter two cars in front of J-man, the old station wagon riding low under the massive weight of the Rhinehalter brood. The windows were fogging up in back. In the adjacent row, Krig spotted the Monte Carlo nosing into traffic and felt a bittersweet pang to see Curtis smiling in the passenger seat. Rita had wrestled her wet hair into a ponytail, and Krig thought he knew exactly how it would smell with his lips pressed softly against the nape of her neck.

But there were too many ifs. Too many buts. Too much waiting around. For the first time in his life, Krig felt that he couldn't afford to drive in circles anymore; even at forty-two grand a year, he'd still be repeating himself. Even if golfing with Don Buford might be better than watching the Raiders by himself on Sunday afternoons. Even if Rita might change her mind, eventually. J-man had it right: sometimes you gotta leave a part of yourself behind in order to move on. And though he was resolved to his new course of action, intent upon his unfolding future, Krig ached all the more for the past, for the familiarity and convenience and timeless consolation of Port Bonita. And more than ever, he ached to possess Rita, as he watched her inch herself into the fray, as one by one, they all inched themselves into the fray and wound their way down the mountain toward home.

there $\quad$ (

January 14, 2007

Dear J-man,

   Aberdeen is cool, but it ain't P.B. I miss the mountains, the
weather kind of sucks, and nobody has Kilt Lifter on tap. But
the truth is, I'm not drinking as much these days, anyway — and
I stopped smoking weed altogether. It's funny how much more
time I spend looking forward now than back. Most nights I just
stay home and read if I don't have practice. I started coaching
Pee-Wee hoops in November. We're in last place, but since we
switched from man-up to a zone, we're 3–0, and I think we're just
hitting our stride. The kids are really excited. Funny, I didn't even
know I liked kids.

   Bad news of sorts: the Goat finally gave up the ghost a couple
of weeks ago. The block is shot. Hated to see her go, but I got two
grand for the body, and at least I managed to save the furry dash
cover — why, I don't know. I drive a little Geo Metro now, and I'm
actually okay with that, even if it's not exactly a chick magnet. In
some ways, it beats that old gas hog.

   Thanks for the Christmas card, and congrats again on the
baby! He looks just like you! Say hi to the gang at High Tide — and
tell Hoffstetter he still owes me twenty bucks for that AFC
Championship game. And if you happen to see Rita around, tell
her I said "Hey."

Take 'er easy,
Krig

P.S. I read on the SFRO database yesterday that a guy reported a
couple of class B sightings behind his cabin last week, out near
Lost Creek, which is in the hills just west of here. I know you
think I'm crazy, but I still want to believe. I'm thinking of heading
out that way.

ACKNOWLEDGMENTS

I owe a great debt to many sources, texts, and individuals, without whom this book would not exist. If I've forgotten to list anybody here, let it be a testament to the scope of my debt.

First, Nick Belardes for his super-cool maps; Michael O'Conner for his killer cartoons, though they didn't quite work, to no fault of his own; and also Shannon Gentry for her work on the early maps.

My wife, Lauren, gets her own line for the patience and diligence it takes to survive a novelist (even on a good day).

Though *West of Here* is very much a work of fiction, much of the "historical" material was inspired by my eighteen months of research, which owes a huge debt to many sources. Robert L. Wood's wonderful treatment of the Press expedition in *Across the Olympic Mountains, The Press Expedition, 1889–90,* was nothing short of indispensable to my research (not to mention a great read), as well as James H. Christie's original account of the Press expedition from the *Seattle Press* (July 16, 1890), and Charles A. Barnes's narrative account of said expedition. Also indespensible to my research was Thomas Aldwell's *Conquering the Last Frontier,* Paul J. Martin's *Port Angeles, Washington: A History,* along with *Shadows of Our Ancestors, Readings in the History of Klallam–White Relations,* edited by Jerry Gorsoline, with contributors Lewis L. Langness, Joyce Mordon, Kent D. Richards, Peter Simpson, and Marian Taylor. William W. Elmendorf's *Twana Narratives* was another invaluable resource, and James G. McCurdy's *By Juan de Fuca's Strait* another. Also, Philip Johnson's *Historic Assessment of Elwha River Fisheries* was extremely helpful, and thanks to Steve Todd for tracking it down for me. *Watershed: The Undamming of America,* by Elizabeth Grossman, was another great resource. An acknowledgment is also due to Murray Morgan, who has contributed so very much toward preserving Washington state's rich history, which I have so thoroughly turned on its ear herein. A thin book this would be without the wealth of knowledge and insight provided by all of the aforementioned texts.

I would also like to acknowledge the entire staff of the North Olympic and Bainbridge Island Libraries, the Klallam Tribal Center, the Jamestown Tribal Center, Port Angeles Seafood, the Bushwhacker, the Klallam County Historical Society, Olympic National Park, and the guy who invented beer.

Also, a huge thanks to the following individuals for their editorial and critical insight: Mark Boquist (and Pete Droge and Dave Ellis and Sean Mugrage, too) for first coming up with the title *West of Here* with the 1990

Ramadillo release of the same name. Thanks are due to David Rogers, Michael Meachen, Hugh Schulze, Shelby Rogers, David Liss, Margaret Walsh, Gina Rho, and Matthew Comito for their invaluable readings of the manuscript at various early stages and also to Jerry Brady for his inspiring tales of towniehood in Bowie, Maryland (and for the name Krig), Jessica Regel, Jackie Luskey, Stephanie Abou, Ian Dlrymple, Richard Nash, Mom, Dad, Jim, Jan, Davey, Dan, my nephews (Bob, Buddy, Danny, Matthew), my niece (Angie), Carl (you are dearly missed), Lydia, Tup, Brooks, Justin, Tomasovich, my blogging compadres J.R., D.H., J.C., and the rest of my trusty companions, as well as all my brilliant, colorful, and inspiring comrades from the Fiction Files.

A huge thanks to my brilliant editor and advocate Chuck Adams, who pushed me to do my best work at every juncture. Also, big thanks to Elisabeth Scharlatt, Ina Stern, Craig Popelars, Michael Taeckens, Jude Grant, Brunson Hoole, Kelly Bowen, Katie Ford, Michael Rockliff, and everyone top to bottom at Algonquin, along with super-rep Kurtis Lowe. And lastly, my friend, agent, and trusted reader, Mollie Glick.